Now and then it's good to pause in our pursuit of happiness and just be happy.

—GUILLAUME APOLLINAIRE

FROM RUM TO ROOTS

A NOVEL

LLOYD G FRANCIS

Published by Marway Publishing

Marway Publishing
1388 Haight Street #167
San Francisco CA 94117
marwaypub@gmail.com

ISBN: 978-0-9892161-0-4

Book Cover and Layout Design by *the*BookDesigners

You can contact the author Lloyd G Francis at lgfrancis@rumtoroots.com, or on twitter @lgfrancis. News and events about the novel *From Rum to Roots* can be found at http://www.rumtoroots.com

For further information about Marway Publishing products and events please contact: marwaypub@gmail.com

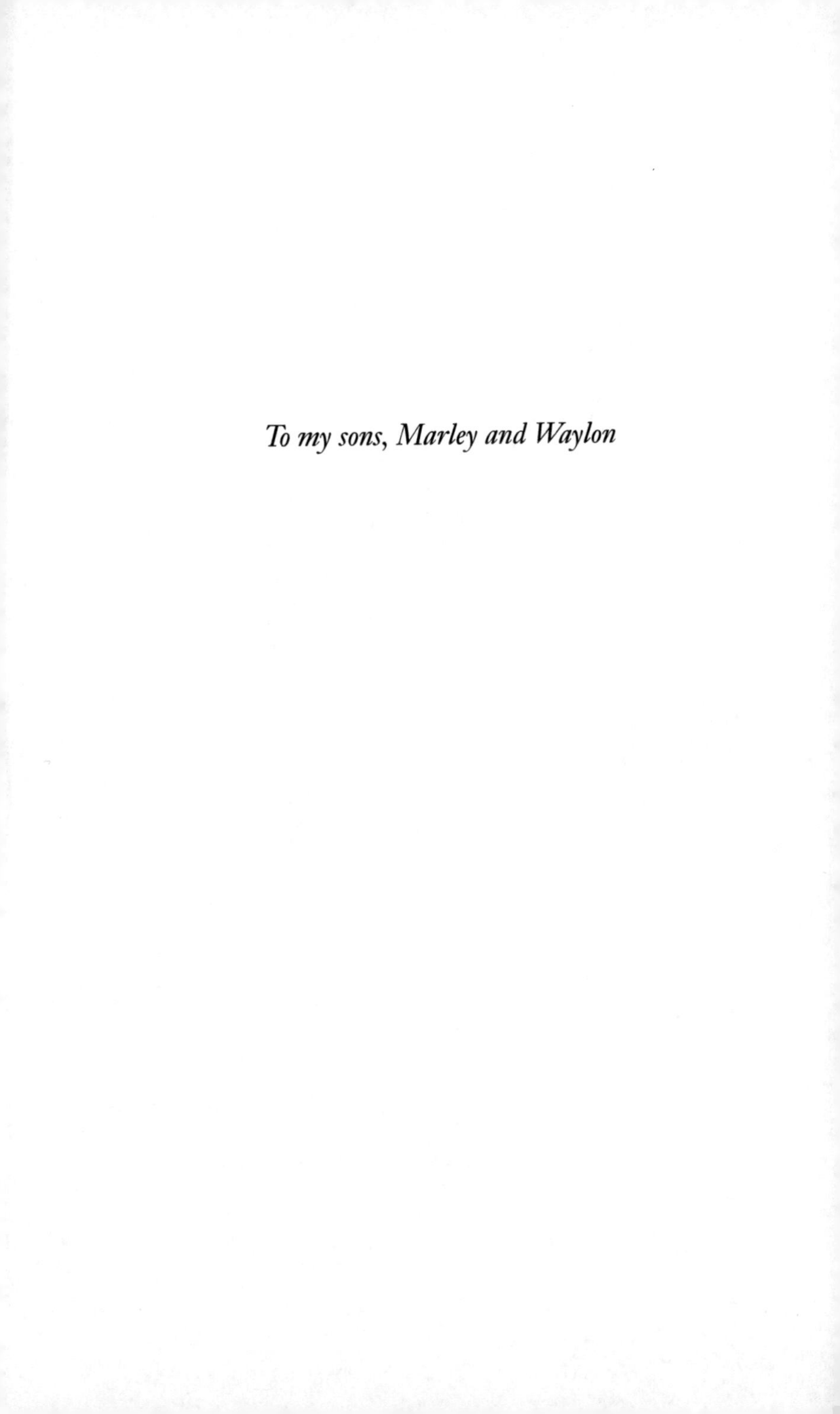

To my sons, Marley and Waylon

RUM

1

DECEMBER 1937, PORTLAND COTTAGE, JAMAICA

The sun hung low on the horizon. Earlier that day, Linton McMann had watched the workers in his gang disappear into a field of sugar cane, hoes slung over their shoulders, their bodies squeezing between the stalks. Enveloped in the sea of tall, green, tropical grass, only the rustling clumps of bush betrayed their locations as they cleared weeds.

Now, Linton stood atop the flatbed donkey-cart, the light casting a long, slender shadow behind him. A bugle announced the workday's end. Beyond, across the Plain of Vere, he could see the stately Blaine House, built on the tallest of three gentle, isolated hills rising from the flat, indolent land. The other structures on the estate -- a distillery, a refinery, and the barn -- were barely defined in the hazy, muted light. The men emerged from the emerald thicket, their shoes caked with moist dirt, in a procession that was the antithesis of the morning ritual.

"Circle up, mon!" Linton called to his workers. "Circle up!"

They gathered around him, black African and East Indian, each man red-eyed and exhausted, each carrying or leaning on their hoes, waiting to be formally dismissed.

"Tomorrow we'll meet in de southwest field. Is de first field to harvest so get plenty res'." Linton bade them a good night and most of the men trudged off to their homes, scattered about the district known as Portland Cottage. The cane waved lazily against the rapidly changing crimson sky. Jamaican fruit bats began to emerge from their caves, wings beating softly in the dusky air.

Linton welcomed the few remaining men on the donkey-cart, and drove them, lurching back and forth along the dirt trail, to their homes in Elysian Fields, the old slave quarters, perched at the foot of cemetery hill, the eternal resting place of the Blaine clan.

It was dark by the time Linton dropped them off and released the donkey. Watching the old beast amble into the night reminded him of happier days when he used to ride donkeys with his brother for fun.

Linton leaned against the barn door and studied his surroundings. He knelt and ran his fingers through the rich soil, trying to imagine the secrets hidden in its loamy darkness. Clutching a handful, he closed his eyes, as a familiar wave of anger swept over him. Small fragments of memory tugged at him, soft flesh against his cheek, his mother's velvet voice, the caress of her hands as she applied a salve to his tender little boy skin.

Why did she have to die? he thought. Leaving me here with Blaine. His real father. The master in the mansion. It was his oft-repeated lament. I'm his secret son! He tossed the handful of earth aside. If only I could go back in time, he reasoned. If only...

"Linton."

"Yah, mon." Pulled from his thoughts, Linton got up quickly.

Before him stood a young servant boy from the main house. "Mistah Blaine wan' yuh inna de back a de house."

"What does he want?"

The young boy turned to leave. "Go 'round and wait by the back door," he called, before disappearing into the night.

The house, a sprawling three-story Victorian, was painted grey with red and white trim, and every window was fitted with thick wooden storm shutters. Tightly cropped croton hedges encircled the structure, their compact green leaves streaked with vibrant red and yellow. At one corner of the house an imposing tower sprang upwards, with a round room at the top, and from this room you could see the entire estate, where five generations of Blaines lay buried in the family cemetery.

Another of the three hills was devoted to the family business, rum production. Two buildings, a refinery and distillery, were located atop the knoll. Surrounding all three hills, cultivated fields grew the cane that was harvested, then prepared for use in the refinery. The cane juice was boiled and the sugar crystals removed, leaving the molasses to be brought to the distillery. In the distillery, large brick furnaces heated the molasses in clay pots. Dunder, yeast from previous distillations, was added. The rum, known in patois as John Crow Batty, was stored in wooden barrels and taken into the cave at the base of the hill to age.

Linton entered the rear garden near the reflecting pool. The patio was landscaped immaculately with mango and breadfruit trees and, of course, ackee trees, a Jamaican favorite that bears fruit all year round. Benches were shaded by trellises. Pineapples, hugging the earth with their sharp leaves, were abundant with fruit. The center of the large patio was dominated by a huge *lignum vitae*, a tree of life. Delicate pink flowers adorned the branches that overhung the yard. Helconia plants with drooping red flowers and distinctive yellow tips and hibiscus blooms of every hue lined the walkways. Linton sat down at a patio table near the back door, painfully aware of every passing second that he was kept waiting.

It seemed like hours until the large wooden door opened and Major Blaine stood before him, tall, with lightly tanned, almost white skin, and dark blue eyes. Linton stood up.

"Come in, boy," Major invited.

"In?" Linton looked surprised. Blaine looked at him. "Come in."

Linton had never before set foot inside the mansion. Following the direction Major indicated, he went down stairs that led into the library.

Despite the house recently being wired for electricity, the library was one of a few rooms left without power. The dark Jacobean wall panels absorbed much of the light generated by lanterns. In the center of the room, surrounded by shelves brimming with books, sat a large circular table on which had been placed a bottle of rum, a pitcher of water, and two glasses. Persian rugs were scattered on the imported white pine floor. The ceiling, crowning the row of tall narrow windows, was painted white to reflect the light and brighten the room. The furniture and somber surroundings gave the room an atmosphere of old world grandeur.

Linton reading the book titles in the lantern light, felt his pulse quickening. There were hundreds of books, maybe thousands. Unable to quench his thirst to read since leaving school four years earlier, twenty-three year old Linton looked at the books in awe. Poetry, plays, fiction, history -- his excitement was palpable.

Watching Linton enjoying himself, Major made Linton an offer.

"Would you like a key to allow you in here to read books in the evening?"

"Why?"

Major sighed. "You *are* my son."

Linton kissed his teeth. "But I'm not your son outside of here."

"Linton! What would people think?"

"Me nuh care wha' dem tink."

"Don't speak *patois* in my house." Major glared at Linton. The truncated speech, missing articles and chaotic contractions found in Jamaican patois annoyed Major. It sounded crude and uncivilized. After sending Linton to May Pen All-Boys Elementary School, Major expected Linton to make an effort to sound polished. He cleared his throat and continued.

"What about my wife Pauline? This news would devastate her. No, Linton, with me you may be a Blaine, but we must play a role for the outside world. Try to understand," Major went on, "I have plans for you. So do you want a key or not?"

"Yes, of course! But I'm wondering --"

"What?"

"Why can't we go upstairs?"

"Linton, other than being welcome in the evenings in the library, you will never set foot in my house. Other than the three servants who work inside, I don't let my employees in the house."

"Employee? I'm your son!"

"You been here for twelve years and you know the answer already."

"Yuh could make up any reason," Linton countered. "My being your *bastard* -- doesn't have to be revealed." Suddenly, he felt self-conscious, wishing he could retract the word *bastard*; to frame it differently so that his bitterness did not foul this rare moment between them. Just being invited in the house thrilled him. The impulse to hug his father was deep in his bones. But the marrow continued to nourish his hatred.

"Were you on your feet all day hoeing and tending cane? How much dirt gets under your fingernails? No," Major answered rhetorically. "There's only one reason why you're the gang driver, Linton. You're my son. Don't you understand? No one knows you're my son. That's why you still have your mother's last name, McMann. If the world would accept you having the Blaine surname, we could express our true feelings, but you're old enough to understand why it's got to be our secret. People here look at you differently if you're a bastard. A child of sin, they will say. And God knows how they might look at me." There was a dead silence. "Besides," he said, "now is time we discuss the plans."

"Fuh what?"

"Tomorrow I want you to report to Busby in the distillery." Major's face brightened. "Busby's expecting you."

"So, me haffi report to distillery?"

"It's time you become familiar with distillation, fermentation, and other basic logistics." Major said. "I don't want you in the fields." Major picked up the bottle of overproof white rum. "Busby, God bless him, is not goin' live forever. Son, come, let's celebrate your advancement."

Linton watched his father pour two large shots of pure white rum dashed with cold water. Lawd Jesus, he thought, as Major pushed the glass toward him.

"To you," said Major, toasting Linton, "the apprentice manager of rum production on the Blaine estate."

Glasses clinked. Linton had never drunk rum before. He followed Major's cue, throwing his head back and taking a long swallow. The rum had a distinctive flavor. He wanted to appear authentic in drinking but the rum burned. He cleared his throat.

Major smiled. "Take it easy, and breathe through your nose."

The lake of fire in Linton's throat was giving way to the warmth spreading in his chest. One sip made him tipsy and his hostility began to dissipate. Surprised, he took another sip. The headiness of the spirits felt good.

"Dis all right mon!

"You've had enough." Major looked amused to see him so easily intoxicated.

He brought out two cigars, cut the ends, lit them, and handed one to Linton. Soon the room was draped in smoke. For a few minutes they sat in an amiable silence, smoking.

Linton glanced at Major through his half open eyelids. Being with his father like this was overwhelming. He felt like a normal little boy, eager to please his Dad. Yet, despite all that, the fact remained that he was still a secret. Looking at Major's wide nose and slightly swollen lips Linton felt his irritation rise. He resembled his father and Major's African features were obvious to anyone who looked hard enough. Sometimes Linton thought he could see Major staring at his dark skin with disdain in his eyes. But he couldn't be sure. The rum continued to work, blurring his mind.

"Linton," Major said, "You're my son." He pursed his lips. "But to reveal our secret would ruin us. I'll always stand behind you, but you know that's what I demand, that you won't talk."

Linton's eyes were closed. "What?" he asked. His voice was slurred just enough that Major knew it was time for him to leave.

"Nothin'. Not anything important," said Major. "It's time for your sleep. Get a full night and meet Busby at the distillery tomorrow at 10:00 a.m.

"10:00 a.m.?" Linton struggled to get up, then sat down quickly, his eyes wide open in amazement. "I'll be fine." Linton laughed. Together they went up the stairs and out into the fresh air. The roar of insects filled the night.

"I will give you the key to the library at the distillery tomorrow," Major said. "Until then, good night."

His heart ached as he watched his son dissolve into the darkness.

The sun was high when Linton awoke. He scrambled about getting dressed and left the house in a hurry. All around, in every direction, sugar cane stretched for acres, tall, broad leaves twitching in the wind. On the horizon lay the Portland

Ridge, honeycombed by caves, the semi-arid terrain dotted with vegetation. He walked past the Blaine House, the structure looming above, emerging from the hillcrest as though it were itself, a force of nature. He eagerly climbed the stairs that led uphill, two steps at a time.

Linton burst inside the distillery, only to find it deserted. Breathless, his eyes adjusting to the dark shade, he peered about for Busby. What he saw filled him with excitement. There were seven square holes in the ceiling, that allowed beams of sunlight to stream in, illuminating dust motes floating aimlessly in air. The structure lacked walls and instead wooden pillars supported the roof every twenty feet. Linton moved through the shed looking at the brick kilns and clay pots in awe.

"Linton!"

Linton caught a glimpse of a short fat black man with slate grey eyes and pure white hair, who paused and then, like a butterfly, was gone.

"Over here!" Busby shouted from outside the shed. When Linton reached him, Busby stepped forward and shook his hand.

"Welcome, Linton," he said.

"Thank you fe having me," Linton replied. "I've never been up here."

"Well from now on, this is where yuh report, and me must warn yuh, we don't have no gang drivers, no foremen, no managers. *Everyone works*." Busby pointed at a pile of wooden buckets. "Yuh can start by placing a dozen buckets next to each clay pot. When yuh done, we need fifty barrels brought up de hill and stacked behind de distillery."

"Fifty?"

"What, yuh hard a hearing, bwoy!" Busby roared with laughter. "Nah sir! Dis 'ere distillery is a place a work. Today me a scrub de pots, and after lunch, yuh will sweep and clean de furnaces." Wasting no time, Busby spun around and was gone.

By noon, as Linton rolled the last barrel against the shed, every muscle in his body was screaming. He went inside and found Busby washing a pot, wet from head to toe, holding a brush and grinning at him.

"Mus' be breaktime," he said, throwing the brush aside. They went outside and Busby shared some fish with Linton, who, neglected to bring something to eat. After they ate, Busby poured two glasses of rum.

"Yuh tired?" Busby asked.

Linton shifted in his seat. "I'm not used to dis."

"It won't take long fe yuh to catch on," Busby said, pouring himself another drink. "I prefer to work alone. It was Mr. Blaine who insisted that you work with me to learn rummaking." Busby peered at Linton as if trying to size him up. "Me can't figure out why he like yuh so much, but if I was yuh, I wouldn't ask. Too many people dem starvin fe lack a work inna Jamaica today." He finished his drink and slamming down the glass, called Linton back to work.

They toiled all afternoon. The alcohol gave succor to Linton's aching body. Busby's girth did not slow him down; indeed he moved like a cat, nimble, light and quick. Linton watched, amazed at how Busby, who had to be at least thirty years older, seemed to move tirelessly, slipping between the shadows till the sun touched the horizon. Linton, grimy from ashes and sticky from kneeling in pools of water, almost wept with joy when he was told to stop.

"Tough day, eh? We haffi be ready next week," Busby said. He showed Linton a diagram of the estate and put his stubby finger on the map. "Here it is, de southwest field. In three more days, we goin' to receive cane from deh." Then Busby reached in his pocket, took out a shiny brass key, and handed it to Linton. "Mistah Blaine nuh tell me what it for," he said. "Him say yuh woulda know."

Linton put the key in his pocket. He continued to clutch it until he reached home and carefully placed it on the dresser. Later, after bathing and changing his clothes he walked to the mansion, and circled around back. Turning the key in the lock, his heart leapt for joy as he opened the door to the library and entered a new world.

Major Blaine observed his beautiful and slender wife Pauline's reflection in the mirror. Her attention was focused exclusively on the brush gliding through her dark tresses. The storm shutters were pushed back to let in the sun and her light coconut colored skin glowed in the morning light. Birdsong floated in through the open bedroom windows.

Major shifted his gaze out the window, to the seemingly endless fields of sugar cane. "The dry months are here," he said.

Pauline stopped brushing her hair. "What dear -- what did you say?"

"The dry months."

She resumed brushing. "It's December, Christmas is coming and all you think about is the harvest."

"My father used the term dry months instead of harvest season."

He moved to a window where he could see the refinery and distillery and the wooden ramps that led into the aging and fermentation caverns.

"Really, Major, your son is returning from the United States tomorrow and you want to talk of dry months and the harvest season?"

"Andrew is planning to stay -- isn't he?"

"Why, of course. I think so."

"Good. He can help us start to prepare for things as we see them in the future."

"Just give him some time to get accustomed." Pauline was well aware of the tension between father and son and anticipated Major's ritual outburst once Andrew arrived.

"Of course, sweetheart. But if he has come home to loaf --"

"Major!"

"Okay, okay." He attempted a smile.

"Please." Pauline got up and left the room.

Major sat down on the small sofa and stewed to himself. Andrew has had it too easy, he thought. It's time that boy stopped partying and sailing with his friends in Montego Bay. When I was his age I was fighting in the Great War. The thought jarred him. He opened his eyes and was surprised to find them moist.

Major filled a flask with rum and went out to the stables. He saddled Ta-La-Wa, his favorite Arabian horse, mounted, and rode off in the direction of the western road. He allowed Ta-La-Wa to canter. As he passed the old servants' quarters, he saw children and adults going about the day-to-day details of life. They're lucky, he thought. Here in Jamaica, they get treated like human beings without fear of being lynched. Without us masters, they'd be a lazy lot.

He took a deep breath, feeling hollow at the thought of his workers' laziness. He knew better. All around him was clear evidence of the many fruits of their labor, including his large, beautiful house, the careful upkeep of the other structures on his land, the neat cultivated fields that sprawled across the acreage. They're not lazy, he conceded. In exchange for their labor, the Blaine family had always put food on their tables and provided a safe place to live. Yet, they complained.

He looked down the road. On either side laborers stooped in the broiling sun, working hard. Some paused to look as he rode by, but he chose to ignore them and pushed Ta-La-Wa to a light gallop.

When he reached the cemetery, Major stopped his horse. Behind an old iron fence a single spire rose up from a marble platform. The obelisk, surrounded by five gravestones was inscribed: *They did not die in vain.* Major lifted his flask. *Neither will we.* To the Blaine clan, he thought, and drank, and then urged Ta-La-Wa on.

Thick smoke billowed from the distillery.

Linton rushed in carrying a bucket of water. His face was contorted with fear. I'll be cutting cane by morning, he thought, as he ran outside to fetch another bucket.

Fifteen agonizing minutes later, the two men surveyed the damage. One of the large clay pots had been destroyed. The dunder, a yeast that is a key ingredient in the distillation process, had burnt up. It would be days before the equipment could be up and running again.

"It's all my fault," Linton moaned. "I'm gonna get put back in the fields fe dis, mon."

"No, it nuh yuh fault. Yuh here to learn."

"Yuh asked me to light de fire, den yuh tell me to keep an eye pon it. It was my responsibility," Linton insisted. Taking a deep breath he asked, "Where is Mr. Blaine?"

"Mistah Blaine lef' dis mornin' with him horse. We haffi tell him when him come home. And yuh must make me do de talkin'. Come now, let's clean up."

Linton slowly dragged himself over to the fire-pit and began shoveling the stinking wet ashes. He threw himself into his work, shoving the spade into the ashes with more force than necessary. There was not a chance he would let Busby take the blame.

Major turned his horse toward the coast. Sugar cane towered above him and he could see nothing but the narrow swath the road cut through the thick green hedges. It was unusually hot for December and the canebrakes provided no relief from the beating sun. Damn, Major thought, I forgot to bring my damn hat.

Soon, the landscape began to change dramatically. The cane abruptly ended, replaced by scattered bushes, shrubs, and stunted acacia trees. On the right side of the road a bog appeared. On the left, Portland Ridge drew near.

Ta-La-Wa slowed to a walk. The road, so narrow it was now little more than a trail, sliced through the bright green guinea grass. Trees and vines closed in around them. Major dismounted, tied his horse to a tree, and began to climb a hill. Above him, on a large limestone outcrop, he could see vines hanging over the yawning mouth of Runaway Cave. When he reached the cave, Major sat down on a large boulder. From this perch he had a splendid view of the sparkling blue waters of the Caribbean Sea.

Major had been coming to Runaway Cave for as long as he could remember and it was here that his father, Peter Blaine, had told him a terrifying family tale, had told it countless times, while sitting on this very rock. Sometimes, late at night, they would build a fire and Major would tremble with excitement, for his father was about to tell the story.

"How old are you, Major?" his father always asked.

"Twelve, Daddy."

"How many times I tell you the story of Runaway?"

"More than I can remember, Daddy."

Peter nodded. "My grandfather, Robert Blaine told me when I was a little boy, and I sat where you are right now, and here I am telling it again. It is a story we Blaine's must never forget." He said in a low voice, "Runaway Cave is the bright spot in what is otherwise a very dark story.

"We left America in 1777. Your great-great-great-grandfather, Winston Blaine abandoned his tobacco fields and sold his slaves in Virginia, fleeing the American Revolution to remain loyal to the King of England. He arrived in Jamaica and established the Blaine Estate. Winston had one son, your great-great grandfather, Gordon. Once Winston grew too old, Gordon ran the estate. His son, Robert was born in 1802.

"The Estate grew and prospered until 1831 when, during the Christmas Rebellion, a band of escaped niggers invaded our land. Your great-grandfather, Robert was in the nearby town of Alley when the mayhem began and from a distance saw the Blaine House engulfed in flames. It was a grander structure then, running the full length of the hill. Everywhere was chaos. Our slaves joined the mob and they rioted and ran pell-mell in a blind and pointless rage.

"All around, Robert could see fires from plantations, the thick, dark columns of smoke rising high into the sky. He and four loyal slaves ran for their lives. What he didn't know was that one of the slaves, his concubine, Ruth, was pregnant with Theodore, my father and your grand-father. They fled south, away from the plantation and away from civilization. They found refuge in this cave for three days, until the trouble subsided. There was nothing to eat except fruit from a few nearby trees. When it was finally safe to return home, they found everyone, the entire family, had been murdered. The mob, in its fury, had torn bodies apart. He buried them in a mass grave and marked the spot with a granite obelisk.

Everything was in ruins. Theodore, was born seven months later while his parents, Robert and Ruth still lived in tents. Theodore was their only surviving son. Theodore married my mother, Abagail, a Scottish woman from Port Antonio." Peter sighed. "Then I came along, and now, Major, I have you."

"What about the house, Daddy?" Major stretched out on the rock and yawned. He and his father had been through this story-telling ritual many times. Major loved coming here with Peter.

"It was a time of hardship in Jamaica. It took ten years to complete the new Blaine House. It's smaller than the original, but suits us very well."

Peter stood up and opened his arms wide. "Your great-great-great grandfather, Winston, found these three small hills and discovered the spring near the rear of the house. The house is a beacon, standing tall above the five-hundred acres of land the Blaine's have owned for five generations and will have forever."

"Forever, Daddy?" Major always asked the same question.

"Forever. To insure our future we must be prepared to sacrifice, and do our duty. Robert, rose to the occasion," Peter told his young son Major. "He met the challenge and *completed his duty*. I took his place when he got old and there will be a time when you, too, will be called, Major. The Blaines always meet the challenge."

Duty, the Blaine watchword. Major was steeped in the concept by the time he could walk. When the British Crown cried out to fight the Huns, Major was one of the first to join as a lieutenant in the British West Indian Regiment.

With his young wife, Pauline, and four-year-old son, Andrew, looking on, watching his mother cry and his over-enthusiastic father wave, Major sailed away, remaining on deck until the island disappeared from the horizon. The warm Caribbean waters merged into the chilly Atlantic. Finally arriving in Cairo, Egypt, he joined General Allenby in the campaign to crush the Ottoman Empire. By the time Major returned home, a war hero, both his father and mother had passed away and Andrew was six years old. But he found it impossible to feel proud of himself. Deep inside he had to acknowledge that during the war, he had neglected someone.

Linton, his other son, was five.

Major took a large swig of the rum, then belched with an abandon he'd have called uncouth had it occurred around others. He took another pull from the flask, and laughed. Okay, he acknowledged, I made some mistakes.

Mistakes?

He could not bring himself to regret the affair, despite how wrong it had gone in the end. It was so long ago. He was in May Pen on business when he first saw Misti, a dark-skinned, brown-eyed beauty with hair cascading down her shoulders. Polite, petite, and poised, she was so small it looked as if a gust of wind might blow her away. Major approached, slipping the wedding ring off his finger. She fell in love, and so did he. Major saw her many times, unable--no, damn it, unwilling--to tell her or Pauline the truth.

He would return home late at night from his trysts with Misti, look in on his young son, then wearily remove his clothes and, still thinking about Misti, would climb into bed with his wife and make love to her. Lying next to Pauline, his heart felt heavy with guilt. He loved her, truly and deeply, and desperately didn't want to hurt her, but he couldn't bring himself to put a halt to the affair. He also, just as truly, loved Misti.

When Misti announced that she was pregnant, Major joined the British West Indian Regiment and in 1916, left for Palestine. He easily convinced others that duty called, but was tormented by the real reason, and the knowledge filled him with self-loathing. After returning home in 1919, Major all but ignored Linton, his bastard son. He never told Pauline about the affair. His son Andrew did not know that Linton was his half-brother.

Even so, these thoughts did not assuage Major's conscience. Misti's death had been unexpected. A routine dental appointment in May Pen led to blood poisoning and her death a week later, leaving their son, Linton, alone. Major attempted to ignore all responsibility for his son, was willing to walk away and cast the boy's fortunes to the wind, had Timothy, a crippled ice vendor in May Pen, minded his own business. After all it was his deeper sense of responsibility to Pauline that kept him from acknowledging Linton. Or was it cowardice? The question brought a frown to Major's face. How Timothy discovered his secret, he never found out. That damn iceman had a way of prying into people's affairs. There was a driving rainstorm, the sound of hooves clattering, and a knock on the door. It was Timothy, with his one hand, grasping the hand of Major's seven year old son.

Now, sitting on that flat rock, Major closed his eyes and recalled seeing Linton's innocent, bereft face. Timothy left and Major went out into the rain, and took the boy down to Aunt Cordy's. On the way, for the first time ever, Linton called him Daddy. That terrified Major.

"Don't call me Daddy!" Major slapped Linton's face, the child recoiling as tears of heartache and grief gushed from his eyes. "Address me as 'sir'." Major regretted hitting the boy and yelling at him, and the memories burned like the fires set in the cane fields to drive away the animals and burn dead vegetation. His progeny. He denied the boy his lineage, his rightful heritage.

Ashamed, he handed Linton over to Aunt Cordy, matriarch of Elysian Fields, the old servants' quarters where many of the Estate's laborers still lived. He never explained to Aunt Cordy, but she knew. Days and months went by and Major tried to forget about the child.

I can't help myself, Major thought, trying to understand the recent encounter with Linton. I'll never publicly acknowledge the boy and he will just have to accept that. But I'll take care of him. After all, Linton's a bright boy, Major argued inwardly. I've given him a basic education and now with access to those books he can try to make something of himself. Like it or not, I *am* his father and as such I have a duty, a responsibility -- no, Major, his conscience retorted, by God you have an *obligation* -- to account for Linton.

Warm air caressed Major's face. His eyes were soft and unfocused, his vision was blurry. "Drunk!" he exclaimed with a giggle.

He drained the flask. Evening was approaching. The sun's descent behind a bank of clouds made the sea lose its sparkle, the blue water appearing gray and foreboding. The foliage and grass, so verdant and inviting in the sunshine, now appeared sinister. Major stumbled down the rocky path to where Ta-La-Wa waited. The breeze, a delightful respite from the heat and humidity, had intensified into a stiff wind, branches crackling, stirring leaves, the sound of hoary threats.

He pushed Ta-La-Wa to a gallop. By the time he arrived back at the Estate he was boiling over with self-loathing, a volcano ready to erupt. He directed Ta-La-Wa toward the barn.

"Sah!"

He turned and saw Busby and Linton approach.

"We have some bad news," Busby said holding his hat in his hand.

"Yes, just tell me what it is," Major snapped, his face darkened with anger.

Linton stepped forward. "I made a mistake and left the fire burning too long. It burnt all de dunder and destroyed a clay pot. Is my fault, sir." Linton looked right into Major's cold blue eyes.

Thwack! Major punched Linton in the mouth. Unexpected as it was, it sent Linton reeling and he fell backwards into the dirt. His mouth gushed blood. Busby rushed to Linton and applied pressure to the gash. Linton moaned, his head cradled in Busby's arms. His eyes were filled with hate.

"Pay attention next time." Major shook his bruised hand and walked away.

Stunned, Busby whispered, "Nuh bother say nothin'. Les get yuh fix up, nuh?"

They slowly stood and stumbled, arm in arm toward Elysian Fields as the red sky darkened into night.

The candle's naked flame was partially surrounded by a Pet condensed milk can cut open and shaped to resemble a lamp. Hot wax pooled in the bottom, the flame sputtering and flaring so close to his cheek, Linton's nerves jangled in anticipation of being burnt. He closed his eyes. His entire face ached.

"Hold steady, nuh?" Linton's lids fluttered open. Sheila, a bush doctor, gently daubed a wet rag on the torn lip. "It really a swell up now," she said.

Busby sat opposite Sheila, holding the lantern aloft to give her light.

"Me nuh hardly have roots, de Chinese store closed, and is too late fe wake up Auntie. It gonna hurt, mon."

"Uhhgh," Linton responded, backing his face away from the lamp.

"Me a go a Aunt Cordy tomorrah an get somethin'," Sheila replied, then disappeared into the next room, taking the makeshift lamp with her. Busby looked at Linton.

"Jus' keep yuh mouth shut, yuh hear," he said. "Him nuh sack yuh yet." But Busby was perturbed by what he saw. "Why didn't yuh let me tell him? Jesus! Somepin else is behind all dis," Busby muttered to himself. "Me nevah see Major act like dat."

Linton kissed his teeth. He winced with pain. I hate him, he thought angrily. One day -- *one* day -- I will pay him back.

The modest homemade lamp cast a bright glow as Sheila came back, banishing the darkness into corners, making shadows dance upon the walls. Linton glanced at the porcelain face bowl with bloodstained water.

"It need stitches," she said.

"Nah doctor here fe help him," Busby said.

"If him nuh get stitch, him lip gwan heal up wit' big welt yuh know. Me nuh even have ice fe help de swelling."

Busby moved the lantern closer to Linton's face and Sheila applied a brown salve. It burned terribly and Linton shivered with pain.

"Alley is de closest place where a doctor gonna be found."

"Yuh take him tomorrow?" Sheila looked at Busby.

"Yah."

"Inna de morning first ting, okay?"

Busby said good-night and closed the door. Sheila kissed Linton's forehead. "Yuh a stay here with me tonight," she said.

Linton looked at her.

"Yuh a sleep right dey, suh," she repeated, and turned down the bed, fluffing the pillows for her guest.

Linton looked bewildered. "Me can make it home, Sheila." He got up slowly, only to be gently pushed back down.

"Me tired too," Sheila whispered. She put the lantern on the bed-stand and helped Linton undress. She peeled down his pants and took off his shirt. Her fingers traveling across his muscular back, suddenly halted as she became aware of the strange knots of flesh. She picked up the candle lantern and turned Linton so that she could see.

"My God, Linton! Who do dis to yuh!" She ran her fingers over the long scars criss-crossing his back. " Linton, who?"

"Shhhh!" Linton put a finger to his lips. He didn't want to talk and could not even feign resistance to her putting him to bed. Sheila tucked him in, stripped down to her underwear, and crawled in next to him. Her earthy sexuality and warm, fleshy curves caused his passion to rise in spite of the pain.

She blew out the lamp, snuggling as close as she could, and smiled as his arm slid around her, pulling her still closer. She let out a deep sigh as he entered her. In the yard the palm trees waved breezily throughout the night.

The morning sunlight, dappled by the trees, cast a soft light on Major's face. He awoke moody, worried about things that were not supposed to matter. He looked at his hand. A painful bruise discolored his index finger. He had surprised himself last night. He never intended to hit Linton. It was the drink that led him to lash out thoughtlessly, on impulse. He regretted it, but would never say that he was sorry. In fact, he admired Linton for stepping forward, feeling a sense of pride for the guts it took for him to take responsibility.

Pauline stuck her head in the room. "Dear, Andrew will be here any moment." Almost as soon as Major noticed her, Pauline was gone.

Major got up, washed, shaved, and stood before the mirror, dressed in black pants, a white shirt and a gray tie. He admired his reflection a moment longer, then joined Pauline downstairs on the porch.

"Why, Pauline, you're as pretty as a picture."

Pauline was gazing at the road. She wore an ankle-length navy blue dress and a flowing white blouse. She smiled at Major's compliment, but her eyes never left the road. His servant, Sheila, poured two tall glasses of sorrel, a sweet drink made from tiny red sorrel flowers. Then she retired to her place against the wall, innocuous, waiting to be called into service. Two more glasses stood empty and waiting.

"Look!" Pauline jumped to her feet.

Major saw a puff of dust rising between the cane fields.

"It's him."

The Landsdowne bounced into sight as it negotiated the potholed road. The cream-colored car stood out in contrast to the green fields, drew closer, closer, and pulled into the brick lined driveway. Before the car had even stopped, a tall man with curly hair, and café au lait skin jumped out and ran toward his parents. Pauline clasped her hands in excitement. Andrew ran to his mother's arms, picked her up and kissed her while spinning in circles. Putting Pauline down, he turned to his father and offered his hand. The moment Major's hand touched his, Andrew quickly drew his hand away.

"*Rahtid!* Dat weak handshake, mon! Shake ma han' like yuh mean it." Andrew grinned and offered his hand again.

"Andrew, the rule still applies here, no patois allowed in the house. It is... beneath us." Major spoke with a firm voice while his face betrayed no emotion.

"Please, Major," Pauline implored.

Andrew's hand still hung in the air. Major extended his own, they shook and Pauline invited Thad, the car's driver, to sit down. Moving in quickly, Sheila poured two more glasses of sorrel and, virtually invisible, moved again into the background.

Thad Williamson was a short white man with blond hair. A native Jamaican, he had lived in Kingston all his life. Pauline greeted him with a hug and Major smiled and shook his hand enthusiastically, a gesture not lost on Andrew.

"How was the drive?" Major asked Thad.

"I haven't made it out to these parts in a while. Me forget how beautiful de countryside really is."

"And your son?" Pauline inquired. "He must be in graduate school by now."

Thad beamed, clearly a proud papa. "He's in medical school and plans to stay in the States after he finishes."

"Oh, Thad, that is wonderful!"

Major leaned over and clapped Thad on the shoulder. "Congratulations!"

"Thanks, mon!" Thad said. "But how about your own boy? A law degree from Columbia!"

"We couldn't be more proud!" Pauline looked at Major. "And we couldn't wait for Andrew to come home."

"Thank you, dear Mother."

There was a brief awkward silence, then Major, with an unanticipated note of enthusiasm said, "I'm planning to be his first client!"

The ice was broken if only for a little while.

"I'm so glad to be home," Andrew said, smiling at the people around the table. "After my academic imprisonment in England, and now that I got my law degree in the United States, I'm glad I spent time in New York. Now is time fe independence. Garvey sow de seeds long ago."

"Seeds?" Major retorted. "I hope you aren't trying to change anything but yourself. It's time for you to make some money, not change anything. Drink the milk, don't count the cows." Major looked at Pauline. "Are we in agreement?" Before anyone could answer he continued, "I never liked Garvey, especially after he did time in prison in the States. They should have kept him there and never allowed him back into Jamaica."

"He gave the colored man hope!" Andrew cried.

Thad laughed sarcastically. "The poor uneducated masses!"

Pauline opened her mouth to speak but was interrupted.

"It's a false hope," Major roared. "Going back to Africa in a boat! What did he call it? Oh yes! The Black Star Liner. What a pathetic joke." He picked up the sorrel and drank while looking reproachfully at Andrew. "Besides, *you* aren't Negro." Andrew ignored his father and stared at the glass of sorrell sparkling in the sunlight.

"Well," said Thad, clearing his throat and slapping his thigh, "We'll never find the answers to the problems of the world over a glass of sorrell, which means I must be off, I've got work to do."

"Thank you so much for bringing Andrew home," Pauline said.

"And I cannot thank you enough," Andrew added. He looked at the car where two servants stood after unloading the luggage. "Ahh, Mother, I forgot!" He approached the pile and began to sort through it.

Pauline joined Andrew but the two men remained seated at the table. Unasked, Sheila fetched the rum for them.

"I like your boy, Major, so full of enthusiasm," Thad said.

"Yes, he is, but sometimes I worry that it will be his undoing."

Thad leaned in and lowered his voice, speaking in a confidential tone. "Try to keep him out here, Major. It's real tense in Kingston. People are going to get hurt, and you don't want Andrew mixed up in it."

"Trouble at the docks?"

"Yah, mon. They're these Communist agitators, Alexander Bustamante and William Grant. The bastards been running all over the island talking about worker's rights and all that Union rubbish. They've been seen around the docks talking about organizing workers. I'll see hell freeze over before I see Unions on those goddamm docks."

"I've heard of Bustamante. Where's he from?"

"He's some moneylender from Kingston. Started making trouble about two years ago. There's a huge row over what to do about him. But the real problem is that William Grant." Thad's jaw was set firmly. "That illiterate, ex-Garveyite bastard is the one who's stirred up all dis trouble in de first place. He's the one who started this damn Union shit. He brought Bustamante in. I guess he needed someone who could read." Thad chuckled. "One thing for sure, I will fire anybody who comes into my business talking that rasclat nonsense!"

"Damn right," Major agreed. "I'm fortunate the Union will never come here."

"Yes!" A sudden shout from Andrew grabbed their attention. He stood, holding a guitar case over his head.

"A real rabble rouser, eh?" Thad laughed. "I better be gone. I'll let you know how this labor thing is going."

"Thank you, Thad." Major forced a smile to his lips. Thad's sincerity produced a bitterness in him. As the car drove off, Andrew began to play the guitar. Major was crestfallen.

A rabble rouser. The words filled Major with shame. Thad's son was studying medicine in the United States while his son, law degree in hand, was living the bohemian life in New York and entertaining wild dreams to change the world. What did I do to have him turn out like this? he pondered.

Major went into the house. The lighthearted banter between Andrew and Pauline, and the guitar's melodious sounds drifted over the patio and through the open windows. Major went past the tall doors and climbed three spiral flights of stairs to the tower office, entered, and with the windows shut, closed the door on the harmonious joy outside.

The hotter the day became, the slower the donkey pulled the dray down the road toward the Blaine Estate. Holding the reins as the wagon creaked along, Busby's eyes were closed. Next to him Linton delicately probed his lip with his tongue. The black thread from six new stitches stuck out like horse hairs, making him look, he feared, ridiculous. His face was bandaged and swollen. The dray lurched, startling Busby. He glanced at Linton.

"Yuh lucky, mon," Busby said.

"Yah? Tell me why."

"Yuh no appreciate it, mon. People a starve inna Jamaica now. Hunger a walk de lan', and only dutty water fe drink. It nuh rain enough. De dirt no good. No jobs. An' yuh a complain."

Linton remained silent. Acres of sugar cane surrounded them.

"Look, mon," Busby said, "Cordy tell me everyting, how yuh bawn dead, an' den yuh come to life. Dem was ready fe bury yuh when de midwife notice yuh start breathe. Everybody say it a miracle. Yuh fadda die inna de Great War. Mistah Blaine tell me all about him. When yuh mother passed on, God bless her soul, Mistah Blaine bring yuh here fe raise by Aunt Cordy. Now yuh luck change. Me fully expeck to see yuh make it, mon, but yuh gotta stay humble an a good tings a comin'."

Linton snorted. Such lies Major and Aunt Cordy had told! Humble. Just another way to say accept my humiliation. Spurred by a momentary generousity of spirit, Linton reconsidered. Perhaps Cordy doesn't know the truth, he mused. Who knows what Major told her.

"Yah, mon," he replied.

"Why yuh nuh let me do de talkin."

"I didn't want to be a coward."

"When me tell yuh fe do somepin, yuh fe do it. I run de distillery, anyting dat happen dey is me responsible. Yuh must tink yuh is a young lion. Why didn't yuh defend yuhself las' night?"

Linton's face showed no expression. The only thing that had kept him from lashing back last night was fear. He was terrified of his father.

"Yeah," Busby continued, "Yuh quiet now."

Linton looked away and rolled his eyes. He was living a lie and he was tired of lying. Yet, he did not dare reveal his secret. He knew what people would say, how they would gossip, and how his father was obsessed with keeping his patrimony a secret. He wondered how much longer he could go on with the charade before something in him snapped.

The sound of Busby's voice again interrupted his thoughts. "Me gonna drop yuh at the servants' quarters. Sheila said she would wait at yuh house."

Linton moved carefully as he got out of the dray and walked up the lane. He looked like a mummy bandaged in white and the children stared at him inquisitively. He wanted to whirl around to grab at them playfully, but the throb in his head was building painfully. Finally reaching his cottage he shoved the door open and saw Sheila. He stepped forward into her arms, and moving to the bed, they collapsed. His head was cradled in her arms. The need to sleep, the heat, his lip, and the lusty scent of Sheila's body were overwhelming.

"You were so quiet at dinner, Major, you hardly said a word." Pauline moved closer to him under the sheets. The window was wide open with a screen keeping insects at bay.

"Yes, I was quiet."

"Why?"

"No outbursts right?"

"Let's just have a simple happy Christmas." Pauline's green eyes shone like emeralds in the dim evening light. "Please?" She buried her face in his chest.

Major hugged her tighter to himself. "Why is the boy so damn bohemian?"

"You have to let him explore."

"Oh! So that's what you been telling him."

"No --"

"What then?"

"I just want to give him a bit of freedom."

"Freedom," Major's tone dripped with cynicism, "comes with responsibility."

Pauline was silent. Sometimes Major sounded like a broken record.

"The boy has a responsibility," he went on. "He has a foreordained purpose. I don't think he will even be there for the Crown, should he be needed. There's going to be a revolt, Pauline, I'm telling you. And Andrew disappoints me talking all this workers' rights nonsense! And independence from the Crown?! Where would we be if that happened? The Blaine Estate is waiting for him, so where is he? Dammit, Pauline, it's time for him to step up and be a --mfff!" Major's voice was muffled by Pauline's kiss. Only then could he hear the birds crying out in the night.

11

JUNE 1937, KINGSTON, JAMAICA

Only three minutes to go. The nun glared at the classroom full of teenage girls who sat like shiny black stones under her scrutiny. Even with every window in the classroom wide open, the unbearable humidity left everyone dripping with perspiration.

It was the longest day of the school year, the Friday before summer vacation. Daisy Wellstead sat at her desk, trying to endure. She could hardly contain her excitement. As the seconds ticked by, the students continued to observe the requirement for silence.

Daisy glanced furtively to her sister, Callie, who sat a few desks over. Not a peep. Less than a minute to go. As the seconds ticked by, the sounds outside the classroom grew louder, the braying of the donkeys in Constant Spring Road, vendors shouting from their fruit stands, the sharp repeat of the peanut roasters whistles.

The nun placed a hand in the small of her back and tried to straighten up. "I want to --"

Riiiiiiing!

The old woman's words were swallowed up by the frenzied outburst of prisoners set free. Daisy grabbed her slate and ran for the door, nearly colliding with Callie. The hallway was choked with schoolgirls pouring from the classrooms.

Moving into the noisy pandemonium, the girls edged over to their lockers. Daisy knelt to open the bottom locker. She put on her white straw jippy-joppa hat and then nearly knocked it off, closing the locker door, forgetting the extra wide brim that always flopped out. She joined Callie and they entered the tide of students trying to leave the hall.

"Lawd, de bell couldn't ring quick enough," Daisy said. "Is like she would nevah stop talkin!"

"Every year she gi' us de same lecture," Callie said. "Go home, don't take wi' de bwoys, go to church an' confession. Me had enough a dis place. Come on nuh!"

Pushing and shoving, the sisters made their way through the crowd, merging with the river of schoolgirls clad in blue and white spilling onto the sidewalk. The school colors tempered the conflicting hot pink walls, red doors and yellow and turquoise trim of nearby buildings. Constant Spring Road was a clamour of horse and donkey carts, small herds of goats, roaming dogs, pigs, and the occasional cow. Every now and then a Landsdowne Triumph Gloria coupe or an old Crossley Golden sedan came down the street, engines out of tune and sputtering. The combined debris of dust, manure and exhaust irritated the eyes and noses of laborers, shoppers and beasts, democratically assaulting everyone without regard to status. It was a perfect picture of regimented chaos.

Daisy, at seventeen, was tall and well proportioned. She was less voluptuous than Callie, but most men found her looks utterly stunning. She wore no makeup. Daisy discovered that men treated her differently when she wore makeup: red lipstick drove men crazy and provoked behavior that she found intolerable. She passed through the clotted crowd with ease, striding forward purposefully against the tides of younger girls.

Scrambling to keep up, stutter-stepping around her fellow students in hot pursuit of her sister, Callie was two years younger than Daisy, and several inches shorter. But Callie's school uniform concealed a well-developed, curvaceous figure, wide hips and strong, athletic legs.

Daisy stepped into line to board the bus and moments later, Callie caught up, cutting in front of Daisy in the line.

"Yuh comin to Parade?" Callie asked, gasping for breath.

"Me nuh have time fe party. Mummaa ask me fe come home quick."

"What? Please, dere's plenty time fe help Mummaa and still go to Parade."

They rode the Number 30 along with most of the other passengers and got off at Parade, a block-square park that was Kingston's most popular downtown hangout. Balloon hawkers strolled the paths, their multicolored goods tethered to a wrist, crying, "Balloons, balloons, any color, any choice, only fe tuppence!" Pushcarts and stationary foodstands sold hot, juicy beef patties and roasted goatfish, and bammy pancakes made with cassava. People with less elaborate setups stood next to open cartons stocked with star apples, sweet sop and sour sop, naseberries, oranges, mangoes and papaya. Along the streets surrounding the park, girls looking to party flirted with passers-by, and impromptu firepits began to smolder with charcoal in preparation for the long night ahead. Mischief was in the air, yet the festivities had hardly begun.

Boys stood around trying to chat up the girls and the girls, shy with inexperience, cautiously gathered in groups and chattered amongst themselves. People of every shade, shape and background waited impatiently for when darkness descended and the groups dissolved into one seething, sweating mass, dancing to the tunes of countless musicians playing their music, playing for money, playing for sheer, wanton abandonment and joy, playing –– for themselves.

Daisy wasted little time gawking and headed home but Callie dawdled, longing to stay. Finally giving in, she ran and caught up with her sister.

"Is gonna be de largest party inna Kingston tonight." Callie grabbed Daisy's arm and drew her closer. "Yuh know, is de end of school party night, is goin' be wild."

"Stop nuh!" She yanked her arm away.

"Mummaa nuh need yuh all night. If we cannot make de party a Parade, dem say dem havin' big party over Hope Gardens too. We can ––"

"No." Daisy was emphatic. Now that her sister's mind was made up, Callie knew there was no changing it.

"Daze, please, Mummaa won't let me go without yuh."

"Too bad. I have work to do. Mumma sey she need help."

"What is it? Me will help yuh."

Daisy stopped, looked at Callie and slapped her knee laughing. "Yuh? Help me?" She started walking briskly. "Yuh so *la-zy*, yuh mus' tink me crazy."

"Daisy!"

Daisy walked ahead while Callie, trying to walk alongside her, avoided the surging cars and carts, the two of them arguing all the while.

In Beeston Street, they passed a long row of women squatting on low stools selling vegetables.

At the pristine white gate of number 42, Daisy paused. "I have plans to be something, Callie. Time for play is ovah. Yuh still a likkle girl, but it's me las' day of school. I'm a woman now!"

"Cha! Yuh can't even keep a boyfriend," Callie snorted. "Besides, who would want yuh hand in marriage? It's so scarred up." She laughed wickedly and ran into the house, dashing up stairs.

Daisy looked at her left hand. A bright scar crossed the knuckles where her fingers joined her hand. Twelve stitches. It marred what were otherwise beautiful hands.

Stung, Daisy bounded up the stairs, in a frenzy to continue the argument, but Callie was already locked in her bedroom.

"Yah servants and garbage-boys," she yelled at the door. "Dats all yuh got!"

"Stop yuh noise!"

Daisy nearly dropped. Spinning around she beheld Wilbur, a paunchy middle aged man with a lazy left eye, carrying a bundle of wood from the inner courtyard. Slowly his scowl of disapproval turned into a mischievious smile.

"If yuh is a woman, yuh cannot run inna de house a shout and scream," he said, his grin broadening in size as he spoke. "Yuh nuh mus handle yuhself like a woman!"

"Yes, Wilbur." Daisy nodded. She didn't really like Wilbur and felt ill at ease around him. With his skewed eye, it was always difficult to know what he was looking at. Sometimes her intuition crackled and she felt his attention, probing, searching her most sensitive areas. But since her father had passed away over two years earlier, Wilbur had become her mother Rose's love and salvation. She didn't know what her mother saw in him.

"Daisy!"

Rose's voice boomed from her room down the hall.

"Congratulations on finishing school." Wilbur patted her shoulder and carried his load into the kitchen.

Daisy found her mother sitting in the middle of the large king-size bed surrounded by envelopes, invoices, documents, and ledgers. In the two years since her husband's unexpected death, Rose struggled to keep up with an ice business here in Kingston, and one in May Pen, thirty miles to the west. But her high blood pressure prevented her from working harder.

Rose anticipated Daisy's help once she had left school, and Daisy eagerly awaited the day that she could stand by her mother's side. Now the moment had come. Daisy felt her chest swell with pride.

"Me so proud to see yuh done wit school," Rose said. "Me feet swell, an' me fallin' behind." Rose shook her head. "I wish your big sister, Iris was here."

"But isn't she coming for Christmas?"

"Yes, but me want her fe stay. Me could use her here."

Offhandedly, Daisy said, "I wish I could visit Iris inna New York."

"Dere so much hatred dey for us, what yuh wan' go dey for? An' don' lie, yuh not going fe no visit, yuh wan' stay. An' yuh stay dere, dem goin' turn yuh inna prostitute. Dey do dat wit' young girls like yuhself."

"That's not what I heard."

"What yuh hear are lies. Iris would have been better off if

she had stayed here."

Daisy watched Rose sitting in the midst of the papers. Rose appeared larger than ever, an imposing figure sitting cross-legged, her head cocked to one side. The impression left Daisy in a respectful silence; she did not wish to challenge her mother.

"I wish I knew more about Iris's husband," Rose sighed. "De husband yuh fe choose is crucial," Rose said, looking sharply into her daughter's eyes. "De only good man me know in me life was yuh father. He worked hard, and then he come home. And him make sure we taken care of. Yuh father always say, me work hard fe me pickney, dem fe have something when me gone. Him struggle an start dis ice business and him lef' it fe us when he died.

"And him was always faithful," Rose said. "A good man, why him haffi die?" Rose looked upward, as though she could see Titus, her dead husband, relaxing atop a heavenly cloud. Wiping the tears, she went on. "Daisy, me is strong on me own. Me corner de ice market in downtown Kingston and now dem wan' kill me fi doing it," she laughed. "But sometimes it's a bit much."

"What will yuh do now?"

Rose kissed her teeth and looked at Daisy. "*We* haffi run de business, dere's no choice."

"We?" A smile crept onto Daisy's face.

"Is time fe yuh to step in fe me and supervise de ice house. Grapples will help. When yuh want something, tell Grapples, and he will see that de men get de message. Remember, de men is goin' fe try to find a way fe test yuh. Jus' deal wit' Grapples."

Daisy threw her arms around Rose. "Mummaa!"

"Nuh bother get too happy gal. Is plenty a hard work ahead." Rose disentangled from the embrace and reached for a manila envelope. "Under no circumstances are you to open this. I need yuh an' Callie to deliver it to Timothy inna May Pen tomorrow."

"Callie! Why she haffi come?"

"Yuh mus' look out fe one another. I'm tired a dis foolishness and fighting between yuh!"

"Mummaa, she nuh do nothin' 'round de house! It all fall 'pon me. Mek her stay an' do somepin 'round here."

"No. She goin wit' yuh. Yuh tink me goin' let yuh mek a trip like dat alone? Yuh mus' be crazy."

Daisy rolled her eyes. "Where me fe find dat one hand man?"

"Yuh know where him is, inna de white house across from de train station. He will be very glad to see yuh," Rose said.

"Him mus' be older den de hills."

"Timothy never too old fe deliver, and him collect plenty money fe me wit' him one han'. Him have his crew dey." Rose got up from the bed and sat down in her rocking chair and closed her eyes. "Me tired now, wan' get some res'."

Smiling, Daisy quietly closed the door.

At daybreak Daisy was busy in the kitchen making breakfast. The room smelled of cinnamon, pimento, and peppers. On the stove, salted fish cakes in bubbling coconut oil sizzled in a cast iron skillet.

From the kitchen window she watched Kingston shake the sleep off its streets. Across the yard, outside the ice house, wagons and pushcarts bathed in rose-colored early morning light, lined up, waiting to be loaded with ice.

Daisy put the plate of fish cakes on the table and stared critically at the breakfast arrangement -- a steaming pot of tea, dumplings, toast, fish fritters, and three bowls of porridge. A delicate yellow hibiscus in the center of the table glowed in a beam of sunlight. She admired her creation. Her face glowed with excitement. Since yesterday, when Rose gave her the errand to go to May Pen, she had been fantasizing about the trip. She could not wait to leave for the train station. Impatient, she started looking for Callie.

"Come nuh!" Daisy cried. "Callie! Breakfast ready, come on, nuh?"

She was only five years old when she last made a trip on the train beyond Kingston and could barely remember the simplest things about the journey. She again leaned into the hall corridor and yelled, "Callie! We leavin' in ten minutes."

In her bedroom, Callie did not respond. She was upset at having to go to May Pen. She had planned to go to a balm yard north of St. Andrew to watch the healers at work. She shivered in frustration as she bent down and tied her shoes. The previous night's argument left her depressed and angry. She couldn't ask her mother to let her go to the balm yard instead of May Pen. Spirit healing was considered outside of the sphere of Christianity and was, therefore, of the devil.

All three of Rose's daughters were familiar with bush medicine due to Rose's efforts to teach them as they grew up. But where Daisy and Iris found it enough to learn about herbs and roots, healing the body, Callie was enchanted with the idea of, affecting the soul as well. Only Obeah, the African black magic as practiced in Jamaica covered both body and soul. It picked up where bush medicine left off with incantations, love philtres, poisons, amulets, and spells that dealt with the mysterious forces in higher and lower realms.

"Yuh fe steer clear a dem evil African foolishness an' black magic," Rose admonished Callie, but her advice fell on deaf ears.

"Mummaa, please let me go to St. Andrew," Callie had begged last night.

But Rose was firm. "Yuh mus' go wit' Daisy. Is time yuh leave de rubbish alone and take an interest inna something real, like de damn business."

Daisy had quietly smirked.

"In de morning," she'd said, "we fe catch the 8:30 train to May Pen. No worries Callie." Daisy looked at her haughtily. "I've been on this train line before."

Rose kissed her teeth and frowned at Daisy. "Me sending yuh both, fe look out fe one another. Please, don't either of you disappoint me, jes' get along."

Callie came out of her room, went into the kitchen and hurriedly ate breakfast, then waited for Daisy at the foot of the stairs. She decided that it would be better to keep quiet rather than vent her anger. Daisy slowly came down the stairs. As she approached, Callie moved ahead, left the yard and strode down the street toward Kingston Station. Daisy hurried to catch up.

"Excited, eh?" Daisy said cheerfully, but she was met by Callie's stony silence. They continued together without saying another word, purchased their tickets, boarded the train, and sat, in different rows, as if they were strangers.

Clickety-clack, clickety-clack…. The sonorous, hypnotic beat of the rails intensified Daisy's excitement. She sat with her face close to the window observing the transformation from city to country as the train labored over the Liguanea Plain toward Spanish Town. Meanwhile, Callie stared vacantly, sulking, dwelling on why she should have been allowed to go to the balm yards. Each revolution of the wheels carried her closer to the parish line between Saint Andrew and Saint Catherine. The unrelenting rhythm deepened her funk and she avoided looking out the windows, as if to deny that she were on a train to May Pen.

Clickety-clack….

The train crossed the steel truss of the Rio Cobre Bridge. Daisy could hardly believe the broad sweep of the river, majestically swollen from recent rains. Spanish Town bordered the river bank and as the train pulled out of the station, Daisy opened the window and closed her eyes. Sultry tropical air blew across her face. She could not understand Callie's dark disinterest. She was thrilled to be going to May Pen.

When the distant mountains appeared, even Callie could not resist a furtive glance. She began to see vegetation she recognized only from pictures: a trumpet tree here, a blue mahoe tree there, sweeping expanses of wild guinea grass. Finally as curiosity took hold, Callie wondered where, exactly, she was. How will I know I'm in Clarendon Parish? Callie wondered. Ahead, a plateau spread out before them, huge fields of sugar cane. It had to be Clarendon. She watched the cane bowing and bending in the draft of the rapidly moving train and, for the time being, surrendered her resentment.

A forest of telephone poles heralded their entry into May Pen. Homes, some little more than shacks, dotted the landscape. As they approached the town center, the girls gawked at the bustle. Finally Daisy made her way over to Callie and took a seat next to her.

"We must get off at May Pen station," Daisy said.

Daisy's voice rekindled Callie's resentment. "I know that," she snapped. "Let's do what we here fe do, an' go home."

But Daisy wasn't listening. Nearly bursting with anticipation, she stared out the window and waited for the train to come to a halt.

Pshhhhhhh! Releasing billows of hot steam, the locomotive had slowed to a walking pace. Along the track siding, bananas, the deposed king of yesteryear's international commerce, were piled up to be shipped to Kingston. Well-muscled men, clad in tight pants and sleeveless shirts, lazed on crates. As the train jerked to a halt the men sprang to life to either load or unload cargo. Adding to the tumult, vendors crowded the platform, pushing and shouting, vying for customers, selling everything from chicklets to breadfruit, ackee, and sweet sop.

Walking through the station and feeling unsure of themselves, the girls held hands in spite of their mutual irritation. The smell of ginger root, bananas, peppers, cigarette smoke and stale sweat made Callie feel ill. She was impatient to get outside. But the melange of aromas invigorated Daisy. She breathed deeply, trying to take it all in.

Walking over to a stand where an old, dark-skinned woman sat, Daisy surveyed the array of fresh and dried herbs: vervain studded with purple blooming flowers, Jamaican medina, front end lifter and bizzy and many others, all neatly packaged in brown paper bags. She was pleased with herself at being able to identify the herbs by sight. The old woman smiled, smoking a cigarette, her cheeks puffing out, showing two rows of perfect white teeth.

"Yuh goin stand dey, or yuh goin' buy something?" Callie asked, trying to get Daisy moving again.

Picking up some shiny brown nuts, Daisy asked, "De bizzy 'ere, how much?"

"Haypenny a sack, penny fe three."

Daisy tossed the bizzy back in the basket. "Yuh nuh here fe higgle, yuh here fe thief!" She took Callie's hand and headed for the exit.

Callie mumbled, "We'll never find Timothy inna dis confusion."

"He lives cross de street." Emerging from the station Daisy motioned toward a blue and white building. "Dere de place is."

At the side of the house stood an old man, his white hair glistening in the hot sun. Timothy, known as the Ice-man of May Pen, was a tall dark skinned man who carried himself with a gentle pride that was accommodating to others. His left hand was horribly disfigured, with the thumb and pinky missing and only three fingers protruding from a mangled stump.

But his smile was his trademark. Six gold teeth glittered when he grinned, even making Callie feel gleeful. He opened the gate and urged them to enter. "Daisy, Callie, is been two years an' me nuh see yuh since yuh faddah pass." They hugged and he led them through the yard, past flowering bushes, a breadfruit tree, and the small shed that housed the cooling unit for the ice-house. Young men using grappling hooks to move the ice momentarily stopped work to observe the attractive young guests, while the girls shyly avoided their gazes.

Timothy showed them to a table on the zinc-roofed open porch. "I was expeckin' yuh," he said holding a chair for each, in turn, to sit.

"How so Mas' Tim?" asked Callie. "Is impossible."

"Yah, mon." He flashed a golden smile. Timothy was barefoot; his pants were cut to resemble a long pair of shorts and they hung from him loosely, concealing his scrawny legs. A white undershirt accentuated his belly. Yet his face had not one wrinkle, making him appear at least twenty years younger. Only the white hair suggested his advanced years.

"How could you expect us? We didn't phone, and we didn't send a telegram. So how yuh know?" asked Daisy.

"News travel fast inna de country." It was difficult to tell if he was serious. "News travel faster here dan in Kingston." He nodded, making Daisy think he was pondering the fact. "Ahhh," he said abruptly, "I'm actin' like a terrible host. Yuh mus' be thirsty."

"Oh God, yes," Callie said. Daisy stared as if looking right through her.

"Tis too hot not to have refreshment -- Margaret!"

A young girl, perhaps fifteen, appeared in the doorway. She was dressed in a ragged blouse that was too small for her well developed body, and a long flowing skirt. She'd been napping and yawned widely, shaking the sleep away.

"Unnoo wan' eat sompin'?" Margaret asked.

"What?" Daisy, accustomed to a Kingstonian accent, had difficulty unraveling the Clarendonian lilt. "What yuh say?"

"She ask if you wan' eat," Timothy interpreted.

"When must we get back to de station?" Callie fidgeted with impatience.

Daisy seemed determined to do the opposite of whatever Callie wanted. She shot Callie a dirty look. "Thank you, Mas' Tim, we will be happy to eat." She opened her briefcase and extracted two envelopes, and handed them to Timothy. "From Mummaa."

Timothy gave one to Margaret to open, and using his teeth, opened his envelope, extracting a large sum of money while Margaret read the other one silently. When she looked up, she said, "Rose is closing us down."

"What?" Daisy couldn't believe her ears.

"Why are yuh so surprised?" Timothy asked, sticking the cash in his pocket.

"Mummaa just said I was going to help her with the ice business!"

"In Kingston, yes. But out here in May Pen business is not good any longer. There is too much competition now and the prices are falling. Me tell yuh mudda to consider closing dis place and concentrate on Kingston. Is why I was expeckin' yuh fe come close we down."

Daisy crossed her arms. Clearly, this old man did not understand the complexities of business. He may have been her father's friend, but he was only a bumpkin at best. Yet, in an outward show of respect she held her tongue, having been raised to respect her elders.

Margaret soon returned to the porch and they slaked their thirst with tall glasses of chilled sorrel. Overhead, clouds gathered, partially obscuring the sun and reducing the heat. After a few more minutes, Margaret emerged with hot food. Once Callie tasted the rice and peas, and boiled green banana smothered with a rich, spicy, Jamaican curried goat, her impatience was transformed. She forgot about the train. Daisy, too, ate with gusto. Both girls complimented Margaret enthusiastically on her cooking.

Time passed quickly and before they knew it Timothy said, "Is time fe go.

Passing through the gate, the girls turned to wave. The table was already cleared, and Margaret was nowhere to be seen.

"Daisy!"

She walked back to Timothy who waited for her.

"Did yuh forget something?" He offered Daisy a scrap of paper. "I believe Rose goin' want yuh to account for all dat money. Yuh want a receipt?" Sheepishly, Daisy took it from him, sticking it in her pocket, and ran across the street to join Callie, leaving Timothy waving good-bye.

On the train ride back to Kingston, the hard wooden benches inside the coach prevented Daisy from dozing. Callie, next to her, seemed oblivious to the discomfort, and her head dipped forward with sleep.

In years past the two sisters had been close but now Daisy's resentment of Callie was growing. She thought back to when Callie was still a little kid, maybe eleven years old, being beaten up by a class bully. Daisy jumped in and defended her little sister, pummeling the classmate to the ground. It took a crowd to pull her off the girl.

After school the next day, the girl's two older sisters were waiting for Daisy. They jumped her and dragged her to the ground. What they didn't figure on was Daisy's incredible rage. She bit one girl's hand, drawing blood, and kicked the other in the face so hard three of the girl's front teeth were knocked out.

What irritated Daisy now, though, was Callie's attitude. She showed a complete lack of curiosity about the family business, never offered to help, and when she was asked to do something, often left the task half finished. One time, Callie had been asked to stay at the ice house to collect a check for an ice shipment the customer was going to pick up. When the customer arrived, he neglected to pay for the ice but Callie absent-mindedly issued the receipt anyway. The customer, who was not a regular and needed the ice for a special occasion, never paid the bill, but Callie simply justified the mistake by saying she didn't have the temperament for business.

"Me is interested inna other affairs," she'd say.

But the affairs in which Callie showed interest were taboo in Rose Wellstead's opinion. Callie's interests became an issue in the Wellstead household when Rose discovered her pouch of obeah familiars: parrot beaks, fowl bones, some sticks, and a handful of dirt. Black magic, or white magic, it made no difference: the occult was Satan's business.

"Don' bring dem type a tings inna me house," Rose said, throwing Callie's treasures into the stove.

But Callie doggedly pursued her interest. The youngest of three sisters, she felt the need to define herself in a way that would command attention in a female-dominated home. Her quest led her beyond the acceptable boundries to a more traditional African cultural practice that was both feared and sought after.

Roman Catholicism, Rose's staff, did not capture Callie's imagination, nor was she bound to it by fear. Fascinated with making love potions, and casting spells in order help people in romance and money, Callie engaged in a clandestine search for a teacher. The fact that obeah was also used to kill and wreak disaster did not deter her. Callie wanted to help others in their health, wealth, and love, not in achieving personal revenge. The train rhythmically rocked to and fro. Daisy watched Callie sleeping and as time passed, her stare became softer and she, too, nodded off.

In what seemed to be a only a few moments later, Daisy was jerked awake. She opened her eyes to see the train pulling into the Kingston station. The locomotive gave one final jolt and hissed, releasing a cloud of hot white steam, adding to the general misery of the passengers sweltering in the relentless heat.

The stroll home was jovial in contrast to their walk to the train station earlier and they decided to go to Parade. They went back to Beeston Street and Daisy left the briefcase upstairs and then left for Parade with Callie. The sun had long set by the time they climbed the stairs to their house.

As they walked by their mother's door, they noticed that the lights were off. A sigh of relief escaped from Daisy's lips. They were home free. Their bedrooms were just footsteps away.

Waving good-night to Callie, Daisy took firm hold of the doorknob, opened it, and turned on the light.

Sitting on Daisy's bed Rose looked sternly at her shocked daughter.

"*Where* were you?" she demanded, "and where is my receipt?"

Daisy's froze like a marble statue. She was unable to speak.

"Receipt?" Rose repeated.

Daisy suddenly realized with horror she had forgotten all about the receipt for the money she gave Timothy.

"Where is it?" Rose persisted. "Well, gal? Say something! This is business."

"Is in de briefcase Mummaa. I forgot to give it to yuh."

"In de briefcase? What it doin' in dey? Go get it!"

Daisy retrieved the case. But the receipt wasn't inside, and she felt herself wilting with fear.

Daisy walked down the hall to her bedroom empty-handed, Callie stuck her head out form her room. "It's in your pocket," she hissed.

"I heard dat!" Rose shouted. "Come here!"

Daisy dug the bill from her pocket and gave Rose the crumpled receipt,.

"Daisy, dis job is too important," Rose said quietly. "I need responsible, honest people 'round me. Dis," she held out the tattered receipt, "is not good business. I'm sure Timothy gave you a nice crisp reciept, an' yuh treat it like dis? Is our livelihood,

Daisy. There are men who say woman can't run business. Men who -- yuh know, just waiting for us to slip. Yuh haffi conduct yourself as a responsible woman if yuh goin get respect. Yuh deeply disappoint me gal."

Rose got up, went down the hall into her own bedroom and quietly closed the door. Daisy's eyes welled up with tears. The first test and she had failed miserably. But there was little time for tears. During the next four weeks Daisy discovered just how difficult it was to establish herself as the boss of resentful, disrespectful men, most of whom really did know the business better than she. The hours she worked were long. Work around the ice factory started at dawn and lasted till dusk. She had no free time to hang out with her friends or play games with Callie. She started the day by talking with Grapples, a tall dark skinned man with a large head and long arms. As foreman, he always knew how the coolers were functioning, how many ice carts were expected, if there were any unresolved labor problems, or how they would fill an unanticipated half ton order. All of that and more came up during their morning meetings.

Grapples, she felt, tried to assert his imagined authority in a way that annoyed her to no end. She was desperate to find a way to assume total dominance, despite the massive odds against her. Not only was she a woman in a man's job, she was the boss's daughter, and most damning of all, still just an inexperienced kid. Daisy kept a watchful eye on Grapples, worked all day, and by evening, was bushed.

One morning the telephone rang early, before Daisy had even eaten breakfast. It was Grapples and he sounded frantic.

"Missus, we have... a problem down inna here. Jesus! Yuh mus'..."

"Calm down," Daisy said. Her voice was steady and strong. Intuitively, she knew that any big problem she solved would solidify her position in the business.

"But Miss ..." Grapples breath was ragged.

" I'll be down de stairs inna minute," Daisy said calmly. "No need fe big botheration." She hung up the phone softly and sighed. Rose called from her room.

"Yes, Mummaa," Daisy stuck her head in the door.

"What's wrong down dey?" Daisy closed her eyes in frustration. Nothing made it past Rose. "Grapples needs to see me. Nothing important so you mus' relax, Mummaa." Daisy took her mother's hand.

"Thank God fe yuh. Me nuh know how me would do without yuh. Please do me a favor," Rose continued, "an' later today pick up some epsom salts fe me feet."

Before leaving the house Daisy studied herself in the mirror. She was wearing a pretty yellow skirt with an opaque white cotton blouse. Should she change her clothes, make herself look less pretty? Deciding, she crossed the street to the ice house still wearing the same clothes. At the door, she took a deep breath. Her stomach throbbed with butterflies. Forcing herself to breathe normally, she opened the door and entered the building.

It was always a welcome relief from the heat to be in the ice-house. While the soaring temperature and humidity steamed the city of Kingston, the workers in the ice-house on Beeston Street found refuge inside the cool building. *The House*, as the workers dubbed it, consisted of one spacious room with a high, vaulted zinc roof that was pockmarked with holes, the result of years of corrosion. Within this room refrigeration chambers were lined up neatly in rows, freezing large blocks of ice and keeping it frozen.

As Daisy crossed The House, her red flat shoes tipped, tapped, and slid on the concrete and sodden sawdust floor. The men were gathered around the engine. They wore light jackets, dungarees, and work gloves. Daisy felt chills up and down her spine. Towering and silent, the men, stared sullenly at the floor, shifting their weight from foot to foot and sneaking furtive glances at Daisy's bare legs. Goose bumps covered her flesh. She felt apprehensive and exposed, standing before the men, but that was her secret; outwardly she knew she appeared firm and in control. Grapples emerged from the group. He held a small metal object.

"De compression inna de engine *gone*, mon!" Grapples said. "Him over dey," He pointed at a short man who hung back from the others. "Him forget fe open de safety valve, an' de regulation valve mash up! Me wan' fire him. Him is nothin' but trouble. Yuh *rasclat*!"

Annoyed with his swagger, Daisy wisely paused before continuing, managing to conceal her true feelings. She knew better than to chastise Grapples in front of the men. Instead she struck a conciliatory tone, "Mistakes happen," she said.

"Question is wha' we gonna do now?"

She turned her attention to the regulation valve. A protruding post seemed to screw into a joint and if she were to unscrew it, she thought, the regulation valve might open up.

The men were growing restless, waiting for something to do. Grapples stepped forward. "De refrigeration stop work now. De temperature a rise as we speak. Is impossible situation we in." Grapples raised his voice. "Me nuh think —"

Keeping her tone of voice neutral, Daisy politely interrupted Grapples, "Have we sold today's ice?"

"Nah, Miss, we have plenty orders fe fill."

"Grapples, me wan' yuh fe take *charge* a de situation like yuh always do. Have some men go an' start loading de ice orders quick as possible and load de wagon dem up."

Grapples wasted no time. "Yuh three over there, go an' load up de rest of the carts. An yuh two go wit' Erik an get de chill trays ready for de water. De res' a yuh goin pack ice fe de retail customers. Come on, mon *move*!"

The workers casually walked off, their pace a clear statement of what they thought of Daisy giving orders, even through Grapples. She looked over at her foreman and called him outside. Once they were alone she handed the regulator to Grapples.

"Well, yuh have any suggestions?"

Grapples studied the device, turning it over and over in his big hammy hands.

"De gasket blown. Can't be repaired."

"Nah mon!" Daisy said, "dere mus' be a way. Nuthin' less will do."

"It mus' do," Grapples said, handing the device back.

"Didn't you put in de compressor?"

"Gal! It mus' be fifteen years ago."

"What about a hardware store?"

Grapples shook his head. "De gasket made special fe de valve. Yuh mus cable New Orleans fe de part an' dem will send it to yuh."

"So yuh expeck me fe sit here? Mek me go an' see if me can buy some kind a rubber washer fe it."

Looking at Daisy, Grapples rolled his eyes. "Don't go by yuhself, Daisy. Me––"

"Cha! Me gone!" She took off, trotting towards home while Grapples watched her cross the street.

Jus like her father, he thought.

Daisy went straight to the kitchen, got a screwdriver, and opened up the regulator. She knew nothing about refrigeration but noticed the bits of black rubber inside and understood that they were the crumbled remains of a seal. She reclosed the regulator and carefully placed the assembled valve in a black velvet bag that had housed some of her paste jewelry.

In Rose's business phone book she found the factory repair contact. Lingering over a glass of water, she organized a plan of action. The very first thing was to send a telegram to the parts manufacturer in New Orleans, Louisiana. She gathered the bag and left for the telegraph office. After she wired for the new part, she'd try to find a rubber washer that fit temporarily at least. When she turned into King Street, Daisy ran smack into a large crowd of marchers protesting the skyrocketing price of metered water. The crowd, made up of men, women, and children, was noticeably poor; some wore little more than rags. A light-skinned man with straight dark hair led the group toward the government offices, located on the same block as the Telegraph Office, and try though she did to avoid them, Daisy got caught up as the mass surged forward. She cursed her luck. After some minutes, the leader held up his arms, bringing the motley procession to a halt. Seizing the opportunity, Daisy broke free and hurried on.

When she entered the Telegraph Office, she was surprised to find the clerk asleep. She slammed her hand on the counter, causing him to jump, smacking his head on a shelf.

"Lawd Jeesus!" he exclaimed, gingerly rubbing his head. "Gal wha' yuh tryin' to do?"

Daisy's look was sour.

"Cha," he added, "nuh bother act like yuh tink yuh de mayor."

"A telegram to ––"

"Goood marnin'," the clerk spoke slowly, elaborating each word. He gave Daisy a sarcastic sneer. "A wha' yuh need Miss?"

"A telegram." Daisy said.

"Yuh inna de right place, Miss. But," he yawned and pointed at a small table with different colored forms. "yuh have fe fill out de pink form over on dat table."

Daisy filled in the blanks, hoping no one entered the telegraph office before she completed the form. The cable to Carre, Inc. requested that a replacement valve be sent special delivery to her address in Kingston. She smiled with satisfaction; she had even remembered to include the parts number in the telegram. She gave the clerk instructions to send a messenger with the answering cable, thanked him like she meant it and, for added insurance, tipped the man generously.

Outside, the protesters gathered in front of the Colonial Office were cheering and making a ruckus while police, some carrying large sticks, attempted to surround the group. A few rowdies challenged the police to take them and their families to jail.

"At least we will eat!" a voice cried out.

Daisy craned to catch a glimpse of the speaker but was frightened off by a policeman's menacing look. She ran down a side street away from the demonstration. She had her own race against time, she reminded herself. Thirsty and out of breath, she hustled over to the hardware store on Queen Street.

Two frustrating hours later, Daisy had still not found a washer that fit. She had already visited two other stores and tried so many washers, her fingers were black. Her body felt tense as piano wire. Standing in the aisle at Pete and Port Hardware Store, she realized her search was proving futile.

She walked out the hardware store. Maybe Grapples was right, she thought. She turned down an alley that went behind the store and ran into a blacksmith's foundry. For a moment she watched the dark skinned man labor in the heat and pound the metal surrounded by the hot coals.

Her eye focused on the metal that the smith was pounding. With each stroke the metal yielded to the hammer, bending bit by bit. Suddenly, Daisy was struck by an idea. She would need some washers, and it wouldn't matter what their shape was. She hustled off and went back into the hardware store.

"I'll be damned if I give up now," she said out loud and a smile crossed her face. Picking a variety of washers, she hurried to the register and paid.

She ran home, realizing that it was now the hottest part of the day and there was still so much to be done, Daisy passed a crowd of men and women already preparing for the evening block party. When she arrived at 42 Beeston Street, the Ice House was eerily quiet.

"Grapples."

"Yes, Miss?"

"Bring me a small knife, pliers, two candles, matches, and a bowl of cold water."

There was a long pause. "Lawd Miss, yuh-a-get ready fe *obeah*?"

"Get de damn tings dem an' leave me. Yuh know me nuh like witchcraft. Now gwan!"

After gathering the supplies, Grapples returned to his hammock. Daisy sat down at a small table, her lips pursed. She struck a match, lit the candle, picked up one of the new washers with the pliers, and held it over the flame.

"Me goin' cook yuh," she muttered. The rubber threw off blue flames as it sputtered and crackled, and gave off noxious fumes. Her nose burned. Undeterred, she used a toothpick to deftly mold the hot rubber into a wider disk. She was patient and had to start over more than once. Beads of sweat rolled down her forehead and stung her eyes. She picked up another washer, held it to the flame and painstakingly, doggedly, crafted a crude but serviceable large round washer. Gently nestling the rubber inside the regulator valve groove, she screwed the apparatus back together.

She looked at the clock. It was five minutes past three. She made the sign of the cross and looked for Grapples. Together, they went over to the compressor.

"Here," she said handing him the regulator valve. "Put it in and start the compressor."

Grapples did not try to hide his skepticism.

She looked him in the eye and said, "Grapples if I wanted yuh opinion me would a give up by now!" After controlling her impatience for so many hours, Daisy could hardly contain her emotions. She watched restively as Grapples installed the valve.

The engine wheezed and gasped as if suffering from emphysema, then died. The silence was deafening. Behind them, a thousand beams of light shone through holes in the corrugated metal, dappling the wall.

"Try again."

And again the motor coughed and rattled, sputtered and wheezed. It cut out, only to catch again a moment later. A high-pitched hiss began and gradually grew louder and louder, until a *click* sounded. Grapples examined the regulator valve. No gas was escaping. The pressure continued to build, the tone of the motor became regular, and it began to purr happily. Daisy's face showed no emotion. Grapples stared at her in dumb amazement. The ammonia-water refrigeration system had been restored.

"Jeez-ahm lawd!" Grapples exclaimed.

"Grapples, I want yuh to put de water inna de chill trays and make sure de ice start up now."

"Jesus, Miss, yuh done de impossible." For the first time there was respect in Grapple's demeanor. He got busy preparing the water trays.

Daisy sat down at the table, weary, but buoyed by the elation of victory. Grapples was a nice man, she knew, trustworthy and loyal, and had acted as he thought best to keep the business running. She knew he thought she was too young and inexperienced to take over. But now, she realized, she had earned his respect. The power struggle was over. She was the boss. Squinting at the beams of sunlight, Daisy savored her victory against the real adversary in this race: the sun. I beat that old bastard, she thought.

There was a knock on the door. A boy from the telegraph office delivered a telegram and she gave him a penny. She opened the envelope and read, RECEIVED REQUEST [STOP] GASKET ON ORDER[STOP] DELIVERY 1 WEEK [STOP] CARRE INC NO LA [STOP] *WESTERN UNION.*

Feeling content that she'd put in a good day's work, Daisy left Grapples and went home. At the front door she remembered the epsom salts for Rose's aching feet. She turned back and headed for the pharmacy.

The sun was slipping below the horizon when Daisy finally entered the kitchen, epsom salts in hand. The aroma of the brown stew chicken, cooking on the stove, filled the air. She looked out the window at the setting sun, the light brilliant and beautiful. She closed her eyes and imagined the light surrounding her vital and vibrant, carrying her far above it all.

DECEMBER 1937, KINGSTON, JAMAICA

They walked timidly down the gangway, two wide-eyed children disembarking from an old banana boat. The *Allegria* had just docked in Kingston, the capital city of Jamaica, an island colony they had heard about since birth. Neither Clarence nor Charles Knowles could believe their eyes.

It was December, just a week before Christmas, and in New York City, from which they had just come, the wind blew cold and blustery and snowflakes filled the sky. Here a stiff warm breeze kissed the island and it looked like summer. A verdant carpet of green covered mist-cloaked hills and the humidity was comparable to a scorching New York summer day.

Iris, the children's mother, saw Daisy waiting on the pier. She'd felt confident kissing her husband Tom good-bye, and on the train, her excitement at returning to Jamaica had grown with each passing mile. But by the time she left Key West, she was plagued with anxiety. She was returning to her homeland for the second time in fourteen years. She looked up. The sky was filled with clouds, stirring memories of her trip home two years earlier. An image of her father laying in his casket flashed through her mind.

Frowning, she shepherded the boys to the gate. At Immigration, Iris showed their passports and continued on through Customs. With documents stamped and processed, they passed through the exit and Daisy was upon them with hugs and kisses.

"Dahling!" Iris cried. "*Rahtid!* Daisy? Daisy, you look so good!"

"I can hardly believe it," Daisy said. She turned to the boys.

"Boys, say hello to your Aunt Daisy." Iris nudged the boys forward. "This is Clarence and this is Charles." The kids squirmed under Daisy's scrutiny.

"Mah nephews!" she said, squatting and offering a hug. "Ahm so happy to finally meet yuh."

Charles, the older boy, mustered his courage and pointing at Clarence said, "He's eight, and I'm ten." He avoided looking at Daisy and tried to sneak a peek when her attention returned to Iris. Charles, with his full moon face, chocolate brown skin and jet black eyes, appeared as a stranger to Daisy, but Clarence had his mother's face, angular and sculpted, and light honey brown eyes.

They left the terminal and at the curb, Daisy hailed a taxi. The driver loaded the boot with luggage, while everyone piled inside..

Careening through the streets at breakneck speed, the driver raced past pedestrians in the crosswalks. The wind caused the temperature to fall a few degrees, giving Kingstonians brief respite from the eternal heat. Nevertheless, by the time they roared into King Street, the cab reeked of sweaty bodies. Iris took a small cut crystal atomizer from her purse and sprayed herself.

"Lavender water, eh?" Daisy asked.

"Yes, me dear." Iris's eyes sparkled with excitement, "I absolutely love it. It really soothes me, yuh know."

"Helps wit de smell too." Daisy smiled, watching the boys wrinkle their noses. "Tell me, how's Tom doing? We disappointed he didn't come wit' yuh."

A cloud descended on Iris's face, then quickly disappeared. "Oh––he's good. He wanted to come, but there was a business deal happening and he needs to keep close to the negotiations. He always looking for good investments." Iris fumbled uneasily with the atomizer trying to put it back in her purse. "Damn thing," she growled irritably. Then, realizing how foolish she appeared, she closed her eyes and, letting the air escape from her lungs, exhaled all her tension. She picked up the atomizer and sprayed on more lavender water.

"Yuh seem to need plenty soothin'." Daisy's comment hung in the air unanswered.

The cab pulled up to the curb and jerked to a halt. At the top of the stairs, Callie stood waiting to greet her oldest sister.

"Lawd Jesus," she called to Iris.

"Dahling!" Iris yelled back. She hurried up the stairs and before Callie knew it, she was being hugged so tightly she struggled for breath.

"My baby sister get sooo big!" Iris stood back and admired Callie. "Oh! Tell me, where Mummaa?"

"Yuh goin' kill her wit' dat stink," Callie answered, but she was grinning from ear to ear.

"Follow me," Daisy said, taking Iris down the hall.

Callie, recovering from the olfactory assault, studied the two little boys, who had only spoken in whispers to each other since coming into the house. The boys seemed puzzled. The way people spoke was not totally foreign, but the sound was more raw and lyrical. Clarence, the younger boy, projected a confident curiosity and excitement about getting to know this exotic place. But his brother, Charles, seemed put off, standing at a distance and hanging back. Maybe overwhelmed, Callie thought. Or less adventuresome. Probably tired from the long journey.

"Yuh hungry fe a likkle someting?" Callie asked.

"Huh?" Charles wrinkled his face.

"Food, mon," Callie repeated.

Callie could see the confusion on their expressive faces.

"Food, F-O-O-D," she said her hands pantomiming putting food in her mouth.

The boys nodded their heads.

"I'll go an' get yuh a mango." Callie dashed downstairs.

The two boys looked at each other.

"What did she say?" Charles whispered.

Clarence, sounding amazed, responded, "I saw three colored policemen."

"I know. I can't believe it." Charles shook his head. "Can't believe this place."

Daisy tapped lightly and opened the bedroom door a crack.

"Cha! Open de door, nuh?" Rose called.

The door swung wide and Iris entered followed by Daisy. Iris rushed to her mother's open arms and sank to her knees crying, and laughing, kissing Rose all over her face.

After a few moments, Rose held Iris at arms length, wrinkling her nose. "Lawd Jesus!" she said. "Dat lavender?"

"I'm sorry, Mummaa," Iris laughed even as her eyes were brimming with tears. "Is me lavender water —"

"Yuh tryin' fe poison me? Lawd, gal!" Rose tried to help Iris up. "Welcome back! Me nah expeck yuh fe visit us again, yuh know."

Iris sighed. "Mummaa, I'm back. Time will never pass without my comin' to see yuh." She laughed. "Listen to me speakin' patois already an' me back here inna Jamaica less dan a hour."

"Me pray every day fe yuh," Rose said. "Me pray fe yuh fe come home, an' since yuh nuh come, den me pray fe yuh safety. Is dangerous fe negar up dey."

"Mummaa! Is safe inna Harlem, yuh know."

Daisy laughed. But she was listening keenly. She was very curious about her older sister. When Iris was seventeen she had run off and jumped a ship to New York. Daisy was only three. She grew up hearing stories about how Iris had betrayed her family. But when their father learned that Iris had married a successful Harlem businessman, all was forgiven – or at least forgotten. At that point, Titus and Rose couldn't have been prouder. But only three years later Titus was dead and his many invitations to Iris to visit had been refused. His death had been traumatic for Daisy, as it had for everyone. Finally meeting her older sister two years ago, at her father's funeral, confirmed Daisy's suspicion that she had to go to America.

"I want to visit Iris in New York," Daisy said, taking advantage of a pause in the conversation.

Rose gave Daisy a dismissive glance. "Cha! Yuh goin' no whey." Turning to Iris she continued, "Lawd, girl, let me look pon yuh." Iris held her arms out and slowly turned around for Rose. She was wearing a long white skirt, patterned blouse, and black shoes. Rose, reaching for Iris as though she were six years old, adjusted her clothing. Embarrassed, Iris stood stiffly looking at the ceiling.

"How's Tom?"

"Work hard fe -- I mean -- work is hard to get, Mummaa."

Quick to catch the correction Rose needled, "Yuh nuh speak like us no more?"

"Tom thinks we will do better if… I drop the accent."

Rose looked heavenward. "Lawd Jesus, yuh a deny wha' yuh is! Me nuh go America, me fine right heah." She let herself speak freely in a heavy patois. "No forget yuh Jamaican."

"Me nuh forget, Mummaa. Just sometimes not having an accent makes it easier to earn money."

"Me nuh fe sale like dat." Rose looked away shaking her head. "Is de problem wit' America, me hear *everyting* fe sale."

"Mummaa --"

Abruptly, Rose changed the subject. "Whey me grandchildren?"

Magically appearing in the open doorway, with faces scrubbed and hair freshly combed, stood Clarence and Charles, their Aunt Callie right behind them. Iris urged them forward and the boys edged into the room reluctantly. Clarence was so shy he couldn't look at his grandmother.

Already primed, the boys self-consciously mumbled "Merry

Christmas, Grandma."

Rose started to cry. "Look at what de Christmas Breeze blow inna me house! Is yuh first time here. Unno mus' go a Gran' Market an' get some cheer. Let Daisy take yuh down dey."

The kids looked confused.

"Your Aunt Daisy will take you down to the Gran' Market," Iris explained.

"Everyone speaks so strangely here," remarked Clarence. Charles stood off to the side, aloof, looking at everyone reprovingly.

"Yuh pickney grow up nice," said Rose, "Yuh raise dem right."

A week passed and Christmas Eve day arrived like any other, with the sun peeking over the mountains to the east, sending a narrow beam of light into the boys' room. Daisy burst in, crying gaily, "Good marnin! Time for you boys to get up. Tonight's Christmas Eve an' we mus' go a Gran' Market. Get up! Get up! Get UP!"

The children raised their heads, then collapsed back into the covers. Daisy drew back the curtains, casting the intense morning light onto their beds. She was wearing a red, white and green dress, her hair pulled back in a ponytail. Tousled and sleepy, the boys struggled to wake up. Clarence sat up, his legs dangling over the edge of the bed. He looked at Daisy and giggled. She peered at him with mock sternness and said, "What's so funny?"

Clarence studied Daisy and decided to test this aunt's sense of humor. "Who are you? Mrs. Claus?"

"If I was, I would have the elves kick yuh out of bed," Daisy picked up a pillow and swatted them both. She smiled broadly, delighted that Clarence had the nerve to tease her. "Come, we have lots to do today!"

Charles rubbed the sleep out of his eyes. "When is it going to snow?"

"Snow? Yuh inna de tropics, bwoy it doesn't snow here! Master Charles, dis Jamaica and is hot all year roun'." Daisy looked out the window. "Is gonna be a *glorious* day."

The kaleidoscope of blinking lights in Grand Market helped create the unmistakable atmosphere of Christmas magic, bringing holiday excitement and glee to both children and adults. Toys were everywhere –– balloons and stuffed animals dangling from poles vied with overflowing tubs of the small, inexpensive toys that have a universal appeal to young children. Parents rushed about buying last-minute items while their younger progeny whined, nagged and pouted until, occasionally, the parent succumbed and purchased some trinket. The lucky youngster would squeal with happiness, not realizing that tucked in the hidden corners of their homes their parents had already wrapped the real gifts. Daisy and her two nephews strolled down the crowded ailes in the midst of the crush. *Feeeeee! Feeeeee!* Two sales boys pushed through the crowd, blowing whistles and bobbing and weaving like ghosts drifting through the shoppers. "Dem blowin' whistles are called *fee-fee*," Daisy said. "Yuh wan' one?"

Both boys nodded.

Daisy purchased three red, white and blue whistles and each of them blew heartily in three-part dissonance, merging with the distant sound of exploding firecrackers. Turning into a long aisle lined with stalls, Clarence squealed delightedly, assaulted by the aroma of Peanut Pinda cakes, coconut grater cakes, peppermint sticks and tamarind balls, competing with sweet mangoes, papayas, star apples, custard apples, and even American candied apples.

"Look at them," Charles said, hardly able to believe what his eyes beheld.

Misunderstanding, Daisy said, "Yuh don't have such markets in America?"

But Clarence understood completely. "Negroes. Everyone's colored." He grinned broadly, a happy, self-satisfied smile.

"Ahhh...." Daisy was beginning to comprehend how remarkable this must seem to the kids. She led them to a booth, where she bought a little bag of coconut candies. After weighing the sack the vendor dropped a brown chunky candy into Clarence's hand. Charles declined, asking if he might instead have a candy apple. Daisy nodded her approval to the vendor, then continued through the market, stopping at various stalls to buy items for the Christmas feast. All around them, the profusion of aromas, of body sweat, food and candy, blaring music and nonstop noise, sent Clarence into a joyful frenzy. But it drove Charles inward. He was nearly silent.

"I want it!" Clarence exclaimed, pointing at one cheap toy after another.

In stark contrast, Charles wore a glorious scowl on his face. Holding his candy apple, his lips sticky and red, he appeared to be so bored with it all.

Suddenly something like gunfire erupted behind them. A string of firecrackers jumped and danced on the ground behind them, twisting and fragmenting, creating clouds of acrid smoke.

Nearby, a blind man on a stool sat next to a little boy.

"Fireworks, mon!" the man cried. "Cheap fireworks!"

The blind man lit another string of firecrackers and grinned. The boy remained expressionless. By the time the smoke cleared Daisy and her nephews were gone.

The last thing Daisy searched for was salted cod. She finally came upon a small stand attended by a short, wiry, Chinese woman. She smiled when the trio approached, displaying the remaining six teeth in her mouth and the two women nodded at each other as a sign of respect. The boys looked surprised, for the woman was wearing a colorful purple wraparound dress, her hair wrapped in a red cloth tied with a white ribbon, just like any other traditionally-dressed Jamaican woman. When Aunt Daisy asked, "Yuh have saltfish today, Miss?" they nearly dropped their jaws, for the woman answered in a thick patois, "Yes, ma'm, it right ovah dey." The woman pointed at some small wooden boxes. "But me mus' tell yuh, de saltfish marry to de bammy."

Daisy stamped her foot. "Nah, mon! Yuh kyan sell me jus' de saltfish?"

"Sorry but dem is marry today. Saltfish scarce an' bammy plenty."

"Marry?" asked Charles.

"Bammy?" said Clarence.

"Marry means yuh have to buy them both," Daisy told them. "Bammy is de flat white pancakes." She turned back to the woman. "Me nuh happy, but okay, two box a de saltfish." Daisy looked with resignation at the two bags of bammy and gave one to each of the boys to carry.

By the time they finished this last transaction, it was time to head home. Charles walked briskly toward the exit, dragging Daisy by hand with Clarence trailing behind. Just as they were about to leave the market Clarence shouted, "Look!"

Several chickens hung upside down from a line, suspended from their feet while a man with a knife went from one bird to the next deftly cutting their heads off. Blood spurted as their wings flapped helplessly. The butcher wiped off the bloody spray and tossed the chicken heads into a basket. Charles turned aside, sick to his stomach.

"I love this place," Clarence said. "I want to stay in Jamaica forever."

Daisy ushered the boys outside. *Jonkunnu a come!* rippled through an excited, growing crowd.

"Jonkunnu a come!" Daisy repeated.

"Jonkunnu?"

"The Christmas parade. Jonkunnu is a special celebration this time of year," Daisy explained. "Jonkunnu is how we celebrate Christmas."

People carrying pots and pans, ladles and lids, banged them together, creating a rhythmical racket. *Cla-ca-lang-lang-cacca-ca-lang-gang!* Clarence bounced to the beat, enthralled as the energy built, but Charles clutched Daisy's hand fiercely.

More people, seeming to materialize out of thin air, joined the clamor of banging pots and pans. Red devils with pitchforks charged through the crowd, scattering terrified children who were then chased by laughing parents. As the devils passed by, Charles cowered behind Daisy while Clarence stood by defiantly, taking it all in.

Pitchy Patchy a come! Is de Wild Indian... Ho! De Devil! The crowd roared. Pitchy Patchy wore multicolored ribbons; red, yellow, purple, green, that swished and swayed with every move and shimmied with the beat. She looked so massive, spectators doubted that even a man inside the costume was big enough to make it jump and dance. The devil pranced about with his extra long horns, and a train of red attendants holding mirrors threw firecrackers, sometimes even scaring the adults with their menacing gestures.

"Look!" cried Daisy, pointing at a woman who appeared very pregnant. "It's Bellywoman!" Bellywoman, jumping around and obscenely thrusting her belly at the crowd, was also a man dressed as a woman. Behind him was a man wearing a huge cow head.

The crowd seethed in a frenzy of dancing and for a few brief moments, these decendants of slaves were transported back in time and place, temporarily abandoning the colonial yoke and grinding poverty of their routine tropical lives. Jonkunnu was more than a celebration of Christmas, it was a festival of the solstice, the eternal dance between the earth and the sun, mimicked by a human milieu of characters, passion, and rhythms. Clarence jumped and pranced about and Daisy marveled at his fearlessness in the face of Jonkunnu, even as Charles cowered and she protectively held his hand.

She touched Charles's head in a gesture meant to comfort.

He angrily wrenched his hand from Daisy's. "I want to go home!"

The parade was moving on and people began to evaporate as seamlessly as they had collected. Puzzled, Daisy looked at Charles.

"Okay," she said, "let's go home."

Still flushed with the excitement of Jonkunnu, Daisy entered the kitchen, followed by the two boys, each carrying bags. She nearly swooned. It smelled so good! Preparations for the holiday feast were in high gear and the rich aroma of foods, specially savored at Christmas, tickled the olfactories and teased the memory of taste. Rose gently rocked in her chair, overseeing the culinary operation, while the two boys joined Wilbur at a table in the corner quietly started crayoning a coloring book. The kitchen was large and at one of the two stone sinks Iris busily washed calalloo, the big green leaves flapping about and sprinkling the surroundings with water.

Callie, at the stove, browned chunks of oxtail in a skillet for oxtail stew. The aroma of curry, pepper, and bay leaves permeated the entire house. A ham, prickled with cloves, baked in the oven, occassionally basted with a special sauce, the ingredients of which were only known to Rose. One counter was covered with ackee, a perennial fruit with yellow flesh that resembled scrambled eggs when cooked with bell peppers and onions. On a table, pots and baking pans of dumplings, escovitch, stew peas, mackrel, plaintain, and breadfruit waited to be put away in the cooler. Daisy tingled with the same anticipation she felt as a young girl, about to open her presents.

The doorbell rang announcing the arrival of Rose's friend, Sally Maud, coming to help with the preparations. Slender and petite, Sally seemed to fairly glide across the floor. Her skin was faultless, a face sculpted with all the love and kindness nature could bestow. She looked fifteen years younger than she was and only the strands of gray betrayed her as an older woman. A mole above her left lip implied a sultry sexuality in defiance of her prudish attitude, but it was her inner beauty that was truly endearing.

When Sally entered the room, she was warmly welcomed. As at home in this kitchen as she was in her own, she washed her hands, opened the wooden ice-box door and made space for her dish of marinating oxtails.

Sally greeted everyone with a hug and observed Charles and Clarence at the table with their coloring books. "Iris," she said, "yuh have two *handsome* boys."

Iris beamed with pride. "Thanks, Miss Maud. The time goes by so quickly when you have kids." Turning her attention to them Iris said, "Did you say thank you to Miss Maud? She paid you a compliment."

"Thank you, Miss Maud," they said in unison, without looking up from their coloring.

While the preparations continued unabated, Rose sat in a rocker and told stories about what Beeston Street was like when she was a child.

"It was good growing up in Jamaica," Rose said. "We only had a likkle, but it was enough. We never went hungry.

What likkle we have we share wit' one another. We loved each other first."

"All that talk about love and sharing is fine and dandy," Iris said, "but to be honest I am glad I am raising Charles and Clarence away from Jamaica. Better jobs, education, culture and medicine, it's all in the United States."

"Lawd Jesus, where me go wrong raising dis gal?" Rose looked into the heavens.

"Dem boys would be better off here!" Sally countered.

"All dem Americans care 'bout is money," Callie said.

"Last me hear, money *is* important," Daisy retorted. "Yuh nuh haffi work, so it nuh mean nothin' to yuh."

"Stop, stop, *stop*!" Rose shouted. "Nah bother quarrel in me house today."

"De money still fallin' pon de street like manna from heaven in New York?" Sally asked.

Iris gave her a long look before answering.

"We fine."

Sally skillfully cracked a coconut with a hammer and drained the water into a glass bowl, dug out big chunks of coconut meat and grated them onto a wooden board.

"De money nuh flow, eh?" she said. "I remember you sayin' de money an' job jus' dey fe de taking."

"Dat was before 1929," Iris sounded so defeated. "Hard times is everywhere you know, not just inna New York."

"Hard times is good times inna Jamaica!" Rose retorted.

Daisy looked at Rose disdainfully.

Ignoring Daisy, Rose continued, "America nah fe me. Dem hate us. Inna de south, inna de north, inna New York, inna

Chicago –– dem hate us everywhey! Me 'ear plenty story dem. Me a stay right 'ere inna Jamaica whey me can tell *buccra* fe kiss me batty!" Rose patted her butt, laughing and looking at Sally Maud, who nodded in agreement.

"Mummaa, I live in Harlem and is nice," Iris concentrated on ripping the calalloo leaves.

"Is de same mistake all around inna dat country," Rose continued. "Dem always a talk 'bout bad days is ovah, but inna Jamaica we know is different. Bad days nuh gone, dem comin'."

"But Mummaa, we are making ..."

"Cha! Me nuh care wha' yuh a make!"

"... a living."

Rose shook her head. "Oh," she added, acknowledging her harsh interruption. "If times get tough, yuh and yuh husband always have a place inna Kingston."

Iris tore the green leaves roughly. She remembered Tom's reaction when she suggested moving to Jamaica after she returned from her father's funeral.

"Baby those people down there, they's *monkeychasers.* Why would I move to a primitive place like that?"

She remembered how the argument culminated with her leaving the apartment. Outside it was raining and she had a good cry. She stopped tearing the wet leaves, caught by the memory that was pulling her into sad feelings.

"Yuh see," Rose gestured towards Iris, "yuh see America, me will never go dey! Me can't forget what happen to me friend, Netta."

Daisy's exasperation was all over her face. "Please, nah bother tell it again."

"Me would a never forget her." Rose, relishing the opportunity to tell the tale rocked impatiently in her chair. "Like it was yesterday. Dem lef fe go a de United States, de whole family. Two years later dey back, de fadda him dead and gone, dem lynch him. *Dem even cut off his* --"

"Pickney inna de room!" Iris cried.

In the corner, alerted that something was going on that they were not supposed to hear, the boys feigned disinterest, but were keenly alert to the fierce conversation.

Callie got up. "Let's go young men, it's getting late an' we mus' feed de geese,." Wilbur dozed in a chair, snoring lightly and undisturbed by the discord.

After Callie and the boys were gone, Daisy returned to the debate. "Mummaa dat was almost thirty years ago, things have changed now."

"And it happen inna de south, Florida me think. De white people aren't like dat in de north," Iris added.

"They're even more wicked up dey," Sally said.

"North, south, east and west it nah make no difference, de white people dem hate yuh in America," Rose said, rocking slowly in the chair. "Buccra nuh wan live wit yuh. Yuh shoulda lissen an' stay 'ere."

Daisy motioned to Iris to follow her out of the kitchen. They went downstairs and found a quiet area of the courtyard to talk. In the center of the yard, Callie and the kids were tossing grain to the excited geese.

"Nah bother dwell 'pon it," Daisy said, putting her arm around Iris.

Tears stung Iris's eyes and she struggled to contain her

smoldering anger. They could hear laughter coming from the kitchen. Daisy could feel Iris's body trembling. At last Iris collapsed into Daisy's arms and wept.

"Is okay," Daisy whispered, but still Iris cried.

"De truth is," Iris squeaked, "we makin a lot of money. But I'd give it all back to be here with Daddy."

Stunned, Daisy and Iris sat close together, each comforting the other.

The gifts were wrapped and piled in the closet, a small mountain of red, green, and pastel-colored boxes. Daisy and Iris had been wrapping presents for hours. The rest of the house was quiet; everyone was asleep.

"We mus' sing *Silent Night*," Daisy said.

Iris chuckled. "Yes mon –– and bring down holy hell pon dis holy morning."

They giggled. The clock struck 2:00.

"Me is so glad yuh come home, Iris. Merry Christmas."

"Me too," Iris responded, "Merry Christmas, dahling."

Daisy put the finishing touch on a small package wrapped in a golden foil. "This is the last one, for Wilbur."

Iris smiled. "He makes Mummaa happy."

"He makes me feel funny."

"How?" Iris asked.

"It's the way he just moved in on Mummaa like dat. Right after Daddy pass away. Den sometimes I *feel* him looking at me."

"Yuh tell Mummaa?"

"Yuh can't speak bad about Wilbur," Daisy said.

"Him contribute money," Iris said. "Mummaa tell me how him give her plenty money from his battery business. It's hard to speak 'gainst a man like dat."

Daisy put the package down amongst the other Christmas gifts. "What is Tom like?"

Iris sighed. "Tom is a wonderful husband and a good father... like Daddy. He provides for us, yuh know... bettah dan mos' men in New York." Iris surprised herself, the sudden clarity with which she felt proud of Tom and her children.

"Den why did yuh want to come back to Jamaica?"

"It was Daddy." Iris bit her lip. "I dunno." Iris shook her head. "But I don't want to come back here to live," she continued. "I'm lucky I have Tom."

"Yuh lucky."

"Don't go to Mummaa an' spill my business," Iris said.

"Of course not. Is your business. As for me, thank God fe de ice. Is goin' be one profitable business." Daisy gleefully rubbed her hands together.

"Me hate to disappoint yuh but your days are numbered. De business is goin' melt away in a few years."

"Nah! What yuh talkin' 'bout?"

"Daisy, haven't yuh heard 'bout electric refrigerators?" She was startled to realize how behind the times the island really was. "In New York more and more people have them. They're cheap."

"Yuh don't have to buy ice?" Daisy sounded utterly dismayed. With a few brief words the foundation for her future had been kicked asunder.

"Nah, mon. We stopped buying ice since Tom brought an Electrolux refrigerator home. It looks like a regular icebox, like some of the rich folks in Kingston have, but there's a motor to keep it cold instead of ice."

Daisy sat down. She had never heard of an Electrolux refrigerator. There would be no tropical ice empire. It was only a matter of time, a short time, before refrigerators were everywhere in Jamaica. It was the last straw. "Iris," Daisy said gravely, "me mus' get to America."

"It nuh easy."

"Yuh did it."

"I was very lucky. Yuh haffi get visa these days," Iris said.

Daisy's lips were tightly set. "I have to try." Looking at her sister in the muted light, Daisy admired the proud lines in Iris's face, and her bold spirit. Iris, like her, wasn't satisfied with her lot in life and struggled to improve it. That took money. Iris had found a way to get the money to shape her future and Daisy wouldn't be satisfied until she had money of her own. She glanced at the clock. "Let's go to sleep."

The women went down the hall to their bedrooms and the only sound was the click of the latches as their doors closed for the night.

Christmas dinner was nearly over. Iris and Daisy cleared the remains from the table while Callie, in the kitchen, prepared glasses of sorrel and a plate of sliced fruitcake for dessert. Charles sat at the table in a cloud of silence, sulking. He woke up early Christmas morning, only to be disappointed. In Jamaica people observed Boxing Day, the British custom of opening, or "unboxing" presents the day after Christmas. He was enraged but knew better than to complain. It was just one more thing he hated about this place.

The idea of Boxing Day even took Clarence aback.

Charles had not really eaten much of the feast, but Clarence was stuffed. He took on the task of trying everything and found a surprising number of dishes to be interesting. The adults were delighted with his willingness to taste new foods and offered him one tantalizing combination after another. He didn't like green bananas or yam however, in spite of pouring gravy over them to enhance the flavor. Clarence proclaimed, "No taste!" to a roomful of good-natured laughter.

Callie, having served dessert, finally settled down to join the party. She reached for her glass of sorrel, and accidentally knocked the drink over. The red stain quickly spread across her starched holiday dress. Conversation, brought to an abrupt halt, was suddenly broken by peals of laughter.

"Daisy!" Rose exclaimed. "Stop that now."

"Cast a spell!" Daisy hid her face as she laughed, but she could not stop. "Use de obeah, nuh?"

"Obeah?" Clarence chirped. "What's that?"

Crying, Callie jumped up and rushed out of the room.

"Yuh haffi spoil de dinner like dat?" Rose bellowed.

"Yah mon! Dat -- was -- funny!" Daisy could hardly catch her breath. There was pure cruelty in her laughter. It echoed in the parlor and down the hall.

"Get out!" yelled Rose. She was shaking with anger.

Still snickering, Daisy left the room.

"Hmmpph! Well, one of these days she won't have so much to laugh about," Iris offered.

Wilbur wiped his mouth. "This is Titus's fault. Him spoil him dawta an' now him dead an' gone an' de gal a continue fe act up. Yuh remember? Daisy walked around here proud and boasy, and him call her bold. Yuh remember?"

"What's obeah?" Clarence persisted in asking.

"Come, is time to go outside an' play," Iris said motioning to her sons.

Rose, scowling, dropped her spoon on the half eaten fruitcake. "I have a headache," she said. "I jus' wan' lay down fe nap." She kissed her teeth. "Cha –– me vex. Dem girls fight all de time now. They ruined de holiday."

"Yuh nuh hear me! I said it's time for you to be gone.," Iris yelled at her sons.

"Tell me what obeah is first," Clarence insisted.

"None a yuh business!" Rose bellowed. "Gwan wit' yuh!" The two boys scampered away from the table and Rose followed them out, on her way to her own room. A moment later Wilbur got up and followed Rose to their bedroom. Iris left to check on the boys.

When Callie re-entered the kitchen she was surprised to see everyone gone. She had changed into a fresh dress. Putting on an apron, she began scraping the dainty plates of half eaten fruitcake when Iris returned to the kitchen, her honey eyes scowling.

"I've never seen anyting like dis inna me life. We was havin' such a good time. Both of yuh haffi spoil de evening? All yuh a do since we get 'ere is quarrel," Iris said.

Callie carefully put the dishes in the sink. "Before yuh open dat," she pointed at Iris's mouth, "yuh better know about dis *bumboclat* place 'ere."

"Keep down yuh voice––and stop cursing," Iris said.

"Yuh nuh live 'ere," Callie hissed. "Dat blasted bitch! She tink she de boss a de house since she been runnin' tings around dis yard fe a few months dem." Callie struggled to control her voice. "She cruel. She love fe laugh at my misfortune. Everyting funny fe her."

"Dem say yuh a practice obeah, is true?"

Callie hesitated. "I'm still having dreams. I've had them since I could remember." Tears filled her eyes. "But I'm not practicing obeah."

"I'm surprised at you. Leave all dat devil worship alone. You need to go to church and stop hanging out wit' dem wicked people." Iris held her sister's hand, clasping it gently and bringing it to her face in a tender gesture of affection. "We love you and we don't want to see you lose your soul," Iris went on. "All of us, Mummaa, Daisy––"

"I hate her."

Iris looked to the heavens and made the sign of the cross. "Don't ever say dat again," she said. "*An' lef' de black magic alone*!"

Callie frowned. How? She had tried over the years to escape but the visions and dreams sought her out, whispering secrets of things yet to be in her ear. She could not leave the black magic, it was in her, manifesting, sometimes predicting calamity so devastating it was frightening. She had only recently decided to live with her gift rather than escape it. She was studying obeah with a powerful obeahwoman in Half Way

Tree, but told no one about her sojourns to the nearby district. She knew better than to talk of it, and she was determined to continue seeing this woman.

It was quiet. The naked light bulb cast a harsh light. Daisy came into the kitchen and grinned at her sisters. "You need to speak wit' her on dat obeah. Mummaa throw out some rubbish of her's just de other day."

"Grow up, Daisy!" Iris said to her. "Is yuh spoil everyting dis evening."

"No! Is me make dis evening possible. Who yuh tink a keep dis place runnin'? Who is shopping, cleaning, cooking, and managing de men?" Daisy glared at Iris. "A me alone! Me -- by myself, witout any help." She looked at Callie and trembled with pent up rage. "All Callie do is is eat, play, complain, an' practice obeah: goin' to de cemetary a collect dirt fe throw pon people. Den when she nuh get her way, she start bawl like a baby."

"Yuh lie! Me nuh do dat. Is fight yuh wan', fight, eh? Is *bangarang* yuh a look fuh?" Callie charged forward, shoulders squared, while Daisy, her fists balled up, stood ready to scrap.

Iris stepped between them. "Both a yuh, stop! Yuh gwan kill Mummaa wit' vexation. Stop it!" Iris started after Callie, leaving Daisy alone in the kitchen.

Daisy thought of those days when she and Callie were inseparable. But when she studied her hand, she was reminded that it was Callie's cruelty that left that scar. It was still bright nearly ten years later. Remembering that day, brought her back to the smell of the damp earth. She could still feel the wind as it rose signaling a sudden change in weather. Several children, playing a popular game, sat in a circle passing stones around. Lightning flashed, followed moments later by the crash of thunder. Unfazed, the children passed rocks, pounding them on the ground in a distinct syncopation during which they sang a song that was repeated endlessly.

Go down a Manuel road
Gal an' bwoy
Fe go broke rock stone
Finger mash no cry
Gal an' bwoy
Remember a play we a play
Gal an' bwoy

If a hand remained a moment too long, it gave the person passing the stone a license to smash down with all their might. The game continued until, of course, someone's finger was smashed.

A clap of thunder captured Daisy's attention, and her hand had lingered a moment too long. Six-year-old Callie seized the opportunity and brought her rock down ferociously. *Smash!*

Daisy screamed. Huge droplets of rain began to pelt the earth and she watched the gush of blood drip from her hand mixing with the raindrops and forming pools of pink water in the mud at her feet. It took several stitches to close the cut and made her middle finger permanently numb. Daisy never forgave Callie. Even now, in her mind, she could hear Callie's harsh laughter. The rupture between them never fully mended, fueled by Daisy's self-righteous anger.

Suddenly Iris took Daisy's hand, yanking her back into the present. "I think is time to grow up."

"With all I do around this house, I am grown!"

"Shush! Is not what yuh do, is how yuh act, Daisy. De time fe act like pickney is ovah. Yuh teasin' an' laughin like a child when nuttin is funny." Taking Rose's last cigarette from the blue Four Ace's pack on the table, Iris said, "I need some air."

From the window Daisy watched the boys playing in the yard. She saw Iris light the cigarette and release a cloud of smoke and then went back to clearing the table.

Two days later a stiff breeze blew from the east stirring up clouds of dust. A slow-moving cab pulled alongside the Royal Customs Building pier and came to a stop. The riders quietly stepped out.

Clarence wept angrily. He did not want to leave Jamaica and was unable to convince his mother to let him stay behind.

"Yuh must be crazy," Iris said looking directly at her youngest son. "Your father would slay me if I did something crazy like that, left his boy behind!"

Clarence fumed with resentment. He thought about the two big trips they'd made to Alabama. He'd found it unbearable, black people scared of white men and the silent subservience they used to survive in his father's home town. In Jamaica, he had found a proud dark skinned people. He *knew* that was the way it was supposed to be.

Charles, on the other hand, was eager to leave. He helped the cab driver take the bags downstairs in an effort to speed up their departure. He barely kissed his grandmother, and had bounded down the stairs so quickly that Iris called him back so he could say a proper thank you and goodbye to his Aunt Callie. When he finally got to the taxi, he got in and slammed the car door loudly. He was desperate to return to New York City.

At the entrance to the Customs Office, Daisy swept the boys up in a hug. Then she and Iris embraced. "Remember what I told you," said Iris. "Don't be discouraged."

Daisy cried and held on to her elder sister. "I'm comin'," Daisy whispered. She watched them, waving even after the doors slammed shut. The taxi had already left, and Daisy began to walk home just as a cloud of dust swirled up and stung her eyes.

IV

DECEMBER 1937, PORTLAND COTTAGE, JAMAICA

In the dining room, Sheila busied herself with clearing away the half eaten bowls of porridge, plantain, fried livers and onion, noticing, once again that her employer threw away more food in the course of one day than she and many of her neighbors got to eat in a week.

Major dabbed a napkin at his mouth and enjoyed a leisurely cup of tea, momentarily lost in thought. While he sat, Andrew bounded down the stairs.

"Andrew," Major called to him. "What you have planned?"

"Going to the beach." Andrew yawned. "I was planning to relax, Daddy, I'm tired."

Goddamn him, Major thought. Tired at ten in the morning?

"You've been here for a week," Major said. "I need your help at the distillery."

"Can't it wait?"

"No."

"Will it take all day?"

"Yes. Probably three days."

Andrew stared at the floor while Major anticipated his protests.

"I'm ready to start." Andrew noted the look of surprise on Major's face.

"What?"

"What do you want me to do?" asked Andrew.

Major recovered from his surprise and stood up.

"Follow me," he said, turning towards the stairs.

The sheer majesty of Major's third floor office made Andrew feel insignificant. High ceilings, circular walls, and two enormous windows that overlooked the estate, made the room feel tall and narrow. A large oak desk and high-back chair dominated the center. Lining the walls, shelves held hundreds of bottles of rum, some from other distilleries, and some specialty rums. Andrew squinted in the bright expansive whiteness of the room. Major brought a bottle off a shelf.

"I'm closing a deal that will see us ship fifty cases of our oldest rum to the United States," Major said. "If they are happy with that, they are planning to order several hundred cases of white rum over two years." He picked up the bottle, showing it to Andrew. "This rum is thirty years old." He opened the bottle and gave the cork to Andrew, who sniffed it.

"Man! It smells good."

"Indeed, the rum's been aged in burnt barrels for 30 years. See that golden color?" Major held the glass aloft showing off the rich amber liquid. "There are twenty-five barrels containing this very special rum." He gave Andrew a glass and poured one for himself. They drank it slowly, savoring the complicated flavors and enjoying the aroma.

"Amazing!" Andrew said.

"You will be in charge of retrieving these casks from the

cave, taking them to Tablestone for bottling, and delivering them to the Kingston docks for delivery in Miami. Busby will help you while I finalize the deal in the States," Major said.

"How long will you be gone?"

"Two weeks." Major's face was etched with worry. "Let me tell you something. The men will look up to you. They will search for cues as to how strong you are. Don't fraternize with the workers. You must know your place and they must understand their's. To be friendly with them is to invite trouble on yourself and the enterprise. Busby should be the only man you deal with. Understand?"

"I understand, Daddy."

"Good. Go have breakfast and come back in a hour. I'll prepare a list of the lot numbers to be retrieved and information for you about taking the rum to the dock."

What have I gotten myself into? Andrew wondered, as he walked down the stairs.

Major, at his desk, reviewed his recent discussion with Pauline. She was right, he realized, as she so often was.

"Give him something to do," she pleaded, "and Andrew *will* come through."

Major relaxed in a rocking chair, nursing a glass of rum and enjoying the sound of the creaking springs as he tilted gently back and forth. The noisy springs were heard loudest on days when Major triumphed over something or someone. Light a cigar… pour a glass of rum… lean back, feet up… watch the clouds of smoke settle about the room… relax… *creeeak… creeak… creak….*

He daydreamed about the upcoming trip to Miami. We'll close this deal and start shipping 100 cases of rum per month, he mused. He thought about the good old days of prohibition, when boats would meet Busby near Jackson Bay and load up to 200 cases of rum to take back to the Florida Keys. He always managed to circumnavigate the British and American authorities and was never caught. But the end came in 1932, when the Volstead Act was repealed, ending prohibition. His rum business had crashed. Major would never forget the day he had to stoop to selling parcels of land in order to make ends meet. Never, in 147 years of growing cane, had the Blaines abandoned the business of exclusively selling rum. Now, after four long and precarious years, he dared to hope. This deal would revive the Blaine fortunes.

The setting sun cast a pink light on the distillery and with the last cask corked, Busby collapsed in a chair. Linton finished extinguishing the fires while the day disappeared into the indigo skies of dusk, then joined Busby. The smoke and steam from the fires still hung in the air as the men enjoyed a well deserved shot of rum. Linton held the dirty glass, his hands blackened with soot, peering through the clear white rum at the distorted image of Busby.

"Well, Mistah Busby." The voice startled Linton and he splashed his drink.

"Well, now, if it isn't Master Andrew, what a pleasant surprise," Busby said, getting up and shaking his hand. "How are yuh, sah?! Welcome home!"

Glancing at the man next to Busby Andrew said, "Linton!"

He reached out his arm to shake hands. "I hardly recognized yuh! I guess we've both grown up over the years, eh?

"Yuh father make him the new understudy," Busby interjected proudly.

You mean my father, Linton thought. Taking Andrew's hand he said, "Welcome home Andrew, it's good to see yuh."

"It's been a while, eh?" Linton nodded politely. "Congratulations on the new position, mon. Yuh coulda do a lot worse dan study under Busby. But yuh haffi excuse me, Linton. Me hopin' fe sit down wit yuh soon, but right now me haffi speak wit' Busby." He smirked. "Yuh know me daddy. Duty calls!"

Linton watched the two men talking under a trumpet tree as memories spooled through his mind. He and Andrew played together when they were young boys, running around the estate, dashing in and out of the sugarcane fields and riding mules. But when Andrew turned twelve he was sent to England to boarding school and after that Major made sure the boys rarely saw each other. Andrew's leaving had been traumatic and fueled Linton's hatred of Major. Clenching his fists, Linton tried to redirect his thoughts. Memories connected to those days and the scars on his back had been squashed down in a dark corner of his mind and he knew better than to air them. He poured another drink.

Busby returned alone and said, "We got two hundred cases of rum fe bottle at Tablestone. Dis will be tough wuk mon." He punched Linton on the shoulder playfully. "Make Sheila let yuh get plenty res'."

Walking down the moonlit trail toward home, Linton took care not to stumble. At the foot of the hill he saw Sheila on the ramshackle porch, deep in the shadows waiting for him, waiting 'til he stepped up and she reached out to him.

"Lover," she whispered in Linton's ear. "Me lover." She wrapped her arms around his neck and gently nibbled his ear.

He picked her up, swinging her around, both of them dizzy in love, and she surrendered, spinning, giggling, surrounded by the security of his arms. He carried his sweetheart through the door and put her down on the bed. Their hunger had gone unsatisfied all day. Linton stripped off his work clothes, and at the porcelain face bowl, washed off the day's soot. Sheila slipped off her dress, leaving her naked, waiting, expectant. She was always waiting in bed for him, would wait 'til roosters laid eggs if need be. She hated waiting, but it also excited her, his gentle, tender, slow approach was irresistable. She closed her eyes and let her mind wander.

The first time they made love it had been a slow and timid affair. Linton's reticence made Sheila dash boldly into expanding the boundaries of exploration with him. He enjoyed being led, taking his cues from her ministrations. Only now, months later, could he come to the bed and with surety press himself upon her, the contact of their skin sending bolts of excitement through her body, making her shudder and sigh all at once.

Linton blew out the lamp. Beams of moonlight came through the windows, highlighting the satiny darkness of his skin. Only giggles, moans and the rustling of sheets punctuated the peaceful night.

Basking in bed with Linton, Sheila snuggled closer. "I have red-pea soup an' bread. Yuh hungry?" she asked.

"Hungry? Fe what? I jus' had you." He grabbed a succulent handful of her buttocks and gave a loving squeeze.

"Yuh tink yuh funny, but I'm hungry."

Laughing, pulling herself free, Sheila got up and prepared their meal. Linton sat down at the little table and flipped through an old book, in which there were pictures of the world's great cities.

"Yuh wan' travel to dem places?" he asked, showing her a photo of London.

"Maybe. Wouldn't it be grand to get away from here and see the world?" She sighed. "I'd be happy jus' fe see Kingston. Missus Blaine has told me many things 'bout Kingston, how big, an' all de people, and how you can leave Kingston for de States pon boat." Her eyes grew dreamy. "Who knows, maybe one day I will."

"Cha, I'm stayin' right 'ere," Linton declared. "I don't like de city."

"Yuh never live in de city."

"No," he said, "never have. But I know that living amongst dat many people would make me unhappy. Too many people, not enough space."

"Den let's go on an outing on New Year's Day. We can go up de hill an' have a picnic. Besides, me haffi collect some roots fe Aunt Cordy, she almos' outta everyting."

Linton took a sip of the rum. "Go look fe roots? Wit' Aunt Cordy?" he asked hopefully.

"She still not feelin' well." An expression of worry clouded

Sheila's face. "She been stayin in and layin down. Sompin' 'appen to Aunt Cordy, I couldn't bear it, mon. She keeps insisting she nuh have much time lef'. Aunt Cordy is me real mudda."

"But yuh mudda––" Linton hesitated, unsure of how Sheila would react. "Didn't yuh mudda come and take yuh?"

Sheila shivered. Born in the nearby town of Alley, when Sheila was three her mother decided that she couldn't take care of her daughter any longer and left her with Aunt Cordy. Six months later her mother left Jamaica for Great Britain. Eight years later her mother, married with two children, returned to Portland Cottage to take Sheila away. Her stepfather treated her poorly and after her thirteenth birthday, she ran away and returned to live with Aunt Cordy. Luckily she secured a position as a maid in the mansion.

"I have two muddas: de one who brought me inna de worl' an de one who love me." Sheila ached with sadness.

"Aunt Cordy is old now ," Linton said slowly. "I don't know how old."

"I don't think she even know," Sheila said.

Linton's boyhood was dominated by the short, dark-skinned woman, who was already old when he was introduced to her at the age of six. Cordy was a descendant of the Maroons, a fierce group of runaway slaves who escaped from the Spanish and British. In 1739, after a brutal war between the Maroons and the British, a treaty was signed, granting the Maroons autonomy and creating the town of Accompong in St. Elizabeth Parish, where Cordy was born. Growing up, she learned bush medicine from the village matriarch and after getting married, she moved to Clarendon in 1868 with her new husband.

After settling in Portland Cottage, Cordy was summoned to the Blaine Estate to look after a sickly newborn baby. The baby was suffering from a terrible illness and his prognosis was grim. But after Cordy began treatments of bush baths and herbal teas the child became better. The child, Peter Blaine, was saved because of Cordy's cure. In appreciation, Robert Blaine built a cottage and offered it to Cordy and her family. She had lived there ever since.

In his thoughts, Linton could see her dark eyes, smiling face, and the shock of white hair, her fingers dancing as she sprinkled herbs onto the battered scale with its blackened counterweights, creating concoctions for her patients. The trips that they made in search of roots with Aunt Cordy were some of Linton's fondest memories. Now Aunt Cordy was old and frail. Sheila took over collecting roots with Aunt Cordy's daughter Rini, and together they both treated patients with Aunt Cordy's guidance.

Outside, a rooster crowed in the darkness.

Panting heavily, Linton and his partner pushed the last heavy cask up the hill, rolling it closer to their destination. The sun beat down but the heat did not bring them pause. The men worked relentlessly, taking only a few short breaks.

At one point while resting, Linton looked up and saw Andrew sitting under the shade of a blue mahoe tree, sipping a drink and reading a book. Seeing his brother so relaxed while he was sweaty and ready to drop from exhaustion enraged Linton. When they resumed pushing the barrel, he tried to think of something else but he could feel the tears of anger building up in his eyes.

Nevertheless, seeing Andrew led to an epiphany: he realized he had to leave the Estate. But where would he go? And would Sheila go with him? And did he want Sheila with him?

Once the barrel was safely in the truck, Linton looked for Andrew, but he was gone.

"Jus' two more casks," Busby shouted, as he helped the men struggling to roll the barrel up the ramp into the truck. "Les' finish dis," Busby cried, "one, two-push!"

With the last barrel aboard, Busby turned to the crowd of men that gathered around him. "Is now New Year's Eve, mon! 1937 is ovah!" He brought the men over to the distillery and with Linton's help passed out a bottle of rum to each man. The men, surprised by such a gesture, began to celebrate with hand-shaking and backslapping.

"Gwan 'ome! No wuk tomorrah," Busby said, dismissing them. Linton watched them leave while Busby fetched two glasses.

"Yuh surprise 'bout de rum, eh?" Busby said, chuckling. "Is Mr. Andrew's idea. Him sey gi' em a bottle a rum fe de New Year." He poured a drink. "Him is a better mon dan him faddah." He offered Linton a glass.

"Happy New Year to yuh, Busby. Thank yuh fe being me teacher."

They took their time, enjoying the rum, watching the sun sink lower in the sky. Linton shook hands with the old man, then Busby watched as Linton trudged off for home.

Washed up and dressed, wearing fresh, clean clothes, Linton stood at the tall doors in the rear of the huge house. He unlocked the door and quickly entered.

As the hours passed, the library walls grew dark and afternoon merged into evening. Linton lit a kerosene lamp and continued reading an old dark leather-bound journal, his brow knitted in concentration. Grudgingly, he became aware of the intruding sound of a drink being poured. He turned to see Andrew, smiling, holding a glass of rum in an outstretched arm.

"Join me fe a New Year drink, nuh?" Andrew reached for another glass and poured a drink for himself. Andrew's nose was red and he was obviously drunk. Setting his drink on the table, he sat down heavily in a chair.

"Yuh know, I spent entirely too much time inna America," Andrew said. "I'm glad to be home."

"Where yuh was?" asked Linton.

"Oh, New York at Columbia University," Andrew said carelessly. "Hardly any colored people in America is given the opportunity to go to school dey. America is a damn contradiction. One place dem treat yuh as a human being and just ten feet away is someone else wan' spit pon yuh. Is crazy mon. But still, lot of Jamaicans dere. Me like Harlem. Is de one place where we can live like a man." Andrew paused his eyes narrowing. "Here, in Jamaica my African blood makes no difference. In America just one drop a negro blood means dem can treat yuh like an animal. Here, everyone mix up, negro, cooley, white, chinee ... but in de States! Lawd, dem hate everyone wit' color inna dem!" He stopped and drained his glass. "Yuh ever hear a communism?" Linton shook his head. "Well dere is gonna be a revolution inna America and den tings goin' change." Andrew slammed his fist on the table.

Linton took a swig of rum.

"Yuh see how no one here owns any land? Communism is an economic system that will give people like you, de workers, an opportunity to live decent comfortable lives. Communism means labor unions fighting for just wages, taking large plantations like this one and breaking them up so that more people can make a living off the land." Andrew looked at Linton, breathless.

"Well, I don't know—"

Interrupting, Andrew continued talking at breakneck speed as though he'd been saving these thoughts for years, just to tell Linton. "Nevah min'. Look mon, is a big worl' out dere. But I'm interested inna Jamaica. Is time we break wit' England." He paused briefly and took a swallow of rum. "Yuh hear 'bout Norman Manley? I want to work with him in Kingston. It's de future, yuh know, our independence. An' I plan to be a part of that."

By now, Linton was listening attentively. He had never heard Andrew ever say anything in opposition to Major. His cold feelings for Andrew began to thaw. "Who is dis — Manley?" he asked.

"He's a lawyer. He's goin' help people get the vote an' demand their independence. Before Daddy leave for Miami a few days ago, he told me not to mix wid yuh workers. But he made a big mistake sendin' me away to school like he did. After I get de law degree I realize it's de workers me wan' work for. Daddy has a big problem with dat. Big problem." Andrew sighed. "Him also have a problem wit' me patois." Andrew laughed. Linton snickered in spite of himself. "It was my idea to hand out de rum today," Andrew continued. "When I asked daddy if I could give de men a small bonus, him ask if me crazy." Andrew shook his head. "So me tell Busby fe gi' everyone a bottle. Is high time we express our gratitude."

"Gratitude? For what?"

Andrew snorted. "My life of leisure," he said dryly.

"Leisure, like when yuh was sittin' under de tree?"

"I was sittin wit' Karl Marx and watchin all a yuh a cook inna de sun." Andrew laughed like this was the cleverest thing he'd ever said. He gasped to catch his breath. But looking at Linton's expression, he realized, sadly, that the irony of the statement was lost on him.

If Linton had lived near Kingston he might have heard Marx's name at a labor rally. But out here on the plantation? Most people could hardly read. Linton simply didn't have the exposure to education that Andrew had.

Andrew still remembered the fateful day Major told him, a naïve twelve year old, that he was going to attend school in England.

"When do we leave, Daddy?" Andrew was excited.

"We'll be leaving in a fortnight, Andrew." He smiled, happy to see the glee with which Andrew had received the news.

"I'm going to tell Linton that we're going to England!" Andrew cried, running down the garden path.

"Andrew!"

He stopped in his tracks, recognizing the tone in his father's voice.

Major walked over and knelt on one knee, staring Andrew right in the face.

"Linton is not going with you."

"But Linton's my best friend!" Andrew's face was etched with disappointment.

"It's time for you to grow up." Major took Andrew by the hand. "You're too big to be playing with Linton. He's not in our *class*," Major paused, emphasizing the the word, "and you must begin to learn the limits of good taste and social standing. From now on you will have friends more in keeping with who you really are."

Major forbade Andrew from even talking with Linton, and the next day Pauline and Andrew left for Kingston, soon to sail for England. After that, even during his visits home during school vacations, he wasn't allowed to associate with Linton. But he never forgot Linton, sometimes yearning to see him and recapture the pleasures of childhood.

Now, years later, sitting as a young adult in Major's library, Andrew felt a connection far deeper than any friendship he developed in England or the United States.

"Maybe it's because we was friends when we was young pickney." Andrew fiddled with the bottle cork. "I remember the first time we met. Daddy told me about your father, and how he died during the war and of your mother dying so young. I felt sorry for you, but I was always glad you came to the estate because you were the best thing that happened to me. I trust you, Linton. You make me feel comfortable. Really, there is no one for me to talk to, yuh know? Daddy and I disagree about everything. Do yuh know what I mean?"

"Yeah, mon," Linton said quietly. He thought of the polished lies that Major had created. Lies that concealed Major's infidelity to Pauline, smothering him in obscurity. Lies he hated living with. "But you have to be thankful nevertheless."

"Right. I'm sorry. I haffi be thankful fe what I have."

Yes, mon, be thankful, Linton thought. Despite his lingering jealousy, Linton also had good memories about Andrew. Both children had been manipulated by Major.

The evening closed in. The young men got totally drunk and during the next two hours as they laughed and talked about a wide range of topics. Their bellies began to rumble with hunger and the conversation wound down. Linton studied his empty glass. Suddenly impassioned, he almost yelled at Andrew, "I live here all me life, but me nuh wan' die here! I have to get out! I want to see de world."

"Go to America, mon," Andrew encouraged. "Yuh wan' see de worl' den go to New York… de whole worl' is dey all inna one place. Plenty Jamaican live in New York. Go dey, mon." Andrew belched loudly. "Go dey an' learn, den come on back to help me organize!"

Linton, suddenly aware of the hour, looked at the clock. "Is New Year's Eve and I have to get home." He reeled as he got up. "Sheila gonna wring me neck!" he said, laughing helplessly.

"Lesh do dis again!" Andrew grinned broadly. "But before yuh leave, jus' one more ting."

"What?"

"A toast to the New Year and to our renewed friendship. Those times, when we was pickney, playing with Sheila, dey is good memories, mon." Andrew poured two drinks. They clinked glasses and each took a big gulp of the fiery rum. "To 1938," Andrew toasted, "and to seeing our friendship grow for many years to come." Linton tried to imagine Major's reaction when he learned that his sons had reestablished their bond. Well, he thought, even if Andrew doesn't know it, blood *is* thicker than water.

Closing the door behind him, Linton whispered "And to you –– brother," as the lock clicked shut.

Sheila's face was framed by the dappled light shining through the trees. Linton lay beneath her, holding her in his arms. He wanted this moment to last forever.

They lay on a small white blanket surrounded by guinea grass, wild sugar cane, and trees infested with love bush, a parasitic plant whose reddish stems and white flowers hung from the branches. A cluster of lipstick trees, with their large green leaves and brilliant spiny red fruit, surrounded them. Strewn about the edges of the blanket were the remains of lunch and two picnic baskets filled with the herbs and plants they had collected that afternoon. Overhead a passing cloud subdued the unrelenting heat.

"I say you is my woman," Linton smacked Sheila's rump, "and I'm your man! If we could just be like this forever, I would give up all me ambitions and stay here for the rest of my life."

Sheila's cackling laughter came to an abrupt halt. "Ambitions?" Sheila peered into Linton's eyes.

"What would you say if I told you I was leaving?" Linton queried.

"I don't know."

"You wouldn't *come* with me?"Linton's facial expression radiated his disappointment. He sounded crestfallen.

"Wit' yuh? Linton, wha' yuh a chat 'bout?"

"I'm thinking of leaving."

"Den' a 'course I'm comin'. Why haven't yuh spoken 'bout it?"

"I've been thinkin 'bout it for a while and last night I came to a decision."

"Is de first time me hear it. Where yuh wan' go? An' when yuh wan' leave?"

The thought crossed her mind that if she decided to stay, Linton might leave without her, but fear dissuaded her from giving voice to the idea. The woman follows the man, she'd read that in the Bible. That was enough for her. Good advice should be followed, she told herself.

The question hung in the air unanswered. Pulling away from their embrace, Sheila began taking the wrapped herbs from the baskets and spread them out. Reading from a tattered sheet of paper she went over her list.

"...strongback, ram goat rose, shame weed. All we haffi find now is john bush," she said brightly.

They reached a clearing where blue, green, and brown malachite butterflies fluttered around tiny, fragile, light green buds growing in the midst of what looked like weeds.

"John bush!" Sheila cried. "We need plenty. Good fe de feet. Cordy constantly a complain dat her feet hurt."

Baskets full, they walked hand in hand back to the estate, past the Blaine mansion to Aunt Cordy's cottage in the former slave quarters.

It was midafternoon and villagers were gathering at Aunt Cordy's for the traditional New Year's Day tea meeting. Tea meetings were raucous affairs with music and dancing, the rum flowed freely, and there was plenty of food. Many women had spent the day cooking and the aroma of curried goat, baked chicken, rice and peas, fried plantain, and boiled green bananas, hung in the air. Goat head soup, also known as Mannish water, bubbled in a huge pot.

From her rocking chair Cordy watched with deep pleasure as the friends and neighbors she had guided for seventy years filled their bellies and celebrated the coming of the New Year.

"Make sure fe get yuh Mannish water!" she cried. Mannish water consisted of goat heads, tripe, feet, garlic, cho cho, scallions, Scotch bonnet peppers, white rum and spinners, a kind of long thin dumpling. Spicy and flavorful, the soup was well known as an aphrodisiac. Aunt Cordy always served the soup on New Year's Day.

"De men dem need plenty for when dem get home," she added happily.

"Me prefer cowcod soup, mon!" someone shouted.

"No cowcod here, yuh fe get Mannish, mon. Is New Year's!" Cordy retorted, making everyone laugh. Lighting a cigarette, she smoked with the lit end in her mouth.

"Me nuh see how yuh do dat' Auntie," Sheila said. "I remember when I was young, I thought dat me could a smoke like dat. Me bun up me lips when me put de cigarette in my mouth, yuh should-a see me lip, it full-a blistah. I nevah try it again."

"Is de way de ol' timers smoke," Cordy laughed. "Me mudder, me granmudder, all de ol' people dem smoke like dat."

"I jus' wish yuh would stop smoke," said Rini, Cordy's middle-aged daughter. She was a dark, short, stocky woman with her father's build and her mother's stubbornness. "I keep beggin', let's go a clinic inna May Pen --"

"Clinic!" Cordy interrupted Rini, then took a long drag on the cigarette. As the lit cherry disappeared behind Cordy's lips, Sheila shuddered. "Me have never seen doctor inna me life. Is almost over now, so why bother?" Cordy said.

"Is jus' a checkup Auntie," Linton said.

Cordy turned to Sheila, "Where de roots?"

Sheila pointed to the baskets behind her.

"Me learn de healing arts from Nonia," said Cordy proudly. "Back den, dere was no clinic, we had Nonia, de bush doctor. We used to call her Miss Nonny and she knew all de secrets of healing and traditions she say go back to the dawn of time. Is she teach me everyting. We take care-a we-selves in dem days. Now, is de white man cure yuh a look fuh." She snorted derisively. "Keep yuh pill, me a take de bush; me nuh know where de pill a come from."

"Mum," said Rini, "we don' want anyting bad to happen to yuh."

"Lawd Jesus!" Cordy cried, "Yuh goin' prop me corpse up inna de room when me dead? Lemme go, mon. Is long enough. Me nuh know how long me fe go."

The hours passed and the crowd thinned, and eventually everyone had gone home, leaving Cordy's kitchen dark and silent. Tacked to a red post, an aged black and white portrait of Queen Victoria peered across the deserted room, eyes unblinking, staring as she had for decades.

Sputtering, groaning, and rattling down the road, the old Blaine Estate delivery truck pulled a trailer filled with barrels of rum on its way to the Tablestone bottling plant.

When they finally pulled into the plant's loading dock, the supervisor said, "Yuh mus' wait now. Me can have de bottles ready tomorrah in de morning."

"Please, mon," Busby pleaded, "We mus' deliver inna Kingston by 7:00 a.m. tomorrah fe prepare fe export. Please mon, me need yuh help."

The supervisor shook his head. His skin was so dark he looked blue. "Nah, mon, it nuh work like dat. Come back tomorrah."

Busby was visibly upset when he returned to Linton, waiting outside with the truck. Linton knew that when Busby was quiet it meant he was angry and he had learned that it was foolish to imitate Busby's demeanor. Busby had the tendency to explode if you spoke at an inopportune time. The day had begun wrong, with Andrew and Busby quarreling intensely. Busby's plan to leave at 6:00 a.m. was dashed when he discovered that Andrew had neglected to leave a check to pay for the bottling service. Andrew arrived at 8:00 in the morning, drunk after spending New Year's Day in Montego Bay. When Andrew appeared, he was nonchalant, further outraging Busby, causing Andrew to dawdle in response before writing the check. The delay would cost them dearly. Because they were so late in getting the rum to the bottler, it would take a serious stroke of luck to make it there in time to load the ship.

Driving down the potholed road, the engine echoed in

their ears. May Pen stretched before them.

"We gwan stay inna May Pen tonight," said Busby slowing the truck. "Me know jus' where to go."

Linton cooly observed the streets filled with shoppers, livestock and pedestrians. The train station came into view. Busby turned left, parking the truck before a ramshackle white house with blue trim.

"Where we is?" Linton asked.

Leaning against his fence, Timothy watched as Linton and Busby got out of the truck. Wearing sandals, shorts, and a white cotton bush-man's shirt that contrasted nicely with his dark brown skin, Timothy was the perfect picture of a country gentleman.

"*Rahtid!*" Timothy said, coming forward to meet them. "Me nuh expeck fe see yuh today, Busby!"

Soon the men were seated under the shade tree, sipping rum over rocks. Linton took in the house, the yard. It all seemed strangely familiar.

"Yuh remember coming 'ere Linton?" Timothy asked.

"Here?" He looked at Timothy.

"Yah mon. Yuh been 'ere many a time. Right inna dis 'ere yard."

"When? Me can't re ––"

"Nevah min' right now," Timothy winked at him. "Margaret!"

Margaret came out of the house wearing a long gray skirt that did little to hide her splendid figure.

"We mus' make up bed fe two tonight. One on de sofa, and de other on de floor." Timothy noticed how Linton was focused on Margaret. Once she was gone he asked, "Yuh want her tonight, mon?"

"Nah, mon," his ears were burning with embarrassment. "I'm fine."

"Don't be afraid," Timothy went on. "We won't tell Sheila. A man should be free at a time like dis."

Linton looked over at Busby. "You been talking about me?"

"Nah bother look 'pon me mon!" Busby said. "Me nuh say nothin'. Yuh forget, Timothy a *powerful* man. Him *know* tings."

Linton looked back at Timothy who was laughing so hard he almost fell off his chair.

"Who tell yuh?" Linton asked Timothy.

"Yuh would be surprised at what I *know*," Timothy said, then shifted his attention to Busby. "So Busby, wha' de problem?"

Linton watched Timothy, but the two older men, engaged in discussing business, seemed to forget he was there. Across the room, next to the front door, was a picture of a man with a finely manicured beard, wearing a large crown. His demeanor suggested nobility. Maybe a king, Linton thought, or at least someone important.

Later that night, as he lay on blankets on the hard floor, Linton heard, over Busby's snoring on the sofa, Timothy shuffling through the room.

"Mas' Tim, who dat is on de wall by de door?" Linton asked.

The lantern Timothy held was barely lit. The flame slowly bobbed and weaved. "Dat is de Emperor Ras Tafari. Him is King of Kings, Lord of Lords, Light of Saba, the Conquering Lion of the Tribe of Judah. He was crowned King of Ethiopia, but... can we speak bout dis later, eh?" He chuckled softly. "Margaret a wait 'pon me mon." Timothy walked away with the lantern.

Mas' Tim mus' be crazy, Linton said to himself. Dat ol' mon a romp wit' Margaret?! Rolling over, he closed his eyes, took a deep breath, heard a squeak here, a rustling outside the window, a horse galloping down a dirt packed street. Sleepily, he doubted the truth of his perceptions. But his body grew heavier and soon his mouth fell open and he joined the chorus of snoring in the darkness.

It was hard to tell if it was the insistent crowing of the rooster, the whistle of the boiling kettle, or the bright red morning light striking his face that stirred Linton from his sleep. Opening his eyes, he searched for Busby but only saw rumpled sheets. He got up, freshened up, and found Timothy on the porch, smoking a spliff.

"Busby gone to pick up de rum," Timothy said, tossing a banana peel in the yard for a goat. "We need to talk. Me know yuh long time, Linton. I can see yuh restless."

"Yuh *know* me?"

"Bettah dan dat, I unnerstan yuh. I see yuh ready fe pick up an' leave. An' I mus' tell yuh, I'm ready fe leave 'ere as well." He picked up the hot kettle. "Tea?" he asked and poured Linton a cup. "More sugar?"

Linton was puzzled. "I've been here before?"

"Yuh used to play right over dey on dat mango tree. I remember when yuh was just likkle pickney, before...." Timothy stopped, thoughtfully. " But dat is another story. Right now I wan' invite yuh fe come live wit' me. I'm leavin

May Pen, moving to the mountains.

"Where yuh goin'?"

"I'm moving near Bog Walk, near de gorge. Startin' a community based on Rastafari. Yuh should come. I know yuh wan' leave de Blaine Estate, an' I'm tired a Babylon."

Linton studied Timothy, who sat before him clad in torn pants and a dirty tee shirt. How did this man know so much, and he knew so little?

"Well," Linton said, "I want to leave, but…"

"Afraid?"

Linton nodded.

"Yuh will come when yuh ready. 'Til den, remember, in two weeks I'm leaving for Bog Walk."

The sound of a truck interrupted their conversation. Pulling up with a trailer filled with cases of rum, Busby honked the horn impatiently.

"Yuh mus' come and visit," Timothy added as they got up to join Busby.

Flashing his teeth, Timothy said, "Yuh have plenty time, Busby. Stay wit me mon, have tea. Is no problem, de ship nuh leave today, mon."

"Nah sah! Linton come on!"

Timothy grabbed Linton. "Tink 'bout it. Now gwan!"

Linton barely had time to slam the door shut before Busby drove off in a cloud of dust, careening into traffic and speeding around the corner.

"Mistah Blaine gwan be vex!" Busby yelled. "Lawd Jesus him gwan be vex! Dis shipment gwan be plenty late." His voice sounded tortured, "De ship leave today." He punched the accelerator and leaned over the steering wheel, his eyes pasted on the road as the truck lurched toward Spanish Town. Slow down, Linton thought, please, please slow down!

And, indeed, after only a few more miles the truck abruptly came to a halt behind a long line of vehicles. Traffic stretched as far as they could see, up to the crest of a small hill. There had been an accident, a most common occurrence with the arrival of the automobile in Jamaica, between a flatbed truck and a mule-drawn dray. The mule was dead. Yams and bananas were scattered all over the road.

"*Pussy-clat!*" Busby screamed. "It all ovah now. Might as well gwan home." He pounded the steering wheel, turned the engine off, and they sat in a stony silence. It took three hours to clear, the clean-up work crawling along at a snail's pace. Finally the traffic began to trickle past.

Busby negotiated the streets through Spanish Town and while Linton dozed, drove by Half Way Tree and Crossroads. When he awoke they were in Kingston, an alien world with streets more congested with traffic than he had ever seen or even imagined. People were everywhere.

So this is Kingston, Linton thought. It don't get bigger than this. He wanted to walk through the town, eat the food, and brush against the women while wandering through the busy streets. Once they reached the wharfs, Busby stopped the truck before Williamson's World Import/Export shop. Thad Williamson walked out smiling.

"I am so glad you knew," he told Busby.

"'Bout what?"

"A storm's soon upon us and the ship won't sail 'til the day after tomorrow. We have plenty time for paperwork and loading. I tried to get word to you in May Pen."

Linton howled with laughter. Busby stood there, his mouth agape.

"You look surprised." Thad motioned to them to come inside. "Haven't you heard the old saying: red sky at night sailors' delight, red sky at morning sailors' take warning?"

Linton bounded up the stairs snickering. Busby shuffled behind, a sheepish look on his face.

"Come on, mon!" cried Linton. "We nuh have dat much time an' me wan' see Kingston."

Over the next two days the dark mackerel sky unleashed its fury upon Kingston; the rain came down in wind driven sheets, forcing all work on the docks to cease.

After the inclement weather passed, throngs of unemployed dark-skinned men gathered at the docks, filled with rage and resentment and desperate for work. They waited, wretched and tremulous, hoping to be among the lucky few chosen to break their backs all day, loading and unloading ships. The compensation for this good fortune was one shilling, which bought a few morsels of food, enough to assuage the hungry cries of their children and half-fill their own complaining bellies. The work was erratic and there was never enough to keep all of the stevedores employed. The rate of compensation, insufficient to feed and clothe their families, had been set a century ago and had never, in all of those one hundred years, been raised.

When the foreman finally emerged, the restless men pressed forward, attempting to make themselves seen. Papers in hand, the foreman took his time, selecting only a few, then quickly retreating to the safety of the warehouse. Sullen, angry men helplessly yelled at the silent unresponsive doors.

“Me pickney-a starve to deat’, mon!”

“If me nuh wuk, me-a bun’ down de place wit fire.”

“Is time we unionize!”

Jamaica’s finest, the constabulary, strutted up and down the docks, billy clubs in hand. Linton waited for Busby outside Thad’s, anxious to leave. He did not like the tension that was building up around him. A large group of workers, maybe eighty strong, milled about surrounded by the same number of constables.

I don’t like this at all, Linton observed. What’s takin Busby so long?

By the time Busby and Thad came out, the crowd had grown into a mob. They surveyed the scene.

“Bastards,” Thad said with disgust. “*Rasclat* reds, mon.”

“Me nuh wan’ nuttin fe do wit dis.” Busby scurried to the truck, turned the ignition, and the engine coughed to life. Linton got into the truck cab. Once they reached the outskirts of Kingston Busby added, “Me can’t wait fe get back to country.”

Linton did not reply. His attention had really been captured by the scene at the docks. He had never witnessed such a spectacle. When he worked as gang driver in the fields, even when he was, himself, still a field worker, the men were happy to work for wages. It never occurred to him that they might organize to demand a larger share of the profits.

So this is what Andrew was talkin' about! The idea made sense, but he wasn't ready yet to consider joining any movement for change. Drink the milk and don't count the cows, that's what Major always said. Of course Major had plenty of milk while Linton and his neighbors had far too little.

He dwelled on his childhood; he was starved for maternal love like an infant starves for mother's milk. But he hungered for paternal love as well and his father wanted little to do with him. His thoughts provoked questions he had never asked before. How did his mother fit into all of this? How did she meet Major? How was it that old man Timothy knew so much about him?

With each passing mile the scenery became more familiar: small farms, little roadside restaurants and taverns. Linton was grateful that Busby did all the driving. Near Old Harbor, he fell asleep as the truck rolled from side to side over the bone rattling potholes on its way back to the Blaine Estate. Busby took his time, satisfied that the journey had been successful. The rum was on a ship heading for Miami.

When Busby turned off the ignition, silence hovered in the air.

"Thank yuh, mon," he said, "fe put up wit' me foolishness."

Linton laughed. "Busby!" he said, "you did all de driving and after all you––"

"Linton, Busby!" Sheila shouted as she ran toward them. "Tank God yuh back. Aunt Cordy collapsed! Come!"

The three of them, each moving at a different speed, rushed toward the servants' quarters.

Linton reached Cordy's home to find it surrounded by neighbors. They made way respectfully for "Aunt Cordy's boy." Many remembered the youngster who pranced and sang while Aunt Cordy prepared various compounds for her patients.

The air was still and even the croton bushes stood at attention, resembling sentries posted around the house.

Inside, the heat was oppressive. Rini stood at the head of Aunt Cordy's bed, her face wet with tears. A doctor from May Pen busied himself ministering to Cordy's needs.

To Linton, Aunt Cordy seemed impossibly small under the light sheet. Proud frown lines etched her face. Her eyes were closed and she breathed slowly, her inhalations labored and shallow, her forehead damp with perspiration.

The old doctor said, "She's had a stroke. Massive, I'm afraid. It won't be long."

A tear rolled down Linton's cheek. He knelt next to the bed and took Aunt Cordy's small, frail hand and kissed it tenderly. Her skin felt thin as tissue paper.

He closed his eyes and wept with the abandon of a small boy. Aunt Cordy squeezed his hand ever so slightly.

The dark and gloomy room was overflowing with sadness. As the shadows outside lengthened, Aunt Cordy's breathing became progressively more shallow and the time between inhalations longer.

Pauline and Andrew Blaine arrived to pay their respects to a woman who had always been there to help at crucial times in their lives. Pauline, too, wept, a sight that surprised many.

Aunt Cordy was surrounded by the people who loved her when she drew her last breath.

After she passed, Rini took charge of the house, refusing to let anyone disturb anything in the bedroom. She and Sheila assumed the care of preparing the body for burial, washing and dressing it.

"Careful," Rini cautioned Sheila, "if yuh flash wata 'pon her back de duppie will follow you complaining a cold. Yuh nuh need de botheration, cause den yuh mus go a obeah man fe de cure."

I don't believe in ghosts, Sheila thought. Nevertheless, she was careful as she sponged the body. The water was collected in a large basin beneath the table.

Toward dawn, Linton, Busby, and Andrew, silhouetted by the rising sun, stood by the gravesite, gasping from exhaustion, sweating and resting on their spades. They opened a bottle of white rum and, passing it around, each toasted Aunt Cordy, took a healthy swig, and poured some of the clear liquid onto the dark rich soil.

That evening candles leading to Aunt Cordy's house flickered alongside the road. The entire community gathered to sing Christian hymns, play dominoes, and share memories. Andrew and Pauline also came to participate in the ritual.

Two days later they buried Cordy next to her husband, Arthur, the only man she had known and loved, who died thirty-three years earlier, and their three sons. More than two hundred people turned out to say farewell to a healer who had affected so many lives in and around Clarendon Parish. After the burial Rini and Sheila planted calabash trees at the head and the foot of the grave.

For nine nights the residents of Portland Cottage gathered at the old slave quarters known as Elysian Fields on the Blaine Estate, to celebrate Cordy's life. After the "nine night" extravaganza, a party so raucous it seemed bent on raising the dead, the daily rhythms on the Blaine Estate resumed, but for Sheila the world would never be the same. Her grief was especially profound.

One evening she went out, unnoticed, to gather up a specific variety of bushes, branches, and roots. Returning home she heated several pots of water. In deep concentration, lest she forget the proper combinations, she distributed the particular cuttings into each of the pots. Did Aunt Cordy say to add strongback to the second pot, she wondered, or was I supposed to... Soon, brown liquid bubbled before her.

Three hours later, she squatted near the fire in the darkness, carefully decanting the elixirs together into one pot. The fire sparkled in her eyes. Just one week before her death, Aunt Cordy had taught Sheila the secret recipe and method for making roots tonic. Sheila recalled Aunt Cordy's admonition: *Tink carefully who yuh plan fe share dis wit'. Fuh de res' a yuh life, yuh fe share it only wit' one person.*

It was time for a taste. Sheila held the cup in her hands, the moon reflected on the surface of the liquid. She took a sip, savoring the flavor, and smiled.

V

JUNE 1938, PORTLAND COTTAGE, JAMAICA

It was harvest season on the Plain of Vere in southern Clarendon Parish and dark pillars of smoke rose lazily above the burning canebrakes. Throughout the countryside, men carrying torches fanned out to set fire to the fields, incinerating the dross, the dead leaves and weeds, forcing mouse and mongoose to flee before the flames. The conflagration raced through the emerald thickets, followed by an army of laborers, cutlasses in hand, swarming across the smoldering earth, chopping down the naked, scorched cane stalks. These they piled onto the bare soil, to be loaded onto donkey carts and taken to the refinery, and processed into molasses.

For years Jamaican men traveled abroad to places like Panama, Nicaragua, Colombia, and the United States, in search of better wages. There they were paid, if low by local standards, far more money than they could have earned in Jamaica. But in 1929, with the worldwide crash of economies, men returned home by the thousands, resulting in high unemployment and skyrocketing poverty. The white plantocracy struggled to maintain the status quo, but as the years passed, the misery grew out of hand. Children wandered the country roads begging for food, families starved, and men, women, and children stood at the prison gates in Kingston, demanding to be arrested in order to receive food and shelter.

By spring 1938, the hot coals of discontent glowed brightly in the hearts of the island colony's laborers. There were too many men and far too few jobs, and the pay was abysmal. Wages, stagnant for more than a century, gave rise to rage that spread like a rash all over Jamaica and, indeed, the Carribbean.

When a new sugar plant opened in the village of Frome, in western Jamaica, a rumor that the pay was to be four pence a day attracted scores of job applicants, many of whom were given jobs. On Friday evening when management made a surprise announcement that they were paying two pence a day, the new employees angrily refused their wages saying that they expected higher pay. The dispute culminated in gunshots from police. Four people were killed, including a woman who was bayoneted to death, and scores more were wounded.

News of the violence crossed the island and civil unrest spread quickly. Rumors and men's imaginations left Clarendon Parish awash with stories that had no basis in fact. Looking out of his office window, Major Blaine clutched a three day old newspaper, trying desperately to control his racing thoughts.

Damp, smoky air, heavy with the scent of sugar cane, drifted past Major's window. Shafts of light filtered through the hanging smoke, producing an ethereal atmosphere. His eyes stung. Major looked again at the screaming headline: VIOLENCE SWEEPS THE ISLAND. Slowly, deliberately, he crumpled the newspaper and threw it in the trash.

I can't afford this, Major thought. We must fulfill that contract. The estate still had to deliver 500 cases of rum in Miami. The riots threatened to stop him from honoring the contract. The possibility kept him awake at night along with questions about Pauline's and Andrew's safety. He pondered the risk to his family, as well as the loyalty of his crews. The notion of a strike filled him with dread, but in his heart he knew that the plantation workers demands were not unreasonable. Yet he refused to break ranks with the other planters. Paying higher wages would signal a capitulation that was, in his view, a sign of weakness. The tragic history of the Blaine Estate was not lost on him. In his mind he could still hear his father's voice and never failed to recognize his responsibility to his class.

"Your Great-Granpa returned to find everything burnt to the ground," Peter took every opportunity to remind Major, "and our entire family -- massacred."

Shuddering as he sat in the plush office chair, he tried to imagine the slaughtered bodies in the midst of the smoking ruins.

His thoughts returned to the present. He retrieved the crumpled newspaper from the trash, his attention captured by an article about itinerant farmers in northern Clarendon Parish marching for better wages and living conditions.

Major Blaine was having none of it. He would be prepared for the mob this time. The Blaine Estate would not fall victim again. He knew what he had to do. The line of his jaw grew distinct. He stood up and squared his shoulders, and quickly left the room.

Linton was almost finished in the distillery for the night. His arms ached from shoveling wet ashes out of a fire pit, but fatigue didn't slow him down. While he worked, he kept an eye on Busby and Major, who sat outside on stools, engaged in a fierce conversation, and managed to catch snatches of what they said.

"Major, yuh nah wan' dat!"

"What would you have me do? With all of these trouble-makers loose there's no telling what may happen in Clarendon."

"But if yuh coulda lissen to..."

Linton cursed his luck. In the distance a truck grinding its gears, drowned out their words. He hurriedly put his tools away and went back to continue eavesdropping.

"De police jus' excite de people," Busby said emphatically. He rarely raised his voice, especially when talking to Major. "It nuh goin' guarantee a ting!"

"Then nothing will." Major stood up and brushed himself off. "It's time to go."

"Gi' 'em a likkle raise nuh?" Busby clasped his hands imploring Major to listen to reason. "Mek dem feel dem have somepin fe lose, nuh?"

"And what will my friends think of me?" Major replied.

"Yuh friends!" Busby slammed the drink down on a table. "All these years we have known one another, since yuh was bawn. Me grandfadda was hired by yuh grandfadda. For a hundred years we been helpin' you run tings here on dis estate. Two generations *wuk'* fe nuthin'. Me livin' jus' like me grandfadda.

Almos' all of us here is second and third generation. An' yuh a worry about yuh friends! De people yuh should be worryin' bout is yuh family."

"My family always paid everyone on time."

"We is yuh family! Nuh true?"

Major raised his voice. "No! These people don't appreciate what we offer them. We gave plots of land to many of the families, plots most of them don't even bother to farm."

"But de lan' no good and the plot so far away," Busby said, breaking into Major's monologue. "Yuh keep de bes' land fe yuhself." Busby threw the rest of his drink into the dirt. "De poor people haffi struggle jus' fe raise a likkle yam or pumpkin. An' de wages not enough. And with no rain lately, food scarce. People hungry and..." He broke off in mid-sentence, aware that his words fell on deaf ears. Busby felt a wall materializing between them. He realized with some surprise, that he hardly knew Major at all. "Jus' promise me one ting," he said.

"What?"

"Before yuh call police, yuh call me."

"Why?"

Busby sighed. He was weary of the verbal sparring and he looked beaten. "I can keep tings in order, Major. I can keep de peace. Jus' don't call in no guns."

Major put his index finger to his mouth thoughtfully. "I will let you know." The discussion over, Major got up to leave. He motioned to Linton to walk with him.

"When these troubles are resolved," Major said quietly, "I have made arrangements for you to go to Monymusk for training in blending rum." He drew Linton closer. "Don't go getting involved in anything," he whispered, "stay clear of trouble... and keep your mouth shut."

Linton watched Major disappear into the fading evening light. He was startled by a screaming crow. It landed on the roof of the distillery and Busby threw a rock. Cawing, the bird flew off.

"Damn crow," Busby said scratching his chin as he poured Linton a drink. "Good thing is de distillery. De crow pon yuh roof screaming like dat only mean one ting."

"Death?"

"So they say." Busby fell into a depressed silence.

Linton pondered Major's words. No matter what is to happen, he thought, I'm staying out of it. Sipping rum, they watched the ragged purple clouds on the horizon.

"All Major haffi do is gi' de people a likkle sompin," Busby continued. "But him too *bloodclat boasy*. Dey's gonna be trouble." He looked at Linton, his face betraying his hope that Linton would pledge himself to the cause of keeping the peace.

"If dere's trouble me *gone*, mon. I want to leave anyway." Linton swallowed the rest of the rum. "I'm not involved in this."

"Yuh can't leave. Blaine have plans fe yuh bwoy."

"What 'bout mine?"

"Wha'?"

"My plans, Busby! What about my future?"

"Stop talkin' crazy."

"I have my reasons." Linton said.

Facing Linton, Busby put his hands on the young man's shoulders, looking at him tenderly. "Be patient," he said. "De tough times will pass, den yuh can do somepin. Yuh is a young man. Take de time fe get a skill so yuh won' be breakin' yuh back inna de fields."

Busby pushed a cork in the rum bottle and placed it back in a dusty cabinet that he then locked. He thoughtfully scratched his pate. "Yuh is a man now. Yuh mus' start thinking like one, and sacrificing as well."

Looking into Busby's eyes, his father's words rang in Linton's ears. *Stay clear of trouble.*

The next day, under the hot tropical sun, three constables and several gun-toting mercenaries, intimidating men dressed in gray shirts and dark pants, arrived and took up posts around the mansion.

Major stayed in the house, avoiding contact with anyone but his family and the house servants. He was at the breakfast table sipping a cup of tea when a servant came in to say that Busby wished to speak to him.

"I am growing tired of that man," Major said, slightly annoyed. "Tell him to talk to his people instead of talking to me."

Across the table Pauline ate breakfast behind a veil of silence. Major sensed her icy stare. "I take it you don't approve?" he asked.

Pauline excused Sheila from her post. Once they were alone, she answered, "This is an outrage, still being here in this madness. Major, we must go to Kingston or Spanish Town. It's the only thing that will guarantee our safety. Four plantations have been attacked including the Melvins, and they were lucky to get away with their lives. Marauders are roaming the countryside killing people. And you want to stay here because of some stupid family tradition."

Major held up a small nickel-plated pistol. "I bought our protection. Those men know their orders. If something happens, this is for you. Shoot to kill."

"Major! After all these poor people do fe you, *this* is how you treat them?" Pauline looked at him with disgust.

"You have always felt too much for them, Pauline. Treat these people better and it leads to attitude problems and the situations like we have now."

"That's just not true, Major," Pauline interjected. "You did not treat them better and this has happened anyway."

Major sniffed. "Now is the time to remind them of their place on the island. I think Thad is right, we will have communism in the Crown colonies if we fail to be vigilant. Goddamn that Bustamante! The damn dockworkers strike! It's people like that labor organizer Grant who needs to be locked away in prison." He pounded his fist on the table. "These damn *rasclat* workers get paid enough. These lousy, lazy people should be thankful for anything we've given them."

Thankful for *nothing*, Pauline thought. "What did we give them?" she demanded. "Slavery, disease and ––"

"Christianity," Major interrupted, "saving countless souls."

"Oh Major. Jesus Christ himself can't put food in your child's belly or shoes on his feet."

"They learned a strong work ethic, and through slavery they acquired something they did not have till we arrived."

"Hard work?"

"Pauline, now they are loyal subjects of the crown."

"They don't look so loyal now."

"That, my dear, is the direct result of people such as yourself, interceding and tempting the natives to regard themselves as something that they are not."

"Why, Major! Look at yourself. You're a native! What a pompous, ignorant thing to say!"

Major got up from the table and left the room, carrying with him the familiar sense of shame he could not purge.

That evening, in his little one room cottage, Linton sat at the table looking at a bowl of yams and a small heap of rice. Next to him, Sheila shrugged, "Is all we have."

Reeking of rum, his belly burning with anger, Linton couldn't think of a time in his life when things were worse. Drought had brought hardship to Jamaica and the effects were felt most acutely in Clarendon. Without water, crops failed. Food had become scarce and expensive, leaving most people no choice but to look for alternatives. Linton's stomach rumbled as he thought about the many evenings during the past few months spent foraging in the countryside for callaloo or wild yams to eat. The small plots given to the workers who lived on the estate consisted of tough, poor soil that did not yield. The gardens resembled a wasteland, dry and parched. The residents of Portland Cottage had grown accustomed to the dull pain of hunger. It had been months since anyone had put meat on the dinner table. There was a time when Linton and Sheila ate chicken almost daily, but now all the fowl had been eaten, so there were no eggs either. The water from the spring, except a few gallons they kept to drink, went to canefields.

Sharing the food, Linton made sure that Sheila's portion was more generous than his.

"I already ate," he lied, but Sheila eyed him suspiciously. They took the meal in silence, as if to conserve their energy for more important tasks.

After dinner, Linton went out to the porch and looked at the fires glowing in the cane fields. Sheila came out and wrapped her arms around him, hugging him close.

"I'm scared, Linton. Up inna de big dining room me hear Blaine a say him give shoot to kill orders."

"Nah bother worry 'bout dat. Just mind yuh business, an gah-long."

They stood listening to the night insects and breathed the heady aroma of the tropical countryside. Paradise. A perfect moment that was broken when Linton said, "Get me some rum, Sheila."

"Why yuh haffi drink more?" she whined.

Linton turned on her in an instant. "Yuh gwan," he raised his hand to hit her and she cowered.

"Go 'head nuh! Hit me! Hit me!"

The sight of her, cowering, waiting for the fist to strike, stopped his hand, frozen in mid-air. The alcoholic haze momentarily receded. He moved to hug her but she shrank from his touch just as he still inwardly cowered in fear when faced by Major's wrath.

Insistent, he wrapped his arms around Sheila, but even as he held her, she remained rigid and he felt the distance between them growing wider. Maybe, he thought, I should stop drinking. But the moment it crossed his mind, the familiar terror grabbed hold of him, the urge to fill the unbreachable emptiness that formed the core of his being.

The next morning, their neighbors awoke with the perpetual pangs of hunger and prepared their work-weary bodies for another day of sun-roasted, back-breaking labor. The police presence created a tension that grew with every passing moment.

From his office window, Major Blaine watched the motley collection of men, women and children grow more restless as the sun crawled higher in the sky.

"We need fe eat!" they shouted. "Yuh can't just run us up outta we homes!"

"Mistah Blaine yuh come out here an' explain! Yuh owe us, Mistah Blaine! Yuh owe us!"

There was a pounding on the door.

"Who is it?"

Andrew burst in. "Stop this *now*," he demanded.

"And start paying excessive wages, right? It's harvest time, and what is everyone occupied with?" He threw up his hands. "Strikes, riots, disturbances of the worst kind, all timed to hurt us. Troublemakers are responsible for this, Andrew. After they're arrested, people will calm down. In the meantime, I have a responsibility to protect you and your mother -- and the Blaine property."

"The property?"

"Of course." Major motioned expansively. "All this will be yours –– someday." He smiled faintly.

Andrew backed away. "I don't *want* it, Daddy. Don't you understand? You're living in the past and time is passing you by. You think this is the future? I just spent time with the best and the brightest minds, and let me tell you, Daddy, there's no future here." Looking stunned, Major sat down as if Andrew had slapped him hard across the face. Andrew continued, the temper in his voice intensifying as he spoke, "Colonialism is over. Over! For three generations our neighbors have been loyal employees of this estate and you treat them like shit! You expect them to be grateful? My God, Daddy, wake up! It's 1938!"

Major's face darkened with anger. "How dare you," he said, his voice barely audible. "We treated those people well through the years."

"Those people? Yuh forget, *dem a fe we people, a dem blood inna we!* It nuh secret. Yuh love fe deny it. Yuh deny everyt-ing––even who yuh is."

"Get out!" Major pointed at the door. "How many times must I tell you not to speak patois in my house!"

Outside, a sudden barrage of gunfire gave way to screams. Andrew ran from the room. An alarm bell sounded. Clouds of dark smoke billowed into the sky and flames rapidly engulfed the processing plant and the distillery. There was another volley of gunshots. Major observed the chaos through his spyglass, rage distorting his face.

"Shoot them," he muttered. "Goddamn it, shoot them all!"

On the Estate, the guards shoved families from their homes at Elysian Fields and forced workers from nearby groves to the edge of an emotional precipice. In desperation, the crowd threw rocks but the guards simply laughed, mocking the defenseless men and maneuvering the crowd further from the mansion. Busby, running back and forth, exhorted the crowd towards calm and tried to stop the rock throwing. Linton hung back, trying to maintain a low profile, keeping Sheila close to him, determined that they not be separated. Suddenly someone yelled, pointing at the black smoke rising in the sky.

Busby rushed over to Linton. His eyes were wild with fear.

"Look!" he yelled. "De distillery on––" A bullet ripped through his throat, spraying Linton and Sheila with blood. Busby dropped to his knees and toppled face-first to the ground, blood gushing from a huge wound.

More gunshots followed, unleashing pandemonium. Linton pulled Sheila to the ground and lay on top of her. Only yards away two of his neighbors, their flesh pocked with buckshot, screamed in pain and vainly called for help. Next to him, Busby lay still, his blood pooling on the flagstones.

After the gunfire stopped, the screams continued to punctuate the silence.

"Linton," Sheila cried, "get off me!"

"Are you all right?"

"I'm all right, you?"

"Yes." Still he did not move.

"Linton, yuh a crush me mon!"

"Be quiet, I'm trying to hear."

The smell of gunpowder hung over the crowd. Linton slowly raised his head. Three bodies lay in the road.

"Oh God!" Linton reached out to touch Busby. Busby's unfocused eyes grew dim, as he was freed of his earthly moorings. Sheila screamed and in an instant the street came alive with activity. Several neighbors carried the two wounded men to shelter. Mr. Chao, the Chinese shopkeeper, opened his doors and two women guided Sheila, distraught and weeping, inside. Another group of men carried Busby's body into the building through the back door. No one spoke as the crowd melted away, leaving the road empty, save the bloodstained flagstones.

Hours after the skirmish most people had fled to the neighboring town of Alley or managed to return to their homes in the village of Portland Cottage itself. People who lived in Elysian Fields on the Estate were afraid to go home and found shelter elsewhere. The streets were deserted except for some constables, who strutted around, truncheons ready, and beat any unfortunate they came across. From inside Mr. Chao's store, Linton observed them through the window, his eyes filled with hate. He dared not go out. At dusk he and Sheila climbed to the roof and went to sleep. Flakes of ash from the smoldering distillery fire fell like snow, blanketing them as they slept.

At dawn clouds covered the sky. Busby's body, wrapped in linen, was lowered into a freshly dug grave. Dozens of people crowded into the lot behind Mr. Chao's store, their heads bowed, silently saying good-bye to a man most had known since childhood. Two men stepped forward to fill the grave, their spades slicing the soil in a random rhythm, mimicking life with its uncertainties and surprises. Linton and Sheila, holding one another, stared at the fresh mound of dirt, the ashes and the footprints of mourners, and wept.

After a short, hurried service they returned home, hand in hand, defiantly passing through the Estate gate and past the security officers.

"We leavin' today," Linton said. "There's nothin' keeping us here."

"Where will we go?"

"We see Timothy. He will help us."

"I need some time. I can't jus' leave."

"We'll only take what we can carry, and forget the rest." Linton felt an urgency to be as far away from this place as possible.

"Just one day."

"That day is today, Sheila. I am leaving before the sun is down, and I plan to be at Timothy's tonight. I can't wait for anyone. I gotta go."

"Yuh can't wait for me?!" Sheila sounded shocked. Linton took off and she ran behind him. No matter what, she thought, he's not leaving here without me.

They passed the tropical blossoms, usually so vibrant and gay, shuddering under the soft carpet of ash in the gray filtered light. Heading toward their little shack they passed one abandoned cottage after another. At Aunt Cordy's grave the two calabash trees still stood erect, healthy and green. Where is everybody? they wondered.

They found Andrew splayed out on their cottage steps, a half bottle of rum next to him.

"Linton! Sheila! Thank God you're all right!" Staggering to his feet, he hugged Sheila and offered an unsteady hand to Linton.

Linton did not extend his hand. "Busby's dead," he said matter of factly.

"Busby?" Andrew was incredulous. Tears welled in his eyes "How did it happen?"

Ignoring the question, Linton moved past him. "I'm leaving."

Andrew grabbed Linton by the shoulder. "Tell me what happened!"

They went inside and Linton collapsed into a chair, his head in his hands. "We just left the Chinese store." His voice trembled with emotion. "Busby's buried. Dem bastards … shot him." Linton halted, staring into Andrew's eyes and then burst out, "I hate Major! I'm leavin' dis place, right now."

"I don't hate Major, but I do pity him. Linton, he's human, he's not perfect, he gave me life––"

"And a whole lot more! He gave yuh everything."

"I'm his son! My father took care of yuh, too. Nah forget dat. After your father was killed in de war, and yuh mother passed away, Daddy intervened and saved you from a life in an orphanage."

"Yuh know it all, don't you?" Linton said flippantly.

"What?"

"Who takes care of me now? We live in different worlds, you and I," Linton said. "Tonight you go behind armed men to sleep in a comfortable bed in a big 'ouse. *Me?*" he shrugged, "where do I go? You forget that afternoon when Major tell us dat we have to grow up in different worlds, but I remember. You went to boarding school and I went to primary school in May Pen. You were in college in London while I was in the fields, battered by the sun. While you got a lesson every day, I got lashed with a whip. "

"And you hate me because of that?" Andrew asked.

"No," Linton said, "I hate *him* for it."

Troubled, Andrew stared at Linton before he spoke. "Linton, I was a boy. You know if I had it my way, you would have come with me. You're like a brother to me."

Linton snorted and began to sort through clothes. " I have to get busy and pack our things."

"Sheila too?"

"Sheila's my woman. She goes where I go."

From the kitchen area of the small cottage, Sheila listened to the exchange. Finally she heard in Linton's response the commitment that swept away the doubts she harbored about leaving.

"Where will you go?"

"Timothy's. You'll find me there." Linton stood up and shook Andrew's hand.

They watched as Andrew tottered out the door and up the hill toward the mansion. At the crest he turned and gave a strong wave, nearly stumbling, then he disappeared into the house.

Standing alone in the Blaine family cemetery, Major looked at the green rectangular fields of cane, the stalks rippling in the wind, disappearing into a gray wash. His heart raced whenever he pictured the distillery in flames.

He felt numb. He'd come here seeking solace but finding none, stood on the hill, inhaling the acrid smoke, watching the ash continue to fall from the sky, trying to make sense of it all.

I'll rebuild, he thought. In a month, we can salvage the harvest. Busby will help get a crew together. It was only then that he remembered Busby, and he set off to find him.

When he reached the old slave quarters, he was surprised to find them deserted. Turning a corner he spied Linton and Sheila on their porch, packing belongings into large burlap sacks.

"Linton!" Major called out. "Are you all right?" Coming closer he continued, "Sheila? We've been wondering where you were. Are you all right?"

Linton propped his sack on the ground and glanced casually at Major. Sheila ignored him entirely, not even looking up from her packing.

Major finally realized that they were packing travel sacks and stopped dead in his tracks. "What are you doing?" When they did not answer he repeated, "Where are you going? Where's Busby?"

That got a rise out of Linton. "You damn fool." He gave Major a chilling glare. "Busby's dead!"

"What?" Major stepped back as if he'd been slapped. "No," he said. "My God! Not Busby!"

"Yeah, Major, yuh best man, decent, honest, hard working, loyal Busby. He's dead. Your hired thugs shot him in the head. So what now? Who's in charge? We're leaving."

"What did you say boy?" Major's tone changed and he seemed to stand taller. "You're not goin' anywhere except to Monymusk."

Dark with anger, Linton strode over to his father. Major never saw it coming, the right hook to the left cheek. He saw multicolored lights and for a moment felt deeply peaceful. Then he opened his eyes. His ears roared. His vision was blurred and when he touched his mouth, saw blood on his fingers. He sat in the dusty yard, puzzled, and looked at Linton looming above.

"*Nevah!* speak to me like that again--*Father*." Sheila did a double take but clearly this was not the time for questions. They picked up their few sacks of belongings and set off down the road.

Major struggled to his feet. "I'll never let you back," Major shouted. "You'll beg me---you rude bastard!"

Linton put the heavy burlap sack down and reached out to stay Sheila, He turned to face Major. "Bastard, eh?" He laughed dismissively. "Yes, sir, that's what I am. Your bastard, yuh r*asclat!*"

As they walked away, Linton's excitement grew. When his eyes met Sheila's he grinned and felt a strange burgeoning sense of freedom and confidence.

Major watched until they were enveloped by a field of green cane stalks. He walked up the hill to the house. The wind was blowing and it had started raining hard, washing the gray sludge off the bright green leaves and brilliantly hued flowers. Wet and bedraggled, he went inside, slamming the door, his mind hopelessly confused and his heart filled with bitterness.

VI

SEPTEMBER 1944, BESSANWORSE, JAMAICA

After leaving the Blaine estate, Linton and Sheila went to live with Timothy in Bessanworse. Timothy, through means that remained a mystery, had secured a number of hectares of land in a fecund valley near the town of Bog Walk. Accompanied by several others, they established the camp at the head of a spring, near the ruins of an old plantation house.

Timothy invited people to come and live based on the principles of Marcus Garvey, and a nacent religious cult known as Rastafari. Timothy, a former Garveyite, preached that salvation lay in freedom from the white power structure, which he dubbed Babylon. The residents had to agree to participate in an agricultural collective. The money made from the crops belonged to the community.

"Some may disagree," Timothy said, "but we cannot return to Africa in fact, until we return to Africa in our hearts and learn to love one another in communities such as this."

Soon, 150 people called Bessanworse home. Everyone had a job: men worked in a pit making charcoal, refining and bagging it, women sewed and sold garments in Bog Walk, farmers cultivated ganja, corn, bananas, yams, okra, and pumpkin, which were wholesaled to a merchant at Coronation Market in Kingston. The children tended the animals and artisans created crafts that were sold at a stand on the road in the gorge. The profits were turned over to Timothy, provoking some grumbling, but most of the residents were simply grateful that no one went hungry and everyone had clothes on their backs. Timothy promised that one day everyone would get a deed to their homes.

Linton and Sheila harvested herbs and roots, preparing and packaging them for wholesale and making concoctions for people who fell ill. But the one product that everyone especially sought from them, was roots tonic brew.

Sheila had made the tonic for the first time only a week after Aunt Cordy passed away. She continued to brew the roots and it proved as popular as Aunt Cordy's. She kept the secret to herself, pondering a great question: should I share it with Linton? She kept the secret until she became pregnant, feeling it was her destiny to spend the rest of her life with him.

So early one morning under a calm, violaceous sky, Sheila summoned Linton and they went step-by-step through the process of making the brew. When they finished, both the recipe and the method were seared into Linton's memory. He was a quick study, and it wasn't long before he alone made the roots tonic.

Carried by a mild breeze, the scent of bananas and mangoes drifted over hills and across gullies to a small clearing where Linton and Sheila busily searched for medicinal herbs. Perched on the side of a steep hill, their donkey waiting nearby, they could see the Rio Cobre, shimmering like a snake dozing in the late afternoon sun. The meandering waterway had cut a deep canyon known as Bog Walk Gorge, a ragged wound that streaked across the verdant Jamaican landscape.

Sheila stepped carefully on the slope, her full belly protecting their unborn child. Her eyes darted to and fro in search of familiar bush and bark. She stopped abruptly and hacked at the roots of a bush. "Chaney root, mon," she said, pulling the roots from the earth.

Linton stuffed the roots into a sack slung over the back of the donkey. Shirtless, his dark body glistened with sweat. He was trim and muscular, both the reward of youth and the result of hard physical labor. His beard was thick, and his teeth gleamed as he grinned at Sheila. Ignoring him, she continued to study the foliage. Finally, as the sun sank lower on the horizon, she slouched forward with fatigue.

"Have yuh forgotten yuh pregnant? You must think about your condition," Linton said. From behind, he wrapped his arms around her expansive belly. He loved her being pregnant. Sheila relaxed, feeling secure in his strong dark arms. But moments later she was irritated at him.

"Think? It's yuh need to start thinkin'," Sheila said.

"'Bout what?"

"Leavin'. Is time we leave dis wilderness."

"How many times we haffi go ovah dis!"

Sheila spun around to face him. "We've been here five years an' now I'm pregnant. I don't want to be here any more, Linton. I'm tired a de damn country livin'." Sheila's whine set Linton's nerves on edge. "I don't want to have a family here.

We could move to Kingston and stay with Andrew. Den when yuh get a job––"

"Yuh jokin'! Move back inna Babylon?" Linton snorted. "All my life me been without. Without a family, a father or mother, and now, finally I getting something of my own. Years a looking and wondering and now we find a place, we trod de earth and be happy. We're not struggling in Babylon, we're living off a de land. An you want work fe buccra, and give our money to him, and live with de people who a spy on yuh, while de rest dem *su-su* pon yuh. Let Andrew go, he doesn't' think like we do. He chose a different path. He wants to build a better Babylon system. I would rather do me duty to de community."

"He got married, got a job, had a son... Andrew *grew* up." Sheila was frustrated. "Now we expeckin' a child Linton. Now is not de time for foolishness."

"Foolishness!"

"Yes, foolishness. All dis damn nonsense about duty and community. I'm tired a de rasta philosophy."

With a dour expression, Linton took a spliff from the leather pouch that hung around his neck. Bending down, he kissed Sheila tenderly.

"Yuh jus' tired. Yuh need fe res'. Les go 'ome." He helped her get atop the donkey from where she scowled in the twilight.

The path to the hilltop was narrow and treacherous. When they reached the hillcrest, Linton lit the cone shaped marijuana cigar. The sun had sunk low on the horizon and the lingering afterglow stretched across the sky. He put his hand on Sheila's thigh. Taking two deep puffs, he exhaled, watching the wind snatch the smoke as it left his lips. Far below, the river appeared as a slender thread, reflecting the purple sky. Linton pointed to it.

"That is the border between heaven and hell. On this side, in our world, the land provides *sustenance.* We live over here, on our land, with our tribe. On the other riverbank, Babylon waits wit' all its wickedness and a world war." Linton turned to Sheila, his face filled with emotion. "That's why *I and I* work so hard fe this life . Babylon is falling. But our life in Bessanworse is the very best thing to happen to us."

"Maybe de bes' ting to happen to *you*," she retorted. "But what about us, Linton, what about me, what about de baby? Is there room for us in this world between your *I and I?* Even at de estate we lived better dan dis. Now is time to tink bout what is best fe de family."

"Have you been hungry since we here in Bessanworse? You forget how hungry we was in Portland Cottage? When we all do our duty to de community, we is doing for ourselves. We with brothers and sisters workin' fe a common goal."

He waved his hands dismissively. They walked down a trail strewn with boulders, past the ruins of an old plantation house, one of the many that had been numerous in this area of the island. According to legend, many slaves were tortured and killed at this plantation.

As they made their way down into the valley, Linton's exuberance couldn't be contained. Oblivious to Sheila's pain, he turned and gestured toward the endless hills and mountains of Jamaica's interior.

"How can we leave dis?" He patted her belly. "We mus' raise de pickney here, in nature, inna de heart a Zion." He turned from the ridge and clicked his tongue, encouraging the donkey to follow him.

Linton prattled on but Sheila stopped listening. The jerking motion of the donkey made her nauseous but her legs ached when she walked. She looked into the deepening darkness, her heart racing for fear of duppies, ghosts known in these parts for their mischief, and despite her doubts, Sheila preferred to not tempt fate. Even now, she wore an amulet given to her by an obeah man for protection.

In the distance they could hear the faint rhythm of drums and soon, the chanting. The vibrations rolled across the ground and tickled Sheila's belly and prompted the baby to kick.

"Feel dis baby, Linton." He placed his hands on her smooth skin and felt the burgeoning life of his child.

"He must be a boy! Kick it boy! Kick it to the beat, mon!"

Linton started down the path, laughing heartily and in spite of herself Sheila joined in. Linton could always make her laugh, causing her anger to give way to silly sheepishness.

As as they approached Bessanworse, clean, clear spring waters bubbled up from a limestone cavern, creating a stream that passed through the village and a stand of coconut trees. Encircling the village grew cultivated plots of corn, cocoa, banana trees, and ganja. The moon, nearly full, cast a serene glow over the village. Women prepared the evening meal around cook fires while their men, tired from a long day of labor, relaxed in clouds of ganja smoke, played their drums and chanted:

The wicked carried us into captivity
Required from us a song

But how can we sing
Rastafari song in a Strange Land.

When they reached their shanty, a lean-to built of mud and thatch, Linton helped Sheila off the donkey and followed her inside. He tried to help her into bed.

"Linton, stop fussing. I'm just tired." She lay back, her head resting on the pillow. Linton pulled the sheet over her while she tried to ignore him.

"Are you hungry?"

He was gone before she could stop him. Out in the yard he unburdened the donkey, fed and watered him and prepared his resting place for the night. It only took a few minutes but by the time he returned to the shack with a hot plate of food for Sheila, she was fast asleep. He sat down and ate, watching her, thinking about his soon-to-be family. For so many years, he had searched for something to fill the emptiness. Now, with Sheila pregnant, the pieces had finally come together. With his love for Sheila he would build what was lacking, a family of his own.

Linton felt the excitement surge inside him. Fatherhood. The idea sent shivers of pleasure through him. He lay down next to Sheila, spooning her within the safety of his own protective frame, and wrapped his arm around her belly. Please give me a son, a healthy boy, he prayed as his head found the pillow.

After getting a full night's sleep, Linton went outside, to cook roots. Soon water and herbs bubbled in the pots. The familiar earthy aroma took him back to his childhood at the Blaine Estate, playing with Andrew and when Sheila, the youngest of the three, tagged along as best she could.

Stirring the pot, Linton was lost in his thoughts when a tall man approached.

"Roots!" the man said. "Yuh mus' put a bottle aside fe me, eh?"

It was Riddle, a sarcastic man whose long neck and limbs made him appear as a moveable stick figure. Riddle was a malcontent, who could always find something to complain about. His eyes darted back and forth suspiciously, making Linton feel uncomfortable. Linton always did his best to avoid Riddle.

"Wha' goin on?"

Riddle grinned. "We is goin to Kingston in a couple days. Last night Timothy told me dat we goin' with Barris in his truck."

"We?"

"Yah mon, yuh and I fe go down de mountain to Kingston."

A cloud of disappointment descended on Linton's face and he sighed. Seeing this, Riddle moved in and elbowed Linton playfully.

"Yuh can't keep using Sheila as a way to get out of de work." Riddle whispered, his neck craning forward. "Yuh haffi contribute too, jus' like de rest of us."

Linton glared at Riddle. "I didn't say I wasn't going to do it. I have to look after Sheila. She beg me to stay close and I haven't left the camp since she pregnant. It's only a couple weeks more." Picking up the pot, Linton slowly decanted the elixir into a large metal basin to cool.

"Yuh can't make gal control yuh like dat."

"Don't tell me what I can do! And don't worry, I'm going to Kingston." He settled down to sulk in silence.

"One more ting."

"What?"

"Kenneth and I need help bagging and stacking the charcoal onto the truck."

"What time?"

"Afternoon."

Linton rubbed his jaw, thinking about it. "I'll be there."

Later that morning Linton complained to Timothy about being tapped to go to Kingston with Riddle.

"Anyone but Riddle," Linton pleaded. "You know I can't stand him."

"We all have duties here," Timothy said. "We didn't come here to argue, fight, and backstab, we came in search of some way to live free of Babylon's exploitation. Yuh mus' learn fe work wit' Riddle. But Linton, if yuh want fe wait until after de baby bawn to take a load to Kingston, is yuh choice."

Linton's brow knitted with worry. "I'm afraid of what the men will think a me."

Timothy gazed into Linton's eyes. "Yuh nevah goin' achieve anyting lasting in life, worryin' 'bout what men think and what woman goin' sey."

Stung, Linton went to see Sheila, who sat outside their hut, carefully bottling roots Linton had made earlier that morning. They went inside and it took a moment for their eyes to grow accustomed to the gloom. As Sheila's due date drew close Linton knew that she preferred him to stay near. This baby was her first and she'd grown anxious and more dependent on him than he'd anticipated. He didn't mind except it sometimes put him in conflict with the group.

"Sheila, de men not goin' let me skip me responsibilities." He could feel his heart beating. "And I agree," he added.

"What yuh mean?"

"I have to go to Kingston with Riddle and Barris."

"Yuh mean Timothy won't even give yuh a break fe be with me? Goddamn him!"

"Sheila! It's not Timothy, it's my choice. It's only two days."

"What if the baby comes?" Her eyes filled with tears.

"Then you have we baby. Even if I is here, we callin' pon de midwife." He stroked her cheek. "I'll be back in two shakes of a duck's tail. You act like we're not going to see each other again."

"Why yuh haffi volunteer?" Sheila persisted. Turning her back to him, she heard him exiting the hut and yelled, "Yuh can't even stay wit' me for a couple minutes?"

Linton stuck his head back into the dark hut. "I feel it's my duty, Sheila, me duty to de community," he said in as noble a voice as he could muster. "We all do. Bessanworse is too important for us to be selfish. Yuh mus' try and unnerstan, dis is a big thing. We will be de example for de rest of our people to liberate demselves. All of us here, working together. Yuh mus' read yuh Bible," he admonished. "Den yuh will unnerstand." With that he strode off.

The pile of charcoal seemed insurmountable. The men labored, slowly, steadily, whittling the mountain down to a hill, then a bluff and, ultimately, into a patch of blackened bare earth, strewn with tiny fragments of charcoal. They struggled with shovels and bare hands to complete the task of putting all the coal into the burlap bags. The black dust hovered in the air and they coughed up phlegm peppered with coal dust.

Once the job was finished, Linton, Kenneth, and Riddle, sat down together, exhausted, covered from head to toe with black powder. Over one hundred bags of coal were neatly stacked far from the fire pit. The men admired their work, relaxing on the flatbed of the truck.

"*Rastafari!* Is good work men," Kenneth said.

"Yes, mon!" Linton declared.

"I wonder how much is dis worth?" Riddle asked.

"Enough," Kenneth retorted. "Something haffi pay fe de land we livin' off.

"Yuh tink Timothy is payin' fe dis land?" Riddle broke out laughing. "Timothy crooked, mon, I tellin' yuh. We squatters, mon."

"If you think him crooked, an' yuh a squatter, why don't you leave?" Linton looked at Riddle with an air of disgust.

Riddle returned his dirty look. "Yuh naïve."

"Yuh *rasclat!*" Linton retorted.

Kenneth slapped both men on the back. "Yuh can learn a lot from each other," he said. "But is time fe me to go home."

After dinner, as drums reverberated in the background, Linton lit a spliff and inhaled deeply, closing his eyes, letting his mind drift. "Linton?" Sheila spoke up to him.

"Yes, sistah."

"We need to boil more roots. Yuh leavin' in two days an' me wan' do dat tomorrow." She waited, ready to recoil when he gave her all the reasons why he couldn't do it.

"Yes, tomorrow morning, we'll do it. But I want to start before sunrise."

That night, Sheila was roughly awakened by Linton's thrashing about in the bed.

"Linton!"

Witless, trapped in sleep, he continued to flail, defending against the menacing switch brandished before him.

Whiisp!

The sound of air sliced asunder caused him to cringe protectively.

Whiisp! Crack!

The pain always struck him like a bolt of lightning, catapulting him upright and conscious. Entangled in sheets, he was wet with perspiration, and confused. Realizing it was another nightmare he collapsed, exhausted and dazed.

Sheila pulled up the rumpled sheets. "De nightmares is gettin' worse," she said. "Yuh screamin' and carryin' on.

Linton rubbed his eyes, "I'm sorry."

"Tell me yuh dream, Linton. What happened. Please?" She snuggled next to him, stroking the welts on his back. "Secrets," she whispered, "have no place between us." Her lips were pressed against his ear. "I love yuh. Lemme help. Tell me, what happened, love." She lightly kissed his neck.

"No," Linton said. He pushed her away.

Sheila was undeterred. "Let me help yuh, nuh?"

Linton turned over and studied Sheila. What if you *told* her? he thought. Just *do it.* But he remained silent, looking into eyes that awaited an answer. He wiped his brow. "I don't want to remember," he said, the desperation in his voice was tightly controlled. "I must bury me past, and try to find me own destiny."

"Linton, yuh can't disown yuh past and yuh can't run from yuhself." Sheila's expression, a mixture of devotion and love, unnerved him. He lay next to an angel, whose very presence demanded the purest honesty. Since sincerity demanded his delving into repressed memories of the brutal whippings and worst of all, the flogging he received when Andrew left for England, he found refuge in being mute.

He turned away, toward the wall, and was faced with the image of himself as a young boy tied to a tree. His mistake had been to stand up to his father. He directly threatened Major with going to Pauline and telling her the truth about who he really was. He regretted it. Later, after a daylong drinking binge, Major, on horseback, chased Linton through the fields. When he caught Linton he had, face flushed with anger, tied him up and cut the greenest, most supple switch he could find. The stench of rum on Major's breath made Linton's eyes water. These many years later he could still remember the threat in Major's voice.

So... yuh plannin' fe tell Pauline dat yuh my son? Bwoy yuh nuh goin' to England wit' Andrew, and yuh not goin' tell Pauline anyting 'cause -- me goin' kill yuh. Arms stretched around the breadfruit tree, his wrists tied, and tree bark biting his bare chest, he'd felt terror, and the explosion of agony as the switch tore through his flesh. He was almost nine years old. He tried to forget, to live as if it never happened. Just thinking about it made his back tingle with pain.

"Linton, yuh have--"

"No, I do not!" He sat up, upset at her persistence.

Cowering, she touched him, saying, "I'm sorry, baby, I just... I wanted to help."

"There's nothing you can do." Shaking free of her, he got up, and donned some clothes. "I can't sleep," he mumbled.

"Yuh vex?" She looked at him, puzzled and heartbroken.

"Nah, but I don't want to remember such things, Sheila. I jus' wan forget." Putting on his power shoes, made from rubber tires and rawhide webbing, he left the cottage and Sheila.

Outside in the warm starlight, Linton felt a wave of heartfelt gratitude for Sheila. Goosebumps erupted all over his flesh. Cramming down the emotions, he walked toward the center of the village. Why, he asked himself, did she stay with him? His drinking and the fights took their toll on their relationship.

He sat under the tree in the dark, deserted square in the center of the village, and pondered his life. The stark fact that he was to be a father in a few short weeks, the gravity of the situation, frightened him. He did not know what it was to have a father in the fullest sense of the word. Growing up, Aunt Cordy had shown him incredible kindness and raised him with love, but there had never been a man to care for and guide him. Timothy's knowledge about his background puzzled Linton. Unexpectedly a hand touched his shoulder, startling him. It was Timothy. Smiling, he sat down next to Linton.

"I was jus' thinkin bout yuh," Linton said.

"And here I is wonderin' why me ears are burning." He laughed.

"Mas' Tim?"

"Yah, mon,"

"How do you know so much 'bout me? How do you know bout Major being me faddah?"

Timothy glanced at Linton thoughtfully, as if sizing him

up for some important mission. "I was there when you was born. Your father was not. Your mother was a good friend. Yuh forget but I used to play wit' yuh when yuh was just dis high." He held his hand a foot above the ground. "When Misti died, I looked for Major to come get yuh. But he was nowhere to be found. So I took you down to the Estate."

"He was going to jus' leave me, eh?" Linton said.

"I don't know. I didn't wait."

"Bastard!"

"Linton, yuh can't go on a carry de anger like dat."

"What are you talking about?" Linton stood up and stretched.

"Yuh mus find a way to forgive Major."

"How?" Linton stared angrily at Timothy. "Why?!"

"Yuh mus' forgive him; it is your cross to bear in life."

"No! I can't bear it!"

"Jah makes all sorts of crosses," Timothy went on, "some is made a wood, others stone, some iron, others feathers, some, even as light as air. One ting is certain, him make a cross just fe yuh, an' it not too heavy or light. It jus' right fi yuh. An' yuh mus' carry it. Jah will never gi' yuh more dan yuh can bear."

Linton bit his tongue. He would never forgive Major. The mere idea of seeing him again filled him with revulsion. Bitter hatred stirred in the darkest corners of his being and he trembled with rage. Pulling off his shirt he exposed the scars on his back to Timothy.

"How do I forgive for *dis*?" Linton cried. "These scars remind me every day of my life."

Timothy touched the ridged, ragged scars on Linton's back.

"Linton," he said, "yuh will not know happiness without forgiveness. Yuh can't make dem scars on yuh back disappear, but you can make these scars, in here––" he thumped his chest with his fist,"–– dem can heal. Dat's forgiveness. Maybe, yuh haffi lose more before yuh unnerstan."

"Maybe I already unnerstan'. As far as my father is concerned, I have nothing to lose."

"Come," Timothy said, ending the discussion, "is getting' late."

The village was waking up and smoke from breakfast fires already hung over Bessanworse like a fog bank.

"I will be with Sheila today," Linton said. "We brewing roots."

"Make sure me get some." Timothy clapped Linton on his back and winked. "I can surely use it!"

Eager to get started on what would be an all day affair, Linton burst into the hut, pulled off his trousers and climbed into bed. He gently awoke Sheila, cooing words of love and kissing her tenderly, becoming more urgent as she responded.

"Linton! Is too early, Linton!" But she laughed seductively. Her protests were muffled by lips and tongue and her enthusiasm soon equaled to his own. Outside, in the fresh morning sunshine, the villagers of Bessanworse greeted the day.

Taking refuge from the cruel glare of the sun, Linton and Sheila worked in the shade of a huge star-apple tree. It took the better part of the morning to make a tub of roots tonic and after they finished, Linton slept while Sheila lined up the small glass bottles to fill. She sat so her belly hung between her legs. Her eyes were narrowed as she concentrated on the task of decanting the brown liquid tonic.

When she was nearly finished, she kicked Linton, harder than she intended, to wake him.

"Yuh mus' take dis bottle fe Mas' Tim." She pushed a cork into the bottle and set it down on the table, selected another freshly washed bottle, and poured elixir into it.

"Kickin me?" Linton said, rubbing his face angrily. He struggled to his feet.

She frowned. "Smoke too much a dat damn ganja." She pushed the bottle toward Linton. "Here," she said, "fuh Mas'Tim."

Hesitant to leave the shade, Linton looked out into the baking sun, wiped the sweat from his brow, opened the bottle and took a long drink.

"What de hell yuh doin'?" Sheila smacked him on the shoulder. "Now me haffi make another bottle."

"Jus fill it with some water," Linton joked. "After all, he should be careful, lest Margaret kill him."

"Margaret brings Mas'Tim so much happiness." She poured more tonic into the bottle. "All yuh can do is focus pon de vulgar." But a grin broke out on her face and soon they were giggling together. Taking the bottle he got up to leave.

"Linton!"

He turned.

"Ask Mas'Tim for a favor. Ask if I can come with yuh tomorrow."

"Come with us? To Kingston?"

"Yes," she said, clasping her hands over her mouth in excitement. "I could come with yuh to Kingston. I've never been dey."

Linton snapped his fingers. "Why didn't I think of that. You could ride inside the cab, and Riddle could ride in the back." He smiled at Sheila and, with a lightness to his step, went to find Timothy.

Timothy and Margaret were lying together in a hammock, legs entwined. Linton hesitated, unsure of whether to interrupt them.

"Cha, come mon, wha' yuh want?" Timothy said. He seemed slightly annoyed but once he saw the bottle of elixir, his expression changed to one of delight. "Ahh." He uncorked the bottle and took a good swig, wiping his mouth with his wrist. "Jus' in time." Next to him Margaret squirmed provocatively.

"Mas' Tim, let me ask you something."

Timothy nodded, taking another swallow.

"Let Sheila come to Kingston with me. Riddle or I can ride in de back a de truck mon." Before he had even finished, Timothy was shaking his head.

"Nah mon, is no place for a pregnant woman," he said firmly.

"She really wants to go."

"If she gi' yuh trouble send her to me," he said, dismissing Linton and turning his attention to Margaret.

When he told Sheila what Timothy had said, she was deeply disappointed.

"Well, I guess that's it," she shrugged.

"What yuh mean, that's it?"

"Nuttin, baby. Everyting goin' be all right." She concentrated on jamming corks into the remaining bottles. "We should let Timothy know we sellin' de tonic to Chang."

"Why? Timothy will make us stop."

She jammed the cork into the bottle and put it aside. "I don't like to keep secrets from Timothy. Besides, we could try to sell more of it in de open."

"It would sell--quick!" He imagined people lining up to buy it. "I always have people askin' me fe a bottle."

"Just de other day Riddle wife Doris ask me for some," Sheila said. "Two of these is for her." She put the bottles in a basket. "These are all spoken for. Dis batch yuh can sell to Chang inna Kingston."

The late afternoon shadows grew long, bold, then gave way to the oncoming night. They ate dinner and retired early.

It was drizzling the next morning when Riddle and Linton tied down the loaded charcoal on the back of the truck. Sheila and Doris watched as their men made a final check of the vehicle.

Barris, who owned the truck, was hired by Timothy to make deliveries every fortnight. He approached the men and said, "Yuh hear de news, mon, is a big storm comin'. We must hurry."

Linton kissed Sheila passionately.

"I'll be here when yuh come back," she whispered in his ear.

Linton climbed into the truck, followed by Riddle. The engine roared to life. Sheila stepped back as the truck lumbered away. Linton watched as she receded in the rear view mirror, standing a little apart from Doris, her beautiful belly bulging like an egg, waving at the truck as the first raindrops began to fall. Linton shivered, as a chill ran up his spine. Sheila became a dot in the vibrating rear view mirror, then she, and Bessanworse vanished in the mist and rain.

Don't worry, he thought to himself, watching the wipers sweep back and forth, you'll be home in no time. The raindrops hit the windshield resembling tears falling from heaven. The road ahead disappeared into the grey, uncertain fog. As anxiety clutched his heart, he reminded himself that it was his first baby, too, and that there was no need to be afraid, the midwives were near and were prepared to help Sheila. *No need to be afraid.* Nevertheless, the thought made his heart beat even harder.

When they were finally heading down Bog Walk Gorge, negotiating the two lane road in the rain, Riddle sighed.

"I glad we gone from Bessanworse," he said. "Sometimes yuh haffi admit de work is too much fe de likkle benefit. Me hear dem have Rasta camp where dem guarantee yuh a woman."

Linton shrugged his comment off. "Timothy is a good mon," he said. "Why look fe something I have already."

"Indeed," Riddle said.

"Hold on," Barris said. He stopped the truck behind a line of vehicles waiting to cross Flatbridge, the narrow one lane corridor that spanned the Rio Cobre River. The rain came down steadily, tinting the vibrant green leaves blue.

"What a way the weather has turned bad," Linton said.

"I jus hope it nuh wash de damn bridge out," Barris said. "Seem like every other day Flatbridge under water." He pushed the gas pedal and the truck lurched onto the bridge, slowly negotiating the passage only inches above the raging waters.

"I hate how dere is no railing on de bridge. Yuh coulda

drive off de side and never know it."

"Yuh woulda know when de water close over yuh head!" Riddle retorted. "But if it keep rainin', we jus' stay in Kingston, right?" He flashed a crooked smile. "We can only hope to be so lucky."

Pulling away from the bridge on the outskirts of Spanish Town, the truck gears ground as Barris drove up a hill. Linton settled back, sandwiched between Barris and Riddle, watching the rain hit the windshield.

Linton's back ached. He handed bag after bag of charcoal to Riddle, who dutifully took each sack into the shed. He was angry that Barris, asleep in a chair, offered no help. Even more galling, Barris would be paid cash for driving while neither he nor Riddle got paid. The more his back hurt the more resentful he felt. When they finished unloading, Chang, a short stocky Chinese man, came out with a clipboard.

"Is all here and accounted for." Turning to Linton and Riddle, he asked, "Which one a yuh goin' sign?"

"I will." Linton walked with Chang back inside the store. Standing close he whispered "I have seven bottles of roots tonic for yuh."

"Lawd Jesus," Chang said. "Me was wonderin where yuh went. Me nuh see yuh in months."

"Expectin' a child, so me stayin close to home."

"Congratulations, mon!" Chang paid Linton ten shillings, then gave him an extra shilling, saying, "Dis fe de baby."

Grinning proudly, Linton thanked Chang and pushed the money into his pocket. They returned to the truck where Chang shook hands and left them standing in the downpour.

They sat in the cab, sweating and wet, as rain pummeled the roof. Looking skeptically at the downpour, Linton said, "If we lucky we might get home tonight."

"Home!" Riddle looked at Linton incredously. "Look out de window, mon. De gorge full a water."

"Yeah, mon," Barris agreed. "Flatbridge under water now, mon."

"Well, I nuh plan fe sit in 'ere all night," Riddle said. "Dey is plenty woman inna Kingston."

"Who goin go someplace wit' yuh a smell like dat?" Linton crinkled his nose.

"C'mon," Barris said, "me know jus' where to go." He turned the ignition and drove to Orange Street near the downtown club district. Parking the truck, he turned to Linton. "Yuh comin? Don't worry, anyting dat happen is just between us." He winked at Riddle and they burst out in laughter. "We can go to de Glass Bucket," Barris wheezed. "Is always a party dey."

Linton shook his head. "I'm happy right here in the truck," he said. "I don't want to party, and I'm spoken for ." He glanced at Riddle. "Wha' 'bout yuh woman?"

"Yuh a blasted idiot, Linton. Yuh jus' sell dat roots to Chang. Yuh tink me nuh see? Plannin' on keepin' de money? Wait till Timothy hear 'bout dis." He slapped his thigh. "Yuh know de rule, any money made by any of us should be turned over to him for the administration of Bessanworse. Yuh have money yuh can pay fe de gal dem."

Riddle and Barris laughed so hard that Barris began to cough. Linton shrugged, satisfied with his decision to stay. But he was angry that Riddle had seen his transaction. He had done business with Chang only once before. Linton worried that Riddle might tell Timothy to damage his standing. I'll have to tell Timothy myself as soon as I get back, Linton decided. And I will give him the money. His stomach tightened into a knot thinking about Riddle exposing him.

"Come on, mon. Share de wealth, nuh?"

"Mas' Tim knows about me sellin' de roots, and I have to give him the money!" Linton said.

"Forget him," Barris said, reaching across Linton to tug on Riddle's collar. "Le's go."

A few minutes later Linton, alone in the truck, watched as the windows fogged up from his breath. It created an illusion of safety; although he couldn't see out, no one could see in. He had lied to Riddle about Timothy's knowing about selling the tonic. His mistake had been in not closing the door behind himself and Chang. Now, on a day when he should feel victorious, he instead felt anxious and unsettled. He wiped the condensation from a patch of window and looked out at the rain. The truck was parked at the corner of Church Street, just south of Parade. He reached into his pocket and took out the coins. He smiled to himself. He had the power to transform roots and herbs into money through some mysterious alchemy.

The rain was heavy and hardly a soul braved being outdoors. The dull thrumming on the roof was hypnotic and his thoughts turned to Sheila. He was sure it was raining in

Bessanworse and laughed at the idea of her cursing him for leaving her. In his minds' eye, he pictured her complaining to Margaret and bawling out Timothy. But she would be so proud of him when he returned. Eight months earlier it was her idea to give Chang two bottles of the roots tonic and suggest that he try a bottle before bed. The results were fabulous and Chang wanted to sell some. But because of Sheila's pregnancy, Chang had been forced to wait a long time.

The rain was pelting the truck with more force now and the wind picked up. He couldn't pin down the source of his anxiety, why he was so worried about Sheila. She was difficult to understand, but he loved her, loved the basic, primal, instinctive arousal of her touch. Her caress filled him to overflowing. Since being with Sheila, his sense of injustice and bitterness had subsided and he felt safe enough to love, a risk that he did not take lightly. He could not bear to think of life without her. And now with her pregnant, he did not dare imagine life without the baby; their baby, a life he still did not know.

Linton took a deep breath, trying to stop his thoughts for even a moment. To let himself get so emotionally worked up wasn't manly. Sleep, he thought, that's what I need.

In the morning he was rudely awakened when the truck door opened. Riddle clambered in, slapping him on his leg. During the night the rain had stopped and in the sunlight water steamed along the roadway.

"Le's go mon!" Riddle cried. Barris climbed into the driver's seat and fired up the engine. Rubbing the sleep from his eyes, Linton suddenly remembered where he was.

"Yuh miss a helluva *ring-ding* las' night!" Riddle said, as the truck took off.

"Jus' get me home," Linton muttered. He looked up at the sky. Heavy grey clouds still hung overhead but at least it wasn't raining.

Scowling, Linton turned his attention to the passing scenery while Riddle and Barris continued to relive their exploits from the previous evening. Finally Riddle ran out of things to boast of and fell asleep. Only the hum of the engine droned on.

When they reached Bog Walk Gorge, they were at the end of a long line of traffic waiting to cross Flatbridge. The bridge was submerged under the raging waters of the Rio Cobre. It had stopped raining, but waters from the craggy Jamaican mountains continued to funnel into streams and rivers, all hellbent to reach the Caribbean Sea.

"De road close at least till tomorrow," Riddle said. "Le's go back to Kingston."

"Do yuh have de money fe buy petrol?" Barris said to Riddle. "We just sit here, inna de queue."

"Please, don't provide more vexation today," Linton snapped. "We are staying right here until the road opens. Turn off de engine."

"Lawd, mon! Linton have plenty money," Riddle needled.

"I will whip your ass, boy if you keep it up!"

"Instead of being mad at me yuh shoulda ask where all de money from our labors is goin'. We deliver de goods, Barris is paid for using de truck, but who gets paid for all de coal?

Who get de money fe de vegetables an de clothes de 'oman dem make?"

"I hear Chang has an agreement with Timothy," Linton said.

"Dat's right," Riddle said dismissively. "Wit Timothy, Hmmph! When yuh goin see some a dat money?"

"Well, why don't you ask Timothy if you think he's crooked?""

Riddle looked over at Barris.

"Nah bother look pon me," Barris sputtered. "I just' a rent yuh de truck fe de day an deliver and gwan wit' me business. I'm not involved in Bessanworse business, suh."

They got out of the flatbed and Barris and Riddle sat down on the end, legs dangling, but Linton anxiously paced back and forth. The sky was still a solid dark gray but the air smelled fresh, clean and earthy.

"I will ask Timothy," Linton declared. "I can't believe he would steal from us." He looked down the hill at the river, swollen and rushing past. The roar of water was loud even at a distance. He fingered the coins in his pocket. He hadn't had a tuppence in his pocket in quite some time, and had never really had more than a few shillings of his own.

Riddle looked at Linton with pity. "That will answer all your questions. Just ask him. I is sure dat if him is thiefing de money him will tell yuh de trut'."

Barris snickered.

They waited two days for the river water to subside. Locals came with baskets of prepared foods for sale, and they slept on the flatbed. Thankfully the bridge did not wash out. When they were finally allowed to cross, Barris drove like a madman, dropping them off at a junction just a quarter mile from home.

They trudged up the hill, broiling in the sun. Despite feeling worn out Linton walked fast. He couldn't wait to see Sheila. At the crest of the hill they saw a figure sitting at the side of the road.

"Sheila?!" Linton called. He waved and began to run, but suddenly stopped short. It was Timothy. Linton looked at Riddle. "Rastafari! I tink she have my baby already!" But as they approached Timothy, they saw his expression was grave.

"Riddle go ahead of us," Timothy said. "I wan' fe talk wit' Linton."

The joy drained from Linton's face. "Timothy," Linton shouted, "where's Sheila?

"Come an' sit down," Timothy said.

VII

DECEMBER 1944, KINGSTON, JAMAICA

Linton left Bessanworse within days of burying Sheila and his stillborn son. Everything he beheld reminded him of what might have been: the mountains, trees, and bush all spoke to him of Sheila, until the only thing he longed for was to leave Jamaica. He went to stay with Andrew in Kingston, and through Andrew's connections Linton had received an American visa with almost no waiting. He would depart in two days.

Andrew and his colleagues met frequently in the evening to drink, play dominoes and argue about the demise of the decaying British Empire and Jamaica's first general election. But the rum, the fellowship, did nothing to raise Linton's spirits. On a typical night, leaving the group on the veranda bantering about politics, he'd return indoors, tiptoe into his own bedroom, closing the door quietly behind him. Falling into bed and closing his eyes, the room spun in his drunken state. Unbidden and unwanted images arose in his mind: Sheila waving good-bye, Timothy's face as he revealed the savage truth and, worst of all, his throwing the first handful of dirt into the grave where Sheila and his lifeless son lay. He could still hear the hollow sound of dirt landing on the pinewood box. After the funeral he was beyond comfort. Nothing could assuage his guilt for being absent when he knew Sheila had needed him most.

Linton would never forget when he told Timothy of his decision to go the United States to start over.

Acrid smoke from burning tires hung over the village, creating a brilliant sunset in variegated hues of gold and red. Timothy was tired and appeared troubled.

"Timothy, I have something to tell yuh," Linton stammered. "I have to leave dis place, Mas' Tim. I want to leave Jamaica. I'm leaving tomorrow for Kingston to see me brother, Andrew."

"Where yuh goin' go?" Timothy asked.

"I want to go to America."

"New York?"

Linton nodded. He really wasn't sure, but New York sounded like a good place to start. "Yes Mas' Tim. You've been there. I wanted to ask your advice."

Timothy's watery eyes sparkled. He stood up and reached for his walking stick. "Come," he said.

They walked around the village, through the outskirts where the crops, laid flat by the storm, were rotting. They stopped and sat on a crumbling wall that had once encircled the old plantation house, near the spring that now nourished Bessanworse.

"Everyting yuh need is here. Why yuh wan' leave? De grief will pass, mon. Yuh mus gi' it time."

Linton looked up at the hills surrounding the village. "No Mas' Tim. I have to leave. I must start fresh."

"I said de same ting," Timothy replied, "when I went to de States. An' I come back."

"Why?"

Timothy paused. He rolled a spliff and lit it, taking a deep draw and slowly letting the smoke pour from his lungs. "Here, I'm a man. Over dey, dem call me bwoy." He took another puff letting what he said sink in. "Yuh goin face de same ting. But I unnerstan, yuh haffi go. De money good. Jus' remember one ting. Yuh is a Jamaican. Dem goin tell yuh dis foolishness 'bout melting pot. Remember dis, to succeed dey, yuh mus rely pon wha' yuh learn right 'ere, inna dis yard. If yuh forget, yuh goin melt all right, yuh goin' melt away! Money will change yuh! Me see it happen to plenty a Jamaicans dem."

Even in Kingston, Linton was haunted by Timothy's words. He sat up, putting his legs over the edge of the bed, and brooded in the darkness.

He felt uncomfortable around Andrew's friends. In an effort to help him feel at ease, Andrew had introduced him as an expert in the blending of rum and spirits. But he preferred to remain silent, afraid to reveal his ignorance. He was looking forward to leaving. Living with Andrew was made more difficult by the presence of his wife Josephine, and their one-year old. Sadness almost overwhelmed him the first time he saw the three of them together at the dinner table. Throughout his stay there were moments when he looked at Josephine and saw Sheila.

The night before Linton was to leave, he, Andrew and Josephine sat on the veranda, drinking and discussing his plans. Josephine, a beautiful dark woman with almond-shaped eyes, was wreathed in smoke while Andrew sat beside her, puffing a cigar.

"I wish you would reconsider," Andrew said. "We need men like you."

"I did my part," Linton said. He took a sip from his glass and smacked his lips. "I voted… my goodness, this rum is good, mon."

"Has Andrew gone over your itinerary yet?" Josephine asked.

"Oh yes!" Linton extracted a small piece of paper. He unfolded it and read: "In Miami meet Tappie, board train to New York and meet Gene Owl at Penn Station. Go with Gene to my new place in Brooklyn and start at my job on the following Monday." He looked at them, excited.

"Yuh just remember, if yuh need anything, go to Gene. He owes me from way back," Andrew added.

"Who is Gene Owl?"

"Everyone in Kingston knows Gene. He travels between New York and Jamaica. Owns some nightclubs and a couple a buildings in downtown. He's an old friend, but he's tight. I had to lie and told him you were my brother."

The next morning Andrew watched as Linton struggled to close his valise. The old brown suitcase with the initials AB was crammed with clothes that Andrew had given him. A light grey suit lay atop the sofa. Linton sat down next to it and, for the first time in a long time, he felt happy.

They drove across the city of Kingston, together, Andrew taking his time so that Linton could take one last look. The buildings on either side of the street were painted crazy tropical colors. Brigades of pushcarts, groups of boys playing cricket in the park, old women dressed in multicolored wraps selling produce, farm animals and braying donkeys and automobiles, all competed for space along the roads, as they always had.

"I wish you would stay," Andrew pleaded. "Jamaica has a future and you can be a part of it."

"I have to leave, Andrew. There's nothing for me here. Everyting that brought me pleasure, the mountains, the countryside, the people, all of it now brings me sadness. This is my chance, don't you see? I don't know what to expect in New York, but it's my chance––to create something, to build a new life."

Andrew put both hands on the steering wheel. "I'm sorry," he whispered. "I just have to get used to missing you. You're going to succeed, I'm sure of it. Your dreams are going to become a reality, Linton."

Linton wondered what it would be like in the United States. Timothy's words still echoed in his ears. He had heard that the streets were paved with gold, and he did not believe it. But he knew it was the only place that he would ever go where there was a chance for a fresh start.

He also knew that many Jamaicans returned from America saying that it was no place for a free-thinking Negro. Andrew had warned him about the south. Stories of murder, robbery, and lynching weighed heavily on his mind.

"Don't stay in the south one more day than you have to," Andrew had cautioned. His apprehension and elation blended together making him feel nervous and unsettled.

At the departure gate the men shook hands. Then Andrew watched as Linton walked through the swinging doors and disappeared.

"Boy!" The ruddy-faced immigration agent yelled at Linton, who, awestruck, lingered at the front of the line. Chagrined, he lurched forward carrying his bags.

"Passport!"

Linton handed over his passport.

"And you're stayin'?"

He fumbled with a tattered piece of paper. "Yes I'm going to stay with Tappie, 410 North Sunshine Boulevard in Miami."

The immigration officer looked him over suspiciously. "You ever been a member of the Communist Party?"

"No."

The officer stared him right in the eye. Linton shifted his gaze to the officer's badge.

"Go on," the official said, waving Linton past.

Linton put his passport in a pocket and lifted the heavy valise. He pushed the frosted white doors open and walked out into a new world.

A huge crowd was gathered just beyond the doors and, as people recognized their loved ones, rushed in a flurry to embrace one another. Linton walked down the ramp. A slightly built man with straightened hair, wearing a cream-colored jacket and sporting a porkpie hat, held a sign with Linton's name on it.

"Tappie?"

"Linton!" Tappie's eyes were filled with excitement. "Mon, dem tell me what yuh look like but me would a never recognize yuh. Come on mon," he said, holding up the rope for Linton to step out. "Welcome to America!"

Tappie flashed a smile that seemed it could light up the world. "I have de train tickets for New York." Tappie took Linton's heaviest bag and picked up his pace. He walked as if he were trying to go as fast as he could without being noticed.

Linton struggled to keep up. "Slow down," he said, "why yuh movin so fast!"

Tappie looked back at Linton, "We nuh have de time to waste."

Linton was breathless by the time they reached the 1943 Gypsy red and shoreline beige Chevrolet sedan in the parking lot. Cleanshaven, with tightly trimmed hair and wearing a white collared shirt and black pants, Linton clambered into the car, his white patent leather shoes glistening in the sunshine.

"Yuh have any more shoe dan dat?" Tappie asked, opening the trunk.

"No, these are my best shoes."

"With dem shoes yuh look fresh off de banana boat," Tappie remarked. He slammed shut the car door and fired up the engine.

"But I am."

Tappie left the Port of Miami laughing at the top of his lungs.

Linton could not help but be impressed, speeding down the highway, looking at the Miami skyline and Biscayne Bay.

They pulled into the driveway of a one story house in Miami, surrounded by an immaculately manicured lawn and flowerbeds full of bright red and yellow blooms. Tappie took Linton inside where he met Samantha, Tappie's beautiful Jamaican wife.

"Linton, let's get some drinks going," Tappie said, grabbing two barrel glasses from the alcohol cabinet. "Any friend of Andrew's is a friend of mine. We went to school together."

Tappie opened a bottle of white rum, cracked ice into a bucket, poured the drinks, and handed one to Linton, all while engaged in colorful banter that held Linton in thrall.

"Law school, but we actually got to know one another in New York at the Jamaica Progressive League. Andrew tells me you're an expert in the production of rum. What do you have planned for the States?"

"Well me––*my* rummaking days are over. Me plannin' on being in New York, but I don't know yet what my plans are."

"Lawd *Jees-aam* it cold as *hell* up dey!" Samantha interjected.

"We couldn't take a week of it," Tappie added, matter of factly. "It's fine right here in Miami, a bit slower, and that suits us fine. Did you vote?"

"Yeah, mon, Andrew wouldn't let me miss it. I cast my vote. Is only a few parties anyway."

Tappie laughed. " Here is only Democrats an' Republicans. And is best to leave it at dat. Americans are funny about dem politics. Is best fe stay away from de subject." He poured himself another drink. "But the Jamaican election," he paused and glanced at his wife. "Of course I wasn't surprised dat Bustamante's party took twenty two seats to Manley's five. The People's Nationalist Party has always left me with a––"

"Do you have an overcoat?" Samantha interjected.

"Now why yuh interrupt?" Tappie rolled his eyes.

Linton breathed a sigh of relief. He was ignorant of politics. "No, I don't."

"Yuh goin' need one. Is cold in New York. Tappie, go get Linton yuh old overcoat." She turned to her husband. "And avoid politics!" she scolded.

Samantha held the overcoat for Linton to put on. It was small, but it would do. She nodded. "*Now* yuh is ready fe New York!"

One hour later Tappie drove Linton to the Miami train station. He helped Linton carry his bags to the boarding platform and handed him a brown sack of sandwiches Samantha had prepared.

"Don't forget, keep to yuhself, and stay inna de colored areas especially 'till yuh get out a de South––past Washington, D.C.," he added for emphasis. Tappie grasped Linton's hand and left a five dollar bill in his palm. "Good luck mon. Welcome to America." Linton entered the coach, struggling with his luggage. He found a seat next to the window. The stuffy air in the coach smelled of sweat, onions, and chewing gum, making him feel queasy. When the train started moving he looked out the window and saw Tappie waving, getting smaller and smaller as the train pulled away. His mind flashed briefly on Sheila waving to him in the rain as Barris's flatbed truck had driven off.

When the platform had disappeared from sight, Linton turned his attention to the conductor collecting tickets. He was in America! He was on a train headed for New York! He tried to settle in on the hard wooden bench. He yawned, stretched and looked out the window. Here I am, he thought, free, and able to do anything I want. Then he saw it: the sign on the wall above the conductor's head, painted black with bold white letters that said, *Colored Only.*

The train passed through cities he had only heard of––Atlanta, Washington, D.C., Baltimore, and many more that he had not. The sheer scale of these cities impressed Linton, but nothing he felt compared to his excitement as they approached New

York. The industrial landscape of New Jersey was crowded with factories that had begun to lay claim to the Garden State's formerly pristine wetlands a century earlier. Towering smokestacks belched thick clouds of putrid smoke into the air, making his eyes water. On the horizon, through the blue-gray haze, he saw something resembling a crazy fence. The Manhattan skyline jutted into the sky, creating an erratic border of concrete and glass shapes simultaneously looking cold and inviting.

My God, he thought, just before the train entered a tunnel, that must be the Empire State Building. Everyone, even in Jamaica had heard of the tallest building in the world. Minutes later the conductor announced the last stop, Penn Station.

Before the train had even come to a stop, passengers were grabbing their luggage and getting in line, in a hurry to disembark.

Dismayed by the sudden activity, Linton sat on the bench until the doors opened and a cold blast of air rushed into the coach. He leapt to his feet and frantically donned his overcoat, grabbed his bags and stepped onto the platform. A breeze colder than anything he could have imagined took his breath away. Tears rolled down his cheeks and for the first time since he'd left home, he felt afraid. He looked up and down the crowded platform. He couldn't find one familiar face.

"Linton!"

He looked into the crowd. Everyone was bundled up against the cold, wearing jackets, overcoats, scarves, and gloves.

"Linton!"

A short, tubby black man, holding a small battered sign with L-I-N-T-O-N scrawled across it, struggled to make his way through the crowd. Despite the cold, perspiration glistened on his forehead.

"Linton! I am so glad to find yuh!" the man was huffing and puffing from the slight exertion. "Tappie called and told me that yuh would be wearing this overcoat." He paused to catch his breath. "Welcome, mon!" He stuck his hand out to shake. "I'm George––you are Linton aren't you?"

Linton shook George's hand. "Can we get out of the cold?" he asked.

They joined the surge of people walking toward the terminal.

"Gene's sick," George offered, "so he couldn't come."

They lugged Linton's suitcase up the polished Bottocino marble steps, into Penn Station's main concourse. Linton couldn't believe the spaciousness of the room. The dull roar of a thousand conversations rebounded off the glass and marble, and on one wall a huge schedule board kept track of the myriad of trains coming and going. Linton tried to take it all in while trying to keep up with the quick-paced George. Did everyone in America walk fast? They turned a corner and went down a flight of stairs, where George paid for tickets and they entered the surreal underground world of the New York City subway.

Linton couldn't believe his eyes. Before him, endless corridors lit with incandescent bulbs, punctuated by the constant screeching of trains, stretched an underground city complete with news stands, delicatessens, restaurants, shoe shine stands, chocolatiers and flower stalls, and an endless flow of people rushing in all directions. Christmas lights adorned everything. They walked up and down stairs until they reached the platform to catch the train to Brooklyn.

"We not going outside?" asked Linton,

"No need, we can catch the subway to Brooklyn right here." Linton's look of disappointment was not lost on George. "Too cold for sightseeing," he added, rubbing his hands together for warmth. "Yuh goin' have plenty time fe look around."

The Number 3 pulled into the station, screeched to a halt, and the doors opened. Linton followed George but dashed past the doors lest he be caught.

George seemed entirely unperturbed. "Gene will be glad to see yuh," he said above the din. "They lined up a job for you at the mental hospital. I heard it's a pretty good job, and it pays well enough. Gene even has a room in the boarding house ready for yuh."

Linton nodded.

"Yuh lucky. Is easy to find roomates, but yuh own room?" George laughed. "Yuh will see how tings work around here." At Borough Hall, the first stop in Brooklyn, George poked Linton in the ribs. "We just went underneath the East River," he said. "Welcome to Brooklyn." George showed Linton the subway map that hung on the wall in every car, where they had got on and where they would get off. Linton was taken aback at the size of the five-borough city.

Three more stops and they reached Utica Avenue, in the heart of Flatbush. Icy cold gusts of wind burned Linton's cheeks as they made their way up the stairs and into the street.

Brick buildings lined the streets in every direction. There were so many people, and every one of them walked quickly and looked irritable. Linton had never seen so many white people in one place. It was rush hour. Cars and taxis filled the thoroughfares and drivers leaned on their car horns, loudly cursing. A city bus crammed with passengers sped through a puddle of slush, spraying dirty water on pedestrians. The smell of automobile exhaust competed with cigarette smoke that rose from any small gathering of people and for a moment, Linton felt like he couldn't breathe. He wondered if all of New York was like this. Perhaps Jamaica wasn't such a bad place after all.

"Let's go nuh," George interrupted Linton's thoughts. Despite carrying Linton's heavy valise, George moved fast and Linton had difficulty keeping up.

"We haven't much further." Looking down the street Linton could see that it stretched for blocks, an unrelenting line of brick buildings, sprinkled with green, red, and yellow lights twinkling in the distant intersections.

"Dis area of Brooklyn is mostly Italian, and some Jewish people," George explained.

Crunching through the icy pavement, Linton's feet felt like blocks of ice. His shoes and socks were soaked. At the point where he was finding it very difficult to continue, George turned toward an imposing three-story brownstone. The street level floor was occupied by a liquor store with a bright flashing pink-and-white neon sign.

George walked gingerly up the ice-covered stone stairs. Following, Linton held fast to the railing. George banged his fist on the door three times. It seemed like minutes, but the door finally opened and a pretty young woman with cocoa brown skin and straight dark hair stuck her head out.

Opening the door, she pushed George aside. "Ohhh, yuh mus' be cold. Come in Linton, we're expectin' you." There was a slight, pleasant Caribbean lilt in her voice.

He moved quickly into the living room, leaving her near the door, still smiling at him. The living room was comfortable, with cushioned chairs and two sofas that made an "L" shape. But the focus of the room was something Linton had never seen before, a television. He stared at the large wooden cabinet surrounding a tiny black and white moving image with sound.

Linton felt a hand on him again, startling him and making him shrink away involuntarily.

"What's wrong?" the girl asked.

He tried to think fast. "Nothing, it's just, well… I'm sore from traveling." He grimaced. This young woman was far too inquisitive.

"Aspirin?"

A good way to get rid of her. He nodded and the girl shot off to fetch a glass of water and the medicine.

"Mister Blaine."

A tall, gaunt man with a long sad face and bags under his dark eyes approached Linton. His teeth were brilliant white in contrast to his dark lips, and he sported a neatly trimmed pencil mustache. He wore a black and gold smoking jacket and brown fur-lined slippers. He walked slowly, but not because he was frail; to the contrary, he was quite robust

"I would shake your hand," the man said, moving across the room, "but I have a cold. I'm Eugene Owl, Andrew's friend. Please call me Gene." His voice was deep and rich, with a hypnotic quality that made Linton relax for the first time since reaching New York.

George had taken off his jacket and was sitting at the table with four other men about to begin a game of dominoes.

"Linton, come join us fe some bones, nuh?" George invited. "Everyone, dis is Linton, him just get here today from cross de pond."

"Thanks no," Linton said. "I'm very tired and would just like to settle in."

Suddenly the girl burst in the room carrying a saucer with two tablets on it, and a tall glass of water.

"Just for you," she said, winking at Linton.

"Could I have it… without ice?"

She was gone in a flash and returned with a clear glass of water. She gave it to Linton, accompanied by a doe-eyed look.

"Thank you," he said, focusing on Gene. He took the tablets and swallowed them down with a long drink of water. She remained, gawking at Linton until she suddenly became self-conscious and retreated from the room. Gene took Linton into his study and closed the door.

"Don't worry about her," Gene laughed. "At twenty-one she's a little grown up for her age." Linton sat down in a plush chair and Gene sat at his desk. It was a very small room with a small cabinet full of books and a beautiful stained glass lamp in the corner.

"Linton, I have helped you because you are Andrew's brother," Gene said in a baritone voice. "We got a position as an orderly for you at Good Tidings Hospital for the mentally ill. George plans to take you around New York tomorrow and will take you by Good Tidings. It's across the river in Harlem. Your first day on the job is in two days and yuh will need to show up there at 6:00 a.m. sharp. Your room here includes board. It's as good a deal as yuh will find anywhere. From here on yuh pay your way and carry your own weight. Are yuh hungry?"

Linton shook his head. He'd eaten on the train.

"Well then," Gene continued, "yuh probably want to take yuh bags and go to your room." He got up and opened the door for Linton and handed him a neatly folded packet of paper. "Here's a New York City street and subway map. You're in room nine and welcome to stay here so long as yuh pay the rent. The bathroom is the third door on the right. In the morning yuh make your own breakfast and you're welcome to whatever is in the kitchen." As Linton turned to leave, Gene took ahold of his arm. "By the way, there's a fee for finding the job, ten per cent of your pay for ten weeks. I usually charge twenty-five per cent. And it's like dat because yuh is Andrew's brother."

Linton thanked him and with the domino game going strong, he waved goodnight to the players and went upstairs to his room. Closing the door, he put down his suitcase and looked around.

The room was cramped, with a small face basin and a cracked, rusting mirror in the corner. The single bed took up most of the space, barely leaving room for a small chair and desk, a hatrack, and a dresser. The windows faced the street and the flashing neon liquor store sign cast intermittent pink and white light on the walls. He drew the drapes, blocking out most of the light and sighed. The room smelled of stale cigarettes and disinfectant.

He locked the door, put his suitcase on the edge of the bed, and began to unpack, hanging a few clothes and putting the rest in the dresser. He lit a cigarette, took out a small blue bottle and looked at it reverently. It was tonic from the last batch of roots he had brewed with Sheila. He removed the cork and sniffed and suddenly saw her appear before him. His hand trembled. He reached out to touch her and the apparition disappeared. Tears stung his eyes. He fished out two of the eight shillings that he had made from selling the roots tonic to Chang. "Our money," he said to himself.

He put it away. In the morning he would embark on a tour of the biggest city in the world.

VIII

FEBRUARY 1946, KINGSTON, JAMAICA

During Callie's wedding to her fiance, Colin, people sweltered silently, sitting in the ebony pews underneath the huge copper dome of Holy Trinity Catholic Church in Kingston. Statues looked down upon the wedding ceremony, their facial expressions frozen. As Maid of Honor, Daisy tried to maintain her smile, fanning herself frantically. Callie's wedding was almost over. Looking out onto the congregation, Daisy saw their fans all a blur, and dark hands holding dainty napkins, dabbing tears of joy from their eyes. Daisy sighed. After three weeks of helping her sister, Callie with her wedding plans, she couldn't wait to escape. She could smell food cooking outside in the church courtyard. She closed her eyes and imagined sitting before a plate piled high with food.

You may kiss the bride.

They walked through a shower of rice to the reception outside where food and drinks were waiting. Daisy was ecstatic. She hugged Callie with all her might, and kissed her husband, Colin.

"Oh, congratulations! It was just beautiful!" Daisy cried.

"Thank you for being a part of it! Oh Daisy!" Callie kissed Daisy so hard it left lipstick imprint on her cheek.

It was a raucous reception. Daisy danced, partied and drank, releasing all of the frustration that had built up over the past weeks. At one point she grabbed Callie and they entertained everyone by dancing, drunk, on the dance floor to tunes played by a mento band. But at one point, while talking to a friend, Daisy's tongue got the better of her.

"You could consider Colin a dockmonkey," Daisy said, laughing. "Not just anyone can scramble up and down those crates in the hold of a ship!" The comment brought a laugh but before Daisy could continue, Callie announced she was throwing the bouquet.

The eligible women gathered out on the floor with Daisy leading the way.

Glancing over her shoulder, Callie seemed to look for her sister and then, without warning, pitched the bouquet in Daisy's direction. She could not help but catch it. Everyone surrounded Daisy, laughing and joking about her being next to wed. For a moment Daisy basked in all of the attention. She smiled and laughed, but it stoked the fires of resentment in Daisy's heart. The irony was not lost on Daisy that, as a better looking woman, she could have easily have settled for second best. But upon considering her father, Daisy refused to compromise. The man she would marry had to be like him-- perfect.

After the cake was cut and with people still drinking and partying, Daisy decided to leave. She started to make her way over to say good bye, but changed her mind and turned and walked out the door and into the street, on her way home without a word.

Alone in the house, Daisy closed her bedroom door and let out a sigh of relief. She took off her jewelry, throwing the items carelessly into her jewelry box. She disrobed, dropping her blue dress in a heap on the floor. Wriggling out of her girdle, she wondered why she wore one; her stomach was taut and flat, but she worried about her backside. After she shed all of her clothes, she looked thoughtfully at herself in the full length mirror.

The stately lines of her neck swept into gently sloping shoulders, connected by the defined, delicate bones of her clavicle. She felt her breasts. They were firm and high, not too big, a nice handful. She imagined what the touch of a man would feel like. Looking at her reflection she studied the sexy curves of her hips, alluring and suggestive, but thought her thighs were too fleshy, fusing together behind a dark thatch of pubic hair. Looking over her shoulder into the looking glass, she studied her buttocks, considered they were too big, that she might go on a diet again. Even so, she sniffed, my figure is better than most.

What man could resist this? She donned a white cotton robe. Thank God my standards are high or I would end up with some roustabout like Colin.

There was a sudden rapping on the door, startling Daisy from her reverie. Without waiting for a response, Rose entered, closing the door gently. Still dressed in a beautiful champagne-colored formal, Rose calmly walked up to Daisy, her voice barely audible. "How dare you leave before de wedding reception over? *My friends heard you call Colin a monkey!* After Callie gives you the highest honor of leading the wedding party!" Rose's face glowered with outrage. "What is wrong wit' you? Answer me gal!"

Daisy cowered before her mother. There was a knock at the door.

"Rose?" It was Sally Maud.

Rose's arm slowly came down to her side. "One minute, Sally," she replied. To Daisy she whispered, "Yuh know, yuh nevah too old fe me fe knock yuh down!" Rose left, closing the door as calmly as when she walked in.

Shrugging her shoulders, Daisy opened the top bureau drawer. She drew out a bundle of envelopes bound with a yellow sash. The letters, from New York, were dog-eared and dirty from having been read so many times. There were fingerprints all over them. Opening one, she read:

February 17, 1943.
Daisy,
How is Mum? I hope fine.

You must pray for your miracle and God willing, it will come soon. Don't despair. God will carry you across deep valleys. Don't give up hope. Sometimes it's darkest --

Daisy threw the letter down in disgust. She had received it three years ago and during that time daily prayer had produced nothing. She was tired of hearing it. Her patience, worn down after running to the mailbox for five long years, was gone. Numb with disappointment, many evenings she climbed into bed, snuggled under the sheet and wept. She would never admit that her scorn for Callie was rooted in her own jealousy of Callie's incredible good luck. Callie's life seemed to pass with such ease, while Daisy's was fraught with disappointment.

It was midday, when both man and beast moved in languid resistance to the moist heat that drifted through the mango groves and breadfruit trees. Inside the kitchen a fan turned slowly while a fly flitted about in random circles, darting this way and that, buzzing Daisy's ears and making it hard to listen to her mother and Sally Maud as they talked about America and plucked a dead chicken.

"Why people want fe go America so bad?" Sally raised a cleaver over her head, and *bam!* the chicken's head fell off. "I never left Jamaica here! De blasted buccra," she raised the cleaver once again. "Dem white people hate yuh so bad dem jus' a hang us from de-trees dem."

"They will take yuh an make yuh a prostitute." Rose gritted her teeth in concentration while sawing off a drumstick. "I saw two gal it happen to when they went to New York." She flung the drumstick into a large bowl. "They nevah come back again, dem girls. They whore fe jewelry, they whore fe money, they even whore fe social status."

Daisy drummed her fingers on the counter in frustration, "Mummaa! How do you know what happen to dem? For all yuh know dem successful. Is Iris a prostitute? I can make five times in a day more dan what me make here," she said gesturing around her. "I have to go to make some money, honey."

"So wha' yuh goin' sell, yuh *rass* or yuh soul? In de end it nuh matter where yuh live, it how yuh livin' dat count."

"You expect me to be happy here?" Daisy asked. "Iris wouldn't lie. She love it dey. I want to go an' taste de water myself."

A huge smile played across Rose's face. "Your faddah used to say dat. Yuh is like him in so many ways." Her smile disappeared. "Dat's how him kill himself. Him wouldn't lissen."

"Don't be fooled," Sally went on, "dem is sick after drinking de water, it nuh make yuh happy, it make yuh crazy."

"You don't know what's going on. Everything change now. Even the black people have change I hear."

"Change how?" Rose queried. "Is 1946 -- they get more polite?" The two older women burst into laughter.

"Everyone who comes back from America, come back wit' rude behavior." Sally pulled roughly at the dead chicken.

A door slammed and the three of them subtly turned their attention to the sound of heavy footsteps.

"*Oh what a beautiful...*" a man's voice rang out, singing, "m*oorr-ning!*"

Rose ran to the top of the stairs and met Wilbur. He put down an armful of packages and hugged her. Wilbur's belly sagged over his belt. His pate glistened with sweat except for the shock of gray hair on the back of his head. He came into the kitchen with Rose, sat down and began to smoke.

"A beautiful afternoon indeed," Wilbur said, amiably. "Jus' came back from de market dey." He leaned back in his chair and blew thick smoke toward the ceiling. "De place full a sale but all de produce dem marry up wit' some foolishness."

As Wilbur settled deeper and closed his eyes the phone rang. Daisy answered it and became animated.

"Dis evening, yes gal, me *deh deh*!" Daisy hung up the

phone. "Mummaa, is a huge party tonight up-a de Glass Bucket an' I'm goin' to meet some friends dey."

"Good," said Rose. "Yuh too young to be lock-up inna-de house on a Friday night."

"I meet plenty of guys at de church, Mummaa."

"So where are they?"

"They bore me to death!"

"Instead of looking to leave Jamaica," Rose retorted, "maybe yuh should a look for a man fe marry. Like me. De furthest I've travelled is over de other side a de island, to Ocho Rios fe visit Granny Lovey."

Daisy shrugged and left the room. She did not usually attend parties, preferring church functions, but this was going to be one of the biggest parties of the year and young people in Kingston were buzzing with excitement.

"Oh, Daisy!" Rose went after her, "me jus' remember, Callie is coming over dis evening an'..."

"I won't be here!" Daisy said, closing her bedroom door.

Ceiling fans spun crazily, circulating the fetid air. From an archway cut into a wall painted with murals, Daisy watched a multitude of couples, seething with sensuality, the men dressed for the hunt, the women dressed for the kill. On the dance floor, a mass of sweaty bodies moved to a wild, wailing trumpet and the band, a large ensemble playing the latest from the United States, kept up a straight boogie-woogie beat.

Daisy swayed to the sound, trying to convince herself that

she was having a good time. She looked at her friends, dancing and felt a surge of insecurity. Why doesn't someone ask me to dance? she wondered.

Even as the thought passed through her mind a young man approached. "Excuse Miss, may I have this dance?"

Daisy looked him over. He smiled. "Oh no," she sniffed. She turned away to conceal her look of distaste: too short, too dark, too fat, and his eyes are too close together, she thought, wasting no time in judgement. I couldn't possibly be seen dancing with *that.*

As the evening progressed and the crowds thinned, Daisy rejected several more invitations. Simple idiots, she thought.

Then she saw him.

A handsome man sporting a short haircut and wearing a snazzy sports jacket, was staring right at her. Their eyes met and she couldn't turn away. She felt like she was crumbling under his gaze. He smiled.

Her heart raced. He leaned over to whisper to a friend and Daisy's eyes locked on the diamond-studded gold ring on his right middle finger. He approached and her heart pounded against the confines of her chest. Oh my God, Daisy thought, he's coming to talk to me.

"Pardon me––may I have this dance?"

"Yes." Daisy rose from her chair and offered her hand.

It was late and there were fewer couples on the dance floor now. The band, tired and ready to wrap up for the night, played a slow cheek to cheek. The stranger pulled Daisy close, inviting her to snuggle into him. She closed her eyes and yielded to the guidance of his moves. When the dance ended she stepped back and looked at him.

"Miles," he said, reaching out a hand to touch hers. "Miles Menders." The timbre of his baritone voice echoed in her ears, his voice as smooth and mellow as a saxophone solo.

"You're the prettiest girl here and I had to ask for a dance."

"Me?"

"Yes, you."

Daisy laughed, feeling her cheeks tingle with embarrassment. "I'm Daisy." Suddenly she felt like the clumsiest woman in the world.

"Drink?"

"No, thank you. I don't drink."

"Perhaps a coke?"

"Why -- yes, coke would be fine."

They sat down at a table and Miles motioned to a waiter.

Daisy's heart was beating so hard she could feel the pounding in her head. Easy girl, she thought, trying to calm down before she was hopelessly lost. He's bound to betray himself. But as hard as she tried to resist, Miles tickled her fancy. Mind your manners, Daisy reminded herself, trying not to speak patois. It was obvious that Miles refrained from sounding coarse.

When the drinks were served Miles said, "First a toast, then tell me what were you thinking when you saw me?" He held his glass aloft. "To the cutest girl I've seen this evening."

"Why, thank you," Daisy stammered. Feeling a bit lightheaded, indeed nearly swept off her feet, they clinked glasses and drank. At a nearby table she saw her friends watching. Their eyes met. Daisy giggled.

"What's so funny?"

"Oh," Daisy looked back at Miles. "That you think I'm cute."

"I'm not known to be a liar," Miles said. "I tell the truth and I'll prove it; are you free tomorrow?"

"I am," she answered without hesitating.

"Tomorrow afternoon, pick you up?"

"I'll meet you at the corner of Beeston and King."

"Be there at one." With that Miles got up. "Well, good-night, then," and he disappeared into the remaining crowd.

In a small tree-covered meadow, on the shoulder of one of the many hills north of Kingston, Miles and Daisy sat on a blanket, overlooking the construction site where they were building the Mona Dam. Beyond it, in the same visual frame, lay downtown Kingston.

Daisy watched Miles fumble with the latch to the picnic basket.

"Yuh nuh haf' fingernails," Daisy said, "*make*...I mean let me try." She gulped in shame for absentmindedly speaking patois. But Miles didn't notice. He pulled Daisy into his arms and kissed her for the first time.

At the moment their lips touched, her body felt charged with a spiral of electric current. He stroked the small of her back, his fingertips lightly raking her spine, and kissed her neck.

She hungrily responded and again sought the touch of his lips on hers. As her body began to meld into his she realized that she was losing control. She struggled against the tide that pulled at her to abandon the standards that she lived and loved by. Opening her eyes, she shifted her weight and gently pushed him away.

"No," Daisy whispered, "no..."

Miles stopped, but Daisy could see it was difficult for him. He bottled his frustration but did not lash out and blame her for restraint. She kissed him gently on the lips.

"Let's eat." Miles' voice sounded gruff and raw with emotion.

After a wonderful meal of bammy and roasted fish, and ginger beer, Miles edged closer to Daisy but she fought the urge to fall into his arms.

"Remind me not to come to places like this," she teased, "you're too much for me."

"Is it that easy to resist me?"

"Easy?! Actually it's quite difficult. That's what makes it worth waiting for."

Daisy wanted to be alone with her thoughts. She was surprised at herself for letting Miles get so close in such a brief time. Her difficulty in halting his advances forced her to acknowledge his magnetic power, frightening her.

On the ride home, they chatted about nothing of import. Miles pulled up to the house on Beeston Street and asked, "Will we see each other another time?"

"That," Daisy said, "is *entirely* up to you," and got out the car, quickly slamming the door.

After spritzing perfume, Daisy took a moment to admire herself. It was her twenty-third birthday and in a few minutes

Miles, her boyfriend of three months, would arrive in his black Ford sedan. They saw each other at least twice a week, attending parties and dances, and going to the movies. She still found it hard to believe she had fallen so hard for any man. She took pride in her aloofness but Miles forced her to drop her defenses.

When she was little her father called her 'Daisy B', and the B stood for bold. She remembered standing before him, stamping and insisting on staying up late. The adults laughed, Daddy laughing the loudest of all. In her mind she could see his brown shoes, corduroy pants and white shirt, his big bald head, that distinctive nose, and those gray eyes, crinkled with laughter. And she remembered the rum, gasping from the reeking rum on his breath. I ran away, she recalled, away from their patronizing laughter, escaping down the hall to the safety of my room, my bed, burying my face in the blankets and crying.

Daisy opened her eyes. The recollection left her eyes moist with tears. She had loved her father dearly and was too young to understand that he didn't laugh to mock her. He was proud of his brave little girl. But he died before she had grown old enough to understand. Well, she thought, Miles is my shining knight, come to take me away to a better life. Yet she remained afraid of his command over her passion. It was so hard to resist his physical entreaties. Almost every night she dreamt of making love to him, letting go with reckless abandon.

Now, sitting in the kitchen with her mother and Wilbur, waiting for Miles to arrive, every cell in her body was charged with excitement, making her skin tingle delightfully.

"I nevah did think dat me would-a see me-Daisy *in love*." Rose commented.

There was a knock at the door and Daisy went to the top of the stairs to wait for Miles to come up. He kissed her hello and they entered the kitchen.

Miles was dressed in a black button down suit and wing tip shoes. "Missus Wellstead," he said to Rose, "it is a pleasure." He bowed low, causing Rose to giggle like a schoolgirl. When Miles offered his hand to Wilbur, Wilbur grudgingly responded.

"May I speak to your daughter in private?" Miles asked.

They went into the living room but Daisy, anxious about being late for the show, did not sit down.

"Miles," she said impatiently looking at the clock, "it's time to go."

"I have some bad news on your birthday."

"What?"

"I don't have the car today, it's in the shop."

Daisy did not try to hide her disappointment.

"But it's your birthday, so I had to make it up." He took a small box out of his pocket and opened it. It contained a beautiful dainty gold ring. "Daisy, will you –– marry me?"

"Oh my God."

"No baby, it's me, Miles."

Tears trickled down Daisy's face. The smile on her face was so wide she thought her cheeks might crack.

"My *boo-noo-noo-noos*." Miles wrapped Daisy in his arms and kissed her.

She laughed. "A wha' yuh a say?"

"Me say me *wan'* yuh as me 'oman!"

She looked into his eyes. "Yes. Yes, a thousand times ––"

Miles interrupted with a lingering kiss.

"Daisy!"

Caught off guard by Rose's entrance they jumped apart like naughty schoolchildren. Rose looked at her daughter.

"Mummaa, we going to get married!" Buoyant with excitement, Daisy threw her arms around her mother's neck.

"Oh my ––" Rose's mouth hung open.

"Missus Wellstead," Miles stood up smiling. "May I have your daughter's hand in marriage?"

Rose took a little too long to answer and Daisy cringed with uneasiness. "Mummaa?"

Rose hugged her daughter. "Congratulations."

With that Miles got down on one knee, slipped the ring on Daisy's ring finger and kissed her hand.

Rose pulled her valise to the edge of the bed and with Daisy sitting atop the flap, she zipped the bulging suitcase shut. Closing her eyes, she went over her mental checklist again trying not to forget any important item. Wilbur sat at the vanity watching them.

"How long yuh gone for?" he asked.

"Wilbur, I told you I'm going to spend de week wit' Granny Lovey. She so old now and me want fe spend likkle time wit' her." She looked at the clock. "I have five minutes to be downstairs for de driver."

"Don't worry yourself, Mummaa, I'll have everything under control while you're gone."

"Nah bother throw wild parties here," Rose said with a mischievous look.

A few minutes later Daisy and Wilbur watched as the car pulled off, roaring down the rutted street on its way to Ocho Rios.

"*Rahtid!* Now dat she gone, me can have a drink," Wilbur said wasting no time.

"Mummaa don't care as long as yuh nuh go crazy," Daisy replied.

She was making tea when she felt like she was being watched. She turned to see the door close.

"Wilbur!"

"What?"

"Did yuh want something?"

"Nah, me gone."

Minutes later she heard the downstairs door slam.

The following evening, after going to the Carib Theatre to see a movie with Miles, it took everything Daisy had to resist him. Every time he brushed against her there was a shower of sparks, leaving her feeling defenseless and vulnerable. When they got home she was about to kiss him goodnight, when he pushed her inside the cramped alcove, closing the door behind them. They began to kiss with abandon and Miles' hands roamed her body, boldly venturing to places hitherto unexplored.

Caught in a tidal surge of passion, Daisy fought for control. This was not how she imagined giving herself to her future husband. Miles persisted, acting as though he had not even heard her. Finally she pushed him away, using her palm on his face, roughly shoving him. "Stop!"

"Damn woman when yuh goin' stop sayin' stop? I love yuh

Daisy, I want to marry you!" He reached for her, his face a mask of pure lust, his hands grasping her thighs. Frightened, she slapped him and he slapped her back, across the face, hard. She stumbled, falling to one knee.

"Daisy!" Instantly feeling remorseful, Miles knelt beside her. "See what yuh make me do?" He reached over tenderly, but she shrank from him, repulsed by his touch.

"Get out!" she yelled, hiding her face from him.

"I'm sorry, Daisy, please --"

"Yuh bettah get out now!" Daisy screamed. Miles quickly backed out the door.

"I'll call you... sorry--Daisy, cha!"

Daisy slammed the door and ran up the stairs, holding her breath in an effort to not cry. Running to her room she took off the engagement ring and flung it on the bureau, lay down on her bed and sobbed.

Daisy's cheek was still tender to the touch two days later. Sitting in the kitchen drinking tea with Wilbur she tried to understand what happened.

"I seem to trust people too much," Daisy said. "I have to wonder about Miles. Will he beat me? I won't stand for it."

"Sometimes man haffi gi' a woman a good lick inna her batty." Wilbur yawned. "Me ready fe sleep." He poured another shot of rum and drank it, looking at her. Daisy was unsure of which eye to look at because Wilbur's eyes did not properly focus. He seemed to look in two directions at once. After all these years with Wilbur in the house he still made her feel uneasy. She took a quick mental inventory and determined that she had to be imagining things. Nevertheless, something deep in her heart kept nagging her.

"I never know yuh to drink like dis," Daisy said. "Yuh enjoying yuhself, eh?"

"Not yet," Wilbur said smiling. "Me still have a couple days fe work on getting me kicks." Wilbur belched and left, tottering down the hall.

Daisy cleared the table and washed up from dinner. When she finished, she went to her room, closed the door, changed into her nightgown, and fell asleep the instant her head hit the pillow.

She awoke several hours later.

A shaft of light shone through a gap in the curtains, crossing the room and her bed. The light illuminated her face. She blinked and got up. Moving the curtains aside, she looked out of the window at Beeston Street. Dawn was about to break over Kingston. Daisy put on a yellow knee length skirt and a loose fitting blouse. She loved the early mornings in Beeston street, deserted, waiting for people.

Despite her best efforts the memory of her fight with Miles still weighed heavily on her mind. She was so disappointed in him.

Walking downstairs, she gazed at the sky and felt the pregnant excitement that erupts when watching a glorious sunrise: wonder, joy, anticipation.

The geese, awakened by her presence, began to stir and honk for breakfast. She reached the cellar door, pushed it open, and stepped into the darkness. At the bottom of the stairs she pulled the light chain and the low wattage naked light bulb glowed dully. She went over to the tall burlap crocus sack filled with corn and decanted the feed into a pan.

Without warning, the room plunged into darkness.

"Who is it?!" Upstairs the geese were honking excitedly, eager to eat. "Dammit!" She grasped in the dark, searching for the chain, when suddenly a rough hand clapped over her mouth. Another hand twisted her wrist behind her and she buckled to the floor.

She screamed. A dirty burlap was stuffed inside her mouth.

" Dis crocus bag will clos' ya mout' bitch."

The pungent odor of rum, mansweat, and mildew assaulted her nostrils, but she froze in disbelief.

It was Wilbur's voice.

She could hardly breathe and began to struggle with all her strength. Wilbur tore viciously at her clothes. His dirty fingernails scratched her flesh. Sounding far away, the rending of clothes mixed with the sounds of the agitated honking geese.

"Bitch, me will kill yuh," he threatened.

Overpowered and terrified, Daisy whimpered loudly, unable to speak with the burlap in her mouth. She felt numb, yet not beyond pain. Pinning her to the floor, Wilbur forced his way into the tight, unyielding flesh of an inexperienced girl. She was brutally torn. Daisy closed her eyes and waited for the agony to end. Wilbur's ragged, clammy breath left a sheen of moisture on her neck and face and an unforgettable stench in her nostrils.

"Goddamn bitch," he said as his body went rigid.

When it was over, Wilbur stood up and walked out. Daisy had no idea how much time had passed before she moved. She sat up and retched, and spat out bits of dirty burlap. Her inner thighs felt on fire. Her chest and back, her thighs and buttocks were scratched, mauled; her body was bruised and aching.

Wilbur raped me. Unable to sort her confusion and fear, Daisy curled up on the dirt floor. What did I do? she wondered.

It occurred to her that Wilbur might come back. She struggled to her feet and turned on the light. Her eyes darted about, searching for a sheet or blanket, but found none.

Suddenly, Wilbur loomed in the doorway. He came down the steps, into the cellar. Naked and vulnerable, Daisy cringed and modestly tried to cover herself with her tattered skirt.

"Keep yuh *rasclat* mouth shut, bitch." He tossed a dirty blanket at her.

"Please…" Daisy began to cry. "Don't hurt me again."

"Yuh disgus' me," sneered Wilbur. "Is yuh fault dat dis 'appen 'ere." He laughed wickedly and grabbed Daisy by the hair. "Keep yuh mout' shut, slut," he said. "Tell Rosie an' me will kill yuh, sure as Christmas a come. Now get upstairs and clean up yuh *rass*." Wilbur went up the stairs but stopped at the door.

"I'm sorry," he hesitated, "it won't happen again. But yuh can't tell me yuh nuh enjoy it. Dat's what got me goin'."

Fucking bastard, Daisy thought. Wrapping herself in the blanket she followed him up the steps and went into the house.

In the bathroom, she barred the door before succumbing to waves of nausea. She retched until she was empty. She drew a bath and as the tub filled, the soothing warm water engulfed her shocked and battered body. She closed her eyes. She cried until there were no more tears to shed.

Daisy's body jerked involuntarily when she awoke early a few days later and saw the purest yellow light coming through her bedroom window. Her bureau held jewelry boxes filled with paste jewelry. The water in her face basin vibrated in the sunlight. But something was wrong. She could still feel the throb of pain between her legs. How long would this go on? The pain was dispiriting and made her want to lie in bed all day. But she had to get up, who would manage the Ice House? She got out of bed and saw Wilbur sitting in her pillowed, cushy chair, stark naked, stroking a huge erection.

Dreaming. She forced herself awake. Rain was falling on the roof. The pain in her legs and groin were gone but the real pain, she realized, would take forever to go away. Beads of perspiration covered her brow. The nightmares assailed her, waiting until she closed her eyes in search of sleep. Instead she found the dreams waiting in the dark corners of her mind.

Daisy told no one what happened. She avoided Wilbur and in fact, he did seem to make himself scarce around the house. Although she rarely met up with him during the day, he was with her every night in her dreams.

She bathed three, four times a day trying to wash the filth away. But Wilbur's stink permeated the house: rum, musk, man-sweat. The odor of the damp earth and mold clung to her hair.

"Yuh nah yuhself," Rose kept repeating, "tell me, wha' wrong, darling? Where is yuh Miles? Yuh sleepin' good? Dreamin of fish?" Rose gave her bush tea to bring on her period. "Jus in case."

"No," Daisy said, "When yuh dream a fish, it means yuh

pregnant an that's not me." But her paranoia only became more acute and she gulped down the bitter elixir, worried, until, to her relief, her period finally came.

One afternoon, Daisy was washing dishes when Callie silently slipped beside her, donning a towel and drying the dishes. The sisters worked for a while in silence. Then, as Daisy washed the last pot, she spoke.

"I'm sorry Callie... I had too much to drink at the wedding-- I'm sorry."

Callie stopped drying and took Daisy by the shoulders. "Thank you, Daisy. But right now I'm worried about you."

A bolt of terror struck Daisy. "What do you mean?" she asked.

"Yuh is not yuhself. Wha' happen?"

Daisy snorted. "Miles Menders is what happen to me. I had to get rid of him."

"Is that all?"

"Wha' yuh mean?"

"Yuh just look so sad," Callie pleaded. "I'm your sister, Daze. Yuh can always talk wit' me yuh know."

The exchange terrified Daisy and strengthened her resolve to keep the secret to herself. I must stop looking so down in the mouth, she thought. I've got to keep busy.

Daisy did her best to avoid looking depressed. She created fanciful flower arrangements for the kitchen table, cooked all the meals, sewed and mended clothing. About a month after her fight with Miles, she came home from grocery shopping and found him at her front door holding a beautiful bouquet of red and yellow flowers.

Wearing a blue double-breasted suit and a white shirt, Miles looked so handsome he took Daisy's breath away. He appeared nervous, his face resembling a naughty schoolboy's.

"Daisy," he said, weakly offering her the flowers. "Please, Daisy I need to talk to you."

She merely looked at him and said nothing.

"I really love yuh, Daze." He looked down at his feet. "I can't live without yuh." He stepped forward, his arm stretching out to touch her.

"Don't!" she spat. She took the flowers and went into the house, leaving Miles alone outside, crestfallen.

Sitting on her bed, Daisy stared at the flowers. The smoldering anger was dampened the moment she saw him. It was undeniable, she still had deep feelings for him. She was in deep concentration when she heard singing that made her blood run cold.

Dai-sy! Da-isy!
Give me you're an-swer doooo!
I'm half cra-zy
All for the looove of yoouuu…

"Wilbur!" Rose bellowed.

"Yes love!"

Daisy locked her door. She closed her eyes and leaned against the wall. She tried hard not to remember the events that made her skin crawl.

Later, after dinner she went outside in the courtyard. She looked up at the house windows. Wilbur stood in one, alone, his cockeyed gaze focussed on her, a slight smile contorting his lips. She felt naked and looked away, feeling shame and anger. She trembled with fear.

Reentering the house, she slammed the door so hard the windows vibrated. In the bedroom she found Miles' engagement ring in a tray on her dresser. Glad now that she had never returned it, Daisy slid the ring onto her finger. The gold glittered. Beeston Street is not my home any longer, she thought. I will call Miles.

IX

AUGUST 1950, KINGSTON, JAMAICA

Night fell slowly over Kingston as the blue sky turned ocher, and the flaming red-gold sun slipped below the horizon and into the Caribbean sea. In the city's western sector, a blue haze from burning tires hung in the air of Back O' Wall, driving clouds of mosquitos away from the groups collecting on street corners to socialize, swap stories, and smoke ganja. A rough and tumble district, curbside taverns, some hardly more than thatched shacks with open air patios, dominated every alley and street and were jammed with people loitering about, seeking to escape the stifling heat in their hovels. Goats, roosters, and pigs shared the streets with pedestrians and bicycles and the occasional car.

On the outskirts of this slum, near Spanish Town Road, inside a dilapidated tenement reeking of urine, sweat, and burning refuse, in the deep shadows of a cramped one room apartment, Daisy held her infant, Lissette, to her breast. Her two-year-old daughter, Janet, screamed at the top of her lungs. There were circles under Daisy's flat and lifeless eyes, and her breasts sagged from the relentless demands of two hungry babies. The toddler's screams jolted her from her daydreams into the painful awareness of Janet's hunger. Sighing with the knowledge that there was nothing to eat in the house, she sat in the gloom, clinging to the feeble hope that Miles had found work and would come home with money or, at least, a few groceries.

Daisy got the baby bottle, filled it with water, put three teaspoons of sugar in it, and shook it up. She gave it to Janet, who drank it gratefully. Still breastfeeding the baby, she went to the sofa and sank into it. She stared at the ceiling fan, its white blades spinning, creating the reverse illusion of a whirlpool sucking her down, holding her against her will.

Lissette fell asleep in her arms and Daisy glanced at the clock. It's eight o'clock, she thought, how long will I wait for him tonight? She put the children to bed, kissing them tenderly, and returned to the sofa. She smoldered with anger, loneliness, and defeat. Her shoulders slumped in despair. In the darkness, she stared at the sheets that served as window curtains.

My life, she mused, is a nightmare; but at least my two girls make my wretched life bearable. She surveyed the room, crammed with chairs, a kitchen table, a bed, a card table, a sink and counter, and a two burner hotplate. They were lucky enough to have an adjoining bathroom, sparing them the long walk across the yard to the common outdoor toilets and showers. The walk-in closet served as the children's bedroom. Without the closet, clothes were piled up on the floor and the sour smell of dirty laundry lingered in the air.

When Daisy turned on the light, the naked light bulb that hung over the table flooded the room with an uncompromising glare. She put fresh sheets on the bed, hoping to make it look inviting, then opened the cupboard and searched the dark corners to see if she had missed anything edible. Her stomach growled. She hadn't eaten since morning and if Miles came home empty-handed, she would need to ask her mother for help. Miles had worked steadily until Eugene Owl, the owner of several nightclubs in Kingston, made a pass at Daisy. After she rebuffed Gene, Miles found it difficult to get work and Daisy, filled with humiliation and dread, had been forced to ask Rose for money.

She sat at the table and put her head in her hands. I deserve better, Daisy thought. Dim light from the streetlamps outside cast a gloomy pall in the room. Despite Wilbur's death a year earlier, Daisy couldn't force herself to tell her terrible secret to anyone.

On her wedding night Daisy discovered, to her dismay, that she found physical intimacy repellent. Despite her dreams of making love to Miles, she was a prisoner in her own unwilling body. Miles would come home from work and romance her to bed where her memories would precipitate a train wreck. During intimacy, her thoughts became a torrent of disturbing impressions: the mansweat, the feel of Wilbur's ragged breath on her neck, and the taste of the rough, dirty burlap on her tongue. The memories would swamp her, shutting her down, leaving Miles shocked and puzzled.

Trying to understand, he asked her many questions, but she couldn't give voice to her true feelings. Daisy was numb to her own desires and blind to those of her partner. One evening Miles's frustration turned to anger and he took her, entering her brutally, leaving her shattered and even more sexually withdrawn. Her daughters' births rekindled Daisy's feelings of hope, but what was once love in Miles's heart, had become cold hatred. The sight of her stirred his feelings of inadequacy, both as a lover and as a caring husband unable to unravel the riddle that was Daisy.

The tumbler turned in the door lock with a loud click. Daisy jumped. Miles burst in, stinking of rum and stale cigarettes. His mouth twisted into a crooked smile, turning slowly to a scowl.

"Wha' yuh do all damn day?" he asked, scanning the room. "Me leave inna de morning and come back inna de evening, an everyting de same." Miles disintegrated into giggles. "Hey!" he said, "I'm hungry!"

"I'm hungry too," Daisy replied, "Did yuh bring some money? Give it to me, and me will go shop tomorrah morning."

Stumbling to the table, he sat down, his red eyes narrowed into slits. Daisy regretted that she had spoken so flippantly. Would he be a happy drunk tonight? He looked angry and she feared there would be trouble.

He grabbed her wrist, twisting it.

"Yuh 'fraid?"

"Yes––Miles, yuh hurtin' me."

He released her. "What wrong baby, yuh nuh in de mood? Not that yuh ever are, bitch!"

Humiliated, she stared ahead into space.

"Would we have pickney, if I hadn't *insisted?*"

"Please, Miles," she said weakly, "we don't need this."

The naked bulb cast a harsh light across his face.

"Tell me, wha' me fe do? How me lacking?" For a moment Miles's face softened and he looked genuinely perplexed. "Why yuh marry me? It's not like you wanted to *fuck* me. We coulda been friends."

Daisy cringed under the barrage of questions. "Please, Miles...."

"Please what? Yuh gonna fuck me de way yuh always do, lie dere till me done? Yuh goin' endure it? I hate yuh as much as yuh hate me."

Daisy summoned all of her courage. "Miles, what are we going to do for money?"

Miles took a long draw off his cigarette, then ground the butt out in the ashtray. "Yuh mother won't let us down."

Daisy's heart sank. "Yuh keep actin' like she still have plenty money. It's gone, Miles. *Gone!* All a Wilbur's medical bills, and the funeral plot leave her broke. She sold her house to pay the hospital, so now she's just a tenant. We can't go to her. Is hard enough fe her to support herself." Daisy took a deep breath, surprised that Miles let her carry on.

"You're just going to have to find a job den."

"Oh yeah? Who goin' take care a de pickney? Be a man, and get one yuhself. I see yuh in the bar at 1:00 in the afternoon with the rest of the drunks dem––"

Slap! For a moment Daisy saw stars. Here we go, she thought, and braced herself for an onslaught.

"Dere's more a dat if yuh like." The threat in Miles's low tone of voice set Daisy's nerves on edge.

Her lip smarted. She kept her mouth shut, realizing with relief that she wasn't going to be swept away in a sea of physical abuse.

"Yuh lucky I'm tired tonight." Miles lurched toward the bed, sat down and took his shoes off, then laid back with his clothes still on. Daisy watched praying that he would pass out. In minutes he was fast asleep.

Daisy was thankful she only received a swollen lip. Many times, Miles did a lot more damage than just slap her face. Black eyes, bruises and cracked ribs bore mute testimony to what she had endured. Physically she was no match for Miles.

She looked at him spread out on the bed, witless, his body rumpling the sheets. Above him on the wall a lone crucifix hung. She crossed herself, then eased his trousers down, took his tie and shirt off and covered him with a sheet. She put on her nightgown and turned off the light. She felt guilty for not being honest with Miles, for not telling him what happened with Wilbur. She knew Miles had loved her once and had truly tried to understand her sexual revulsion. His anger was justified if not his violence. She had been so innocent when Wilbur attacked her, she knew she must have somehow provoked him and therefore was responsible for what happened. It was her fault. All of it, Wilbur's and Miles's anger, it was all her fault. She crossed the room and and lay down on the sofa.

It had been years since she worked at the ice house, but now that it was gone, she didn't know of anyplace that might have a job she could work. She entertained the idea of moving back in with Rose on Beeston Street, but that would confirm to the neighbors that her marriage was a failure. She still clung to the hope of getting a visa to go to the United States but the odds were against her considering the lottery system used to select visa recipients. Despite this she refused to give up hope. It could be the year my number comes up, she reasoned. If it does, what will I do?

Her children changed the way she considered leaving. She knew it would be impossible to bring them along to New York. She thought of the countless people who had gone to the

United States and sent money back for their families. Now it was her aspiration, to make enough money to send back for Lissette and Janet to go to private school, for them to have all the things associated with more fortunate children. For them to have three dependable, decent meals a day.

Daisy allowed herself to daydream about New York. Her pulse quickened, and she felt a sliver of hope. She thought of Iris's advice to pray. I'll go to Confession tomorrow and church on Sunday, Daisy decided. No matter what, God is in charge.

It was still dark outside and Daisy wasn't sure how it got started. All she knew was that Miles's touch felt wonderful and, for the first time, made her hunger for more. He was loving her, kissing, licking, and nibbling all over her body, exploring, until overcome with desire, she pushed him down on the bed and in the inky darkness, responded to his needs. To *their* needs. His hands, capable of such violence, gently caressed her body as she straddled him, moving up and down, urging him to completion. He responded both quickly and with restraint and now, changing the dominance of their positions, entered her swiftly, softly, deeply, leaving her breathlessly gasping for air.

It was happening so fast. She held onto him, his broad chest covering her as his thrusts intensified, back and forth. This was what she so desperately desired: to make love to her man, feeling him inside her, sharing the communion of flesh. She heard herself cry out, enjoying the privilege of raw, untamed passion. Her mind went blank, she felt herself slipping into a trance, when suddenly she moved beyond control and her body trembled, shook with spasms of pleasure.

Looming above and within, her lover became rigid, his arms wrapped securely around her, as he sought his own summit, his muscles contracting and exploding with potential life and sublime gratification. Afterward, they held each other, suspended in time, the sheets soaked with sweat and the strong aroma of sex permeating the room. Daisy did not want this moment to end. But dawn was coming and the children would soon be up. She sat up and looked into her lover's eyes. What she saw made time stop, and her lips opened in a silent scream.

It was Wilbur.

Daisy awoke abruptly. She felt a deep disgust. Her body had betrayed her. She looked over at the bed. Miles was gone. It had only been a dream. She got up and dressed, then prepared to take care of the children.

Wilbur had died one year ago, but he continued to live on in Daisy's dreams. He had passed away in agony, curled up in a fetal position on his deathbed, racked with abdominal pain and vomiting blood. It was never determined what exactly killed him. In the face of her mother's grief she comforted Rose but took secret pleasure in watching Wilbur suffer. Seeing Rose fret and spend money trying to find a cure upset Daisy, making her pray for Wilbur's death which came, mercifully for him, in 1948. Daisy rejoiced, thinking she was free, but the memories remained, to wander the corridors of her mind. Even now, four years after he raped her, the slightest provocation could set her trembling.

After getting the children dressed, she took them to Rose, and went to church for Confession.

The aroma of incense filled the church and initially she'd felt reassured. She looked at the other parishioners, here for confession. Most were old, dark-skinned women, bent with age, but there were few young people in the motley group. Kneeling in a pew, she fought the impulse to leave. She gazed at the statue of Jesus suffering on the cross.

"Dear God, Jesus," she prayed, "please help me and my children go to America. I will raise my children Catholic, I won't miss church, and I will dedicate meself to the Lord. This I vow before yuh, or if I should forget de vow, may my suffering be multiplied." She opened her eyes and looked into the statue's eyes.

A confessional opened. An old man hobbled out, walking with some difficulty and she helped him to a pew, then entered the confessional. Heavy woven carpet was stretched over a four inch square window that obscured her identity from the priest. Her thoughts wandered over the many sinful memories that ran like gullies through her mind.

Shliip! The priest opened the window.

"Forgive me Father, for I have sinned." Her mouth was so dry and she could not remember what came next.

"How long has it been since your last confession, child?"

Daisy couldn't recall. Her brain was abuzz. "Three months," she said without thinking. Looking around the closed in confessional box, she had a vision of hell surrounded by dark mahogany walls. Tiny flames licked at the dark grain of the wood. She felt claustrophobic.

"Father," she whispered, "can you sin against yourself?"

"Child, sins against oneself are amongst the most serious of all."

Daisy drew in a ragged breath. "Father— I…." Tell him what happened with Wilbur! Tell him! her mind screamed. But her lips remained shut and, she could not make a sound. She imagined everyone seeing her as a young nubile girl enticing a man to such suffering that he forcibly took her to teach a lesson about the wickedness of flesh. It was all her own fault. She was a temptress, a vamp who brought it on herself, a sin made all the more wicked because as she was a woman, she had tempted Wilbur. Was it how she dressed or how she walked around the house? She remembered her dream. Suddenly, she was jerked from her reverie by the voice coming from the dark cloth.

"There is no need to be afraid," the priest continued, "confess your sins and be free."

"I lie," she said, unable to think of what else to say.

"The greatest sin is not to lie to others, it is to lie to oneself," the voice went on, "the greatest gift is that of confession, my daughter. Do you understand?"

"Yes Father," Daisy had no idea what was just said. Her mind conjured up the cellar, the moldy smell and damp earthen floor. She could taste the burlap and feel the fingernails against her soft skin, ripping her clothes away.

"Hello… hello…"

"Father!" Daisy was jolted back to the confessional.

"Did you hear me?"

"I'm sorry Father, my sins…"

"But know that Jesus is Lord, he died for your sins, and now here at the sacrament of confession you can be pardoned. Remember Mary Magdelene? In the face of her terrible sins, the good Lord looked at her and told her to sin no more:

forgiveness, just that simple. I want you to say three Hail Mary's and three Our Fathers for absolution, go in peace, be of good cheer and––sin no more."

Shliiip! The screen slid shut. My God, Daisy thought, he compared me to a whore, an adulteress. Scared witless, she left the confessional and knelt before the main altar to say her penance. The cloud of guilt had crystallized, its sharp edge ripping and tearing her heart to shreds. Leaving the church, she felt worse than before. Her anxiety was unrelenting. She trudged through the streets on her way back to Beeston Street as if she were a condemned convict. She ignored the harried shoppers, hustling shopkeepers, and vegetable vendors hawking their produce, and then the solution struck her: *It didn't happen.*

She stopped dead in her tracks, unsure if she could believe it.

It really didn't happen.

Could she relegate the entire experience to her imagination?

The dream she awakened to that morning flashed before her eyes.

It was impossible and yet something told her that, indeed, the event was just a vivid dream.

She repeated it again: *it never* happened.

She waited expectantly for a bolt of lightning to hit, something to take the weight from her shoulders. But nothing happened. The guilt weighed more heavily than ever. Convincing herself of this falsehood was going to take some time, she reckoned.

Repeating her new mantra, the dream seemed to lose its sharp edges with each repetition. By the time she reached her mother's, the mantra was a blur, already almost burned into her consciousness.

Inside Rose's house it was unusually quiet. Daisy walked into the kitchen, where Rose was sitting at the table, playing with Janet and holding Lissette. When their eyes met, Daisy knew that Rose would help her.

Rose got up to put the children in bed for their naps. When she returned she hugged Daisy. A kettle on the stove began to whistle. "Want some?" she asked.

"Bush tea?"

"Is jus' black tea." She dropped a tea bag in a cup of hot water.

"Gi' me a cup."

They sat in the parlor adjacent to the kitchen and sipped tea slowly from china cups. Bright sunlight streamed through the open windows. An occasional laugh or shout could be heard from the street.

"I'm goin' help yuh," Rose said, taking Daisy's hand. "Firs' we goin' shoppin, den we goin' take de food where yuh live. Three years and I have yet fe see de place yuh call home."

Daisy's heart stopped. She didn't want anyone to see how she lived in Back O' Wall. She always described her home as being on Spanish Town Road, and there was no phone. The idea of having Rose poking around her neighborhood filled Daisy with horror.

"Yuh look scared to death," Rose went on. "I know yuh livin' in Back O' Wall."

"Can't you just help without humiliating me, Mummaa?" Daisy hung her head.

"Long ago," Rose said, "before I had children, me learned somepin dat help me ever since." She looked into her daughter's eyes. "Yuh mus live yuh life and stop wishing fe more. Yuh mus learn to be content."

Content, Daisy thought, with a rapist in your house. Immediately her mind spun around, snarling, *it never happened.*

"Mummaa, content or no, we mus' have money for food." Daisy said. "I tell Miles, yuh nuh have money like dat no more. But he won't listen."

"He's still beating yuh?" Daisy's swollen lip was clearly visible.

Daisy hesitated. "Yeah."

"Then yuh must bring de pickney and move in here." Rose's voice was severe. "Now!"

"And how is that going to make me look?"

Rose exploded. "*But see 'ere!* It always 'bout yuh, Daisy! What about de pickney ? You mus' be crazy. Yuh situation gone to shit and all yuh a worry 'bout is what people tink. Lawd Jesus!" She sipped her tea. "If yuh worry a how yuh look, think of all de times yuh come here wearing dark glasses. You think people don't know already that he's beatin de hell outta yuh? And all de time you're hoping that your lottery number comes up to get American visa, cha!"

Rose called Grapples, who went two blocks to ask Sally Maud if she could come over to stay with the children. Then, suitcase in hand, Daisy and Rose boarded the Spanish Town bus and got off near Back O' Wall.

The blazing noontime sun created a shadowless world as they walked to Daisy's home. Rose looked at the children on the streets, so many clad in rags, playing in and around mountains of trash beset by clouds of flies. In a little strewn yard, sparsely carpeted with green patches of grass, Rastas kicked a ball. The smell of smoke and food and ganja mingled with the breeze. The two-story tenement where Daisy lived wasn't as bad as some, and was indisputably more secure than some of the shacks people called home. They went upstairs and Daisy unlocked the door.

Rose gasped from exertion. "Is de damn smokin'," she said. "I have to stop." She glanced around the room and looked at her watch. "We have plenty time," she said. "Let's get to work."

Three hours later, with the afternoon light streaming through the window they sat together at the table sipping fresh cups of tea. The room was still in a chaotic state and the dirty dishes were piled up in the sink, but the suitcase bulged with Daisy's belongings.

"Yuh should never be afraid to ask for help from family." Rose took another sip of tea. "That's all yuh have in the world––family. I always say yuh is born wit everyting yuh goin have in life, and everyting yuh have when yuh born is what yuh will take when yuh die. Daisy, I have to tell yuh, bad luck is followin' yuh, and I know why. You're never content. Look at Callie."

"She lacks ambition!" Daisy cried. "Where was she when yuh needed her? She is lazy, superstitious and jealous. You're comparing her to me?"

"She's happy." Rose sighed. "All we really have in this world is each other, and I've seen you distance yourself from everyone. You're in trouble now, and who do you come to? If I wasn't here you would go to Callie."

"I will never call on Callie for help, so help me God!"

"There's a saying, never name a well from which you will not drink. One day, you're going to need Callie."

"To cast an obeah spell? Cha! I leave such people alone. I've already apologized to Callie, but since then, I have no business with her."

"Is getting late," Rose said. "We must go."

When they returned to Rose's, Sally Maud was waiting excitedly. She handed an envelope to Daisy.

It was from the State Department of the United States of America. Daisy, feeling weak in the knees, took the envelope and sat down at the table. She drank a glass of water, then opened it. With hands trembling, she read the incredible news.

"They're going to give you a visa," Rose said. "Congratulations, you've been waiting a long time."

Lissette's lusty wail intruded from the hallway and Daisy's look of pure jubilation faded to one of despair. "My girls," she said. Entering her old bedroom, she saw Lissette squirming next to Janet, still fast asleep. Picking the baby up, she offered her breast and sat down in the dark room alone, suddenly unsure if she could leave her daughters behind. She could not even consider taking them with her financial situation.

One thing I know for sure, she thought, there's no future for my daughters here. She rocked Lissette and watched her suckle. Tears threatened to spill from her eyes. She had dreamt of this moment for years. It had always seemed that on being granted a visa, she would feel nothing but joy. But now, holding the letter, clutching her baby tightly, she felt engulfed in sadness. Lissette had fallen back to sleep and Daisy dozed off. She was startled by a knock at the door.

Rose sat down next to Daisy. "I won't act like I did toward Iris," her mother said. "But I must tell you that I don't want you to go. But I know in the end it's your choice. So, just tell me what yuh need."

"And if I choose to go?"

"Then leave dem two children with me––until you send for them or come back. But what about Miles?"

"I don't know," Daisy said softly.

"When yuh goin' tell him?" Rose asked her.

"Tonight, Mummaa. I'm goin' back home to talk to Miles. De pickney can sleep here."

"Be careful, Daisy"

"He's my husband, and I know him best."

"Den let me get yuh a cab," Rose said.

"No, me takin' a bus, me need time fe think."

"Yuh nah leavin' dis house talkin' bout no bus! Yuh takin' de taxi!"

A few minutes later, Daisy turned the key to her apartment door. The house was empty, undisturbed since she'd left. She sat down on the sofa and waited in the dark.

She tried to stay focused on how to tell Miles about the visa, but she couldn't. Visions of her life with Miles played out in her mind, the bruises, the slaps, the punches, shoes hurled in anger, terrifying times that made her want to leave and never return. Yet, she remained rooted in the seat. It was defiance, something Daisy had almost forgotten. She was angry, but she hadn't figured out who should be the target of her wrath. The air seemed hotter and stickier than ever and the hint of smoke burned her throat. Come on, she thought. Hurry.

It was actually not long before Miles walked in. He turned on the light and scanned the room, his red eyes blinking. He smelled like a distillery. When he saw Daisy, he became belligerent.

"What de *fuck* yuh a look at?" he demanded. "Where de pickney?" He looked at her menacingly. "Maybe is a *bangarang* yuh lookin fuh."

Daisy's heart pounded and she watched his every move. Seeing her situation deteriorating, she cursed herself for not hiding a weapon: a knife, a stick, anything to use for defense. It's too late now, she realized, I might as well get this over with.

"Miles, I got the visa today."

"*What?*"

"It arrived in the mail at Mummaa's." Daisy paused cautiously. "I can go to New York. I want to talk with you about that."

"Yuh have nuttin to talk about! Leave me, here? Yuh must be outta yuh *rasclat* mind, gal!"

"But if you would *listen*––"

"Anyone leavin' is me," Miles said, stroking his chin. "If yuh leavin'––it'll be over my dead body." He stared into her eyes, smoldering with anger.

Daisy glanced at the kitchen. There were pots and pans on the counter, a skillet hanging from the wall, knives in a cabinet drawer. Miles stood up. She took a deep breath.

"Yuh forget who carry de *wood* inna dis 'ere 'ouse," he said, lewdly grabbing his crotch. "Me goin' haffi remind yuh."

He flipped the table and, grabbing Daisy by the hair, flung her into a corner, breaking glass, turning over lamps, and piles of stacked clothes. Knocked in the fray, the light bulb swung wildly, making the shadows sway crazily on the walls.

Daisy got up from the floor, dazed. Her shoulder burned where it had hit the wall, and her hand bled, cut on a piece of glass. But she had little time to catch her bearings. Miles was upon her, slapping her hard across the face. Bloodied and crumpled before him, she blinked, disoriented and confused. Miles grabbed her chin, twisting her head, forcing her to look at him.

"Yuh lucky de pickney nuh here tonight. Cause dem woulda hear yuh squeal like a pig--*ahhhhhh!*"

Daisy bit him and he hurled her to the ground. Seeing her chance she made for the door. She felt her clothes ripping in resistance to her forward plunge.

"Yuh nuh a go nowhey' bitch! When I'm done, yuh won't dream a doing dis again." The bulge in his pants nearly froze her with terror. She cautiously backed away from Miles, her chest bare, the scratches on her back smarting from where his fingernails dug into her skin.

Not this time, she thought. Not if I can help it.

"Yuh goin kill me?" Daisy asked.

"What a waste dat would be," he laughed wickedly. "No, but I could use yuh fe make a son." He circled near. She picked up a cup and hurled it at his head. He lunged.

They collided with the wall and hit the floor heavily. Daisy was jammed beneath Miles. Miles's hands were around her neck. He was choking her.

"I put yuh to sleep and den fuck yuh!" he hissed as he bore down.

She couldn't breathe. Spots began to dance before her eyes. She was crushed between Miles and the wall. With her right arm still free, she groped in search of a weapon. Miles had become evil incarnate: red-rimmed eyes, bared teeth, spittle flying, and the rum on his breath overpowering.

Her hand was getting heavier, searching more slowly. The spots before her eyes were changing colors and she was feeling comfortably numb.

"Bitch!" Miles cried. "Try fe breathe, jus' try it!"

So I'm going to die, Daisy thought. A vision of Janet and Lissette playing in Rose's yard passed through her mind. Her hand touched something, grasped it as tightly as she could, and she brought it down with all the force she could on Miles' head. The impact caused the object to fling from her hand but Miles fell limply upon her, releasing his hold. For a moment she saw rich colors, passing reds and yellows, and a strong shock of violet, then everything went black.

She flashed back to the cellar. Was this Wilbur, still beside her? Opening her eyes, she saw Miles slumped on the floor, an iron skillet near his bloodied face. Daisy still didn't understand. What had happened? Why was her neck on fire? She touched it gingerly and was surprised to see blood.

Blood.

Everything came rushing back to Daisy, including her rage.

Kill him.

She wriggled out beneath Miles, who lay semi-conscious, blood trickling from his nose.

Smash his skull.

"I'm goin' kill yuh!" Daisy cried. Power surged through her, still on her knees, half-naked and sobbing. "Yuh bastard! she yelled again, "I'm goin' kill yuh!" She picked up the skillet and raised it high to smash down on his skull.

Hard as you can.

Someone grabbed her hand.

"Don't do it! Don't kill 'im Miss Daisy," Grapples said. "Tank God me get here in time." Daisy dropped the skillet, her rage replaced by a violent surge of modesty. She grabbed a sofa cushion to cover herself.

"I followed yuh an' got lost in the alley. Is yuh neighbors bring me here. I had to stop yuh."

"You could have knocked!" Daisy said.

Flustered, Grapples found a shirt on the floor and threw it to her.

"Hurry. Get your things and let's go," Grapples turned his back, affording Daisy privacy to get dressed. "Hurry!"

The room was a wreck. Broken glass littered the floor, pots and pans and broken furniture was strewn about the room.

Daisy got dressed. Miles on the floor, groaned. She kicked his groin and his body jerked into a fetal position. He wailed in pain.

"Enough!" Grapples pulled her hand. "Let's go!"

In a final act of defiance, she spat on Miles. Holding onto Grapples, she stepped over the wreckage, out of the ruined apartment and into the night and, for Daisy, into a new life.

ROOTS

X

JUNE 1956, BROOKLYN, NEW YORK

Linton leaned out his apartment window and watched the river of taxicabs, delivery trucks and cars sitting bumper to bumper in traffic, beneath the incessantly blinking traffic lights. The sidewalks echoed with the syncopated sounds of countless shoes slapping the cement and harmonized with music that emanated from other open apartment windows. Everywhere he looked, he found the same kind of vibrancy and commotion of life as in Jamaica. He felt his pulse quicken. It was the first Friday of summer.

Across the street, harried shoppers converged on a green grocer stand, searching for the perfect head of lettuce, early corn, or cherries. His attention was captured by a tall, slender woman squeezing tomatoes thoughtfully, as if trying to divine their flavor through touch. She was calm, walking through the din of activity, carrying herself with elegance and poise and, for a moment, he imagined himself at Sheila's side. A smile slowly crept across his face. He watched her, until a man came up from behind her and, wrapping his arms around her waist, swung her around and gave her a smart kiss on the lips. The enamoured couple laughed and Linton turned away, pained by the sight.

At his bureau, he opened a drawer and pushed numerous old bills and letters out of the way, until he found a black and gold velvet pouch. It contained an envelope with several shillings and an empty blue bottle stoppered with an old cork. It had been a long while since he'd taken the time to study it as he was doing now. Inside the bottle were dregs of the last batch of roots tonic that he and Sheila had made. After twelve years, it still seemed like the nightmare had unfolded only yesterday. Will I never get over her, he wondered. Shuddering, he put the pouch back in the drawer and went to the mirror to make some last minute adjustments to his shirt and tie.

He peeked out the window. The couple was gone and produce was being lovingly replenished by the gray-haired grocer who owned the stand.

The gloomy face that greeted him in the mirror was a sharp contrast to his appearance just minutes ago when, strutting in from a bath, he had looked forward to the evening ahead. But whenever Sheila came to mind a nervous tension infused everything he did. It sapped his spirit and gnawed at his soul.

There was a knock at the door and George stepped in, dressed in a dark double- breasted suit, eager to hit the road. Seeing Linton, he paused.

"What's wrong?"

Linton looked at the floor. "I'm thinkin' bout stayin home, mon."

"Goddammit!" George slammed the door behind him. "These tickets are hard to get, Linton, and they cost a small fortune--"

"Okay!" Linton threw up his hands, "I'm comin'! Jesus!"

"Linton," George clapped his hands on Linton's shoulders, "all work and no play makes you dull and boring. You need to have fun sometime. All you do is work at the insane hospital with crazy people, and sit up in your room. What kind a life is that? What about a gal, mon? What about Shirley?"

"That shovel-mouth gal?" Linton looked at George indignantly. "Please, I don't need people like her in my life."

"Well, believe me, this new woman Daisy is no shovel-mouth gal!" George chuckled. "Wait till you see her." He picked up Linton's bottle of cologne and splashed some around his neck.

"I'm not ready to settle down," Linton replied. "I don't want to be serious."

"If we can't be serious, how 'bout some fun?"

"All you care about is fun," Linton retorted, donning his jacket. But seeing George's reaction, he relented. "You're right, let's go have some fun!" He slapped George on the back. "And don't use up all my cologne."

The kitchen smelled like raisins and cinnamon. Daisy burst into the room, clad only in her underwear and hair curlers. From the oven she withdrew a perfectly baked sweet potato pudding. Placing it on a rack on the kitchen table, she took off her oven mitts and stood back to admire her creation. Behind her, Ethel burst in from her bedroom, adjusting her clothes and checking her appearance. She looked stunning, dressed in a splendid strapless blue dress. Ethel looked at Daisy with horror.

"Lawd, chile, we goin be late! Look at the time!"

"I had to get the pudding ready for the church social tomorrow!" Daisy dashed into her bedroom and slammed the door.

"The only thing you think about is that damn church." Ethel's voice was muffled by the closed door but Daisy couldn't hear her in any case. She was struggling with a beautiful emerald green and black evening dress that was caught in her hair. After fumbling about, she put the dress on properly, coiffed her hair, and admired herself in the mirror. She put on black pumps, opened a box, and took out a fur-lined green shoulder wrap that Iris had lent her for the evening. It was the *coup de grace.* Daisy's outfit and understated make-up would make her the envy of all the women. She looked again in the mirror, searching for a fault, a flaw, something in her appearance to criticize. Dabbing powder on her nose and checking her lipstick, she felt satisfied that she could do no better. The sensation of the wrap on her shoulders made her feel complete and confident.

She glanced at a small picture of her daughters. In two days she would be sending them another barrel of supplies that were so expensive in Jamaica: clothes, books, and day-to-day sundries-- toilet paper, laundry detergent, napkins--and a cashier's check for ten dollars. Sadness stabbed her heart. She made the sign of the cross and went into the kitchen. God had blessed her. Her job binding books paid a decent wage but not enough to satisfy her wish to bring her two daughters to live with her in New York.

"Put me to shame!" Ethel said, standing back admiring Daisy. "That stole is unbelievable."

"It's my sister's," Daisy said, turning from side to side modeling it for Ethel. "It goes great with this dress, doesn't it?

"It's perfect," Ethel exclaimed. "C'mon we have to hurry or we goin' be late. Everybody should be there with plenty of dancing tonight."

Daisy smiled at her friend. "You're always in a hurry,"

Turning off the lights they left the apartment and headed for the subway, their high heels clicking on the sidewalk, while streetlights flickered in the growing dusk of a fresh summer evening.

Across the street from the Audubon Ballroom, Linton and George waited for their dates. They watched the long line grow shorter and shorter as people, clad in their Saturday night suits and evening dresses, went in. George looked at his watch impatiently and scanned the street for Ethel and Daisy.

"An hour late," he said, kicking a pebble across the sidewalk. "Is like they've never left Jamaica."

"The only thing Jamaicans are on time for --is money," Linton deadpanned, prompting them both to laugh.

The men were still laughing, slapping their thighs, when George suddenly noticed Ethel standing next to him.

"Money, huh!" Ethel looked at him with mock disapproval.

George was so surprised, he straightened up too quickly and ripped his pants. The sound of the rending cloth was followed by a pregnant silence.

"Lawd! Him get so meek he bust his pants!" Ethel crowed, and they all laughed with relief.

Linton's attention had already been captured by the beautiful young woman in the green evening dress. Their eyes met, and for a moment he felt a long-dormant tingle in his spine.

George gingerly felt around for the tear. "It's not that bad, just a seam. It doesn't show, does it?" He turned to Linton without waiting for a response, he continued, "Hey! Linton, you know my fiancee, Ethel, and this is her roommate, Daisy."

Daisy barely heard George. Her heart pounding. She was impressed with the handsome young man being introduced. For the first time in years, she felt excited. She knew better than to invest in her feelings, but she stood her ground boldly, daring to have hope.

Linton watched himself as if he were in a dream. He could hardly think of anything to say; indeed, his mouth went dry and he felt nearly speechless. When he led Daisy to the dance floor he was so self-conscious, he failed to experience Daisy's grace. He stumbled around, trying to keep up with her and feared he looked like a clumsy oaf.

For the first evening in longer than she could recall, Daisy forgot about her troubles. The feel of Linton's hand on her back was reassuring and she loved the way he led her as they moved about the dance floor. She danced all evening with Linton, turning down all other requests and surprising Ethel, who had never seen Daisy behave like this. Tired from dancing and needing a break, Ethel asked the men to get fresh drinks, giving her a chance to talk to Daisy.

Ethel leaned in close. "He's nice don't you think?"

Before Daisy could answer a loud voice said, "Daisy! Is that you? From Kingston?"

Reflexively, Daisy turned and to her horror, saw Gene Owl. Several people accompanied him.

"Yuh know, Miles, he's still lookin' for yuh." Gene grinned. "Whatever happened to--"

Knocking over an ashtray, Daisy got up and dashed across the crowded dance floor. Ethel rushed after her.

"What a shame," Gene said, "I was going to ask Daisy about her girls." The group moved on, looking for their table in the dimly lit ballroom.

Minutes later Linton and George returned to the table, drinks in hand. Perplexed, they surveyed the crowd, looking for the two women. But it was fruitless; the girls were nowhere to be found. They had left the table in such apparent haste that Daisy's dark green wrap was still on the back of her chair.

"I can't believe they would run off like dat," George said.

"Maybe they went to the ladies room?"

Disappointed, they sat down and nursed their drinks, scanning the ballroom impatiently. When their glasses were empty Linton asked, "How much longer we goin wait?"

"They wouldn't have left us like that. Something gone wrong. Daisy left her wrap". George looked at his watch; they had been waiting nearly an hour. "Besides, she liked you."

"Let's go," Linton said. "I'll take her stole. We'll find out what happened."

They left the building, Linton clutching the green cape. I'll see her again, he thought with satisfaction.

Still in the ballroom, tucked in a quiet corner, Daisy cowered. When they finally returned to their table it was occupied by another party who had not seen Linton or George. The green fur-lined wrap was gone.

"*Rahtid*!" Daisy yelled, "They just left us here!"

"What do you expect, Daisy? We been gone more than a hour and dem nuh know where we is."

Daisy started to cry. "What am I goin' tell Iris? I can't replace that wrap, it was so expensive..."

"Calm down, nuh?" Ethel was exasperated at how the evening had unfolded. "Is your hysterics that lead us into dis." She handed Daisy a tissue. "I'm sure there is an explanation."

"I just hate that man!"

"Linton?"

"Not Linton...Gene Owl." Daisy spat out his name.

"What do you have to do with Gene Owl?"

"He betrayed a friend."

Daisy was remembering that party in Jamaica, one evening after she and Miles had married, when Gene Owl tried to seduce her. After she rebuffed him, Miles began to find it difficult to get work in the more popular clubs in Kingston that Gene owned. Without work, the situation between Daisy and Miles really deteriorated. Not only could Miles not satisfy his wife's physical and emotional needs, he could no longer provide for his family. Daisy hated Gene Owl.

Early the next morning, Ethel burst into her room.

"Gal! Wake up!" Ethel cried, "you're wanted on the telephone,"

Clearly not wanting to be disturbed, Daisy got out of bed and went to the phone. It was Linton.

"Daisy?"

She rubbed her eyes.

"I have your shoulder wrap," he said. "I work all day, but maybe we can meet after work?"

"Oh, thank you!" Daisy turned to tell Ethel, so excited she accidentally ripped the line out of the wall jack. The phone went dead.

"Hello... hello?" Daisy said. "He hung up!"

Ethel picked up the broken phone line. "You tore the phone line out of the wall." She rolled her eyes. "Now we'll have to walk downstairs until it's fixed."

"Sorry," Daisy said, but her apology was belied by the joy on her face. "Where we fe meet dem?"

"Don't worry about it," Ethel said irritably. "Come on," Daisy grew exasperated. "I'm sorry about the phone. Now, tell me, where we meeting them?"

"Lenox Lounge, next Friday night," Ethel said studying the broken phone jack. "Now I have to go downstairs to use the pay-phone."

Daisy was sorry about Ethel's telephone woes. But Iris's shoulder wrap was safe and now she was sure that she found Linton extremely appealing. She was glad she had left the wrap behind.

Idlewild International Airport was unusually busy. Trapped in traffic and sealed inside a cab, Ethel anxiously looked at her watch. "We goin' be late," she muttered.

Daisy was resolute. "We'll make it," she said. "The Delta Airlines cargo desk closes at 5:00 pm."

Ethel looked over her shoulder at Daisy. "I'm talking about

meeting George and Linton. Why do you have to send this stuff this evening?"

"Nothing has ever stopped me from sending me pickney their barrel on the first, every other month, and nothing ever will. They're expecting it to arrive at Palisadoes Airport tonight," Daisy said. "I've done this for three years, and my pickney love getting the gifts I send."

Ethel couldn't argue with Daisy. Almost every day she bought something for her daughters: a toy, a dress, books, so many that Rose actually asked her to stop sending so much.

The cab finally pulled to the curb and let them out and they got to the cargo desk with only minutes to spare. A few minutes more and Daisy had filled out the shipping bill, and they were outside the airline terminal, hailing a cab and heading to their rendezvous with Linton and George.

They emerged from the taxi in front of the Lenox Lounge, a well-known Harlem watering hole that was frequented by the famous and the "wannabes," actors and their followers, and the just plain curious.

In the Zebra Room, dubbed that because of the striped black and white wallpaper that covered an entire wall, the women found a table and waited impatiently for Linton and George to show up.

"They're thirty minutes late," Ethel said, looking at her watch.

"And you wanted me to put off sending the barrel. At last Daisy glimpsed Linton, struggling through the crowd, carrying a brown package over his head. Leaping from her seat she waved excitedly, "Here!" she cried, "Linton! George! Here we are!"

Linton wasted no time presenting the box to Daisy.

"You saved it," she said, "thank you."

"Linton is the hero of the day." George clapped Linton on the back. "He stopped anyone from taking it––he held them back with him bare hands!"

Laughing, Linton shook his head.

"He even put it in a box with a bow on it," Ethel observed. Daisy leaned over to kiss Linton on the cheek but, unwittingly, he turned and she planted a firm kiss on his lips.

"He deserves it," Ethel pronounced. "The first round a drinks is on George."

Surprised but not to be outdone by Ethel's boldness, George said, "What'll it be?"

Later, while George and Ethel cut the rug, Linton and Daisy sat at the table, talking and laughing together.

"I could stay here and talk with you all night."

"Really?"

She shrugged, shyly. "I can't say I've ever met anyone in a club, and I don't really like clubs. But I like you. Since moving to New York, I've become a churchgoing woman."

"I don't like coming to clubs, either." Linton sipped his drink. "But it's not like we really *met* in a club, it's just where we were *introduced* to each other. I'm a country boy at heart."

"A country boy, eh? From where?"

"Clarendon. I've been here for eleven years, living in the same place in Brooklyn. And you?"

"I grew up in Kingston."

"Do you like New York?"

"It's too big but the jobs are here. I don't want to complain.

It's better than Jamaica."

"That's not saying much. There has to be a better place. These white people will only hire you for certain work."

"Where else can you go?" Daisy inquired. "Canada?"

"California! That's where the real opportunity is. George has applied for several jobs in California and he might get a sweet job with de government. He's an engineer!"

"All Ethel talks about is moving to California!" Daisy replied. California seemed even more out of reach than getting to New York from Jamaica. "What kind of work do you do?"

"I'm an orderly. It's a dead-end. But I'm an American now-- I can quit that damn job and live anywhere I want."

"Where you work?" Daisy asked.

"Glad Tidings Hospital."

"Dat's near where I live," Daisy said.

Smiling, Linton leaned in closer. "Where do you work?"

"Ohelburger's Book Binders. I bind books." Daisy backed away slightly from the table.

The band started to play a slow number. "Come on." Linton took Daisy's hand. Tugging her gently, they moved to the dance floor.

Daisy melted into Linton's arms. She felt his firmness of hand and sure step. She was riding a whirlwind. Not so fast, she told herself, looking up at him. Their eyes met, and then their lips. I'm already lost to this man she realized. Her mind swirled while her body moved in response to Linton's.

At the end of the dance, they returned to their table. The air between them was so charged with desire it crackled. Ethel slid into the booth next to Linton and when she accidentally touched his arm he jumped as though he'd been electrically shocked. Looking at Daisy, he tried to suppress the stupid grin that punctuated his face.

George suggested they get something to eat before calling it an night. The men went ahead to hail a taxi and outside, George said, "You're smooth, mon!"

"Hush up!" Linton retorted, but his self-assured smile betrayed his true feelings.

The ladies came out of the club as it began to rain hard. The water-slick streets reflected the multicolored lights of Manhattan, distorting the images of cars as they splashed by. They caught a taxi and were soon eating in a small restaurant near Washington Heights. Later, while the men were in the lavatory, Ethel said, "Daze, I've never seen you so light-hearted."

Daisy took a napkin and on it scrawled: *Shemberger's Deli, Monday through Friday, lunch 12:30 to 1:00 pm.*

When the guys returned they paid the bill and left. They mosied to the subway station, lingering to peer into store windows and gawk at a newsstand's magazines. At the subway entrance, Linton took Daisy's hand.

"Thank you for a wonderful evening," she said. "I had so much fun!" She grasped Linton's hands, pressing the napkin into his palm. "Let's meet for lunch," she whispered. "I'm there every day."

Linton read the napkin and broke into a huge smile. "I'll be there, God spare me life!"

"Linton!"

George was at the bottom of the first level of the stairs to the subway. "I hear the train comin'!" Linton called goodnight to the women as he dashed down the stairs.

"Sometimes I wished he lived in Harlem," Ethel said. "Brooklyn is jus so far."

Daisy put her hand on her friend's arm. "I'm not going to get my hopes up, Ethel." But even as she said this, Daisy knew her hopes were soaring.

Meanwhile, on a subway train speeding beneath the streets of New York City, Linton was busy reproaching himself for his clumsy dancing and overall oafish demeanor. George listened, exasperated.

"So what if she gave me this note?" He looked at the crumpled napkin. "See a phone number? If she was serious she would have put down her phone number. I looked like a fool tonight, didn't I?"

"You look like a fool now! You already have her phone number and her phone is broke!" George snorted. "What wrong with you mon? You've hit one out of the park. She smitten."

"We'll see." Linton was afraid. He had had affairs, but he always remained somewhat aloof. Falling in love scared him, but despite his best efforts, he was drawn to Daisy like a moth to a flame.

When they arrived home, a note was pasted to Linton's door. He read it and sat down. Good news! Andrew was in town. They had stayed in touch by mail, but after leaving Jamaica in 1945, Linton never expected to actually see Andrew again. What would bring him to New York? He considered telling Andrew about their real relationship. He had hesitated in the past but now, with Andrew's mother Pauline dead, he felt more at ease with the idea. I'll do it when I see him. Linton thought. He has a right to know.

Linton prepared for bed, trying to imagine Andrew's reaction. But once between the sheets he lay there, unable to sleep. He tried to go back in time, to see his past, but discovered that before he was brought to the Blaine Estate, his memories evaporated. He was so young when his mother died. All of his childhood memories were of Andrew, Sheila, and of their adventures around the great house. And, of course, of Major. He recalled the flutter in his heart when Gene Owl told him that it was because he was Andrew's brother that he was being taken care of in New York. Did Andrew already know? Had Major told him? What if Andrew didn't know and didn't believe Linton? His initial euphoria was collapsing into dark apprehension.

Andrew called the next morning and arranged to meet Linton after work, outside Glad Tidings Hospital. Surrounded by sterile white walls, crazy people, and a demoralized staff, Linton's shift dragged through the morning and into the afternoon. Free at last, he changed into street clothes and rushed to meet Andrew.

Dressed casually in black slacks and a yellow short-sleeve shirt, Andrew smoked a cigarette while he waited for Linton. He looked slimmer than when they'd last seen each other, but there was a healthy glow to his deep honey-colored skin. Happily, they shook hands.

"What brings yuh dis way, mon?" Linton asked.

"Independence for Jamaica." Andrew's eyes were wide with excitement. "I'm one of the Jamaican representatives for talks about the fate of the glorious British West Indies. But right now, I could care less about that. Damn it's good to see you, Linton! How are you?"

"This city is too big, my deadend job is driving me crazy, and the winter is too cold, but other than that, I can't complain!" He smiled. "Actually," he confirmed, "I'm moving to California soon. I heard dere's a lot more opportunity out there and better weather. When are you returning to Jamaica?"

"Tomorrow night."

"Tomorrow?! You just got here."

"Yeah, A quick business trip. I'm staying at the Hotel Theresa."

The Hotel Theresa, located at Seventh Avenue and 125th Street, was a gray, august building that loomed over the Harlem skyline. It served as a locus of activity for the northeastern Negro community.

"At least I'm free tonight," Andrew continued, "come, mon, let's get some dinner."

"Good. We can make an evening of it."

Linton was clearly happy to see Andrew, but what he wanted to tell his brother gnawed at him. The men ate at a bar and grill across from the Apollo Theatre. Linton had a few drinks to try to build up his courage, to tell Andrew his secret, but still he could not. Maybe later tonight, he thought.

After dinner, they bought a bottle of white rum and went upstairs to Andrew's hotel room. Linton kicked off his shoes and relaxed on a sofa, resting his feet up on the edge of the coffee table. When he closed his eyes, he could feel his heart pounding in his chest. I've got to tell him, he thought, unable to broach the subject.

After a few minutes of light chatter, Linton glanced at his watch, "I have work in the morning." He started putting on his shoes.

"Hold on. The hotel is closer to your work than Brooklyn," Andrew took off his tie and unbuttoned his shirt. "Don't leave, we have to talk." Andrew poured two drinks. "We have a lot to share," he said. He handed Linton a drink. "Would you consider coming back to Jamaica?"

Linton shook his head. "I can't, Andrew. I could never be happy there."

"We're getting ready to build something great, Linton. You should reconsider."

"I have no business with saving the world." He fished a cigarette from his pocket. "I learned the hard way, I have to take care of myself ."

"How can you say that about your homeland?"

"My homeland? I'm an American citizen. When I raised my hand five years ago and took the oath, I was born again. Now, I don't owe nothing to no one." He paused. His heart pounded and his eyes narrowed. He walked over to an ashtray and ground out his cigarette. He suddenly felt consumed with bitterness. "My Daddy left nothing for me."

"But your father was killed in the Great War when you was a baby."

"So you say. But Andrew! The truth is--Major is my father and we two are half-brothers, mon. To keep the affair from Pauline, Daddy rejected me after my mother died." Linton took off his shirt and exposed his scars. "Major beat me to make me keep the secret."

Andrew's mouth opened in shock and disbelief.

Now that he was speaking, Linton was amazed at how easy it was to tell Andrew his secret. He cocked his head and looked at his brother. "Didn't Major tell you that we was different." Linton pointed at them both.

Andrew sighed. "Yes but––"

"Listen to me." Linton took hold of Andrew's shoulders.

"You remember that morning," Linton went on, "when you left de Estate for school?"

Andrew remembered the profound sense of loss that day, when Major told him that Linton wasn't going to the school with him. It was a major turning point in his life.

"The day after you left I was so upset, I threatened to tell your mother the truth unless Major sent me with yuh to England. Major chased me through the cane fields and when he caught me, he tied me to a tree and flogged me. He said he would kill me if I told Pauline."

Stunned, Andrew sat down slowly on the bed. Linton could feel his confidence coalesce and he breathed deeply, sensing that he had finally achieved his long-sought opportunity to free himself from the shackles of the past.

"He told me that I would never be publicly acknowledged and that I had to accept that you, Andrew, would be the only recognized son he had." Andrew watched as Linton paced back and forth. His face was pale.

"Yuh me brother?!"

"Yes Andrew, and yuh are *my* brother. I'm sorry if I hurt yuh with dis news."

"Hurt me? What hurts me is being denied my brother. What hurts me are those scars on your back. Dat son-of-a-bitch." He propelled himself forward, hugging Linton, "Goddammit!" He stepped back, holding Linton at arm's length.

"Why didn't he tell me? Why didn't *yuh* tell me?"

"Because of Pauline. I think Pauline never knew and Major was scared she'd find out. Pauline was a kind woman, I didn't want to bring her grief. Besides all that, Major threatened me and he beat me. I was scared. As I got older, well, what was the point? You were gone."

"I'm so sorry, Linton," Andrew said. "I believe my mother would have welcomed yuh into our family. He looked at Linton angrily. "My father --*our* faddah--has always been a coward, concerned only with what other people think." The men sat, drinking white rum, momentarily alone with their thoughts. "Why tell now?" Andrew asked.

"It's his secret, not mine, and I'm tired of living a lie. Aunt Cordy and Timothy knew. Cordy told me not to disobey Major. She told me that maybe the day might come when I could tell you the truth. But she warned me not to say a thing to anyone."

"Is that why you don't want to come back?" Andrew asked. "But I can help you in Kingston. Your job here is a dead-end. You know these white people aren't going to let you move up. Your possibilities are limited here. I can make things far easier if you come back. I'm working with Norman Manley on a plan to create a United States of the Caribbean. There will be plenty of work to go around."

"Andrew, don't you understand, I don't want your help," Linton said. "Here, in the United--or at least in some of the States, I can still become whatever I want. But even here, in New York, I don't feel free enough."

Andrew put his drink on the table and lay down on the bed. He laughed. "My dark- skinned brother. You know, Daddy still *denies* nigga blood runs in our veins? Our great-great grandmother was a black slave. Yet, he denies it." He curled his lip in disgust. "He is so damn colonial. Still," Andrew looked at Linton, "we must find a way to forgive him. He is our father."

"Is easy for you to say," Linton said. "Look at you."

"Then come back! Confront him! Free yourself and make him accept what he's done!"

"No, Andrew. I want to leave my past behind." Linton sat down on the bed. The room spun. "I'll never forget your kindness, you and Josephine. I think it's true: blood is thicker than water."

"*Bumboclat*! Blood thicker dan mud, mon!"

Linton sprawled next to Andrew, listening to his erratic breathing. He felt free as never before. His relationship with Andrew felt solid. The *truth*, he realized, *is–– was freedom*. Soon his eyelids grew heavy and he fell asleep, the two brothers side-by-side for the first time since they were young pickney, their lives torn asunder by the very man who should have been their protector.

Linton woke up the next morning with his neck aching, hung over, and hungrier than a prisoner of war. He got out of the bed and looked out the window at the Manhattan skyline. His brother still slept. He decided against waking Andrew to say good-bye, wrote a note, and left it next to the can of Colgate tooth powder.

"Good-bye, my beloved brother," Linton whispered. He rubbed his sore neck. Outside the hotel the sun, still low on the horizon, cast deep shadows and glowing morning light. He hailed a cab to take him to Glad Tidings and as it negotiated the rush hour traffic, Linton began to feel the full and wonderful impact of at last being able to acknowledge Andrew as his brother. Of being able to acknowledge who he was, opinions be damned. And he finally knew that he had an ally in life.

Linton looked through the window of Shemburger's Deli searching for Daisy. For two days he had been dwelling on this moment.

He entered and walked from one end of the crowded deli to the other, but she was nowhere to be found. I should have known, he thought as he returned outside. He glanced at his watch. He had only twenty minutes left. He snorted irritably, took his sandwich from his bag and, biting into it, started walking back to work.

"Linton!" a voice cried from behind him. He turned and almost collided with Daisy, as she ran to catch him.

"Oh, I'm so sorry, I got held up at work," she said, gasping for breath. "Thank God I saw you!"

Linton had to laugh at himself, so unprepared for the sudden change in his feelings. A moment ago he could not have sunk any lower into the slough of despair and now he was soaring with the endless possibilities life offered.

"Well I figured as much," he said, not missing a beat, "so I was heading to Ohelberger's to see if you were still there."

"That's funny," Daisy teased, "my work is in the opposite direction."

Linton hung his head, grinning.

Daisy beckoned him to follow her. "Come on, let's go to the park across the street and eat real quick."

They sat on a park bench situated underneath some trees in a square across the street from the deli. With only a few minutes left, they wolfed down their lunches and barely had time to talk.

Daisy glanced at her watch, "I'm so sorry, I won't be late next time."

"You mean tomorrow?"

She nodded. "Why not every day?"

"Why not?"

"Tomorrow, then, right here, five minutes after twelve." They stood up, each to return to work. "Bye!" she said over her shoulder as she dashed off.

Feeling satisfied and happy, Linton whistled a tune as he walked in the opposite direction, back to Glad Tidings. They had hardly said a word, yet the meeting had felt laden with purpose.

Over the next three months, their lunches became a habitual rendezvous. They were dating exclusively, going to movies and dances every weekend. Linton never once pressured Daisy to sleep with him. Late one night at Daisy's house, it took all he had to resist her. Daisy was sorry he'd gone home, but only after he left.

Early one hot, muggy morning Linton received a telegram. He shuddered instinctively, fumbling with the yellow paper until he got it open. His heart sank as he read: TIMOTHY PASSED AWAY [STOP] 9-11-56 6:34 PM KINGSTON JAMAICA [STOP] ANDREW.

Linton sat down on the bed, breathless, like someone had punched him in the gut. Timothy dead?! It was unbelievable, impossible. His throat tightened. Tears threatened to break the dam. But he suppressed the emotion.

He remembered shaking Timothy's hand as the dawn light kissed the rooftops of the village huts and smoke from the breakfast cook fires dappled the morning sky. He had walked over the hill and never looked back.

A single tear breached the barricade and trickled down his cheek. He brushed it away and glanced at the clock. I better get out of here, he thought, I've got to get to work. Springing into action he changed his shirt and headed out the door.

The Western Union telegram lay on Daisy's table next to a crumpled pile of damp tissues. Timothy had passed away.

Daisy's memories of Timothy were vague. She recalled her father, Wilbur, and Timothy playing cards together when she was a small child, and she remembered relaying information to him in May Pen when she was a teenager as he ran her mother's ice business. She had been taught to respect him and thought of him fondly.

When the telegram arrived, Daisy was alone. Her roommate, Ethel, had moved out two weeks earlier. She and George had married and moved to California. She felt abandoned.

The next day when Linton and Daisy met, as usual, in the park across from Shemberger's Deli he was surprised to see her looking so morose.

"A friend of my family's died last night," she confided. "My father and he were close."

"What was his name?" Linton's eyes were as big as saucers.

"Timothy. Mas' Tim we used to call him."

Linton could hardly believe his ears. "I don't believe it!"

"You know Timothy?"

Linton nodded. "My God! Him know me all my life," Linton said incredulously. "He used to run an ice business but moved to the mountains where I lived with him."

"That was our business!" Daisy said proudly. "Me mother owned it. This makes me feel like I've known you for a long time." Impulsively, she kissed him. Differently from before. Passionately.

That kiss sealed Linton's fate. Linton was, by nature, a worrier, a man who could always detect the cloud on the horizon. All of his doubts and insecurities vanished. When he finally opened his eyes and looked into hers, it registered that this was a moment to remember.

Lightheaded, Daisy took a deep breath and glanced at her watch. Lunch break was nearly over and she hurriedly gathered her things.

"Five o'clock in front of Ohelburger's." She gave him a peck on the cheek. "Don't be late, I really need you."

Linton floated back to work. He was surprised by the coincidence of them both knowing Timothy, and stunned by the important role the man had played in both of their lives.

Daisy ladled more soup into her bowl. She and Linton were in her kitchen eating dinner and talking about Timothy.

"He was always there for me," Linton said. He spoke with a mouthful of food. "That community in Bessanworse... I couldn't stay there." Caught up in memories, for a brief moment he thought he smelled Sheila. Chills ran down his spine. "I lost..." He stopped, his voice choked with emotion.

Reaching across the table, Daisy touched his hand. "What?"

"When Sheila died, she was pregnant with our baby. Timothy had sent me on an errand in Kingston and a storm closed the bridge for a couple of days. I wasn't there... *I wasn't there for her* when she died!" Daisy came around the table and sat in his lap, hugging him.

Linton continued talking and for the first time in his life shared with another person the events that shaped his story. He told her of Major's affair with Misti, his mother, and how it grieved him that he could hardly remember her. He told her about Andrew and how they were brothers at last. He described Bessanworse, and his many adventures with Timothy.

Listening to him, Daisy knew that for her it was time, that this was the man for whom she would risk loving. She was with a man with whom she felt safe. She, too, wanted to tell her story and as the afternoon shadows gave way to the dark of night, she did, stopping short of disclosing the most traumatic event of her life. The rape was a gap in her past, a missing link that she believed revealed a wanton, promiscuous side of herself that she despised, and she would have nothing to do with it. She continued, about to speak about Miles and her children when Linton gently put his finger over her lips and then gently guided her chin upward. She closed her eyes and they kissed. The words that were on the tip of her tongue lingered momentarily and then disappeared.

Their lips parted, and Linton turned on the record player.

The needle settled on the record and the mellifluous, crooning voice of Johnny Mathis filled the room.

Linton took Daisy's hand and in the dimly lit, quiet apartment, they began to dance, swaying slowly as they glided across the carpet. Daisy held Linton tightly, her head against his chest. In an instant her mind took her back to their first dance together at the Audubon. Bewitched by the heady masculine scent and strong, sinewy muscles of his lean body, by his vulnerability to her and the sense of comfort and safety she felt in his presence, her last chance to escape with her heart intact, evaporated. She resigned herself to fate: she was hopelessly love-struck. But did he feel the same about her? She looked at him and Linton kissed her, dissipating any lingering reservations and anxiety. Clinging together in a tight embrace, laughing as they lock-stepped to the bedroom, they tumbled into bed and began to make love. It was shocking for Daisy to realize that she was responding without hesitation or fear––without *revulsion* to Linton's touch.

And for Linton, too, enveloped in Daisy's arms, kissing and loving her, he felt secure, that he was meant to provide for this woman's needs, her wants, and desires. His memory of Sheila impinged on the moment and he could not help but compare, but in Daisy's arms he felt, at last, Sheila's forgiveness, her letting him go to build a new life. In her arms he found the thrill that had been missing for so long after Sheila's death. Daisy would be his woman, his wife, his empress whom he would serve without fail. The question struck him, how had he survived so long without love?

As they peeled off layers of clothing, Daisy's hands caressed and lingered on the scars on Linton's back.

"What is this?" she quietly asked.

"My father beat me," he said, in no mood to discuss it.

Even as Linton made her queen of his universe, Daisy discovered his role in her life: liberator.

But later that evening when Linton invited her to his apartment, Daisy steadfastly refused to go, perplexing him. Finally he got her to tell him it was because of Gene Owl.

Daisy squirmed. "He knew me when... when I was married. He was friends with my former husband. They had a falling out and he hurt my ex-husband's career, that's all."

"That's all?" Linton's eyebrow arched upward, wrinkling his brow. "That's quite a bit."

"Yes."

"Tell me more"

"I have two daughters. Janet is eight and Lissette is six. They stay with my mother in Kingston."

"Jesus, Daisy! How could you tell me so much about yourself and forget to mention yuh two pickney!" It was the first time Daisy had heard Linton speak to her in a tone of irritation.

I was about to tell you, but you kissed me first and—"

"Where is their father?"

"I don't know," Daisy replied, with a hint of desperation."His drinking got out of hand and he was a mean drunk. Cruel. I left him in Jamaica and I alone support my children. I didn't tell you sooner because...." Her voice trailed off leaving the obvious unspoken.

"So he doesn't help you take care of his pickney?"

"Mummaa does what she can. The ice business went under, because of refrigerators. Mummaa spent almost all of her money taking care of Wilbur when he was sick and dying. She sold the house and lives there as a tenant and has very little money left. I try to help in every way I can." She shrugged. "One day I'm going to bring my children here with me."

Daisy's words provoked a strong reaction in Linton. His gut tightened. The thought of abandoning a child repulsed him. He had been abandoned. He could feel his rage rise from within, bubbling just beneath his skin. *So many absent fathers.* Taking a deep breath, he suppressed these feelings.

"I guess that's all you can do then, work and save money and maybe one day have a strong family."

Late one evening, a few months later, Linton sat looking out the window of his little rented room, at the streets abuzz with lights and traffic, with people, and snippets of conversation. His face was illuminated by the liquor sign that hung next to the window, the neon flashing each letter in the word L-I-Q-U-O-R before the entire sign lit up in pink and white.

He held a letter from California, from Gladstone, a private institution for the mentally ill, informing him that he had been hired as an orderly. He had expected to feel ecstatic when he received the news, but instead his heart was heavy. He didn't want to leave Daisy. Unsolicited, his body sprang to life as he thought about touching her, the soft undulating invitation of her flesh. He entertained the idea of their living together.

She has to come with me, he agonized. She has to. His mind began to race. Unable to sleep, he lay back in bed and watched the ceiling fan spin lazily as the night slowly passed.

At the same time, in her apartment across the East River, Daisy, too, felt uneasy. Sleep teased her, staying just out of reach as she restlessly lay there.

In the darkness, she became acutely aware of the fact that she was alone in bed.

Sleep gradually crept up on her like a shimmering haze that pushed aside her worries. The room dissolved, the furniture becoming dark, gloomy, indistinct figures in a blue emptiness over which she drifted, in some sort of sluggish current. The strange forms dissipated giving way to a vast emptiness.

Then, in the distance, something glowed, becoming brighter as it drew closer. It was the largest school of fish she had ever seen. The fish engulfed her, brushed against her, and she shivered. A buzz filled her ears. The light grew intense. The fish moved so quickly they began to melt, creating long threads of spinning light.

Fish! Daisy woke up abruptly, covered in sweat.

She looked at the calendar: November 15, 1956. She wasn't even late.

Yet, she knew.

Her body tingled.

Even as he rang the doorbell to Daisy's apartment, Linton felt the urge to run. He had spent the day psyching himself up, rehearsing how to tell Daisy she had to come with him to California. In an effort to banish the negative thoughts, he struggled to imagine them together in California.

When Daisy opened the door, Linton was struck by how sensual she appeared. Inside the apartment it was quiet, the radio off, the record player silent. Linton kissed her and sat down on the sofa.

"It's awfully somber in here," he said.

Daisy sat next to him. She snuggled closer and he put his arm around her, holding her tight. "That's because… I mean," she said hesitantly, "you might not want me around, and––"

"I didn't tell yuh!" Linton sprang to his feet. "Who told yuh about California?"

"California?"

"Don't you worry, baby," he said, "I want you to come with me wherever I go. Including California."

Daisy pushed him away. "California?" she said incredulously. "That's not why I asked you to come over." She began to cry.

"Honey!"

"Sorry. I get all emotional," she said. Just above a whisper she added, "I'm pregnant."

"What?!" Linton froze. "Yuh pregnant?" It was his worst fear, yet was what he wanted most of all.

"I knew it… you don't want it… what a mistake!"

"No it's not what yuh think! This is wonderful news––but me… Jeez Daisy, what a surprise! I would never abandon you! Not you, not my child. You *both* coming with me to California," he said triumphantly. "You're never leaving my side. I love you." A Cheshire cat grin creased his face. "Pregnant!" he continued, "I'm scared, I can't say that I'm not. You must see a doctor right away. This time I'm taking care. Daze, we makin' a baby of our own, we are a *family!* "

"Once we send for Janet and Lissette, they can help me with the baby," Daisy said.

Linton shifted in his chair. “Wait a minute, Daisy.”

“What you mean?”

“We… can’t afford it. We’ll have to make something else work.”

“But I *am* their mother! We will make it work.”

“Daisy, I don’t make enough to feed five. You’re pregnant. Soon, pickney a run ‘round de house. You can’t work.”

It slowly dawned on Daisy that Janet and Lissette would be in school. She would have to stop working. Her heart froze.

“We can’t raise them, Daisy. They are fine where they are, with your mother in Kingston. And we have to talk about all the money you’re spending on those things you send to Jamaica. Soon, you’re going to have to stop workin’. There won’t be a dime to spare after we take care a de pickney inna Jamaica, feed de baby, an’ ourselves.”

Daisy carried a dirty dish to the sink. She could feel tears stinging her eyes. Linton was right. It would prove financially impossible with his wages, even if he got a higher paying job like a night watchman. They were all menial low-paying jobs.

“Let’s send them this barrel and see what we can do for dem later on,” Linton said, seeing how upset she was. “But right now, with our child on the way and us moving to California, it’s going to be difficult. Can they wait to come over?”

Daisy clung to any hope, any shred of possibility. “You mean after we settle in California?”

“Of course, dear, once we get situated,” Linton said. His mind was already thousands of miles away, in San Francisco. It would require some real logistics, but he felt sure that George would help him get an apartment. I've got to keep my eye on the goal, he thought.

The next afternoon, after hours spent cleaning the house Daisy sat down and looked at the result. Sweeping, dusting, and organizing cabinets were her favorite pastime when she was upset. The physical activity relieved her suffering. The situation her daughters were in tortured her conscience.

I'll make it up to them, Daisy thought. We will bring them to the United States. And in the meantime, we will support them. I'll always find a way." Patting her belly, she found comfort in the fact that she wasn't sacrificing her daughters so much as providing for the unknown life within her. That's the way it is, she thought. She dragged the cardboard barrel from her closet and resumed packing it. This isn't the last shipment, she insisted, packing up books and clothes for her girls.

Two days later, Daisy looked over her shoulder at the barrel sitting beneath the Delta Airlines cargo counter, bound for Kingston. Walking through the terminal, holding Linton's hand, she grit her teeth in an effort not to cry.

A few days later to salve her conscience, Daisy decided to call Rose and speak with her children. She rarely called Jamaica, preferring to write letters. When the operator made the connection, the telephone rang so loudly it jarred Daisy. "Hello!" she cried, into the receiver, only to hear the sound of the phone ringing in Jamaica.

"Just one moment ma'm," the operator said. There were loud crackling and hissing noises on the line.

"Hello?" Daisy heard her mother's voice.

"This is the ITT operator. I have a person-to-person call

for Rose Wellstead.

"Yes, mon! Dis is Rose."

Daisy's heart trembled. "Mummaa, it's me."

"Daisy!" Rose cried, "me is so happy fe hear yuh voice! We receive de package at de airport yesterday. Yuh pickney here wan' fe tank yuh!"

Daisy took a deep breath. "Mummaa, I have some news... good news. I'm pregnant."

There was a moment of silence that Daisy thought lasted forever. Then she held the receiver from her ear as Rose shouted into the phone.

"Oh God!" Rose's voice suddenly grew faint as static roared on the line. Daisy vainly tried to hear her.

"Who is... good...?" Rose's voice faded in and out. Suddenly, the line was free of noise and Daisy could hear Rose clearly.

"...and how long have yuh known him? Please nuh hang pon man cause yuh desperate."

"Mummaa stop worrying about me, I'm a big gal, yuh know."

Rose snorted, "You was big when yuh met Miles too."

"Where are my pickney?"

Rose called to her granddaughters. She gave Janet the phone.

"Hello?" Janet's voice was tentative.

"My baby! How are yuh?" Daisy's heart soared and she sat erect in the chair as if a vital force suddenly inhabited her.

"Mummy?"

"How's my baby? I love yuh!"

There was a pause, "I'm fine," Janet whispered. "Are you comin home?"

Tears came to Daisy's eyes. "No baby, not yet. But soon I

will come and get you." Daisy waited for Janet to respond but there was only the sound of commotion in the background.

"Thanks for the clothes and books Mummy." Janet's voice sounded brittle. Resigned. "Hold on, here's Lissette," she handed Lissette the phone.

"Lissette! How yuh doing baby!"

"Yuh coming home now Mummy?" Lissette's voice was soft and distant and Daisy struggled to hear her.

"No honey, but soon, I promise, are you being good?"

"Yes Mummy. We always try to be good for Dearma."

The operator broke in, saying there was only a minute left for the call. Rose took the phone from Lissette.

"Mummaa, we have less dan a minute," Daisy said.

"Take care a yuhself. Yuh should tink about staying home while yuh is pregnant. When will we hear from yuh again?"

"Soon, Mummaa," Daisy said. Struggling against her impulse to weep, she could not bear to tell Rose there would be no more packages. She bit her lip as a wave of nausea struck.

"Let's get off de phone," Rose said.

"Mummaa?" Daisy halted, taking a deep breath, "I won't be able to send anything for a while––till me have de baby."

"Is no problem, Daisy. De pickney can survive fe nine months."

The nausea was overwhelming Daisy. "Mummaa, I have to get off de phone. I'll write. Kiss de pickney fe me." She hung up and hurried to the bathroom.

In March 1957, Linton and Daisy left New York for San Francisco. They sent their belongings by truck and took the train cross-country. They received a proper send-off at a party thrown by Daisy's sister, Iris, and her husband Tom, who kindly lent them money to make the move. In San Francisco, with George's and Ethel's help, they found a small two-bedroom apartment on Haight Street, across from Buena Vista Park. And Linton started his new job as an orderly at Gladstone Hospital.

By now Daisy was seven months pregnant. Linton obsessively pestered her to take it easy, insisting that she lift nothing heavy. He dutifully accompanied her to the doctor for the pre-natal checkups. As the months passed Linton sought to make Daisy's life effortless: no request was too difficult, no effort too great. When their infant boy was born in June, Linton wrote an ecstatic letter to Andrew telling him the good news. Andrew's answering missive was twelve pages long. Andrew was excited at the prospect of being involved so deeply in the independence movement, and his letter went on to tell of this and many other things in his life. But what caught Linton's attention was contained in a small paragraph near the end of the letter:

> *Brother, since seeing those scars on your back I have been in pain. I've confronted our father many times about it, but he still categorically denies it, claiming that you are a liar. I won't speak to him again till he begs your forgiveness.*

I miss you and we should see each other soon, hopefully here in Jamaica with your family. We can't wait to meet them.

Reading this, Linton felt light-headed, deeply touched that Andrew so fully supported him. He bit his lip to keep from being emotional.

In the subsequent weeks, Linton and Daisy basked in the pleasure of their creation, little Samson, a truly energetic baby who seemed bent on escaping the constraints of his own babyhood and exploring the world on his own. Linton cooed and sang to Samson, but sometimes he found himself irritated with the infant.

"I wish him would hush!" Linton said, "de pickney loud, mon."

"He's only three months old," Daisy defended, "he's discoverin' his voice." Scooping her son into her arms, cradling him, she would offer Samson a bottle. Holding the bottle still felt strange to Daisy; she'd breast fed her first two children. But despite the awkwardness, she took comfort in the fact that the doctors believed that breast feeding wasn't best for infants and that formula had been designed to provide the most nutrients. Besides, what would she look like breast feeding her child amongst civilized people?

One evening the phone rang. It was Gene Owl in New York, and he sounded frantic.

"It's Andrew," Gene sputtered. "There was a train crash. Andrew and his family are missing."

The Kendal train disaster in Manchester Parish, Jamaica was worse than authorities initially thought. Members of St. Anne's Church, including Andrew, his wife, Josephine, and their son Marty were aboard. According to reports, around midnight the townspeople of Kendal heard three shrill whistle blasts, then the horrific screeching of brakes and crashing metal as the train derailed and went over a cliff. At that time, in 1957, it was the second worst train disaster to have ever occurred. Close to 200 people died. It took days to retrieve the bodies and weeks to identify them. The exact cause was never determined.

Throughout the ordeal, Linton maintained hope. Quiet and reclusive, he went to work, going through the motions robotically. I can't risk taking time off from my job, he lamented, and I can't afford to go to Jamaica. He bought newspapers and magazines and read all he could about the accident. As time passed and news coverage diminished, it became difficult to keep abreast of the latest development. He brooded, paying little attention to Daisy or Samson, sitting at the apartment window and looking out at Buena Vista Park. He walked alone in Golden Gate Park and welcomed the fog as a shroud.

All his life death had been his constant companion. First it was his mother, and then his hopes to have a relationship with his father. There was Busby's death and the loss of Linton's career when the distillery burnt to the ground. But by far the biggest blow had been Sheila's and his son's death. It had drove him to seek a new start. Many evenings he reverently took the bottle out and thought of what might have been. The memory of the green valley and the village with it's well kept shacks and tiny cookfires made him long for bygone times. He remembered the many evenings that he and Shiela brewed roots, how the aroma seemed to give him energy. Linton took a deep breath. It had been such a long time since he brewed some roots, he wondered if he could even remember how to make it. More than once he had imagined trying to sell some but it would be impossible to make without the ingredients. Linton shuddered. I must stop pining for the past, he thought and turned his attention to Daisy and Samson. They were all he had and he did not want to lose them. He saw how his withdrawal frightened Daisy. She tried to encourage him, to cheer Linton up, but met with no success. His grief had been unbearable for nearly a month.

Linton sat down on a park bench. He relaxed and he gazed at the eucalyptus trees that towered above him, disappearing into the mists above. He yearned to know what his future held but he knew one thing for sure. He loved Daisy with all his heart and the perpetual funk he was in made her distant. He decided that in order to shake off the malaise, he would ask for her hand in marriage.

The next morning Daisy awoke with the aroma of burnt bacon assailing her nostrils. Startled, she turned to wake Linton, but he was not in bed. She jumped up and dashed into the smoky kitchen to find him, his shirt askew, pajama pants high on his belly, holding a plate with small black strips of what used to be bacon. A foolish grin creased his face. He bowed with a flourish. "Marry me, OK?

The scene before Daisy was beyond absurd. "This is how you ask me?" She burst into laughter.

Linton put down the spatula and walked over, taking one knee before her. He grasped her right hand gently and brought it to his lips.

"Oh, Daisy! Please forgive me for behaving like a common ruffian," he said in a half joking, but serious tone. He kissed her hand once more and looked into her eyes. "Indeed there is no ring, but I wish to ask you for your hand in marriage. Take this," and Linton got up and putting a slice of burnt bacon on a plate he put it on the table before Daisy. "I'll bring home the bacon, and you can cook and with Samson, we'll be a team."

Daisy roared with laughter. She got up and threw her arms around Linton, "Yes, yes, yes, a million times!" Samson awoke, his high-pitched wails adding to the dissonant chorus.

Later that day Linton borrowed George's spanking new '57 Chevrolet Bel Air, and they drove four hours to Reno, Nevada. He'd heard of Reno's reputation for quick weddings and wanted to waste no time. They spent the night at a small motel in a small room furnished with little more than a bed and a dusty Gideon's Bible. The next morning they ate breakfast at a western cowboy-style cafe and in the afternoon chose a small wedding chapel, one of many offering quickie weddings. A sign on the chapel window said *Get Married, Get Going, Cheap!*

"Dis look like de place fe me," Linton said, pulling into the parking space and turning off the engine. The chapel was in a very small building with an exaggerated, vaulted roof surrounded with pink trim. Above the entrance, at the roof's apex two wedding bells were affixed by wire to a rusty nail. Behind this building stood a motel with the parking lot about half full.

"Back in a second." Linton went inside and a moment later motioned for Daisy to join him. She entered an ordinary, tiny office and was greeted by the whitest woman she had ever seen.

"Cute baby," the woman remarked, walking up and making a face at Samson. "May I help you?" she asked. Her smile was generic.

Before they had a chance to answer, a tall, gaunt man with a red face came in through a side door. "Howdy folks, welcome," he said. "I'm Reverend Richard Noversas and this is the missus, Emily, but folks just usually call me Reverend Rich. You can see," he said, taking them through the double doors, "we are a full service chapel."

The chapel was a diminutive hall decorated with garlands of pink and white plastic flowers. There were a few rows of pews and a raised gazebo embellished with a kind of altar. Almost without stopping for air the Reverend Rich continued, "We offer several packages with one sure to fit your budget."

"We just wanted something basic."

"Say," Reverend Rich said, clearing his throat, "I detect an accent. Where are you from?"

"Jamaica."

"Ahhhh, the perfect honeymoon spot for the wealthy and well to do," he crooned, "but here we offer the best in affordable honeymoon suites available by the evening." He looked at Linton and then glanced at Daisy. His wife's smile never wavered throughout the entire spiel. "Are there any guests coming?"

Linton and Daisy looked at each other. "No."

Reverend Rich nodded and wrote something down on a pad of paper. "Will you be needing bridesmaids or groomsmen?"

"Bridesmaids?" Daisy looked confused.

"I have two daughters and two sons, ma'am," the Reverend explained. "For a small fee they will be glad to stand in your wedding."

"Oh no," Daisy exclaimed. "The two things you don't want strangers in, your wedding and your funeral." Everyone laughed.

"No problem," said Reverend Rich, "it's your wedding."

The ceremony was simple. Reverend Rich stood with Linton, who wore a tuxedo two sizes to small for him. The Reverend maintained a frozen smile on his gaunt face throughout the ceremony. On a small battered upright organ that had seen better days, his wife played Richard Wagner's *Treulich Geführt*, also known as the "Wedding March" or "Here Comes the Bride." Daisy walked down the aisle, cradling Samson instead of a bouquet of flowers. Tears streaked her make-up.

The vows were said, rings were exchanged and in a matter of thirty minutes Linton, Daisy, and Samson were on Interstate 80, following the taillights headed west. Sitting next to her new husband, Daisy gazed at the craggy, snow-covered peaks and cliffs of the Sierra Nevada and thought about Janet and Lissette. She cradled Samson, an exoneration from her feelings of remorse and guilt. She had a new family with new responsibilities. She put her head against Linton and closed her eyes. After years of broken dreams and shattered hopes, life was finally beginning to work in her favor. As Linton sped past the state line she dozed off.

Driving home with Samson asleep and Daisy dozing against his shoulder, neither Linton nor Daisy were yet aware of their second child already forming within Daisy's womb.

XI

FEBRUARY 1961, SAN FRANCISCO, CALIFORNIA

After enduring the long flight from New York to San Francisco, Iris sat in the backseat of the car with Daisy's two children encroaching on each of her thighs. Her husband, Tom, entertained three-year-old Magdelene with his pinky ring, while four-year-old Samson quietly watched the windshield wipers squeak across the dry windshield.

The car rounded a bend and the City came into view.

"Welcome to San Francisco." Linton turned off the wipers and gestured toward the beautiful skyline.

"I just couldn't wait to see you two," Iris said kissing each child on the cheek.

Daisy sneezed. "Well, I couldn't wait to smell that damn lavender water." Lines of worry creased her face. She had been disturbed by Iris's demeanor in the airport terminal.

The sisters had not seen each other since Daisy and Linton had boarded the train to go to San Francisco. Daisy remembered kissing Iris goodbye and hugging her, a tight, firm embrace. She imagined that she could feel Iris's heartbeat against her breast. Daisy had repeatedly invited her sister to come to San Francisco but the anticipated visit took five long years to happen. The plane touched down in dense fog and was the last to land before authorities closed the airport. When Daisy saw Iris's gray hair, she gasped. Iris looked older and even resembled their mother, Rose, with her large frame and expansive waistline. She briefly considered her own condition. She, too, had gained weight, her breasts sagged with age, and a small shock of white hair hung over her left temple.

Daisy threw her arms around Iris and was taken aback when she barely responded. Looking into Iris's angry eyes, Daisy was dumbfounded.

Yet, hugging the two children, Iris appeared genuinely happy. Tom, always congenial and polite, talked about the flight and cracked jokes as they walked to the car in the airport parking lot. Linton laughed heartily, but Daisy felt uneasy. Iris was holding something back and Daisy's curiosity only intensified during the car ride home.

At the apartment, Daisy tried to pull Iris aside to ask what was wrong, but Iris avoided her. All evening the feeling niggled at her until, finally, everyone had retired to bed and the sisters sat in the kitchen, drinking hot cups of tea.

Iris scrutinized Daisy's face. "You wouldn't know that you have more than these two children." Iris finally said. "Mummaa write me so upset yuh nuh visit de pickney in eleven years. *Eleven years Daisy.*"

"I send them as much money as I can, Iris."

"They don't need money. *They need you.* How can you treat dem so bad?"

Daisy hung her head. "Money hard to come by. Linton hates his job. He doesn't make enough and God knows, we barely make ends meet." She took a sip of tea. "I told them all this already," she whispered, looking vacantly into space.

"Daisy when are yuh sending for them? Those girls are growing up witout yuh! When are you going to see them? I don't see yuh doing anything to remedy the situation!"

Daisy knew it was true. Sometime ago she had abandoned her hopes of ever being a mother again to Janet and Lissette. She could never admit it, but her older children had become foreign to her life in California. Her resolve to bring them to live with her waned with every day. She struggled to send enough money, trying to relieve her burning conscience, but her regret continued to torture her. She tried to alleviate her guilt by praying for the girls, but even then they always seemed to come as an afterthought.

With Linton's income it would be difficult for Daisy to visit Jamaica; to establish themselves on the west coast they had borrowed money and had only recently finished repaying the loan. They weren't hurting, to be sure, but there was still way too little money left over for "extras." Her mind travelled back to when she arrived in the United States, sleeping in a closet in Iris's apartment, working jobs she hated for a year before finding her job at the book binders. Looking out the window at the park across the street, Daisy realized how far she had come since the evening when she left Miles.

The new life she had sought was her's at last. She considered what it would mean to bring her other children from Jamaica. What would the neighbors, or the parishioners at church think? Why should I drag the past into my life now? I came here to begin anew; I've found a husband and created a family. The past is the past. I see no reason to dwell in it. This is my life and nothing's going to stop me from crafting it as I see fit. After it's secure, she reasoned, I'll bring Janet and Lissette to California.

She realized that Iris was still waiting for her to say something.

"Their time will come," she muttered, "I'm over here trying to better myself so I can help them." Abruptly changing direction she asked, "How are Clarence and Charles?"

Iris shook her head, conveying her immense disappointment, and even disgust, with Daisy. After a pause she answered, "Clarence is doing great. He's graduated from business school and is working for a rope manufacturer on Long Island. Charles decided against going to college even after we told him we'd pay for it."

"What? Doesn't he understand how important it is?"

Iris sighed. "He won't listen, we're disappointed, but he's still our son. The most difficult thing is that he's taken up a drug habit."

"No!"

"For a while we tried to do something. It took a while to see that there is nothing we can do. He's on his own." Iris paused, her eyes brimming with tears. "We've told him he can come back after he's cleaned himself up. We're waiting and hoping."

Daisy listened and shuddered at the thought of Samson on drugs. Both Linton and Daisy were doing everything they could to prepare their children for their lives, emphasizing education. Many times she engaged Linton, speculating about what colleges the children would attend.

The week that Iris and Tom spent in San Francisco included visits to all the regular tourist spots. They drove down Lombard

Street, reputedly the crookedest street in the world, went to museums, had tea in the Japanese Tea Garden in Golden Gate Park, and ate steamed crabs at Fisherman's Wharf. Linton took a few days off from work and George kindly loaned him his car, allowing them the rare opportunity to explore the east side of the San Francisco bay. They discovered the variety of neighborhoods in Oakland, many of which Daisy found quite charming, and she coveted the privacy that detached, suburban homes could provide. Fueling her desire to leave San Francisco, George and Ethel had moved to Oakland a few months before. They were thrilled they'd made the move. But it also meant seeing Linton and Daisy less frequently and Daisy missed the social interaction.

Looking at Lake Merritt, Daisy said, "Let's move here, Linton! It's cleaner and there's more space for the kids."

"Where do George and Ethel live?" Iris asked.

"George is an engineer, not a orderly," Linton muttered, checking his blind spot while merging onto the freeway. The conversation continued but Linton was irritated by Daisy always coveting things he could not afford to give her. She was forever whining about what she wanted and he found it tiresome. Driving across the Bay Bridge, listening to the others chatter about the suburban life, he fell into a funk.

That night in bed Daisy brought up the idea of moving once more.

"Daisy, I'm getting vexed with yuh."

"Don't be vexed with me." Daisy sat up and withdrew a few inches away from Linton.

"I'm tired of hearing you pine after this thing or that, always asking me for things we can't afford." For a few moments only their breathing broke the silence.

"The problem is money," he continued. "And for me to make more, I have to be more than a orderly. I'm thinking 'bout maybe starting a business.

"What kind of business?"

"Remember me telling you about how Sheila and me used to make roots?"

"You still know how to make it?"

Linton sighed. The thought of roots provoked bittersweet memories. "I could never forget," he said, snuggling under the covers and pulling Daisy close.

"I love the idea, but... You think these people here in America will drink roots?" Daisy asked.

"One sip and people was hooked," he snorted. "Leave it to me." He closed his eyes. He had said too much already.

The idea of starting a roots tonic business came to him a few months ago while watching Magdelene and her friends make mud pies. They pretended to sell the pies, a concoction of dirty water, leaves, moss and sand, to each other. Watching the children play, Linton recalled Timothy's advice: to succeed in America he must rely on what he had learned in Jamaica. It struck him that he needed to reconsider the gift that Sheila had given to him, the roots formula. How would he find the ingredients? Could he sell it here?

As the weeks passed, he pondered the problems he would face in starting a business. One day he approached a local Jamaican businesswoman, Connie Silverstamp. She owned a very successful neighborhood restaurant ingeniously called Connie's West Indian Restaurant.

He and Connie struck a deal. She would let Linton use her kitchen facilities at night, when the restaurant was closed, to make the brew, and she would offer it on her menu. When the roots started to make money Linton would pay her an agreed upon fee for the use of her kitchen. However, Connie was not willing to invest any money. Iris's and Tom's visit also allowed Linton the opportunity to talk with Tom about his idea and to ask him face-to-face if he'd invest. He decided to take everyone out to dinner at Connie's.

Connie and her restaurant were Haight Street institutions. The place was always crowded with students, artists, bohemians, and a few homesick Jamaicans looking for fellowship and a familiar meal. On one wall above a booth, a large fish tank filled with tropical fish gleamed under a fluorescent light. In the rear of the restaurant, a simple kitchen overlooked the entire restaurant. From there, when Connie was not circulating in the dining area greeting customers, she watched her employees hustle. Columns of steam rose into the air from bubbling pots. Bells rang and the cooking staff functioned like a well-oiled piston, pushing plates of aromatic spicy food onto the counter for the waitresses to whisk away. Connie's eyes constantly swept the restaurant, taking note of potential problems.

The night before Iris and Tom would be returning to New York, they, Daisy and Linton, and George and Ethel gathered at Connie's for dinner. They went in and were quickly seated.

Connie, a rather large woman, waddled over to their table. "Well, *do re mi !* Linton! I didn't even see you come in." Connie's moonlike face was dominated by two brillant black eyes, and it was these eyes that people remembered. She had a way of putting people at ease with just a glance. For some she was a surrogate mother, a person who listened to problems and dispensed sound advice. After Linton made the introductions, Connie pulled up a chair and joined the little group.

Tom leaned over and whispered into Daisy's ear. "What does she mean, do-re- mi?"

"It's an expression she uses when she's pleased or angry," Daisy answered. Tom laughed out loud at an image of this rotund woman, angry at her employees.

"Whey de pickney dem?" Connie asked, looking about.

"They're home with the babysitter," Daisy replied. "We wanted our last evening together here without the pickney ."

Everyone was in a festive mood. The general hum of the restaurant and conviviality from nearby tables turned up the voltage in the nearly electrically-charged energy that filled the room. Conversation ranged broadly, finally coming around to the subject of work. George, as a civil engineer, designed freeways. Several of his projects were being built in the Bay Area at the time.

"I'm so lucky," he said. "My father moved to New York twelve years ago and I got my visa to come here only because of him. I have no idea what I would be doing in Jamaica right now if I had stayed, but I sure wouldn't be designing six lane freeways. I love my job."

Linton lit a cigarette, blowing a column of smoke into the air. "Speaking of work, I want to make an announcement. We came together tonight to celebrate Iris and Tom's visit, but I also have been in discussions with both Tom and Connie and have something to say this evening. I'm starting a business," he said, "a roots tonic business. I've made arrangements with Connie to make and sell it here."

A waitress walked up with a tray of drinks, innocuously serving them without interrupting Linton. Connie smiled at her, pleased that she had trained her wait staff well. Unimpeded, Linton said, "Tom has agreed to loan me the start-up money. I--we, Daisy and I--want to start selling the roots that I learned to make in Jamaica."

Tom slapped Linton on the back. "It's a great idea, Linton! I got tired of taking orders a long time ago. That's why I started my own business. I'm honored you've asked us to help finance this." Tom picked up his drink and held it aloft. "To roots!"

Linton looked at this close-knit group of people and smiled proudly.

"To success!" George cried out.

"And to family!" Tom added.

Everyone drank a shot of white rum.

Daisy took a sip and her eyebrows shot up. "I can't drink this," she wheezed.

Linton put his arm on her shoulder. "I'll help," he said, draining her glass.

"What's the name of the company?" Ethel asked.

Linton was still nervous about discussing his idea. "I'm not sure. We haven't come up with something I like yet."

"Well you really need to think about it," Connie said. "You want to have a name you can live with. I started this restaurant with nothin' but a wing and a prayer and a little money three friends lend me. But the name, it took a month to settle pon de name." She gestured proudly. "Connie's. Clever, eh?" she chuckled. "I've been 'ere since 1949 and let me tell yuh, opportunity like this don't come often. Even in America."

Later that night, in bed, Linton and Daisy talked about the business.

"What should we call it?"

"Tom's toast got me to thinking," Daisy answered. "I asked myself, what is the most important thing in the world to me? My family. So I thought of the family tree. You know, trees have roots that keep them alive."

Linton's mouth opened with surprise. He took Daisy's hands in his own. "Brilliant!"

She continued, "I think we should call it *Family Roots.*"

Linton went over to the bedroom wall and took down a black and white photograph. "This is what I work for," he said. "My favorite picture of us." The portrait showed Daisy, seated, holding both children on her knees. Linton stood behind her beaming. "Daisy, let's name the company Family Roots."

"Family Roots," Daisy murmured drowsily, stretching and yawning.

Linton gesticulated excitedly. "The advertising pitch could be, 'Drink Family Roots Tonic, good health from our family to yours!'"

"Sounds kinda corny."

Linton gave her a skeptical look and scribbled the phrase on a piece of paper. Turning off the light, he got into bed.

"Daisy, what do you know about herbs and roots?"

"Mummaa taught us enough to buy at the market so she could make her teas."

"This 'ere roots comes from an old secret formula that's from Africa. Long ago in Bessanworse, Sheila revealed the secret to me, but there was something else."

"What?" Daisy, always on the alert when Linton mentioned Sheila, was now wide awake.

"I was the only person she told this secret to. Aunt Cordy told only Sheila and told her she should not ever share it with more than one person."

"That's silly."

"No! Daisy, you *have* to listen! Aunt Cordy always said there was more to this roots tonic than meets the eye. The potion contains magic, a creative force. Just a few drops and you feel refreshed. Give a man a drink and he will be able to make love all night." Linton snickered and wriggled against Daisy. "A glass in the evening, will refresh you and give the greatest energy. I have drunk other roots, but Aunt Cordy's is special."

"Roots is roots," Daisy said. "I drink different types. Everyone claim dem have a special brew."

"Is magic, me say! You'll be right next to me just like I was next to Sheila when we cut the roots and boiled them. But it's a secret and you must promise me you'll never tell anyone, not till I die."

Daisy turned the idea over in her mind. What Linton asked for seemed so silly, there was no magic at all, it was simply a popular drink in Jamaica. In Daisy's mind her doubts about the roots had more to do with satisfying American tastes. But if that was his condition for getting this business going––and she did agree it was a great idea––she'd promise. And a promise was a promise. She'd never tell. "All right," she said. "I promise."

He kissed her tenderly. “I can’t wait to drink some with you.” Linton embraced Daisy tightly and they made love with a fervor they had not experienced in quite some time.

It took a few weeks to locate and gather the ingredients necessary to start production. Connie put Linton in touch with an importer in New York who arranged to have the dried roots shipped to San Francisco. The kitchen was properly stocked and they were ready to brew. With the restaurant closed up for the night, Daisy stood at Linton’s side, their children asleep in a nearby booth. Linton poured a measured amount of water into three large pots. He turned on the gas burner and explained what he was doing as they cleaned the vines, and chopped up the roots and leaves.

“There are six primary ingredients, and three strong spices.” Linton stopped Daisy from writing. He took the crib sheet and tore it up. “You cannot write any of dis down, Daze. You mus’ work wit me till you remember it,” he said.

“It sounds like obeah to me,” Daisy said drily.

Linton smiled. “Who knows? I was told to never write it down. Sheila taught me a song when she brewed the roots.” He began to chant.

Dese ‘ere roots come a long long way,
From times of ancient past
Its secrets veiled in de mist,
‘Tis immortal. May it last.

Let us begin with Bridal Wiss.
And if you please, don't write dis down.
'Tis important we not make a sound
This secret so arcane.
Sarsaparilla, Man Back, and Iron Weed.
Some more Milk Wiss just the same.
Do not forget de All Man Strength,
Good fe bamboo, twill make it stretch.
And last to finish fetch your Junction Root,
Seven measures is de best.

When Linton finished there was an eerie silence. For just a moment, while he was singing, Daisy felt Sheila's presence, could hear her voice, and saw Sheila reflected in Linton's dark eyes. She threw her arms around Linton.

"Thank you for sharing this. I know this is probably the most precious thing in the world," Daisy whispered.

Linton skewed his face in mock frustration, "Baby, family is the most precious thing. But this is a most special thing. We must protect it, keep it to ourselves. The secret lies in our method. It's like no other. But to make sure, we will never leave the Junction Root nor the spices here when we are finished brewing. We don't need Connie to try an' figure this out."

"Yes, yes, I understand," Daisy insisted.

Linton measured out the ingredients and soon the three pots were bubbling on the stove. When each had been properly steeped, Linton poured the contents of the three pots into one huge cauldron that they bought specially for the brew.

Outside the fog swirled about, concealing Haight Street in

a pall of soft gray. The familiar earthy aroma pervaded the restaurant and as it intensified, Linton became both more excited and circumspect. So many memories accompanied the scent. One moment he felt an overwhelming sadness and the next, indescribable joy. He felt chills telling Daisy the secret, and felt proud for successfully completing his task of carrying the tradition forward.

At last the aroma grew so pungent, Linton opened the front door to ventilate the room. After the brown elixir had sufficiently cooled, Daisy ladled it into fresh containers to enhance its cooling. Finally, when the liquid was warm to the touch they decanted it into clean glass milk bottles.

By the time they finished it was 3 a.m. and they slumped, exhausted against the counter. Linton had to be at work at 7 a.m. Daisy poured a few ounces of the tonic into a glass and offered it to him. Her first brew! He sampled it and his throat tightened with emotion. What a gift Sheila had given him, a gift that would impact his family's security and succor all who drank the potion. He took another sip. The tonic was perfect: earthy, sharp and sweet. He closed his eyes, swallowing slowly, savouring the rest of it.

"How is it?" Daisy asked.

Linton's eyes sparkled. "You have time fe some lovin'?" he teased.

Daisy put her arms around his waist. "It haffi be quick!"

Caressing her hair, Linton kissed her forehead. "While we both live, you must never share what you learned with anyone. Whichever one of us is left will have to choose one person." They began to clean up the kitchen. "You will know who and when it's time." He paused to dwell for a moment in the past. "After all these years, I've finally shared it."

The sun was peeking over the horizon when they locked the restaurant door. The weary parents carried their sleeping children home. Practically sleepwalking, Linton crawled into the shower and a short time later, joined Daisy in the kitchen. She served him toast and a cup of roots tonic. He quaffed the drink and within minutes began to feel rejuvenated. As usual he barely made it to the bus stop on time.

The roots were a smashing success. Connie gave out free samples at the restaurant and within two weeks, the drink's popularity skyrocketed. Within six months roots tonic had become a signature drink at Connie's and the demand for it was such that Linton quit working as an orderly and took a job at her restaurant. Americans as well as West Indians enjoyed the beverage, served chilled without ice. Each week Linton received two checks: one for his hourly wages, and the other, his share of the profits from the sale of the roots. He could hardly believe it.

On Sunday, the fifth of August, 1962, Connie's Restaurant, festooned with a rainbow of balloons and black, gold and green streamers was closed to the general public. But the place was packed with people. Almost 500 years had passed since Columbus declared Jamaica a colony of Spain and shortly thereafter the island came under British rule. On the morrow the Union Jack would be lowered for the last time and Jamaica would celebrate its first Independence Day.

To commemorate the occasion Connie had set out bottles of white rum, whiskey, gin and beer, and non-alcoholic bottles of Family Roots Tonic, the white and red label emblazoned with a large tree and the words, *Family Roots: From a Strong Family Tree.* Countertops and tables were filled with platters of Jamaican cuisine––tubs of rice and peas, cooked yams, jerk pork and jerk chicken, baked chicken, fried chicken, bammy, roasted fish, ham, turkey, and even green banana and oxtail stew. The air was redolent with the aroma of spices, grease, cigarette smoke and alcohol. Calypso music blared from a small RCA Victor record player spinning 45s, the records stacked on a spindle and dropping onto a rotating platter, playing tunes with barely an interruption, one after the other.

Behind the counter a bartender mixed and served drinks at a furious pace. Near the back, at a corner table, Ethel and Daisy sat out of the fray with their children, Samson, George Jr., and little Magdalene. The place became so crowded that Connie had to stop more people from coming in for fear of violation of fire codes. People on the sidewalk peered through the front window longingly, their faces pressed to the glass.

George, a bit tipsy, made his way through the crush to talk to Linton. Shouting, he said, "Mon, yuh mus' come have a drink with us. Tomorrow we free."

Linton looked at him cynically. "I hope Jamaicans are ready to pay dearly for that freedom. As for me, I enjoy being free here in de States." He laughed good-naturedly at George, who was getting drunker by the minute.

"Lissen!" George interrupted.

A tinkling glass could be barely heard above the din. Connie stood on a chair, holding a glass high. Soon everyone quieted down. Bottles of rum were passed from person to person and glasses filled, while Connie spoke.

"Tomorrow," Connie said, "Jamaica will be a free nation. Jamaica's independence is the final step in a struggle that has taken centuries. We cannot forget the mother of our native country, Nanny, who led the Maroons in the first fight for freedom over 200 years ago. These escaped plantation slaves provoked many other rebellions, but it was not until Sam Sharpe led the Christmas Day Rebellion of 1831 that the British were convinced to abolish slavery in the Empire. The end of slavery ushered in a new era of hope.

"But Jamaicans," she continued, "weren't satisfied. The fight for equality continued through the heroic efforts of Bogle and Gordon, and Marcus Garvey, and now today, through Norman Manley and the new Prime Minister, Alexander Bustamante. So let us toast, to honor all of the men and women, alive and dead, who embarked on this journey from slavery to freedom. May we strive to repay the huge debt we owe them." Connie took a sip from her glass and everyone drank, followed by a few subdued moments.

When she broke the silence she cried, "Remember, Connie's will be closed tomorrow––for Jamaican Independence Day!" The entire room roared with approval and the chaos of conversations and merriment resumed unabated for many hours.

At the corner table Daisy held Magdelene, who slept deeply, oblivious to the surrounding noise.

"I'm ready to go home," Daisy said. "It's hard to keep the

kids up this long without a nap. I've been going since early Mass this morning at Saint Agnes. And it was so noisy last night on Haight Street!" She glanced at Ethel. "Yuh ready?"

"Come on," Ethel agreed, "let's get out of here."

A few minutes later they entered Daisy's apartment, only three blocks from Connie's Resaurant.

"Finally, peace and quiet." Ethel gratefully sat down on the couch. The boys, normally best friends, started to fight, waking Magdelene. Assessing the situation with the acuity of a toddler, she started crying. It took some doing but the children were finally settled and the women sat down to cups of tea. All the rooms in the apartment were, by now, furnished nicely. Beautiful curtains hung in the windows. The kitchen cabinets stored quality cookware and dishes.

"I hate this city," Daisy said. "I want to move to the East Bay."

"We still love it there," Ethel said. "It's warmer too. And the room!" Ethel clasped her hands, "When Georgie and the neighborhood kids get to be too much, they go in the backyard to play. A lot better than when we lived in San Francisco."

"Owning your own house is better than paying rent," Daisy added.

"That's right," Ethel sipped her tea. "You've been doing well selling the roots with Connie."

"Linton always worries that something bad will happen and he won't be able to pay the bills. Really, he is a good man, responsible about taking care of me and the kids. I shouldn't complain. But I want more for us and I don't want to raise my kids here in this city." Daisy went to the window overlooking Buena Vista

Park. Her body, in remarkably fine form after four pregnancies, was outlined by the sunlight streaming through the window.

"We've all come so far," she continued. "I keep thinking I'll be happy when I get this, or when I do that, and there's always one more thing before I can be happy. But I can tell you this Ethel, I deal with my unhappiness a lot better with money than without it. In Jamaica I was unhappy and poor. I am blessed to be here." Daisy made the sign of the cross and looked heavenward. "We'll be okay as long as Linton keeps the money flowing. Flowing and growing. We can do anything with money, we can be anything with money, it's money that secures the future in this world and I want our future to be secure."

"Money is important, certainly, but it isn't everything, Daisy."

"Money is the real world, Ethel. It's what drives your husband to get dressed in the morning and go out to that freeway he's building, and it's what drives my husband to stay up all night brewing roots, then work during the day promoting it."

"It's not just money, Daisy," Ethel said. "What about purpose? Work gives our lives meaning, or at least it should. After all, I think––"

There was a shriek from the bedroom and Magdelene came out crying, followed by the two boys, repeating over and over about how sorry they were. The ladies answered motherhood's call to action and in a few minutes the tears were dried, and the kids made up and were back in the bedroom playing.

Daisy put water on the stove to make more tea. "My children have to understand that having a job that earns decent money is important. They'll go to university, but not to study music or art or theater. No, it will be a proper profession, like a doctor or a lawyer. But Linton really dreams of Samson getting an MBA and working with us."

Ethel shook her head. "I just want Georgie to be happy. His father talks of college all the time, but I don't care how he does it, as long he makes a living and he's not in trouble. You have to trust children to find their way."

"The way is too dangerous in today's world," Daisy countered. The kettle began to whistle and she poured the steaming water. Uninvited, thoughts of Janet and Lissette intruded rudely, interrupting Daisy's train of thought. A pang of guilt pierced her heart. She thought of Magdelene. She may have let down her two older daughters, but she wouldn't let down her baby girl. She would be there through thick and thin.

Daisy continued, "I know I am going to have to shepherd Magdelene every step of the way. I'll give her everything she needs. Education, clothes, lessons, all of this costs money. My daughter will never find herself lacking."

The Independence Day party ended near sundown and Connie's was now empty save for Linton, George, and Connie. They sat at a table cluttered with beer bottles, glasses and half eaten plates of food. George let out a belch, then settled back stuporous and content.

Connie, looking tired but satisfied, rapped her fingers on the table. "Nah bother with the clean-up," she said, "Tomas will be in tomorrow to get the place ready fe business on Tuesday.

Thanking Connie and saying good-night, Linton and George left the restaurant. At the corner, Linton reminded George that his wife had gone home with Daisy and was waiting for him there. Linton was going to take a walk. He did not invite George to join him. They shook hands amicably and went their separate ways.

Linton headed up the hill into Buena Vista Park. Eucalyptus trees towered overhead, swooshing gently in the evening breeze. Concealed behind a green screen of bushes and plants, he found his favorite bench and sat down. The lights of San Francisco twinkled through the trees and he imagined himself amongst the stars.

He was on top of the world. In twelve years he had totally reversed his fortunes, from being a destitute peasant in the Jamaican countryside to being a family man living in a major city in The United States, with a job and a thriving business of his own.

Family Roots! The name gave him a thrill. His heart soared as he repeated the name over and over again until it sounded strange on his tongue. It would always be in the family, he thought, trying to see into the future. Between Samson and Magdelene, who, he wondered, would inherit the formula? The idea of telling them both crossed his mind. Why not, he went on, there are two people who know it now. Telling them both would ensure that it stayed in the family.

Linton started down the hill, his head whirling with ideas. He wanted to open a large production plant and expand Family Roots in the Bay Area. By the time he reached home he envisioned an organization that included his son, his daughter, future grandsons, and great-grandsons. He told Daisy about his forty-year plan for Family Roots.

"That's pretty ambitious," Daisy said. "But before yuh go

and imagine your great-grandson mixing Family Roots, I think you have a good idea passing the recipe to both Magdelene and Samson. Anyway that's a long way off," Daisy concluded. They went into the living room and watched the 10 o'clock news.

Nineteen sixty-two faded into 1963 and while Linton's days were filled with waiting tables at Connie's, Daisy stayed busy raising their children. Many days she could be found at the park with Samson and Magdelene, or at lunch with Linton on his break at the Panhandle Park. Their evenings were spent together brewing roots at Connie's restaurant after closing.

In September, Samson started second grade. Linton was so excited, he asked for time off to take Samson to his first day of school. But the next month, when President Kennedy was murdered in Dallas, Linton rushed home after Connie closed and spent the next three days watching TV with tears in his eyes. At first, Linton was puzzled at his reaction; after all, John Kennedy wasn't family. But it dawned on him that he, Daisy and their two children were a part of a larger family: Americans.

A few weeks later, after a long day's work at the restaurant, Linton joined Connie sitting in a booth. The afternoon rush had ended and she was taking a breather.

"Linton," she said, "me need fe chat 'bout a proposition me have fe yuh."

As Linton sat down, Connie leaned across the table and whispered, "How would yuh like to be rich? I want to make yuh an' offer and buy de roots from yuh."

Linton forced a polite smile.

"Wait!" she went on, "just gi' me a chance to explain. I have two wealthy investors, who love the roots. Along with me, we'd like to begin mass producing this drink. Of course we'll have a primary partnership position for you, I think that's only fair."

"No."

Surprised by the finality of Linton's response, Connie inhaled deeply, leaving an uncomfortable silence between them. After a moment she said, "Let me explain something to you Linton. Here in the States it is common to start a business and then sell it for a big profit. Is what yuh work for, profit. We don't work to become sentimental."

"No one will ever know how I make it," he replied. "It's not for sale."

"Maybe yuh don't understand," Connie said, her voice growing louder.

"I understand perfectly well. The drink is mine." He stood up and gathered his things. His head was pounding. He wanted to be as far away from this place as he could.

A frown wrinkled Connie's face. "I thought we were in this together," she said. "For two years you've been using my kitchen and now I ask for just a little piece of the action, and you look offended.

"I am offended. I have paid for the use of the kitchen and I have paid you a fair portion of the profits." Linton took a deep breath. "And now, I quit. I told you that this was my drink, my roots. You asked me for the formula, and I told you that I could not share it. You wanted to put your name on the drink and I told you no. But now, you ask for far too much." He headed to the restaurant entrance.

"Yuh a fool!" Connie called out after him.

Once outside, Linton stood there, stunned. He blinked in the bright sunlight and didn't know where to turn. He was astonished at the fury that had swept over him. The roots was like his child, his responsibility, and he felt as if he had just protected it from being kidnapped.

Walking toward home he felt like he had just lost everything. Not having a job terrified him. I have nothing! he thought, no kitchen, no way of distributing, not enough money to do it all himself. Waiting at a stoplight he started going over his options and realized he had more than he thought. They had always repaid their loans from Iris and Tom on time and with interest, so surely they would be able to borrow from them again. And the roots had been a smashing success, developing a reputation in just two years. Indeed, Connie's finding two well-heeled investors confirmed that fact. By the time he reached home, he had regained some confidence, but was unsure of how Daisy would take the news of him being unemployed. On hearing it, she kissed him.

"I'm proud of you," Daisy said. "Everything is going to work out."

"Can you believe it? She thought money would make me sell out." Linton sounded incredulous. "There's no amount of money that will *ever* entice me."

"You don't need her."

"I'll call Tom," Linton said. "If we can get the money to rent a space, we can make the roots and sell it ourselves."

XII

JANUARY 1964, SAN FRANCISCO, CALIFORNIA

Over the next few weeks, Daisy doggedly called up liquor stores, restaurants and groceries, trying to schedule appointments for Linton to pitch his drink. In a matter of days, he signed up five liquor stores and Jack's, a small West Indian restaurant in Berkeley. Jack's owner had long wished he could sell the tonic that Connie sold exclusively and jumped at the opportunity.

They rented a small professional kitchen in the East Bay and were able to fill these early orders, but it was soon obvious that they would need to move to a larger facility. They cultivated a loyal clientele, which grew on the reputation of the drink, and within six months, moved into a new bottling plant. Soon, they were able to begin repaying the loan that Tom and Iris had given to them.

Daisy was ecstatic. They had bought a car and drove to Oakland every day, where they worked at the production plant. Days turned to weeks and weeks became months. As their lives grew ever more comfortable, Daisy grew ever more adept at ignoring Janet's and Lisette's plight. She absolved her conscience by sending more money.

One evening she saw Magdelene and Samson, kneeling next to an open suitcase, looking through her jewelry and family keepsakes.

Magdelene held up a photograph of two girls. "Mommy, who are they?" Daisy, shocked, knelt down, and took the picture.

"They... are your sisters." Magdelene and Samson did not know they had two half-siblings. Indeed, they knew only that their parents hailed from an island called Jamaica. Their sudden knowledge provoked a mixture of anger, sadness, and incredible guilt in Daisy.

"Wow," Magdelene whispered, pointing at a tall dark-skinned girl. "She looks just like you."

That's Lissette," Daisy said. "The older girl is your sister Janet."

"Where are they?" Samson inquired. "Where is this?"

"They live in Jamaica." Daisy rose to her feet, put the photograph in her pocket, and glared sternly at the children. "You kids know better than to go in our suitcases like that. You should respect people's privacy. Don't go into them again." Magdelene dashed out, but Samson lingered, still curious about his mysterious sisters.

"How old are they?"

"Lissette is twelve and Janet is fourteen. Now stop asking so many questions," Daisy surveyed the keepsakes on the floor. The trinkets reminded Daisy of bittersweet moments that she had buried deep within. She hastily gathered the keepsakes and placed them back in the suitcase.

"But Mom, why aren't they here?"

Daisy slammed the suitcase shut, and took a deep breath. "Samson, darling. Mommy used to live in Jamaica––"

"I know."

"It was a long time ago and I had a family. Janet and Lissette are your sisters. My daughters. Their daddy died, and we were very poor. I came here so I could work and make money to bring them here to be with us. They are with your grandmother in Kingston."

Samson looked puzzled. "Are they coming to live with us?"

"One day, soon, they will be here." She kissed him on the cheek, blinking in an attempt to hold back the tears. "You run along now. We'll talk about it later."

"Hey! Magdelene!" Samson shouted, running out the room. "Our sisters in Jamaica are coming here!"

That afternoon Daisy decided it was time for her older daughters to be in California with their family. I've waited too long, she thought, and now my younger children will ask why I left their sisters behind. And if I would do that to them. No! Soon they must be here with us, where they belong.

When the children were in bed, Daisy plunged headlong into discussing her daughters with Linton.

"I had some difficult questions to answer today, Linton," she said. "Your children want to meet their sisters, and I want my children to come here to live with us."

Linton cooly observed his wife.

"If you saw how our children looked at that photograph. We have no right to deny them knowing their sisters."

"We?" he scoffed. "Look in the mirror, Daisy and ask yourself how can *we* do everything *you* want? You want a car, you want a house, you want to move to the East Bay, you want music lessons an' God knows what else, and now you want your two daughters to move in with us!" Linton started to raise his voice. "You want every damn thing on this planet but Daisy, we don't have all the damn money for that."

Daisy halted, crestfallen. He was right. She wanted desperately to move out of San Francisco, to get a house, and Linton didn't even mention the private school where she wanted to send Samson and Magdelene.

"So?"

She dreaded answering the question. Her answer would reveal what she really was. With her heart thumping, she tried to postpone her inevitable rendezvous with the truth.

Linton threw up his hands and sat on the edge of the bed, waiting. Finally, seeing the tears welling up in her eyes, he touched her shoulder gently.

The moment of truth had come and gone. Daisy's silence was complicit, a resounding response to Linton's choices. Janet and Lissette were not as important as her younger children. She couldn't understand the overwhelming force that allowed her to compromise her most sacred promises. After all these years the memories of Miles had faded, but the thought of seeing Janet or Lissette seemed to restore the disturbing picture she still had of their father. It was not the children's fault. If anything, they were the ones who suffered most. And yet, Daisy ignored the impulse to see them, to visit, finding refuge in the money that she sent to Rose. So the girls waited, and waited, while Samson and Magdelene received her attention. She was afraid to ask herself why she avoided Jamaica, but could not escape the fact that she considered Jamaica to be part of a terrible past that she was loathe to visit. Comfortable in her new life, she resisted dragging any vestige of the past into it.

The McMann family quickly adapted to house hunting on Sunday mornings instead of going to church. So much to do, so little time! One day they looked at a house in Hayward. Daisy fell in love with the place. They settled on a price of $15,000, found a lender, and closed escrow. Owning a home was no longer a dream.

Daisy exulted in the achievement and Linton's chest swelled every time he thought of it. They went to dinner at The Castaway, an expensive restaurant in Jack London Square, to celebrate. Linton had never imagined himself in such a position and he revelled in it. He organized a housewarming party and even considered hiring a band.

With their belongings packed in boxes, and the move imminent, Daisy received a person-to-person phone call from Jamaica. Rose was on the line. Shocked to hear her mother's voice Daisy's ecstatic mood turned somber.

"Daisy," Rose articulated, "yuh mus' come see me. De Doctor sey me have uterine cancer. Him sey me only have a few month lef'… Daisy?... Daisy?"

Dazed, Daisy leaned heavily against the kitchen sink. She felt sick to her stomach.

XIII

JULY 1964, HAYWARD, CALIFORNIA

Linton, Samson, and Magdelene watched Samson's brand new red, white and blue Lionel train speed around a circular track in the living room of their new home. Lost in the pleasure of the train, they were startled by a series of sharp explosions near the front yard. Daisy came into the room, her face pinched with worry. Linton suspiciously peeked out the window. A group of teenage boys, tossing lit M-80s, marched down the street carrying an American flag.

"Firecrackers," he said, stating the obvious.

"I hate those beastly things!" Daisy cried, disappearing again. Linton followed through the kitchen and into the backyard.

"You okay?" he asked. "The look on your face could draw blood from a stone."

Daisy sat down at the picnic table. On it, stretching on a long cord through the kitchen window, sat the telephone. She glanced at it. "I just talked to Iris. She is arriving in Kingston three days after we do."

Sighing, Linton put his arm around Daisy and held her tight. "We're going to take care a everything, don't worry."

He kissed her on the forehead and they went back inside

just as the doorbell rang. The Anthony clan came into the living room: George, Ethel, George Jr., and the newest addition, Anne, who was barely old enough to walk. Georgie came to a standstill when he saw the train set and releasing his father's hand, sat down next to Samson. The boys, best friends, became immediately engrossed in a discussion about electric train technology. Magdelene, delighted to have a real baby to play with, took little Anne into her bedroom, and the women moved Tupperware bowls filled with food from the kitchen to the backyard. Soon, meat sizzled on the grill, the patio was filled with the aroma of food, and the families were gathered at the table, eating, talking and enjoying a typical all-American Fourth of July barbecue. After a sumptous meal, while the women prepared dessert and afternoon snacks, Linton and George moved a couple of lawn chairs to the front lawn to visit in the relative quiet.

"Welcome to de American Dream!" Linton declared.

George stretched back in his chair, eyes closed, basking in the sun. "I don't know 'bout dat, Linton. I'm busy chasing me own dreams."

"I have been a citizen of this country since 1951," Linton continued, "and in less than the ten years since I stood in that ceremony and took the oath, I have become somebody. I have a wife and two children who love me, own my house, own a business, and best of all, I make enough to support my family and still save money.

"Come on Linton! You were *somebody* years ago when I met you at Penn Station in '46."

"Don't misunderstand me. You can't deny that in this society, a man must provide for himself and his family. I couldn't support myself then." He paused. "*I was nobody.* And dere was no hope of my ever becoming somebody in Jamaica. But here," he thumped his chest, "I am a new man. I work for myself. To own the means by which you make a living is a great deal. I'm even thinking of expanding my operation and setting up a plant on the East Coast. It's what I love about America ––about being American. I don't miss Jamaica. Time is wasted there; things are far too slow. You dare not reach higher than the class you're born in. That leads to lack of ambition." Linton slammed his fist gently into his palm.

"Ambition, for what?" George asked bluntly. "To dream of making money? Did you hear what you just said? You have it all backwards, mon."

"I don't buy all this modern day beatnik shit about free love and sharing with your brother. Everything in this world cost money, George, and everything has a price."

"Happiness can't be bought!" George retorted.

"Happiness may not have a price, but when the chips are down, having cash insures that I can choose my misery." Linton grinned, satisfied with having made a joke of it all.

"*Rasclat!* It's not funny, Linton."

"Yeah––well," Feeling uneasy, Linton changed the subject, "We going to Jamaica next week."

"Wow!" George sat up. "Your first trip back since independence?"

"Yeah mon, taking the whole family. I want them to see Jamaica, and... I want them to meet their grandmother, Rose, Daisy's mother. She's sick."

"Anyone from your side of the family still in Jamaica??"

"No, my mother's been dead a long time," Linton said.

"Sisters, uncles, aunts?"

"No. I had a brother, but he's dead now."

He glanced at George, who was watching him. Linton felt a pang of conscience. He had seldom talked about his life in Jamaica and even less often shown any interest in knowing about George's life.

As if to make amends he asked, "How's the construction business treating you?"

"I've been working on a bridge in Oakland, on the MacArthur Freeway, but like you, I'm tired of taking orders. I'd love to start my own company."

"You goin' start a business?"

George looked discouraged. "The banks won't even consider giving me a business loan, not to start an engineering firm. But they'll loan me money to start a gas station."

"Racist bastards. When I return from Jamaica let's talk about it. Maybe there's something we can do." Linton looked at his watch. "We better get inside, George, before the women start to feel ignored."

When darkness fell, they regrouped in the front yard. The children played with sparklers and the men lit fountains that shot multicolored sparks into the air. From nearby yards bottle rockets screamed overhead, exploding in mid-air to the amazement of the children. Up and down Bayview Street families and friends had gathered to celebrate Independence Day. The smell of gunpowder hung in the air, phantoms danced before geysers of fiery sparks, and firecrackers exploded. Laughter echoed throughout the neighborhood. Over the bay, municipal fireworks began.

Linton's arm was draped around Daisy. Her mind was engaged with the challenges awaiting in Jamaica. "Happy Fourth, baby," he said. "Maybe later we can make fireworks of our own." His smile was meant only for her.

She snuggled closer. They felt like Americans more than ever.

XIV

JULY 1964, KINGSTON JAMAICA

The once cluttered room was nearly empty and where the old furniture had stood was distinctly outlined on the drab gray wallpaper. Two teenage girls stood next to the bed, where Rose lay dying of cancer.

"So, is de big day." Rose scrutinized the girls, looking for flaws. "Lissette, go change yuh socks to white, me tell yuh again and again, is white yuh fe wear wit' de yellow dress." Lissette hurried off to change her socks.

Janet sat down on the edge of Rose's bed, anxiously picking at blanket lint. "DearMa, I used to believe Daisy's letters, dat say she comin' soon. It's been years since I care. Now she comin' an' I'm scared. I don't know who she is. The only thing me can remember is a white dress with red dots."

"Yes. De dress she wore de day she left fe New York." Rose smiled when Lissette returned, wearing white socks. "I tell yuh girls dat she comin' back one day to take you with her."

"When I get to California, what I want to see is snow," Lissette declared. "I hear dem have snow inna California an' dat is what I wan' see."

"Snow an' beach, desert and mountain, I hear they have it all," Rose replied.

Janet shifted her weight back and forth nervously. "I wish de two other pickney weren't coming. It's the first time me see--*Mummy* in so long." She felt strange calling Daisy Mummy, but was trying her best to become accustomed to it. "I wanted her to ourselves."

"Is yuh sister an' bredda. They are part of yuh," Rose answered. "I promise, you girls will get enough of yuh mother."

"I've been dreamin' bout this day forever." Lissette looked at a picture of Daisy. She was eleven months old when her mother left and had no memory of the woman.

"I used to dream," Janet retorted. "Remember the packages we used to get and the letters? But it all stopped once she met *him*."

Rose raised her voice in protest, "Janet, how many times --"

"DearMa," Janet cut her off, "it's true, yuh tell us many times dat Daisy never forget us, that she loves us. But how long can I go on believing *that* with nothing but a phone call or letter every month? Sure, she remembers our birthdays and Christmas, sends money, but that's about it."

Rose sighed. Janet was right, and despite her best efforts to shield the children from her own opinions, both girls sensed that she agreed with them.

Janet hesitated. She was angry, afraid, and yet couldn't wait to be wrapped in her mother's arms. "I'm not sure," she admitted. "You're the only mother I know." Janet hugged her grandmother carefully and left her alone in her room. Rose, once so robust and strong, had become tiny and frail with illness.

Rose let out another deep sigh. She leaned heavily into the

pillows and stared at her bony feet, sticking out from under the white sheet. She put on reading glasses and retrieved a letter sent by her physician. Brief and to the point, it said that based on her symptoms, it was uterine cancer.

The first time she read that the shock sent tingles up and down her spine. It said she had six months to live. She'd stumbled to the sofa, feeling as if she had awakened from a strange and frightening dream. She told no one of the contents, but a few days later she hemorrhaged and was hospitalized. The cancer was far worse than the doctor had realized. He revised his prognosis. She would not likely survive three months.

Uterine cancer. Since there was nothing they could do, they sent her home.

Overnight, plans became a call to arms. Rose was broke. The ice business had collapsed with the arrival of refrigeration sixteen years ago, and when Wilbur fell ill, she had sent him to Miami for treatments, paying for it by first mortgaging, then losing the house. She had continued to live in the house ever since, as a tenant.

Rose was deeply disappointed about Daisy's treatment of her daughters. She always talked highly of Daisy to the children, but she knew the girls loved her, not Daisy, as they would love a mother. She had nurtured the hope that everything would work out. But the years dragged on and the girls' memories of their mother, already based on little more than the checks that arrived every eight weeks, grew dim; keeping the faith proved impossible. Then cancer shattered what little sense of security the children felt. It crushed Rose's hopes for her granddaughters.

She rolled over, sleepy and fatigued, and disappeared into a narcotic dream. A little later Callie tiptoed in and covered her with a thin cotton sheet. It was hot. A small, battered fan whirred faithfully in the corner of the room. Sitting down next to the bed, Callie opened the Bible, kissed an amulet hanging around her neck, and began to read.

Flying over the Caribbean sea, they saw the island of Jamaica emerge from beneath the placid waters, its green mountains rising like emeralds on an endless blue horizon.

The plane began to descend. The seat belt lamps flashed, prompting Samson and Magdelene to crane their necks, trying to glimpse the terrain below. Billowing clouds passed by the airplane window. Banking for its final approach to Kingston's Palisadoes Airport, the plane dipped, allowing them to see the cars moving along the roads. Linton watched his children, then looked out the window at Jamaica. Why was he so tense?

The plane touched down and the McManns were soon standing outside the terminal, luggage in hand, assaulted by the humid heat and the taxi drivers looking for fares. Linton, his jaw slack as in a trance, was engulfed by a wave of emotion. The ghosts of his past were here, and they joined the parade as he passed through the gate. Around him people shouted and haggled over money. Then Daisy's voice, pestering him to hurry, penetrated his wall of defense, prompting him to take action. Motioning to a driver, they loaded the baggage and in minutes were racing down the Palisadoes peninsula, bound for Beeston Street.

Sand dunes and water were visible from both sides of the road. In the distance hills appeared, which seemed to relax Linton. He smiled.

"How does it feel to be back, Daisy?"

"Too soon to tell." She looked across the bay toward Kingston and despite the heat, shivered.

The taxi turned left, leaving the peninsula behind, racing west along Port Royal Road. It slowed down as it passed through Rockfort; the road was teeming with man and beast. The automobile traffic was so heavy that at every intersection, a policeman directed flow.

"Daddy, is everyone here black?" Samson stared out the car window, astonished to see such a spectacle. He studied everything, trying to keep mental notes of everything he saw.

Linton chuckled. "You're in God's country now, boy." He looked towards the hills. Melancholy swept across his face.

"What?" Daisy touched his arm tenderly.

"Just thinking."

Daisy flashed a half-hearted grin. They continued into the crowded streets of downtown Kingston. The car swung into Beeston Street and there it was, her two-story childhood home. Her heart leapt, the cab stopped, the driver jumped out and opened the passenger door.

Getting out, Daisy blinked in the bright sunlight. The door to the house opened and a huge, smiling, still lean, six-foot man came bounding out.

"Miss Daisy, it's me, Grapples!" The old man hugged Daisy,

shook Linton's hand and made a funny face at the two children.

"Grapples!" she cried.

"Gwan upstairs, all of yuh!" Grapples said, waving them away. "I'll bring up de bags."

At the top of the stairs Callie waited, grinning, her short hair, plump belly, and wide hips, shaking as she jumped up and down. The sisters shrieked with laughter and hugged. Daisy squeezed Callie, thrilled to see her, but could only think of her two daughters. Where are they? Daisy wondered, looking down the hall.

"Callie, dis is me husband, Linton, and Samson and Magdelene."

Someone tapped Daisy's shoulder. She turned and to her surprise, it was Sally Maud. Daisy could hardly believe her eyes. Sally was very old but looked younger than her age. Her cheeks swelled as she grinned, throwing herself around Daisy.

"Welcome home," Sally said.

But as Daisy embraced Sally, she was scanning the room, looking helpless and lost. Callie could see the destitution in Daisy's eyes.

"In Mummaa's room," Callie whispered, giving Daisy a nudge. "Go see dem alone."

With her heart in her throat, Daisy walked slowly down the hall, each step echoing off the walls and filling her ears. Placing her hand on the doorknob, she took a deep breath and opened the door. She was startled to see a young woman, no longer a child, but a blossoming sixteen-year-old girl.

Janet stared at Daisy, in amazement.

"Janet, is that you?"

The youth could not utter a word.

"Janet!" Rose exclaimed from where she lay in bed, "is yuh mudda!"

"My little girl!" Daisy picked Janet up, swinging her around in circles. She felt her daughter's tears dampening her blouse. Tears streamed down her own face.

"Mummy?" Janet pronounced the word like someone who tries on a brand new dress.

"Yes, baby, is me." She held Janet at arm's length. "You're so grown up, let me look at you." She looked Janet up and down, turning her around, pawing at her hair, and then burst out laughing, again hugging and kissing the girl. "You're beautiful."

Janet glanced at Daisy, then quickly looked away. "Thank you––Mummy." Janet's face was calm, but she clenched her teeth in frustration. She stared across the room, afraid that what she might say would bring her mother discomfort, or worse, offend her. Daisy just carried on talking, unaware, or worse, refusing to acknowldge her daughter's tepid response.

"Where's Lissette?" Daisy asked abruptly, as if noticing for the first time that she was absent.

"In the cellar... hiding...." Janet's voice was barely audible.

"Go get her," Rose said. "She always a go down dey."

With Janet gone and the door closed, Daisy became aware of Rose's heavy hoarse breathing. "Oh Mummaa." Rose had become so small and fragile, Daisy barely recognized her. But the sour expression on Rose's face was familiar. She sat down on the edge of her mother's bed, anticipating a barrage of invective.

"Have yuh no shame?" Rose said, her forehead furrowed in disgust.

"Shame? Oh God! Listen to––"

"*God?*" Rose's face grew tight with anger. "Yuh? Yuh nuh fear God. Look at how yuh treat yuh own pickney dem. Fourteen long years, Daisy! The last time yuh stood before me was 1950. Yuh must tink we stupid. As soon as yuh take up wit––"

There was a timid knock at the door and Janet walked in.

"Go 'way!" Rose spat the words from her mouth like bullets from a gun. Immediately Janet disappeared, closing the door.

"Since meeting dis Linton," Rose resumed, "yuh plan fe leave yuh pickney 'ere. Is wrong, Daisy, wrong! Me hear yuh have big business inna California. Iris call me, tell me say, yuh a buy 'ouse. A 'ouse! *Bombo!* Me abandon yuh?"

"What did Iris say?"

Ignoring Daisy's question, Rose continued the tirade. "How can yuh forget yuh two daughters? Is like yuh a reptile, yuh jus' lay yuh eggs and go? A leave pickney fe fend for dem-selves?" Rose halted, exhausted by the rush of emotions.

"What did Iris say?" Daisy could hardly believe her ears. Iris had promised absolute confidence. She had trusted Iris not to tell anyone about their puchasing a home. Iris had betrayed her. A hot rush of anger surged through Daisy.

"Yuh buy 'ouse! Wha' yuh tink she sey?" Rose's mouth was turned in disgust. "It mus' be more important dan yuh pickney, dem. Yuh a liar, 'bout yuh have no space."

"*Now* we have space fe dem... an' we workin' on getting dem––"

"Workin? *Rahtid!* I shoulda know yuh plannin on leavin' dem. Yuh can't do dat Daisy. Dey no time lef', me gone soon! Dem haffi leave, yuh know me payin rent and dere will be no place fe dem fe stay. Callie's husband crippled an' dem is living on barely nothin'. Him make a likkle from his art, but dem can't feed two more mouths."

Daisy's mind was racing, her stomach was tied into a knot. There was a clatter at the door and Janet stood there stiffly, Callie right behind her.

"Lissette won't come out. She inna de cellar," Callie told them.

A chill ran down Daisy's spine. "Then I'll go to her," she said.

By the time she reached the cellar door, Daisy's heart was pounding. It felt as if it would leap from her chest, sprout wings and fly away like a doctor bird. Her stomach groaned. The cellar door was open, but rather than light flowing in, the darkness seemed to spill out. The darkness was so silent, impenetrable and frightening that it made Daisy dizzy. She held onto the door jamb for support and leaned inside.

"Lissette!" Daisy called. "It's your mother, Lissette, it's Mummy."

Silence.

Daisy's first step into the cloying darkness was tentative. With each step the wood creaked and moaned, complaining of her weight. For an instant she smelled the mansweat, looked into Wilbur's cold eyes, and suffered the mental anguish that comes from being helpless. Yet, with her heart rising in her throat, she continued her descent, all the while whispering loudly, "Lissette, where are you? It's Mummy." Reaching the bottom of the stairs, Daisy pulled the chain, switching on the lightbulb, flooding the room with light.

Lissette looked at her mother. Before Daisy stood a tall

and slender dark-skinned girl who looked just like her. Daisy let out a gasp.

"Lissette!" She hugged and kissed the fourteen-year-old. "Lissette," Daisy said, "I missed you so much!"

"Mummy?" Lissette could hardly believe her ears. "Yuh miss me fe true?"

"Of course," Daisy said, taking Lissette by the hand. "Come on, baby, let's go join de others."

"Wait," Lissette yanked her hand free and smiled coyly. "We comin' to California fe true?"

Daisy turned to Lissette and cradled her face.

"We goin' work somepin out. But now it's time for yuh fe meet the biggest surprise of all, yuh new brother and sister!" Together they hurried up the stairs, forgetting to turn the light off and leaving the door to the cellar wide open.

Callie, Samson, and Magdelene were in Rose's room. Linton, in the kitchen with Sally, sat at the kitchen table while she turned to the task of cleaning ackee with a sharp knife. Daisy had swept by him on her way downstairs to fetch Lissette. He was mute, waiting for her to return, and nearly jumped out of his skin when Grapples stuck his head into the kitchen and announced he was going to the store. Alone with Sally once again, the only sound between them was the shucking of the ackee. From down the hall he heard Rose express her delight in meeting Samson and Magdelene. Wiping the sweat from his brow, he stared into space, his back turned to Sally. In the kitchen doorway, Callie materialized before him.

"Welcome, Linton. It got a little hectic in the hallway." She extended her hand. "I'm Callie, an' dat's Mrs. Maud,"

"Linton McMann," he lightly shook Callie's hand and turned for the first time to look at Sally. He nodded his head, acknowledging her.

"Do you care to come and meet my mother?"

Struck by her reserve, Linton was at first taken aback.

Barely audible, he said, "I'm waiting for Daisy."

"Thirsty?"

"No, thanks." With that, Callie disappeared in the hall.

She reappeared shortly, with Janet. Callie introduced them. He was struck by the longing in the child's eyes, sensed her desire to impress him, to be accepted, to be loved. It moved him, but his feelings were tempered by his own doubts, making him appear hesitant and awkward.

"Mr. McMann," Janet said, extending her hand. "After all these years I'm happy to meet you."

"Likewise," Linton replied. He was at a loss for words and felt like he was swimming against a powerful current that threatened to suck him down. "You are so pretty, Janet, and polite." He could think of little else to say.

The uncomfortable moment was relieved when Daisy and Lissette came noisily into the kitchen.

"Oh--good. You've all introduced yourselves. Lissette, this is your stepfather, Linton."

Lissette smiled and shook Linton's hand with such enthusiasm that he forgot his awkwardness and returned her wide grin.

"C'mon," Daisy said to Linton, "is time for you to meet Mummaa."

At Rose's bedroom door the older girls stared at their little siblings. Samson was on the bed, next to Rose, and Magdelene was curled up in her grandmother's arms. Daisy gently nudged Janet and Lissette forward. "Samson, Magdelene, it's your two big sisters here." Samson jumped off the bed and hugged first Janet, then Lissette, and each warmly responded to his embrace. But Magdelene stared at them and tucked a little more deeply into her grandmother's arms.

Callie stepped forward and reached to lift Magdelene from the bed. "It's time for the little ones to eat." She glanced at Janet and Lissette. "That include big pickney as well."

Everyone tromped out of the bedroom, leaving Rose, Daisy, and Linton behind. As soon as the door closed, Rose's smile evaporated, the light conversation shattered by Rose's sharp voice.

"So? What's de plan?"

"Mummaa!" Daisy sounded shocked. "I'd like you to meet my husband, Linton. Linton this is my mother, Rose Wellstead."

"How do you do, ma'am," Linton said unenthusiastically.

Rose paused and smiled, nodding her head, acknowledging Linton's presence. "Now we dispense with de formalities, I'll repeat de question. What's the plan?"

"The girls will be coming to California soon. There are just a few difficulties left," Linton said.

Rose raised her eyebrow. "De new 'ouse nuh large enough?"

"Everything is moving as quickly as possible," Linton went on. "The immigration lawyer will get in touch with you. That's why we are going to make sure they have everything provided for them by the time we leave."

"Ohhh! I thought dem was leavin' with you," Rose exclaimed, "Wha' dem need before dem leave Jamaica?"

"We can only move as fast as the system will allow," Linton said, avoiding her question. "Now if you will excuse me." Linton gave an abbreviated nod of his head and left.

Rose glared at Daisy. "Him mus' tink me *really* stupid!" she said. "If you had already done all the things him a talk about me girls woulda be inna California by now. I know his type," she said. "Him remind me a Anancy de spider. Cunning promises that be broken."

"Mummaa, you just don't understand."

"Gal stop! Yuh think I'm a idiot?! Dem girls dem a yuh flesh an' blood. Him marry yuh, him marry yuh flesh an' blood. I can't believe yuh woulda sell yuh children dem out like––"

"Sell out?" Daisy was incredulous.

"Compromise everything but yuh children. Yuh should tell him, marry me, an' yuh marry dem." She shrugged her shoulders. "I seen it all before."

"You should see how we try, and then de money––"

"Liar!" Rose shouted. "De money, de money! They don't need money, dem need yuh. Get out a me sight!"

Wounded, Daisy wheeled around and left the room.

When Daisy awoke in the hot, sticky darkness, she found that Linton, too, was awake. The bed sheets lay in a heap on the floor. They were no longer acclimated to the heat and humidity.

"What are you doing '?" she mumbled.

"Is too hot to sleep. I was thinking."

"'Bout what?" Daisy yawned.

"I'll get an immigration lawyer. We're going to get them in California. But they can't come right away, you know."

"Why?"

"Daisy, they might have to wait a couple years. We have to expand Family Roots. It's going to require money to do that and extra work for both of us."

Years! Daisy couldn't believe what she heard. "What do you want them to do in the meantime? My mother won't be here for much longer."

"I know. I know we mus' get dem a place to live." Linton was irritated by Daisy's rapid fire inquiry. "You asking too much questions!"

"Damn right. We need to get this straightened out. They're children, and I can't jus' leave them with anybody. My mother all over me about it."

"I've got problems too, you know," Linton replied. "It's hard being here. Seeing Kingston makes me yearn for Andrew. The mountains remind me of Sheila. And there's my father; I have to go to Portland Cottage. Maybe I can find the answer to my question there."

"What question?"

Linton paused, "Oh, forget it."

"We'll come with you."

"No."

"Why? The kids should meet him. He's their grandfather!"

"Are you crazy! The pickney not comin' and that's final. I

have to go. *Alone.* There are things I must find out--by myself."

Daisy didn't press. This trip was proving to be more difficult for Linton than she had thought it would be. She harbored questions about Sheila, about her terrible demise, and longed to know if her spell still lingered over Linton. But she dared not ask, for other than sharing the formula, Linton barely spoke of Sheila. She remained mysterious and shrouded, and Daisy had always wanted an opportunity to take a closer look.

She rubbed Linton's back and in a small, sad voice asked: "Linton, do you love me?"

Linton laughed. "Daisy! You are my woman from now until forever, of course I love you!" He kissed her deeply, then, with a slap on her bottom and a grin on his face said, "Don't worry 'bout me." He collected some fresh clothes. "I'm going out for a walk."

Daisy watched as he dressed and left the room, neither saying another word.

Closing the door behind him, an emotional wave crashed over Linton. Struggling to maintain his composure, he walked down Beeston Street in the predawn light, thinking about Sheila and her untimely death in Bessanworse. He pictured the raging river and relived the anguish of that fateful day. Tears stung his eyes. He felt like a helpless robot who could do nothing but march toward his fate. As he drew near to Parade Square, he saw a woman holding a young child and his attention shifted to memories of his own mother. He barely remembered her smell, her soft skin. It grieved him that he could not recall the sound of her voice.

Mommy. Sorrow so acute it stabbed his heart. He remembered the dark evening of his mother's nine-night funeral celebration. The mento band played and people danced, drinking and smoking, having a great time. But Linton, crushed by his mother's death, retreated into silence. Seeing the boy's sadness, Timothy sat with him, putting his arm around the little boy, prompting him to relax, letting his emotions take him to tears.

The memory of that night left Linton reeling. Strange, he reflected, how a memory could cause an adult to respond with the sense of abandonment and terror of a six-year-old child. Throughout all of the time he had spent with Timothy in May Pen and Bessanworse, he had not remembered the man's efforts to console him when he was a bereft child.

Entering the park, he sat down on a bench. Dawn touched the horizon with its red glow, and warm tradewinds enveloped him, yet he felt stiff as though from cold. Across the way he saw the black, gold and green Jamaican flag fluttering atop the flagpole. He thought proudly of Andrew.

God, he missed his brother! Shopkeepers began to open their doors, people took to the streets, and more cars appeared. He stared at the line of idle taxis. He checked his wallet. He had plenty of money.

Despite pronouncements from Linton, Daisy found it impossible to keep from obsessing over Janet's and Lissette's situation. She tossed the options back and forth, with only one result: increasing confusion. She could not understand her own detachment. She cared about her older daughters, but had conceded her hope of ever raising them long ago. In an occasional unguarded moment she admitted to herself that it was easier that way.

The day before, when she had greeted Janet with a hug, Daisy felt acutely aware of the gulf between them, confirming her deepest guilt. They were no longer her children. Biology was all that bound them. Shame swept through her. She took out her rosary, turned the black beads over in her hands, contemplating the crucifix. She no longer attended church regularly. Frowning, she took a deep breath, walked over to the open window, and flung the rosary as far as she could. For years she had depended on church teachings to help her sort it out. But in spite of her prayers, her votive candles, and her endless recitation of the rosary, her emotions remained hopelessly tangled. If anything, she suffered now more than ever.

The first rays of sunshine breached the window, brushing her face. Where was Linton? Am I too hard on him? she wondered. He's been through so much. She got dressed and left the house, walking toward Parade. Why am I so uneasy? In all of their years together Daisy had never gone out looking for him. When she reached the park, she spied Linton getting into a taxi.

"Linton!" Daisy cried, running toward him.

He rolled down the window. "I'll be back."

"When?"

"In a day or two!" With that, he tapped the driver on the shoulder and the vehicle lurched out into traffic.

"Wait!" Daisy yelled, trotting next to the car. "Where you going? Can't I go with you?"

"No!" He leaned forward and said something to the driver and the taxi pulled away, leaving Daisy in a cloud of exhaust, hands on her knees, gasping in an effort to catch her breath.

He needs me, she thought. Damn it, he needs me! Feeling abandoned, she watched the cab until it disappeared from view.

Callie lived in a pleasant, modest, yellow and white cottage, on a quiet dead end street across from an open field. After enjoying a splendid lunch, she and Daisy sat on the porch drinking cold glasses of plum juice while Callie's husband, Colin, and Magdelene napped inside. From their vantage point, they could watch Samson play soccer with some neighborhood boys in the street. Across the way, in the field, a dust cloud approached.

"Cattle," Callie explained. "I love livin' 'ere. They drive them through every day around this time."

Long-horned zebu meandered down the street, led by a man carrying a stick. The boys stopped playing and watched the procession. The livestock ambled past, through a gate held open by the herder.

Observing her sister, Callie wondered if Daisy would burst into tears. She suspected that Daisy's sadness was not because of her daughters' plight, but was something far darker. But Callie held a secret of her own, one she dared not divulge to anyone. The thought of sharing it with Daisy had crossed her mind, but Callie remembered well how her sister might react and she discarded the idea.

Still, she was curious about Daisy and finally asked, "What's botherin' yuh?"

"Linton. He took off this morning," Daisy said. "He's

upset 'bout everything: his father, his brother... my daughters. Coming here only reminds him of tragedy." She stopped, her throat too constricted to go on.

"Hello dey!" a cheerful voice interrupted, and a woman carrying a baby walked up to the house. "I'm here to pick up my package, Miss Callie." She came up the stairs and dropped some coins into Callie's outstretched hand. Callie got up and disappeared into the house.

"Yuh 'ere fe Miss Callie?" the woman asked. She leaned forward and whispered, "Callie a de bes' inna dis 'ere part a Kingston. She makes de bes' love potion, me a tell yuh!"

Reappearing with a small paper sack, Callie handed it to the woman and bade her farewell.

"What was that about?" Daisy asked.

"Nothing , it's just a woman come for some bush medicine."

"Bush medicine? She told me it was a love potion."

Callie's expression became indignant. "Is none a yuh business," she snapped.

"Well I don't like obeah, nor the people that practice it. An' apparently you practice obeah. And you are my sister, so now it become my business."

"If you don't like it, then leave me!"

Magdelene came to the door, rubbing the sleep from her eyes. Daisy stood up. "I'm leavin' right now! Samson!" she yelled, pulling on Magdelene's hand. "You consort with the devil to make some money. Have you no shame? Will yuh do anything for money?"

"I know yuh abandon yuh own pickney for money!" Callie stood up.

"Yuh jealous a me, Callie. You always have been and you always will be. I have a husband who works to make a good livin'. An yuh goin' to hell for money!"

"Who do you think you are, Daisy? You're just like the rest of Jamaicans who leave and then come back thinking they're better than us. Yuh no better dan me or anyone else here. I don't care how much *more* yuh have, is *yuh who going live inna hell*!" Callie shouted. "*Yuh* should be ashamed. *Yuh* abandon yuh own daughters! Me, jealous of yuh? Nah suh! *Bumboclat!*"

By this time, Daisy was almost running down the sidewalk, holding her children's hands. Stung, she swore never to forgive Callie for talking about her in front of them.

Callie watched until Daisy got into a taxi. A stupid, selfish woman, Callie thought, and I was considering trusting her. I'm glad I didn't tell her a thing.

The road to Portland Cottage mirrored the Salt River, an aqua blue swath cut through sunburnt landscape. Linton's chest grew tight as they drew closer to the Blaine Estate. He asked the cabbie to stop at a roadside tavern, where he quickly drank two shots of rum. Inhaling deeply, he observed his surroundings. He had changed, but the land was still the same: hot, flat, dry, denuded fields fresh from the harvesting of sugar cane. Strings of women walked along the roadside. Groups of men, gathered under gnarled acacia trees, passed the time while the hot sun journeyed towards the horizon. Blasted idlers, he thought.

"Yuh ready fe move on boss?"

The driver looked at his watch, irritating Linton. He gave the cabbie a dirty look and ordered another shot. "You don't need to fret," Linton said. "I'll pay for all of your time."

After nursing the drink, Linton got into the taxi and they continued to Portland Cottage. Shortly, the three familiar hills appeared on the horizon. As they drew closer, trees obscured his view of the Estate. What would he find? Would he be allowed inside? Would Major finally acknowledge him as his son? And the question that loomed largest for Linton: did any of this matter?

The taxi came to a sharp bend in the road and Linton directed the driver to pull over. Hastily opening the door, he jumped out. The cabbie, watching as Linton stormed through the underbrush, shook his head. Jamaicans coming back to visit were amongst his most troublesome customers, demanding the greatest patience.

The wrought iron gate that opened to the Estate driveway was gone. Near it were remnants of the well-traveled path. To the left, the bare earth was littered with the tattered remains of burnt cane. As Linton rounded a bend, what he saw brought him to a standstill.

The great house was in ruins. The servants' quarters, Elysian Fields, were gone. On the adjoining hill, the cemetery fence had fallen and bushy overgrowth obscured the headstones. The once proud obelisk, marking the mass grave for the Blaine clan members who perished in the Christmas massacre of 1831, leaned at an obscene angle, ultimately destined to come to rest, prone, upon the muddy earth.

Linton walked up the hill to what remained of the mansion. There he found the manicured gardens crushed beneath the constant creep of tropical vegetation. He looked at what used to be the house, its crumbling walls and framework stretched upward like arms reaching for the sky. Half of the building had been badly burnt in a fire. A recent earthquake had collapsed what was left, and all that remained was the chimney, a column of bricks teetering precariously above the wreckage.

The once mighty tree, the tree of life that had dominated the back yard was dead: broken branches and a shattered stump was all that remained. Linton went over to the stump and saw a fresh green shoot growing out of the rotting wood. He kneeled down to take a closer look.

This tree is still alive, Linton marveled. His memories of playing with Andrew underneath the tree began to play out in his mind, bringing a wry smile to Linton's face. The recollections were made bittersweet knowing that Andrew was dead, and probably his father too. I am a Blaine, Linton mused. I'm the *last* Blaine left, Linton realized. He stared at the fragile young sapling, its leaves trembling in the breeze. I'm like this tree, Linton thought, the hidden root that keeps the family alive.

Linton got to his feet, still unable to comprehend the surrounding decay. The extent of the devastation seemed unreal. He thought of looking through the debris, of looking for anything familiar, but only the distant naked cane fields fit his recollection. On the adjacent hill, the cracked concrete foundation was all that remained of the distillery. The caves had all but disappeared. In his mind, he heard Busby and smelled the rum on his hot breath.

Surveying the property from atop the hill, Linton's thoughts turned to the confusion and anger of his youth. Since arriving in Jamaica he'd felt the ghosts of the past dogging his every step, but now he felt alone, more alone than ever in his life. He slowly made his way down the hill. He recognized a few old trees that brought to life afternoons spent playing with Andrew and Sheila, and with the other children who called the old slave quarters home.

Looking at this destitution, he found it hard to believe that twenty-six years earlier, when Major invited him inside the mansion for the very first time, there had been no greater thrill. He remembered the awe with which he'd entered the library. He had so desperately wanted his father's attention. Then a realization struck him like a left jab to his jaw: after all these years, goddamn him, after all these years *I hate him but I still need his approval.*

He reached into his pocket and felt the long brass library key that Major had given him so many years ago. Why is this key so important? he asked himself. He had a sudden impulse to throw it into the bushes. No, he thought, I will wait.

He returned to the taxi and they drove less than a quarter mile before pulling off at the old Chinese grocery, still in business after forty years. Mr. Chao, sitting in a high chair near the open door, recognized Linton immediately. The grizzled old face lit up excitedly and he ushered Linton inside the store. Mr. Chao introduced him to Mitchell, his son, who now ran the grocery. Over Guiness Stouts that Linton bought, they filled in the years for him.

"Major was never de same after the riots in 1938. Him wife Pauline die inna car accident a year later, and den tings really start go downhill. Busby, him dead, an him son Andrew, him nuh interested inna plantation work. Major went a likkle crazy, yuh know." Mr Chao paused. "And den dere was 1957."

"The train wreck, when Andrew died," Linton said.

"And den de earthquake, oh Lawd." Mr. Chao was momentarily lost in memory. "All de caves up dey collapse and half de house tumble down inna sinkhole. After dat him move to May Pen where him have him first stroke. Him been dey ever since. A nurse a look after him."

"When Mr. Blaine leave, squatters looted the place and de house bun down four years ago," Mitchell said. "But worst of all, Mistah Blaine didn't pay him property taxes fe many years," Mitchell shrugged his shoulders. "De government take de land dis year, and dem just sell it off fe pay de taxes. All de cane fields belong to Appleton now. De Blaine Estate is no more."

"Sad," Mr Chao said.

"Is so it go," Mitchell added.

"Is Busby still buried behind the store?"

Mr Chao smiled. "Yes mon! We placed a monument above it with him name. Mr. Blaine paid for dat outta him pocket."

What a kind son-of-a-bitch, Linton thought. He went behind the store and found Busby's grave. A large angel carved from granite was praying atop a large concrete slab. Biting his clenched fist, he found himself once again seized by rage over Busby's untimely death. He was probably the most generous man Linton had ever known, generous and without ulterior motives.

It was getting late and the taxi driver appearing sour and sullen, leaned against the car. Linton returned to the store and asked Mitchell for directions to find Mr. Blaine. Then he thanked him and said goodbye.

The taxi reversed direction, at times slowing to a crawl on the main road, to avoid potholes that sometimes resembled bomb craters. Linton watched the once familiar landscape move past his window.

XV

JULY 1964, MAY PEN, JAMAICA

By the time they arrived in May Pen, it was too late to visit Major. They drove downtown and Linton bought a bottle of rum. He secured a room for the night, gave the cabbie money to get a room himself, and instructed the man when to pick him up in the morning. He stopped somewhere for dinner before returning to the hotel.

Linton sat on the edge of the bed with the open bottle of rum on the night table. He stared through a thick barrel glass, pondering his own emptiness. When he started this journey, he had been full of hope. He'd planned to face down the demons, to transform them through confrontation. But the ghosts of the past were proving mightier than he'd anticipated. He poured another drink, filling the glass to the rim. The alcohol burned his throat, making him recall his very first drink of rum with Major in the library.

He reached an arm around and fingered the scars on his back, still tender after all these years. The scars defined his relationship with his wife, his children, and even his employees. Sometimes he hated himself for his brutality but he would never admit to being too harsh. Once he slapped Samson so hard he drew blood. Linton suffered only a momentary sense of shame at the time, escaping it by blaming the entire affair on Samson's talking too much. In truth he was so ashamed he transferred his embarrassment onto his son. Violence was easy and felt so satisfying. With a pang of guilt he remembered hitting Sheila. Sweet, gentle Sheila who would have done anything he asked to please him. He'd never hit Daisy. His experience with Sheila gradually led him to an epiphany: the thought of a man hitting his mother filled his heart with hatred and he did not want his own children to hate him. He vowed never to touch his lover in anger again. Not that he had not suffered the impulse. He poured another drink and took his time, sipping it uneasily.

Half drunk and annoyed by the humidity, Linton barely slept and in the morning downed four shots of rum before going to meet the taxi. The desk clerk gave him directions to Lillian Lane and a few minutes later the cab pulled up to a small white and green house.

Taking the old library door key from his pocket, he fingered the dull brass, thinking about how he had pined for Major's love. That key was Major's fleeting invitation to Linton to come closer into his life. It was the singular positive experience he could remember between himself and his father. With no positive follow-up, only bitter memories had accumulated. At least Major had tried to accept him, sort of. It didn't work, but that key proved he had tried. Linton gasped. How pathetic that he loved this man, that he had so desperately wanted his father's love that he'd clung to this slight, almost insignificant gesture. But Major was so caught up and bound by what others might think of him, he was never able to be honest, not with himself, not with Pauline, or Misti or Andrew, not with friends and not even with strangers. In his mind, Linton could picture the strapping, tall, light skinned man, his blue eyes coolly observing his bastard child, making his heart jump with hope.

In response to his knock on the door of the green and white house, Linton encountered a short, young, energetic nurse. Her compact body seemed to conceal some kind of high energy spring that she used to propel herself around the room.

"Mr. Blaine hasn't had visitors in years," the woman said, her words coming out in rapid succession. "When his son died he kind of gave up living. He's had several strokes and now is bedridden." She smiled cheerfully. "Are you related? I didn't think he had any living family."

His son. Her words struck Linton like a double edged blade. "No--I'm a friend."

"Well, come, nuh?" The nurse seemed to ricochet off the desk and with a flourish led him down the hall. The shiny linoleum floor tiles sparkled and Linton was impressed with the tidy appearance of the house. "Here we are." The nurse stopped before Major's door. "Dis is Mistah Blaine's room," her voice dropped to a whisper, "can I tell him who is calling?"

"Tell him Linton McMann is here."

The nurse tapped lightly, then disappeared behind the door.

Linton waited, shifting his weight from one foot to the other. He wanted this to be over. His heart seemed to beat weakly in his chest. His head was spinning. There was a loud click as the door opened and the nurse came out.

"I've never seen him excite like dat!" she said. "He can barely talk, so you'll have to bend over to hear him. I told him your name and he lit up."

Linton took the first tentative steps into a simply furnished room. There, in an ordinary bed, lay the stunted frame of Major Blaine, his head propped up on two fluffy pillows. The right side of his face drooped from the strokes. He was almost bald and looked at Linton with watery eyes. Linton was shocked at Major's cadaverous appearance. The once youthful, vibrant skin was sallow and wrinkled, hanging loosely from his bones. His breathing was labored, and yet Major was smiling, his eyes displaying sparks of life. Nearby, an open window admitted a breeze that rustled the curtains and bathed the room in muted sunlight. Linton felt a lump building in his throat.

He fingered the key in his pocket. He had kept it for decades and now could not remember why he'd brought it with him. He saw the nurse still in the doorway, watching, and closed the door, ensuring their privacy.

Major's voice was so feeble, Linton had to put his ear to Major's lips. "My son," he whispered, "my son… my… son… so glad to see you."

"Daddy?" The word popped out, thoughtlessly. Tears stung Linton's eyes. Major was actually crying. Linton touched his father's arm.

"Why?" Linton gently grasped Major's shoulder. "You didn't even tell the nurse, even now you can't acknowledge me."

"I'm sorry… I've been wrong Linton."

"Why you make me wait so long to hear you say that?"

Major shook his head. "You don't understand."

"I understand all too well! You denied it before Andrew."

"I did, and I regret that."

"*Rahtid!* Listen to me, mon! You regret it because Andrew was angry at you. Did you speak before him pass away? Because he knew. You realize that? *I told him.*"

"Please Linton, give me a chance." Major was terrified to see the hatred etched into his son's face.

Hands shaking, Linton undid his shirt, fumbling with the buttons, pulled it off and turned his back to Major.

"My God!" Major gasped, closing his eyes. Memories, long-buried, resurfaced. The insane satisfaction he'd felt flogging his son in a drunken rage.

"*Look at dem!*" Linton hissed. "This how I remember you. *I will never forget.*"

"Forgive me, Linton, please. Forgive me so that I can die in peace. I have nothing left. Only you."

"And now that I am the last, you want to claim me? No, sir. No, sir! I don't want your love. I don't need your love."

Linton put his shirt back on, taking his time to tuck it neatly back into his pants. He withdrew the brass key from his pocket. "Remember this?"

Major examined the key and looked quizzically at Linton.

"That was your one pathetic attempt to be my father. It was the key to your library."

Major smiled. "Yes," he said, "I do remember."

Tears streamed down Linton's cheeks. He took Major's hand into his own, holding the key to his palm.

"That library opened up the world to me. And there was one other thing you did for me. You taught me 'bout rum, and

Aunt Cordy taught Sheila and me 'bout roots. I've started my own business Major, you know that? It's called Family Roots, because the real roots of my family run deep, and are hidden underground. Hidden! And you know what? It's a success! I've gone from rum to roots, from Portland Cottage, Jamaica, to Oakland, California, from being the broke bastard son of a rich plantation owner, to owning my own successful enterprise."

Major appeared to be barely breathing. Linton leaned closer, his voice barely above a whisper. "How can I forgive you, Major? I wanted to tell you to go to hell... and now..."

Linton straightened up. He towered over Major. Time had been cruel enough. Major had nothing left. Struck by the man's emaciated frame and frail limbs, Linton remembered being tied to the tree, his own thin, weak arms holding his limp body against the trunk. I was helpless, Linton thought. But the man who lay before him was no longer the man who flogged him.

It was he now who was helpless.

The whirling thoughts in Linton's head disappeared. He would face it. He still loved Major. An incredible feeling of power took hold of Linton. He gently hugged his father. Linton had done his best to forget, only to discover that he could not. With his father in his arms, it dawned on Linton that it took more strength to care, to love-- indeed, to forgive-- than it did to carry around a festering ball of hatred.

Major tried to speak, tried to reach out, but his arm was spastic, uncontrollably shaking.

"It's all right," Linton whispered, calming the old man. In the silence he held his father's hand. Comforted, Major slept.

Without another word Linton quietly closed the door. In the living room, he asked the nurse if Major needed anything and gave her his mailing address, a wad of money, and left. Getting into the taxi he did not even glance in the direction of the front door. His issues surrounding his father had been cauterized. He lightly tapped his pocket, confirming that the key was still there. Taking a deep breath he smiled. He was free. He ordered the driver to pull over and bought another bottle of rum. As they took off for Beeston Street in Kingston, he drank straight from the bottle.

JULY 1964, KINGSTON, JAMAICA

Fluffy, towering thunderheads floated above a children's amusement park in Kingston. It was a splendid day for a picnic. Janet, Lissette, Samson and Magdelene had finished eating and after packing up, headed home. The older girls had spent the earlier part of the day with their younger siblings, taking them on rides, and playing games of cat and mouse, throwing rings around small bottles, trying to win a prize for Magdelene.

Magdelene did not like what she saw. The livestock wandering the streets, open air markets, pushcarts hawking food, and the dust hovering in the air; so much of it was frightening and made her sick to her stomach. She preferred the clean, orderly existence of her own neighborhood in California.

The general confusion on the streets seemed to excite Samson, however, who kept pointing out things he found strange: goats, gold teeth, the aroma of spices, the lilting accent, and the sheer number of black people surrounding them. His enthusiasm knew no bounds, providing entertainment for Janet and Lissette. Magdelene stayed close to her big brother and regarded Janet and Lissette with great suspicion. It seemed when they were around her mother, they received most of her attention. It had upset

Magdelene from the start, and she immediately reacted with her own attempts to recapture Daisy's attention. But pouting and sulking had no effect, Daisy just continued laughing with the adults and coddling those two girls.

Magdelene looked at her older sisters, sitting across from her on the bus and their eyes met. Janet turned toward Lissette and nodded. Magdelene thought she was competing for Daisy's motherly love. As Janet pointed out, you can't honestly compete for anything with a cute five-year-old. Petite, reserved, and born with an engaging smile, Magdelene appeared to be quite grown-up for her age. But in her silence and indistinct voice was hidden a nasty attitude borne of indulgence.

They got off the bus and walked home. After the picnic utensils were cleaned and put away and Samson and Magdelene were playing dowstairs, Janet sat down at the kitchen table, exhausted.

"I never knew it was so much work to look after pickney," Lissette groaned.

"I nevah meet such a miserable pickney," Janet replied.

"What a *virago*!" Lissette cried. "She's so spoiled!"

"Nothing makes her happy," Janet went on. "I wonder what she's like at home?"

Lissette stood before her sister, thinking of living with Magdelene. "Still," she said to Janet, "I'd love to have a younger sister and brother!"

"You're going to have to wait," Janet said. "You know, I don't believe we're going home with them anymore."

Lissette nodded, her eyes glassy with tears that threatened to overflow and run down her dark cheeks. She had been the optimist, believing that their mother was finally coming to take them home *with* her. Last night, after Janet broke the news to her, she cried, unable to believe that life could be so cruel as to encourage her to entertain hope.

"Lissette," Janet said, "Don't fret. *Is so it go.* After graduation, me should be able to get a job somewhere. But no matter what, we're going to make it."

"But what about my school?" Lissette wiped her tears.

"I'm sure she will continue to send money. We just haffi learn to be content here in Kingston. Daisy has abandoned us."

"What about Aunt Iris? Can't she help?"

Janet shook her head. "Why should she? Aunt Iris and Aunt Callie have been kind, but we have to depend on ourselves. Soon it will only be you and me."

Lissette left for her room and Janet wondered if she really understood the dilemma they could find themselves in.

It was early afternoon and after arriving in Kingston late the previous night, Iris's husband Tom and son Clarence were still fast asleep. Iris, in the living room, readied for a busy afternoon of grocery shopping and work around the house.

"You ready?" Daisy asked, walking in.

Iris sprayed herself with lavender water and looked in a mirror, making sure that her make-up was perfect. "I can't believe it," she said. "I hardly get in the door last night only to find out that you and Callie are quarrelling, Mummaa's mad as hell, refusing talk to anyone, and you have no idea where your husband is. What kind a place is this? What is wrong with everybody?"

"I don't want to have any business with Callie's obeah," Daisy said. "And yuh talk too damn much. Why did you tell Mummaa I bought a house?"

"De pickney is everybody business," Iris hissed. "You can't just leave them here for strangers to take care of. With Mummaa gone what's going to happen to them, eh? Have you thought about that?"

"I'm not just going to leave them here!"

"*Daisy*, Mummaa told me you came here without a plan."

"No!"

"And then you go over to Callie's house and insult her. She's entitled to her beliefs."

"Don't talk to me about her. I don't associate with people like that."

"Daisy!"

"If she want to practice obeah, there's no need for me to speak to her."

"Criticize her if you wish, but she has had to a struggle to raise *every* one a her pickney. You do that? So much sacrifice and you're still not happy."

"I am quite happy."

"Happy with two out a four?" Iris snapped.

"I expected you, of everyone, to understand," Daisy said, her voice dripping with bitterness.

"I understand," Iris sniffed. "But you crossed the line long ago. Plenty people left Jamaica for America and leave their pickney behind and *don't* forget dem. Things are good for you, Daisy. We both have our own businesses and they're thriving, thank God. But you forget and put everyting ahead a your two daughters. I know how important children are. I can't forget, now that I've lost my eldest, Charles. Children are the most precious! You remember saying that Daisy? I remember you saying *exactly* that when you came to New York last year for Charles's funeral? Yeah, you remember then, but now yuh forget, and return to Jamaica with attitude, an'––Daisy, I don't think I ought to say much more." Iris left the room and left Daisy fuming.

It was too much for Daisy to bear. Iris's admonishment hurt. All her life, Daisy had admired her older sister. Indeed, the example Iris set many years ago, leaving Jamaica, getting married and having children while achieving wealth, inspired Daisy to embark on a search that led to her own current lifestyle. Watching her sister cope with losing Charles to a heroin overdose had been heart wrenching. Tears sprang to her eyes. The criticism from her mother and sisters' drove her mad. She saw the skepticism in Janet's eyes and felt both girls' reticence. Her husband had disappeared. With nowhere to turn she went to her room, locked the door, lay down on her old bed and fell asleep.

Some time later a knock at the bedroom door jolted Daisy awake. Linton was finally home. Half drunk, disheveled and tired, he lumbered into the room and sat down on the bed. Daisy wrapped around him, putting her head in his lap.

He saw her red eyes and streaked mascara. "Daisy," he said, caressing her. "I had to go alone. Please try to understand."

"I do, baby," Daisy said. "You all right?"

"I saw my father," Linton declared. "I did what I had to do."

"How is he?"

Linton lips twisted into a tight smile. "Major is behind me." He drew Daisy closer, tentatively tugging her shoulder. "How are things here?"

"No one understands. We aren't going to let de pickney live on de street. They must know that we're going to do something for them." She started crying again and sought the comfort of Linton's arms.

"Have you figured out a plan?"

"I spoke to Miss Maud, she has room at her house in Pembroke Hall."

"That's the nice housing development in north Kingston. Good. We'll give her some money an' everybody's happy. Come on, let's go to bed."

Pembroke Hall was a quiet, relatively modern neighborhood on Annandale Avenue. Linton, Daisy, Janet, and Sally Maud sat on the shaded porch of Sally's house, sipping ice cold sour-sop juice. With her own two children grown, Sally had two bedrooms available and she was happy to invite Janet and Lissette to move in. Daisy was visibly relieved and after working out the details, the only topic to be settled was financial.

"Lawd Jesus, we lucky," Janet said, wiping her brow.

"No, yuh is fortunate," Sally said, looking at Daisy from the corner of her eye. "If yuh mudda was takin' yuh home, den yuh would be lucky."

"Hold on," Linton said. "Everything––"

Daisy slammed her glass down on the table so violently the

drink slopped onto the table. "I didn't come here to be lectured. Miss Maud, I appreciate what you're doing, but I plan to compensate you for the trouble."

Sally snorted. "Yuh jokin'. I don't expect clean wine from a dutty bottle. You don't have to pay me a thing."

"How dare you! I try to better meself in order to help me pickney and all I hear when I come back is how me abandon them, how I don't love them." Daisy gestured wildly toward Janet. "Is me flesh an' blood, me nuh abandon no one!"

"Lef' behind fe de younger two," Sally went on, her face hard as stone. "I'm old enough to tell yuh de truth. Yuh shouldn't lie to yuh pickney. Yuh tell Janet you buy a 'ouse?"

"Jealousy!" Daisy narrowed her eyes. "I see it in all your eyes here in Jamaica. A real envy!"

"Bumboclat!" Sally's voice was sharp as the crack of a rifle. "So many lef' dis 'ere island and forget dem pickney. I would show shame when I returned, not be so proud and boasy. Yuh have no conscience. Dem yuh pickney, dem can't say it, but I will. You is too out of order! I know you since you were born, and it's long overdue for you to feel remorse."

Daisy sprang up from the table, rising so fast the glass crashed to the floor and shattered. "It's time to go," she said, quickly descending the porch steps.

Reluctant to enter the dispute, Linton chased after Daisy and summoned their taxi. When it pulled up, Janet was standing on the porch with Sally. "You best get down 'ere now!" Daisy yelled.

Janet hesitated, urged by Sally to go. Janet got into the cab and they took off.

"I'll never be so happy to leave this God forsaken place," Daisy sputtered as the cab drove back to Beeston Street. Linton sat in the front seat, staring at the passing traffic, while Janet, seated next to Daisy in back, kept her head down.

"She must think she's my mother," Daisy continued. Then, without warning, she slapped Janet's face. "And you, standing there after she insults me. All of you are ungrateful brutes, that's what every one a yuh is!" She yelled at Linton as though he was two cars ahead, and not in the front seat. "Call up de ticket office an' let's leave early! I had enough a dis 'ere place suh!"

Janet shielded her face with her forearm, her lip smarting and the impact still echoing in her ears. But she knew better than to talk back; one word now would invite a barrage of physical abuse.

Daisy's anger proved impossible to contain. At Beeston Street she went directly to her room and closed the door. Janet found solace with Rose. Sicker than ever and overwhelmed by weakness, Rose nursed her own broken heart and comforted her oldest grandchild, who wept bitter tears.

Later that evening, Linton waited for the Knowles family to return home from visiting friends in Spanish Town. He planned to make a bold move and offer a position to Clarence at Family Roots. The proposition was risky and Linton wasn't sure if Clarence would want to take a chance with him in business. The task of introducing a new beverage in a competitive market like New York would be daunting. Linton sat in the living room, fidgeting, trying to pass the time without looking worried.

"Mistah McMann, Dearma wan' speak to you," Janet said, sticking her head in the door.

Walking down the hall, a heavy silence permeated the house. Once in Rose's room however, Linton found her reading a letter, smiling and cheerful.

Rose removed her reading glasses. She looked at Janet. "Please go and check on de pickney dem," she said, then turned to Linton.

"Why yuh haffi leave early?"

"Daisy feels like she's being persecuted. Yes, we bought a house. We could not have Janet and Lissette come to live in a two-bedroom apartment."

"I understand that,"

"People seem to think that we are rich but we are far from it," Linton went on. "We couldn't send for them. We didn't have enough money when I met Daisy, but I tell you now, them girls is coming to California and soon."

Rose looked at Linton like she was looking at a strange specimen in a lab. "I have no choice but to believe yuh," she said. "Just promise me, yuh won't abandon dem, yuh won't leave dem to de fate dat will be theirs–– two young girls trying fe survive here in Kingston." She took Linton's hand, squeezing it.

"I won't let you down, Mrs. Wellstead."

"I'm relying on yuh mercy and kindness fe dem two," Rose said.

"I promise yuh can depend on me," Linton said. Outside they could hear Iris, Tom and Clarence coming upstairs. He paused, considering whether or not to divulge his plan to Rose.

"I'm expanding the business and opening a plant in New York. All of this will help speed up getting the girls to the States, with us."

"That's wonderful news," Rose said. "I hope it all works out."

Their discussion concluded, Linton moved to the door. Rose asked him to send Iris in. She lay in the bed feeling worn out. Her ability to influence and even sometimes coerce, had come to nothing. She did not believe Linton. Even more heartbreaking was that she did not believe Daisy. Her daughters' plan to leave early had upset Rose terribly. She desperately wanted her three daughters by her side.

In the living room, Linton clapped Tom and Clarence on their backs and offered them drinks.

"Tom, you remember that night at Connie's restaurant?"

"When I offered to finance your new business? I couldn't forget that," Tom said.

"Well I want to return the great favor you gave me. I have a proposition for Clarence." Linton poured three drinks and passed them off. "I want to offer you a job."

Clarence was caught by surprise. "What kind of job? Uncle Linton? In San Francisco?"

"Better." Linton took a long sip, clicking his tongue as he swallowed. "There is a large Jamaican community in New York. The roots sell well in San Francisco and it's tiny by comparison. Help me expand to the East Coast. I'm sure Family Roots will be hot in New York City. I need a point man, someone to help me to organize this thing from the ground up. You interested?"

"Are you kidding? I'd love to do it! I'll quit my current job pronto! When would you want me to start?"

"As soon as you wish. I'll pay you better than what they are giving you and of course I'll give you raises as the company grows. Come on, let's drink to this," Linton said refilling the glasses. "After we get home we'll have some long discussions to work out how to proceed. You can give notice at work. For now I just wanted to know if you were my man." They raised their glasses. "And you are. To the Family." They clinked their glasses, and drank.

The men whiled away the next few hours talking about the Family Roots expansion plans. Linton beamed. These people were his family. Their opinions *mattered.* He basked in the glow of admiration. He looked at Tom and Clarence and thought of Samson's future. There was no doubt looking at Clarence that Samson would get his four year degree one day and be at his side.

In Rose's room, Iris and Rose could hear the men's laughter.

"Mummaa, we've spoken to Daisy till we blue in de face. She won't listen."

Rose sighed. "Still we mus' try again an' speak to her. Maybe a different approach, maybe we listen and let her explain." Rose shifted painfully on the bed. "Lawd knows me nuh have much time lef' an' Callie won't come 'ere unless Daisy is gone. I don't want to quarrel now. No time lef' fe dat. Gwan an' bring Daisy 'ere."

Minutes later, with Daisy in the room and the door closed, Rose launched her appeal to Daisy's reason. There was a hint of desperation in Rose's voice, an urgency that made Iris cringe.

"Look pon me Daisy," Rose said. "We'll never meet like dis again. Me wish Callie was here, but yuh and her fall out and now neither of yuh speakin. Is so it go. But Daisy..." Rose stared into her daughter's eyes, "promise me yuh won't abandon de pickney dem. I cannot res' until I hear dat from yuh."

"Mummaa, I'm telling you, I'm here for Janet and Lissette." Something in Daisy's plaintive tone of voice put Iris in a rage.

"Then take them with you!" Iris cried. "My God, how many times--"

"Hush up, Iris," Rose cut her off and pointed to the door. "Iris, yuh mus' go. Daisy, nah bother worry 'bout no one else. Is between yuh an' me."

Once they were alone, Rose took Daisy's hand. She looked so sad.

"Now, I want you to listen to me carefully," she whispered. "Yuh plannin' to put de girls in Pembroke Hall with Sally. Please, don't leave them there. It's wrong how yuh do dem -- it's wrong I tell yuh." Rose paused to make sure that Daisy was listening.

"I never expected you to stay in Jamaica once yuh got de visa. I never expected yuh to make enough to bring dem dere wit' yuh either." Rose's voice was soft and firm. "But I did expeck yuh to come visit yuh pickney. You sent money but you never came back to visit. You sacrificed yuh pickney fe a better life an' now yuh have it, an' yuh still expect dem to wait. Yuh goin' suffer for that, Daisy. Yuh goin' suffer terrible.

Rose stopped for a moment to breathe deeply, gasping for air, exhausted by the effort to speak. Then she went on.

"My time is come and my life is over. Please don't let dem

two girls down. Watch out fe yuh pickney. Don't sell yuhself fe nothin."

Daisy kneeled next to the bed. "Mummaa, you have to believe me." She gently squeezed Rose's hand. Rose put a finger across Daisy's lips.

"Shhhh! Enough. Jus' draw up a chair and sit wit' me for a while." Rose looked more tired than ever. "I have one las' ting to ask of yuh."

Daisy turned the overhead light off and turned on the lamp, casting a feeble yellow light across the bed. She moved a chair next to the bed, sat quietly.

"Daisy, don't leave yet. Stay a little longer. I'll be soon gone." Rose's voice cracked.

Daisy avoided looking at Rose. The lump in her throat threatened to choke her.

"Mummaa. I have to head home. I'll find a place fe de pickney, and Linton have plenty work waiting fe him in California." Her heart skipped a beat when she saw Rose's disappointed expression.

"Den jus' sit 'ere wit' me." Rose settled into the bed, closing her eyes. Soon she was asleep, her breath rasping in her chest.

Daisy considered telling Rose about what Wilbur had done to her. She's dying, Daisy thought, I should tell her the truth. But even the finality of death was not enough to shake her well-guarded secret loose. The impulse to expose her most terrifying secret was countered by experience. It would just upset her and she'll never believe me, so what is to be gained by telling her? Forget it. Daisy remembered thinking that Wilbur was never coming back. Only he *did* come back, he was always there and despite his death, she still lived in his shadow. Here in Rose's home, Wilbur cast a shadow Daisy could not avoid. Rage began to rise inside her. It was time to leave.

Daisy patted Rose's hand and with as little noise as possible, made her exit from the bedroom.

Janet, Lissette and Daisy stood on the second floor balcony. The aroma of jerk chicken wafted in the hot, heavy air and they watched as children played cricket and the adults gathered in congenial little groups. After the acrimony between Daisy and Sally, a deal was struck. The girls would move out of 42 Beeston Street to go and live with Sally in Pembroke Hall. But when Daisy told her daughters that they were moving and she was leaving, Lissette became indignant.

"I'm leaving tomorrow," Daisy said, holding the girls' hands.

"As long as you don't tell us that you'll be back," Lissette said. "I wouldn't believe it."

"But I will send fe yuh," Daisy insisted. "Is what this trip is about, setting yuh up to come and be wit' us in California."

Janet turned angrily on her mother. "You must think we're still likkle pickney. For so long you kept us waiting, believing, and hoping and now you want to leave us with another empty promise. You're not our –– mommy." A tear rolled down her cheek.

"Sweetheart, I love you. These things take time and I told you long ago, a mommy is like an elephant, she never forget." Daisy tried to put her arm around Janet, but she pulled away.

"The only mother I know is Dearma, an' she dying."

"If yuh nuh forget, den yuh just don't care. You're ignoring us," Lissette broke in.

"We know you're not the only one. So many of our friends have been abandoned," Janet went on. "All we ask is that you be honest with us."

"I'm being honest," Daisy replied. She searched frantically for something to say that would redeem her, and could find nothing.

"It's Miles isn't it? You know that he drank himself to death seven years ago! We hardly knew him. Still, when you look pon us you see him."

"Please, stop it, Janet." Daisy was at the end of her wits. "Can't we just have one nice day? Linton and I are going to bring you to California as soon as we can."

Janet went back into the house.

"How can we believe your words?" Lissette asked.

"Lissette, I'm trying for all of us." Suddenly Magdelene burst onto the balcony. "Mommy!" she cried, snatching her mother's arm from around Lissette. The child stared balefully at her sister. The usurper.

"I'm hungry," Magdelene announced.

"I'm sorry, Lissette." Taking Magdelene's hand, Daisy left Lissette standing on the balcony under the darkening sky.

Just two weeks after returning to California, Linton sauntered into his office, tossed his briefcase aside, and looked through a pile of mail. One envelope in particular caught his attention.

It bore a Jamaican stamp and the return address from Major's home in May Pen. He opened and read the letter. Major had passed away. Denying the impulse to cry he stuffed the letter back in the envelope and put it in his desk drawer. He resumed sorting the mail, but couldn't concentrate. Perhaps I'll take the day off, Linton thought and gathered his things to return home.

The drive felt longer than usual. Sunlight, along Lake Chabot Road, shone through the eucalyptus trees, dappling the light that fell on the asphalt. He surprised Daisy at home and in no time they were in bed, making love, taking advantage of a rare moment without the kids. Afterward, Linton felt cleansed, his need for intimacy sated. He told her about Major's death. They spent the rest of the day together. Speaking to Daisy helped Linton to sort through his conflicted thoughts. Accustomed to ignoring his feelings, he discovered he was unable to avoid the pain. But deep inside he was comforted that a lifetime of seeking his father's love and approval had finally led to Major's acknowledgement and apology.

Only a few weeks later, Linton came home to find Samson and Magdelene sitting quietly at the kitchen table. Another telegram had arrived from Jamaica.

"Grandma died," Samson said, holding the telegram out to him. "Mommy won't come out of her room."

Taking it, Linton read: *Rose passed away [STOP]*

"Don't worry," he said to his children, "Mom's going to be all right."

"Are you going to die?" Magdelene asked.

Linton kissed her forehead tenderly. "Everyone gets old and dies, Magdelene. It's natural. But Mommy and I are going to be around for a long time, a really, really long time." Patting Samson, he said, "Let me see how Mommy's doing, okay?"

Thinking of the day he learned Major had died, he knocked on the bedroom door before entering.

XVII

MAY 1970, YOSEMITE NATIONAL PARK, CALIFORNIA

As the sun kissed the rim of the sheer granite walls surrounding Yosemite Valley, Daisy checked the time. Long shadows crept across the valley floor, a harbinger of nightfall. Waiting for Linton and Samson to come back from fishing left her feeling resentful. Linton insisted that fishing was a "guy thing," and she was never invited to join them. They had never actually been successful catching fish, always returning empty-handed. Nevertheless, she was consigned to a boring afternoon trying to entertain Magdelene while Linton and Samson were off having fun. With a sullen expression she put the valuables in the trunk of the car and, holding Magdelene's hand, walked to the Camp Curry Market.

Almost a mile away, Linton woke up to the squeal of a mosquito in his ear and the roar of the Merced River. On the riverbank, Samson patiently held his fishing rod, praying for a bite. Next to him a tether held a two pound trout that Linton had caught. Reluctantly, Linton realized that it was time to head back to camp.

Just as Linton got ready to call Samson, the boy's fishing pole jerked erratically.

"I got one!" Samson shouted.

"Set the hook!" Linton yelled, jumping up.

Samson pulled the pole back abruptly, setting the barbed hook in the trout's mouth. The ten pound test line zigged and zagged across the river as the fish desperately tried to free itself. Samson's face grew tense as he spun the crank of the reel.

"Keep the tip of the rod above your head! Steady… smooth now… take your time… now hurry… Samson, you got 'im!"

Linton fetched the net to scoop the trout out of the water. "That's my boy!" he cried, holding the writhing net aloft. "God! What a beauty! It's at least three pounds. We're eating fish tonight. Just wait till your mother sees this. Just wait!" He extracted the hook while Samson retrieved the tether, then struck a blow to each fish head to mercifully knock it unconscious.

Samson carried the fishing rods and Linton carried the tackle and the fish. As they neared the campground Linton yelled, "Come nuh, I'll race ya!" They sprinted down the road and reached the deserted campsite.

"Mom must be at the market. Let's clean these fish and get em ready to cook before she comes back."

Linton spread newspaper on the picnic table, gutted his fish and scaled it. Samson paid close attention, trying to glean the secrets of handling the knife. When Linton finished, Samson picked up the knife, trying to imitate his father's work.

"Like this," Linton said, holding his hand over Samson's to guide the cut. "First slit its belly so that you can gut it… and to scale it, hold the knife like so." He handed the knife back to Samson and watched as he scaled the fish. "You're getting the hang of it."

Samson beamed. Nothing gave him a greater thrill than being recognized by his father.

When Daisy and Magdelene returned, the fish were spiced and floured and the butter was ready to be melted in the saucepan.

"Madames," Linton said in a mock refined tone. "Dinner will be served shortly. On de menu is fresh rainbow trout."

Daisy set the bag of groceries on the table and smiled. "I don't believe it." She inspected the fish. "They are beauties. I'm glad I didn't buy much."

"We got plenty," Linton said, proudly. "Samson caught the big one."

"You caught those fish?" Magdelene asked, "or did you buy them?" Everyone burst out laughing.

The meal of fried trout, potato salad, and chips was unforgettable. Ater the meal, the children played Chinese checkers while Daisy washed up and Linton fussed with the gear and enjoyed a glass of roots. Finished with chores, Daisy read a bedtime story to the children and put them to bed.

Finally alone after a long day, Daisy joined Linton, sitting on the ground between his legs and leaning into his chest. The campfire crackled.

Wrapping his arms around Daisy, Linton closed his eyes and basked in the warm glow of satisfaction. During the past three years he had made it a habit to take the family camping twice a year, with one of the trips reserved for Yosemite National Park. He wanted his children to know the natural world, not just concrete and organized parks. They made the trips over Daisy's objections to the dirt, the mosquitos, and the smoke from the surrounding campfires. Before every trip she complained about going, and during every trip she thanked him for insisting. As twilight deepened, they listened to the buzzing of nighttime insects, the beating of bat wings, and the occasional laughter from nearby campers.

"Linton?" Daisy spoke softly. "You hear from the immigration lawyer?"

Linton shifted his weight, trying to get more comfortable. "He thought he could have the girls here between this June and next February."

Less than a year, Daisy thought. Janet was nineteen and Lissette was in her final year of school. Where had the time gone? Hardly a minute ago Mummaa was dying and Janet was sixteen years old. Now it was 1970 and Sally Maud, with whom the girls had been living in Kingston, was three months dead, and Daisy's daughters were on their own. The only saving grace was the low paying clerk job at the Bureau of Statistics in Spanish Town that Janet held, but it was not enough to support herself and Lissette. Goaded by guilt, Daisy sent money to help the girls make it in their day-to-day life. Sally's adult children intended to sell the apartment, so the girls would soon have to move.

"Have they thought about what they want to do once they're here?"

"They're interested in nursing," Daisy answered.

"We will pay for their schooling. Give them a good start."

The fire crackled and popped, sending sparks into the sky. Relaxed and enjoying the rare quiet time, Daisy began to doze and leaned against Linton heavily. After a few moments he woke her.

"I am going to call that private high school tomorrow,"

Linton said. "It's got a good reputation for college prep and many of their students go on to universities like Stanford. I think it's the right place to send both Samson and Magdelene."

Daisy sighed. "High school already? I'm barely getting used to him being in junior high."

"I only wish I could have had an education."

"And I wanted to play music... You promised to buy Magdelene a piano."

"A grand piano, no doubt," Linton rubbed his eyes.

"Why, yes, of course, I want the best."

"I thought the piano was for Magdelene." He poked her ribs.

"Everyting a joke fe yuh! The kids should have started lessons already."

"They have plenty of time," Linton said.

"I'm glad we're raising the children here."

Surprised, Linton looked at her. "Why?"

"Our children are Americans. I don't ever want to go back to Jamaica. I don't have good memories of *that* place."

"Neither do I."

The next day, on their way home, Daisy announced that they were buying a piano.

Magdelene clapped her hands with excitement. "Lessons!" she squealed.

"I don't want to learn piano," Samson said. "No classical music for me."

"Just give it a chance," Daisy pleaded. "I think if you do, you'll love it."

"We sure will," Magdelene added. "We'll play duets!" She elbowed Samson playfully, making him laugh.

Not long after, the new Steinway grand arrived. Daisy touched the ivory keys, making the piano tinkle softly. It was the crown jewel in her fully furnished house. Walking around the instrument, she inspected the shiny black finish, carefully looking for scratches or dings. It took the movers three hours to get the piano inside the house and despite all the care and furniture pads, Daisy remained suspicious of damage. But before she could finish her inspection, she heard Ethel honking the horn, dropping the kids off after school.

"Is it here?" Magdelene cried, running into the house. "Oh my God!" Magdelene's mouth hung open as she looked at her mother standing next to the august Steinway. She banged on the keys. "Lessons!" she cried, "when do we start?" Without waiting for an answer she ran off, looking for Samson.

The front door slammed and Daisy heard Samson's book-bag hit the floor.

The children burst into the family room, Magdelene dragging Samson to the piano. "Let's play a duet," she said cheerfully, "Come on, I'll show you how to play chopsticks."

Amused by Magdelene's enthusiasm, Samson sat down and they played a hackneyed version of chopsticks, each of them using only one finger.

Within two months, both children had mastered playing simple duets. Samson was astonished to discover that he *loved* playing piano. He marvelled at the melodies and took a liking to Bach. It was thrilling to feel the growing command over the music he was producing. In his brief life he had been searching for something that was his to control or master. Everything about his life fell under Daisy's guiding hand. Even his friends had to meet her approval. He did not hang out with any of the neighborhood kids, for instance, because Daisy had determined they weren't the type of children with whom he should associate.

All of this led to a growing resentment, but with the introduction of music into Samson's life, he found something his parents approved of, knew nothing about, and couldn't interfere with. He became obsessed with music.

One day Linton went into Samson's room and was shocked at what he saw. Sitting on the bed, studying a musical score, Samson was listening to Brahms' Hungarian Dances.

"I have to try this next," Samson told his father. "I like the rhythms."

"I'm glad you like it. I was wondering if you might be interested in going to the symphony."

Samson replied eagerly. "Dad! I'd love to go."

The following weekend the McMann family took their seats at the San Francisco Symphony. The performance of Beethoven's Third Symphony left them breathless, and they joined the audience in a standing ovation. Subsequently, Samson pestered his parents for season tickets to the Symphony, which they bought, and he did not miss one concert, even when it meant attending alone.

Samson quickly found thirty minutes of practice a day to be inadequate. While Magdelene had to be reminded to practice, Samson had to be forced to stop.

"What about your homework?" Linton would ask, closing the piano lid.

"It's done."

"Go get it. I want to check it."

Samson rolled his eyes. He knew that his father would find something, anything, and would make him return to his desk to work on it some more. Invariably, he would eye the homework with disgust etched into his face.

Linton went to the bar and poured himself a shot of scotch. He rarely slipped into patois any more, unless he was drinking.

"Wha' type a crab-toe writing, dis?" he asked, tossing the work back to Samson. "This time write neatly, like yuh care! The only ting yuh gi' a damn 'bout is dat blasted piano. Well let me tell yuh now, dere ain't gonna be no damn lazy, dope smokin' musician inna me family. Dat is not what me spend me money fuh! A few years from now how do yuh expeck fe get through business school? College is no joke. When yuh done, come show it to me."

Samson gathered the papers and returned to his room. At his desk, he looked at the music books he had checked out from the library: *Jazz Improvisation*, *Mastering Music Theory*, and *The Intro to the Circle of Fifths*. He had been studying them in secret. Putting the books back in the drawer, he opened his writing tablet and hunkered down to rewrite the book report.

The letter informing Daisy that Janet's and Lissette's visas had been granted lay unopened on the nightstand for three days. One month later, Daisy purchased two one-way tickets from Kingston to San Francisco. Samson waited impatiently, memories of his older sisters among his most cherished from early childhood. He loved Jamaica.

Magdelene found her sisters' impending arrival more difficult to accept. She did not dare express her disapproval, but she remained unenthusiastic. The closer it came to their arrival date, the more she found herself in stores with Daisy, shopping for items for the guest bedroom, and for clothes for Janet and Lissette. She felt miserable, but she went along, smiling and trying to act like she was interested.

No one was home when Daisy pulled the brand-new black-and-gold Mercedes Benz into the spacious two-car garage. She shut the engine off and paused, taking a deep breath. After a day of shopping in San Francisco, her feet and back ached, and she was hungry. Wearily, she retrieved the bags from the trunk and went in the house.

Five shopping bags of merchandise from Macy's and I. Magnin surrounded Daisy in the dimly lit family room, but she was too tired to unpack them, and relaxed with a Sprite instead. Feeling exuberant over her daughters' imminent arrival, she had spent nearly $500 on items for the house and on clothes for herself. The girls were arriving the next day and Daisy had tirelessly prepared the house for them.

Feeling refreshed, she began to unwrap her purchases: a stunning, blue Diane von Furstenberg jersey wrap dress, a pair of black pearl earrings, and sportswear from Yves St. Laurent. Ususally, bringing home new clothes, bedding and towels made her happy, but today she found no thrill in looking at her purchases.

In fact, looking around the room, Daisy found no happiness in the expensive furniture, the Waterford cut crystal, or the luxurious jewelry on her neck, wrists and fingers that Linton had given her. She often felt melancholy, walking through her house. All of these things, the very house itself, were at the expense of seeing her two oldest children grow up. She shifted uncomfortably on the couch. It was a rare moment of honest reflection for Daisy. And there was another truth: the closer the time came to welcome her daughters, the more her exuberance turned to anxiety.

Janet and Lissette arrived at San Francisco International Airport on a rainy February night. Janet was a stunning girl, delicate and petite, with a coffee and cream complexion, and brown eyes. Peering through thick eyeglasses, she looked like a bookish college co-ed. Dark-skinned Lissette towered over her older sister. In Jamaica, she had been a high school track star. But she was not just the champion of the 100 meter dash, she was an extraordinary student, consistently making the dean's list. If Janet appeared a little too serious, Lissette's face was frequently creased with a smile and she seemed always on the verge of a laugh. Seeing them come down the ramp from the plane and into the airport waiting room, Daisy felt like she was looking into a rear view mirror at her troubled past. Her daughters were no longer children. Hugging her girls, Daisy reluctantly acknowledged to herself that she had traveled further down the road of life than she'd imagined.

"Welcome home!" Daisy cried. "I told you, I'd never forget you."

"I never thought I'd see the day," Janet replied.

"I can't believe how big dis place is," Lissette said, staring at the airport terminal. She could hardly believe her eyes. During the plane's final approach she glimpsed the San Francisco Bay Area and its sprawling suburbs. The sight of the San Mateo bridge took her breath away as she marveled at the slender strand of concrete that stretched across the water.

Linton greeted them warmly, kissing both girls on the cheek, and Magdelene and Samson hovered around them, curious about their foreign half-sisters.

"God it's cold!" Lissette blurted.

We brought coats for you," Magdelene said, offering them two leather jackets. Putting his arm around Janet, Linton led the way to the car. Soon they were driving across the San Francisco Bay Bridge.

Once they had arrived home Magdelene wasted no time taking Janet and Lissette into the living room to see the grand piano. While Lissette and Magdelene frolicked on the piano, Janet stood quietly, coolly taking in her new surroundings. Fine crystal, a silver serving set, expensive china, and opulent furniture surrounded her. This was far more than she even dreamed of in Jamaica. She had long suspected that Daisy was living in relative comfort compared to their lot in Kingston, but this went beyond her wildest imaginings.

"What a lot of records!"

Janet turned to find Samson thumbing through a stack of 45's.

"Dang! These don't even have real labels. They're all hand-written. Can we play one! Please!"

"No." Linton walked in with a tray holding six glasses of roots. "Your mom will be here in a minute and she wants to show the girls to their room."

"Is that the famous Family Roots?" Lissette asked.

"Indeed!" Linton replied. "Have some."

"Is truly excellent," Janet said smacking her lips. "Which rasta teach yuh how to brew dis?"

Linton shifted uncomfortably. "No rasta taught me how to brew roots."

"Her boyfriend was a rasta," Lissette said. "He made roots too, but nothing like this. This is really good!"

"Rasta?" Samson asked, looking up from the records. "What's that?"

"What!?" Janet cried. "Yuh don' know about Rastafari? Yuh gon' hear about dem now."

"Don't bother yourself with dem, Rasta is nothing to look up to, Samson," Linton said. "They're just black hippies who live in Jamaica."

"I beg to differ," Janet began, but a knock at the front door brought the conversation to an abrupt end. Linton thankfully brought in his next-door neighbor, Robyn Tyler. She brushed past Linton, a rather short fat woman, tossing her blonde hair from her blue eyes.

"And who are you young ladies?" she asked, smiling and reaching out a hand to shake. "I'm Robyn."

"I'm Janet."

"I'm Lissette." She stood up from playing the piano. Her height took Robyn aback. "We're--"

Suddenly, Daisy burst into the room, interrupting Lissette. "My daughters," she answered without missing a beat. Breathless, Daisy looked at her daughters. Swept up in the spirit of the moment, she beheld her daughters with pride.

"Why, Daisy, you never mentioned they were coming. Are they staying with you?" Robyn asked politely.

"Yes." Daisy, put her arms around the girls, who stood there like set pieces, eyes downcast. "If you could excuse us, I want to show the girls to their new rooms."

Sensing that she had come over at a bad time, Robyn said, "I came over to borrow your blender."

"In the top cabinet." Daisy pointed to the kitchen.

"I hope you girls don't mind," Robyn said, turning back to the sisters. "I'm a little busy during the next few days, but if you're staying here, we'll get a chance to visit soon."

"It's nice to meet you," Janet said.

Picking up two bags, Daisy led the girls to their bedroom in the rear of the house.

Closing the door carefully, she dropped the bags.

"Sit down."

The girls took a seat on the adjacent beds. Daisy drew up a chair and placed it between the beds. Taking each of their hands into hers she looked them in the eye.

"I can't tell yuh how glad I am that you're finally home," Daisy gushed. "I know yuh probably lost faith in me. But I told yuh that one day yuh would be here with us as part of my family. Finally that day has come."

Lissette hugged Daisy. "Me glad fe be home wit' yuh," she said. Janet remained sitting on the edge of the bed. Turning to her Daisy took Janet by the shoulders.

"I'm sorry," Daisy whispered. "I know I took too long to bring you here." Taking Janet into her arms, Daisy squeezed her gently before releasing her. "This is your room, your home, and your family forever. Yuh probably want to sleep after such a long trip so I'm going to leave yuh both now and we'll see yuh in the morning."

After Daisy withdrew, Janet turned to Lissette and said, "Yuh see? Look how they're living, while we lived hand-to-mouth in Kingston. She forgot about us. And now she wants to make it up to us, Lissette, hoping I'll forget. But I won't. I never will."

"I'm just glad to be with Mommy," Lissette replied, taking off her clothes for bed. Later that night, while everyone was fast asleep, Daisy peeked in, unable to sleep, wondering what she had to do to win her daughters' hearts.

As the weeks passed, Daisy made it clear that Janet and Lissette were her top priority. She took them to local vocational nursing schools, paid their tuition, and introduced them to her friends. But while all the attention softened Lissette's heart, Janet only grew more critical of the bourgeois lifestyle, and Magdelene grew outright hostile toward her sisters.

Magdelene looked upon her half-sisters derisively. Their

accent was strange and she could hardly understand them. Worst of all, Janet and Lissette absorbed what little attention she was given by her parents. Already reeling over Samson's success at playing the piano, she feared that Janet and Lissette would also outshine her.

The two girls bonded quickly with Samson. Instead of playing on the piano with Magdelene, Lissette joined Janet and Samson, dancing to the slow steady beat of reggae in Samson's room. The throbbing bass drove Magdelene into her room and beyond–– to the edge of madness.

"How am I expected to study with all the noise?" she'd whine to her father, who would go into Samson's room to pull the plug on the stereo.

Other times Samson could be found sitting quietly listening to Janet and Lissette swap stories of Kingston. It was Janet's tales about Rastafarians that caught Samson's fancy.

"All over Kingston," Janet said, " You'll find rastas selling their own unique blends of roots from roadside stands."

"But none of dem can hold a candle to Family Roots," Lissette interjected.

"Really?" Samson was fascinated. "Our drink is that good?"

"Maybe yuh will open a Family Roots branch in Montego Bay," Janet said.

"Wow," Samson considered the possibility.

"Yuh father never tell yuh 'bout Rasta?" Janet asked.

"No. He said roots came from Africa, and he learned it in Jamaica. So roots is a part of this rasta tradition?" Samson asked.

"Roots is a part a Jamaica," Lissette replied. "And Rasta is part a both."

Samson pestered his father to learn more about roots. Linton was delighted. But when he questioned his father about Rastafari's connection to roots tonic, Linton hesitated.

"You never told me that Rasta and roots are one," Samson said.

"Roots have been around long before Rasta," Linton replied. "Roots come from Africa and there are many ways to make it in Jamaica."

"Yes, but it's Rasta making it today inna Jamaica," Janet added.

"So what!" Linton snapped. "When I was a little boy, people were making roots." Linton grit his teeth. Janet was getting on his nerves. Her extolling the virtues of Rastafarinaism was influencing Samson. Linton was ashamed of his past association with it. The Rastas were simple, poor, ignorant, lazy, no-good ganja smokers. Successful expatriate Jamaicans such as he looked upon Rastas in Jamaica as evidence of the growing lawlessness on the island, and he found it alarming that Samson was being exposed to its ganja-fueled, Pan-African philosophy.

"She has to stop." Linton complained to Daisy. "She is trying to fill his head up with all kinds of foolishness."

"She doesn't mean him any harm, Linton!"

"Do you want your son to grow up a Rasta?" Linton slammed his fist on the table. "Or maybe you want him to go and join the Black Panthers? This has to stop, *now*. Or else she has to move. I don't want her here trying to undo what we're doing. I'm trying to raise a responsible man."

"Linton!"

"One that values hard work. Not someone sitting around smoking ganja and beating drums. Dammit! At least Magdelene has the good sense not to fall for that crap," Linton muttered.

"But Samson's has been working *hard* at Family Roots," Daisy pointed out. "You said you were happy about that."

On one hand it was true that Samson was interested in the business, even volunteering to work on weekends, chopping roots at the factory.

But there were other changes in Samson's behavior that concerned his father. The teenager, a fine pianist, having been introduced to reggae, had abandoned the classical music that he used to play to his parents delight. Now Samson was in love with reggae's smoky, relaxed, upbeat, ganja-inspired lyrics and the hypnotic beats. Influenced by the revolutionary ideas, his aspirations changed, as did his dress, and his friends.

A few months later, after vacuuming the entire house, Daisy sat down, exhausted. She took comfort in cleaning the house. It always helped to distract her from whatever was bothering her most and right now what she dreaded most, was dealing with Janet. Since her daughters arrived, the tension between Linton and Janet had become unbearable. In the interest of peace, Daisy had decided to rent an apartment three blocks away for her daughters. It was not a decision she had made lightly and her conscience was smothered with guilt.

She walked over to a display case and looked at her distorted reflection in the wine glasses. She loved them being around, but having her older children in her house had proven problematic. Anger began to well up inside Daisy. Just a week earlier, Magdelene had come into the kitchen, holding several small gold foil packets.

"What are..." Magdelene paused, reading the label "condoms?"

Daisy stopped washing dishes. Water dripped from her hands. Magdelene handed the packets to her mother.

"Where did you get these?" Daisy asked.

"In Janet and Lissette's room."

"Young lady, what were you doing in there?"

Magdelene cast her eyes downward, "I was looking for some lotion. And found it in Janet's dresser drawer. Condoms? What are they?"

Daisy was unprepared to tackle the subject of sex with her pre-teen child. "Condoms are a form of birth control." Daisy stumbled over her words. "You're only twelve years old, Magdelene. We'll talk about this when you get a little older." This was not how she wanted to approach the subject of sex.

"How does it work?"

Daisy frowned. "Never you mind, there are some things that shouldn't be discussed with little girls." She ushered Magdelene to her bedroom and closed the door, her mind flashing on how she had been brutally forced to surrender her virginity. She looked at the task of discussing boys with Magdelene with deep and utter dread. How would she explain the evil and filth that lurked in the streets, the many men with one-track minds, the loose women who would try to entice her to become sluts like them. Daisy had struggled to shelter her children, and the thought of what Magdelene had been exposed to since her older daughters had moved in made Daisy swear.

When Janet and Lissette returned home, she exploded.

"What yuh need fe bring condoms inna me house fuh?"

"Magdelene had no business in our room, looking through our things," Lissette protested.

"What about our privacy?" Janet demanded.

"You want privacy, then move out! When Linton finds out, God help you!"

But Daisy couldn't tell Linton about Magdelene and the condoms. He was angry enough about Janet's influence on Samson. Her fear made her feel like an accomplice against her husband. She could not tolerate it. Yet, Daisy could not bear to tell Janet and Lissette to leave. She bit her finger in frustration and suddenly became aware that she had been standing there, her hand in her mouth, staring off into space. She looked around for something, anything to do. Her attention was caught by some water spots on the wine glasses and she hastily retrieved a clean rag to polish them.

Was it a mistake to bring them here? Daisy wondered. She vigorously rubbed the fluted crystal. No! Her hands were shaking as she buffed the glassware. Jamaica wasn't a safe country anymore. Kingston had changed since she lived there. Stricken with poverty and crime, Kingston was a place where gangs and posses ran entire neighborhoods. Besides, there was her promise to her daughters to bring them to the United States. Bringing them here was one of her proudest moments.

After she polished the glasses and closed the case, she sat down on the sofa. Tomorrow night they would tell Janet and Lissette about their plans to move them into their own apartment. Daisy tried not to worry in the face of her increasing dread.

The next night the sisters and parents sat on opposite sides of the kitchen table. A seam ran across the table like a battle line between opposing armies. Lissette stared vacantly at the table. Sitting at her side, her jaw set defiantly, Janet was resolute and steady. As the oldest, she had always taken the lead.

Neither Daisy nor Linton looked at the girls. Their faces were somber, as if they were attending a funeral. The uncomfortable silence was broken when Linton suddenly came to life.

"After almost a year of trying to live in peace, your mother and I have come to a decision," he said, and looked at Daisy, as if to tell her to continue.

"We have found an apartment for you," Daisy went on, "we're going to pay your rent while you're in school. Things are getting tense in the house. We thought this might be a good compromise."

Janet glanced nervously at Lissette. "Well Mom, we have something we wanted to say," Janet said. "We don't really like living here either. We talked about it and... we're moving to New York."

"Both of you?" Daisy's voice cracked. "New York? Why so far away?"

"Mom," Janet said, "I don't want to be so far removed from my people. There are hardly any Jamaicans here, and the whole neighborhood is white. I'm constantly watching what I say around my brother, and my sister is going through my room and searching my things. I can't stay here. I'm going to New York."

"And I'm going with her," Lissette added.

"You can't leave like this," Daisy cried. "New York? You'll break my heart!"

"Like you broke mine?" Janet retorted. "Momma, I'm almost twenty-two years old. I'm a big woman."

"But what about school?" Linton asked.

"We'll go to school in New York," Lissette replied.

"It won't be cheap," Daisy said. "Stay here and we'll help you."

"But I don't want your help," Janet replied.

"But I love you," Daisy said looking from Janet to Lissette. "You don't love me?"

"Love you? We hardly know you," Lissette said.

"God knows you've really tried, but how do you make up for twenty years?" Janet asked. "You don't know me. You're asking me to constantly watch what I say around Samson, but Mom, *that's who I am.*"

There was an uncomfortable pause. Finally Daisy broke the silence.

"When are you leaving?"

Janet sighed. "We're not sure. We want to do this soon. We'll stay with Aunt Iris until we get on our feet."

Daisy was crestfallen. "But I thought we were building a relationship," she whispered. "One based on love and––"

"Love? *We don't know you.*" Janet replied. Her tone gave Daisy the chills; it was so measured, even, and honest. "You gave us life and that was it! Why didn't you visit?"

"You never gave me the chance to make you my mother!"

Lissette added. "I was eleven months old when you left. I barely remember you."

"Dearma raised us on the principles of the Bible," Janet continued. "And it tell me say: honor thy father and thy mother so your days will be long upon this earth. It doesn't say love. It says honor, and that's what you're getting from me, but little else. Me love is reserved for Dearma, who raised me. It's reserved for Miss Maud and Aunt Callie, who took care of us when we had no where to turn. Is too late for me to get to know my mother."

The girls got up and excused themselves, leaving Daisy and Linton sitting at the table.

Later that night after everyone was in bed, Daisy sat alone in the darkened family room. Conflicting feelings of betrayal and relief at knowing that her girls were leaving for New York brought fresh tears to her eyes. She glanced at the family portrait sitting atop the grand piano. The family portrait that didn't include Janet and Lissette. Staring at the image of Magdelene, her heart trembled. Clasping her hands, she made a vow. As God is my witness, she promised, Magdelene will never live in need for anything if it is in my power. She said a prayer and it struck her that she had not prayed, nor gone to church in quite some time. Her heart felt no lighter but, indeed, seemed to weigh more heavily than ever.

JULY 1974, HAYWARD, CALIFORNIA

Linton and Daisy were getting gray. As the autumn of their lives dawned upon them, they were forced to pay closer attention to their health. Linton finally gave up smoking cigarettes, but not before he suffered his first mild heart attack. After that he tried to become more conscious of his health, insisting that everyone eat well-balanced meals.

Family Roots had become a mature, successful company that was growing, and Linton was eager to move the Family Roots headquarters into a new building. He worked so hard that his cardiologist asked him to take it easier. Linton looked to Samson, his seventeen-year-old son for help. Samson had grown into a strapping, dark-skinned teenager with an engaging smile.

Linton and Daisy were looking forward to seeing their son graduate from high school. They were proud of their daughter, a sophomore, who had made the honor roll each semester. Throughout their children's lives they had stressed the importance of education. It wasn't considered a choice but a duty to attend school, study hard, and upon graduating from high school, study something that could lead to a business degree.

Late one afternoon Linton received a phone call from the principal's office, informing him that Samson had been caught in possession of marijuana and was suspended for the week. The news caught Linton and Daisy by surprise. Linton was enraged. He picked Samson up and brought him home. They sandwiched Samson at the kitchen table, with Daisy sitting on his left, and Linton standing on his right, towering over him.

"Marijuana! Samson, drugs lead to the grave," Daisy proclaimed, lecturing her son. "Look at what happened to Iris's eldest son, your cousin, Charles!"

"Marijuana never killed anyone, in fact––"

"It's killed plenty people!" Daisy shot back. "If it didn't kill them it left them in the gutter."

"Why? Why would you disgrace my name with something illegal like that?" Linton thundered. "I send you to school to learn and what do you do? Smoke ganja? You must tink me is an idiot!"

"I'm sorry," Samson, replied, "I didn't intend to––"

"Sorry? Everyone is trying to help yuh better yuh life and yuh gone, an smoke ganja, an' all yuh can sey is sorry? *Bumboclat!*" Linton's face fell into the palm of his hand.

"We're worried about you Samson," Daisy continued. "Your friends, the music you listen to, and this Rastafari business. It isn't good."

"None of that is going to help you get inna a good university!" Linton cried. "Instead of listening to that crap you ought to worry about getting into a good school."

"It's not crap!" Samson interjected. "You guys don't realize that times have changed. The old ways are gone. Rastafarians represent a new way of thinking."

"Nonsense," Linton snorted.

"They're dirty," Daisy added.

"And all dem do is smoke dope all damn day and loaf around. Is that what yuh want? Linton asked.

Samson sighed. "Plenty of dreads are doctors, and lawyers," he said. "But like I've told you again and again, I want to work with roots."

"If you want to work with us, just get your MBA."

Samson got up and left his parents in the kitchen.

"Do you think this will affect his getting into a good university?" Daisy asked.

"Who knows, it's too late to wonder about that isn't it?" Linton went to the doorway, cupping his hands and yelling down the hallway after Samson, "Suspended from school! Well yuh won't be loafing. Yuh goin' move de furniture inna de new Family Roots office tomorrah morning. I hope yuh is ready fe work!"

"I'll be there!" Samson said just before going in his room.

"Worthless bastard! Bringing down de McMann name," Linton muttered. "Him goin' a college? Yuh mus' be crazy." Linton paced back and forth. "Dey only one place he'll end up, prison, or dead like him cousin Charles!"

"Please stop," Daisy begged.

"Stop wha'? Me send dat worthless bwoy a school an' him a smoke ganja! Me nuh haf time fe dem type a people inna me life!"

"Stop it with de patois, please?"

"Daddy?"

Linton turned his attention to his daughter. Somehow, without his noticing, Magdelene had become a slender, alluring, pubescent female version of himself. "Yes, honey?"

"I won first place in the Science Fair today."

Linton's face bespoke embarrassment. He took Magdelene's hand. "Oh Lord, Magdelene, I'm sorry. With all this madness today I forgot about your science fair. But I'm *so* proud of you, honey." He hugged her. He looked down the hallway and continued, "If dat boy doesn't change he's going to end up in a cell. I just know it." Confused, he kissed Magdelene on the cheek and retreated to his bedroom, wondering how he could have forgotten something so important.

The next morning Daisy lay in bed watching her husband get dressed. It was moving day and, as company bookkeeper, she was uncomfortable with taking the whole day off. More so, she worried about Samson and Linton working together. Linton insisted that moving heavy boxes and funiture was men's work.

"And stop worrying about that boy," he added.

"You put so much pressure on him." She sighed, resigned that father and son might never see eye-to-eye. "Maybe he needs a chance to think."

Linton adjusted his tie. "There's no time to think. Samson's almost out of high school and has yet to choose a university. If he doesn't major in business, I don't want him managing Family Roots. When I was his age, I was breaking my back out dey in de sun. I wasn't some bohemian, smoking ganja all damn day, playing the piano."

"Well, today he was out the door before you even woke up."

"Good!" Linton smiled for the first time all morning. "I'm depending on him. Imagine dat Daisy! We movin' to de fourteenth floor of de Kaiser Building. We came to dis country with nothing. We should be enjoying de American Dream." He shook his head. "Instead, that dream is jeopardized because my son is too selfish to accept his *duty* to our family."

Driving into West Oakland, Linton looked at the Family Roots plant, a cinderblock structure nestled amongst old, shabby Victorian homes, streets littered with trash, and clusters of unemployed men. Some of the men waved at Linton and he waved back, but in their faces he saw a desperation that chilled his soul. Why can't they just get it together, he wondered. All they do is stand on street corners drinking, smoking and complaining about the white man. They've given up. Linton refused to give in to despair. Timothy's words came to mind. *Remember, to succeed, yuh mus rely pon wha' yuh learn right 'ere inna dis yard.*

He thought of Jamaica and of the crippling lack of opportunity on the island. He was so grateful to leave Jamaica, to arrive in Brooklyn. Grateful for a chance to begin anew. He observed a group of men engaged in a dice game. They are just too lazy to take a risk on anything other than gambling. Linton did not fail to notice the jealous eyes that were cast in his direction. He got out the car and slammed the door, happy to be leaving this crappy, depressing neighborhood.

The Family Roots business office was empty and the rooms looked forlorn and abandoned. The firm had relocated the office to a tony building in a tony neighborhood, and Linton would no longer be embarrassed to invite associates to visit. Samson had taken everything to their new digs and only a few men remained to clean up the old space. The production plant would remain in this building downstairs, pumping out bottles of Family Roots Tonic for the West Coast market. The larger Brooklyn plant supplied the expanding accounts along the Eastern Seaboard and would, one day, serve the Midwest and South.

He drove over to the Kaiser Building, took the elevator to the 14th floor, and walked through the new Family Roots office. It consisted of two spacious rooms, one for the secretary and reception area, and one for himself. He was struck by the relative quiet. He sauntered along the outside edge of the room, walled in by a giant plate-glass window, and gleefully looked out over Lake Merritt. After years of hard work, worry and fear of failure, here he was, enjoying a pure moment of unbridled happiness. He closed his eyes and savored the moment. A knock at the door interrupted his reverie.

Samson hesitantly entered the room but Linton was so happy he failed to notice the cloud on Samson's face.

"Nice job," he said, shaking Samson's hand. "How do you like our new corporate home?" They gazed at the lake. "I was just thinking about how we can expand the office in four years to make space for your desk." His hand clasped Samson's shoulder. "I'll even pay extra rent to make sure you have a view like mine. That is why I get so angry with you, Samson. I want Family Roots to be yours one day. I didn't raise you to smoke ganja and live your life as a black hippie."

"A black hippie?"

"You know what I mean," Linton snapped. "This Rasta business. It's no good."

Samson nervously fingered the frayed edge of his jacket.

He had been both intending to and avoiding talking to his father for quite some time.

"Dad, Rasta is not about being a hippie. There's something I want to tell you, and I want you to try to understand. I'm not going to university next year nor the year after and for now I don't have any plans to ever go. I'm not going into business administration either. I want to work at Family Roots." Samson took a deep breath, surprised at his own verbosity.

"*What?*"

"I just want to start working, and work my way up. After all, one day you're going to tell me the recipe and--"

"I'm not telling you anything! You *have* to go to business school. You can't work for us if you don't go to school."

Samson sat down on the edge of the desk, hardly able to believe his ears.

"Your joking right? After all these years of my working here, and cutting roots, and mopping the floors, you suddenly don't want me? I'm suddenly worthless because I won't go get a degree?"

"You must have a degree in today's world."

"You don't have one!" Samson shouted.

"And I suffer to this day for it." Linton opened a small gold and black velvet bag and withdrew a shiny brass key. "See this? It's the key to my father's library. He gave it to me so I could educate myself." Linton put the key away. "Ever since you were a baby I've always sworn that I would give you what I never had. You cannot refuse! Look at George's boy, he wants to attend engineering school, just like his dad! What will people think if you don't get a degree?"

"I'm not going to devote my life to living your dream."

"My dream?" Linton laughed scornfully. "I thought it was your dream. I've watched you work all summer, chopping and shredding roots. I can't say you're lazy. It's that damn Rasta, is what it is. Life is not fun and games, Samson. Yuh gwan a run up and down a shout 'bout Jah and Selassie an' all dat foolishness. All me life me been slaving to give yuh something. I'm doing this for you, can't you see that?"

"This has nothing to do with me!" Samson answered him. "You don't have a degree yourself, Dad, can't you see that? This degree thing is all about you. *It's your dream, not mine.* I don't care what people think about me. I don't need to be rich. I just want to live my life. I just want to work with you. For years now I've wanted to work with roots. But you cannot seem to get over my interest in Rasta." Samson hesitated. "I don't know if I should tell you this... but I just don't see myself working in the Babylon system." Suddenly Samson smiled. "But I don't see Family Roots as a part of Babylon either and that is why––"

"Wait till your mother hears this."

"You've never understood me," Samson said, walking through the door. "Mom will."

But later that evening, Daisy had trouble understanding his decision as well. As she cleared the table after dinner, she expressed her disappointment.

"After all we've done to make sure yuh succeed and yuh goin' choose Rasta before an education? I can't believe yuh would do dis to us."

"Do *what* to you?" Samson asked, "I just want to live my life. Dad doesn't have a degree."

"Exactly why you need one," Daisy answered. "You claim you want to help run the family business, but look at you. We work hard and buy decent clothes an' look how yuh dress." She glared at Samson's jeans and tee shirt. "Instead of goin' to school you wan' go Rasta. If you grow dreads, don't bother showing your face around here. I don't want any Rasta in my family."

"If yuh don't enroll in a university," Linton said, "then you won't be working at Family Roots. It's up to you."

In September, when the fall college semester began, Samson had not applied to college, and Linton fired him. Samson got a job in a music store and within a month had moved from home.

Stung by what they perceived as rejection, Linton and Daisy focused their attention on Magdelene, who thrived in school. Linton bought her a brand new Camaro during her senior year of high school. He paid her an extravagant salary for working in the office at Family Roots during the summer months. But Magdelene wasn't interested in the physical roots. She worked in the office, paying bills and keeping the books with Daisy.

Magdelene went on to receive her MBA from Stanford University, a day that saw Linton and Daisy bursting with pride. Watching her walk back to her seat, degree in hand, Daisy and Linton never felt prouder. They felt the satisfaction of accomplishment as much as Magdelene. Best of all, their family was about to grow.

At the graduation party thrown by Linton to commemorate his daughter's graduation, Magdelene stood with her fiance, Gaylord, a young, handsome, copper-skinned investment banker. Daisy couldn't have been happier. Magdelene had not only graduated with her MBA, she was going to get her "Mrs."

degree with a man who she deemed worthy of her daughter. It was clear that Gaylord was going places. Many times she found herself wondering why her own son couldn't have been more like Gaylord. Linton was so impressed he even discussed investment opportunities with Gaylord.

In March 1980, Magdelene and Gaylord were married in an opulent wedding that included a Rolls Royce Silver Shadow limosine. The reception was a raucous affair that incuded food, drinks, a live band and hundreds of guests.

While the band played Chic's cover song, *Good Times*, Linton, wearing a white tuxedo, nursed a glass of champagne while Daisy nibbled on some cake. On the dance floor, Magdelene bobbed and weaved with Gaylord across the dance floor. Her cream colored wedding dress sparkled in contrast to her husband's dark tuxedo. Daisy's dream had come true. Her daughter was in good hands. She saw Samson ten feet away, talking to a young lady at the edge of the dance floor. She glanced at Lissette, dressed in a flowing yellow dress and dancing with a handsome young man. Daisy felt a pang of guilt. Janet had refused her invitation.

After Janet and Lissette moved to New York, Daisy continued to reach out to her daughters. Initially she supported them while they lived at Iris's apartment. But even after they had established themselves, Daisy insisted on keeping in touch, visiting them several times. Nevertheless there remained a gulf, a rift between her and Janet that seemed unable to heal. Daisy invited them to visit her in California, but while Lissette had made the journey several times, Janet had always refused. Daisy hoped Janet might come for the wedding. But it was not to be. Janet had yet to get past her childhood, while Lissette had found a way to forgive her.

Sitting there watching people gyrate on the dance floor Daisy felt incredibly empty. Her children were grown. Trying to cheer herself up, she nudged Linton. "How does it feel to be just a couple again?"

"You and me? I've forgotten," Linton said with a twinkle in his eyes. "I guess now that Magdelene's married and with Samson out of the house, we're done."

"No!" Daisy laughed, "we're not done, we're just starting out." She leaned over and kissed him. "Look," she said.

Ethel was dancing with Samson, who was leading her around the dance floor. She was wearing a shimmering green formal dress, and for a woman in her sixties she moved with ease. Samson's dreadlocks were concealed underneath a black head wrap.

When Linton looked at his son, he saw himself thirty-five years earlier in Bessanworse, young and strong, with dreadlocks. Linton thought of his relationship with Major and a cloud crossed Linton's face.

"What's wrong?" Daisy inquired.

"Nothing," Linton said, straightening up and adjusting his posture.

Daisy took his hand. "You might not be happy with Samson's path, but he is successful. You can't deny that. After three years of working he is managing that music store. He's done well for himself. Now if he would just get married."

"It's not him," Linton replied. "It's me."

"What?"

"Never mind," Linton answered. His mind remained preoccupied.

XIX

AUGUST 1986, SAN FRANCISCO, CALIFORNIA

When Linton awoke, he was looking into the auburn eyes of a petite blond stewardess. He was already drunk but did not resist another glass of champagne. As recently as maybe five years ago he was still almost embarrassed to fly first class. Being waited on hand and foot made him nervous, but he had to visit New York every three months to mix a fresh batch of roots tonic with Clarence. If he didn't, the plant in Brooklyn would cease operations within five months.

Now, as he usually did on his return trips from New York, he felt relaxed and he allowed his mind to wander.

Since establishing the company in Brooklyn twenty years earlier, Clarence had earned Linton's respect by doing a terrific job, introducing the product in New York City. Clarence had done far more to propel the drink's popularity than just depending on word of mouth in growing Jamaican communities. He invented savvy marketing techniques, including giving cans of spray paint and cash to few a creative youngsters who proceeded to emblazon company slogans all over metropolitan New York, creating waves of copycat graffiti. It was almost free advertising, and by the time City authorities and civic-minded citizens began to complain, the trademark name of Family Roots was on the tip of everyone's tongue.

Since its founding, Family Roots had consistently earned and enjoyed a sterling reputation for high standards in sanitation and employee safety. On the brink of its twenty-fifth anniversary, Family Roots sold well in the San Francisco Bay Area and in all five boroughs of New York City. The Port Authority Concessionaires Department had recently authorized Family Roots to open juice bars in several subway stations and at La Guardia airport.

Clarence had given a stunning sales presentation put together by Magdelene, bewitching the Port Authority officials. They agreed to a most generous contract. Clarence had become like a second son to him, and Magdelene had finally come into her own. Immediately after the meeting he announced that she would become the acting CEO while Clarence would maintain his position of authority over East Coast operations. Linton wanted to take it easy, to retire and enjoy his life with Daisy. Worried about their health issues, he felt a growing urgency to slow down.

Sipping the champagne, Linton stared out the airplane window. In one week he was throwing a Family Roots anniversary celebration. 1986 was going to be their most profitable on record. He was at the pinnacle of his achievement, yet felt unsure about the future. Real happiness remained as elusive as freshwater in the middle of the sea. It seemed only continuing success lay ahead, yet his heart was emptier than ever. Having Magdelene as CEO gave him more time to relax, but the leisure time had not brought him the happiness he'd anticipated. He longed to be closer to his son. Samson was unemployed, his job lost when the store he was managing closed down. Linton felt a lump in his throat. He wanted to reach out to Samson, but how?

The pilot announced that they were approaching San Francisco, interrupting Linton's thoughts. Despite all his achievements, nothing could assuage his disappointment in Samson's not attending college and joining him on the executive team. He stared at the tray table, unable to remember the last time he had sought out Samson, just to spend time or to talk. Shifting uncomfortably in his seat, he realized he felt remorseful. Linton had taken great effort to conceal his past from his children, hiding the fact of his being a bastard, and of his once being a ganja-smoking Rastafarian. He feared that Samson's knowledge of his father's past would make his hypocrisy even more unbearable.

The seatbelt sign went on. Linton looked out the window at Yosemite Valley. Before long he would be at home with Daisy.

The plane made its final approach and landed. The flight attendant announced that luggage would be claimed at carousel three. Linton was the first passenger to disembark and he eagerly walked to the luggage carousel to claim his valise. Suddenly, he felt confused, unsure of which carousel served his flight.

Seeing a security guard he asked, "Excuse me, I'm looking for where my luggage would be?"

"No problem," the man replied. "What flight did you arrive on."

Linton's mind went blank. "I--I don't know."

"What city are you coming from?"

Horror seized Linton as his mind drew another blank. Embarrassed, he looked around and saw a few familiar faces from the flight. "Oh there it is," he muttered, "I see the luggage. Thanks!"

Shaken, he claimed his bag and went outside. The curious memory lapses were becoming more frequent and worrisome. He climbed into a cab and left for home, feeling confused and scared.

When Magdelene arrived home, the late afternoon sun was streaming into the kitchen window where Gaylord peeled potatoes. Only a year ago they had purchased a house in Blackhawk, an exclusive neighborhood known as Hidden Oaks near Danville, California. It was a five-bedroom house on a half-acre lot, studded by several oak trees. With her handsome salary from Family Roots and his income as an investment banker, they enjoyed the luxury of having time to spend together.

Slamming the door shut, Magdelene walked into the kitchen. Gaylord stopped working, washed and dried his hands, came over and kissed her.

"Hey baby...."

She threw the car keys on the counter and sighed.

"What's the matter?"

"It's Dad."

"His heart again?"

Magdelene shrugged, blinking back tears. "Mom wants

me to call a doctor because … Dad's losing his memory." Magdelene hesitated. "I'm calling a doctor to make an appointment for him."

"His memory! How do you know?"

"Mom said he's getting lost driving home. He even got lost on the way to the office!"

Gaylord went back to peeling potatoes. "Has it affected his remembering the secret roots formula?"

"Yes." Magdelene replied. "Mom told me he actually called her, unable to remember it!"

Gaylord let out a whistle. "I could never figure out why Linton has not sold this formula yet. He could make a lot of money. I'm reading about successful mergers and sales of companies like Family Roots all the time." Gaylord set off toward the refrigerator and brought back two packages of chicken. "What are you going to do?"

"I'm not sure." Sprinkling salt on the chicken parts, she thought about the potential millions that they could make by selling the formula. For two years she played with the idea. This could be her chance. Rolling the chicken parts in flour, Magdelene dropped each piece in a skillet to fry.

Her last major triumph had sprung from a near disaster. As she watched the chicken fry she recalled her humiliation during the sales pitch to the Concessionaires Managers of the New York Port Authority.

The debacle began when Linton called Magdelene into his office and said, "You're always asking for important things to do." He handed her a thick manila envelope. "Well, I've finally got something *big* for you."

Magdelene's eyes lit up and she seized the packet. "Just tell me, and consider it done."

"Good. I'm getting old, Magdelene. I need you more than ever."

She opened the envelope and whistled. "The New York Port Authority? This could be huge, Dad." She rifled through the pages. "We're going to land this account."

"Yes, with your help I believe we will," Linton replied.

"I'll pull out all our old marketing pitches. Atlanta, Los Angeles...."

Linton could practically see the wheels in Magdelene's brain spinning. He beamed at her proudly.

Basking in her father's praise, Magdelene got up to leave Linton's office, but at the door turned back to him, "Dad, can I ask you a question?"

"Sure."

"The formula. This isn't easy to talk about, Daddy, but don't you think it's time to tell me?"

Linton laughed, his gray-haired head bobbing back and forth. "Don't you worry, little girl," he crooned, "when it's time to tell the secret, I will."

Magdelene gritted her teeth and controlled her temper. During the next few weeks she put together a good, solid, sales pitch.

On the day they were to give the presentation in New York, Magdelene was dismayed to discover that Linton had been drinking. She was beside herself. "How do you expect to make a good impression smelling like a whiskey bottle at 10 in the morning?" She helped her father into a taxi and they headed off to the Family Roots office in Brooklyn. When they arrived, Clarence was waiting anxiously for them.

"Boy, I was getting worried you wouldn't make it," he said. "Where's the presentation?"

"Why?"

Magdelene glared so fiercely, Clarence took a step back. "Take it easy, Magdelene," he said gently. "I need to review it. Didn't Uncle Linton tell you he wanted me to give the presentation?"

Magdelene felt the ground give way from under her. She felt numb with fury.

Clarence looked from Magdelene to Linton. "Did we get our signals crossed?"

Linton laughed. "Absolutely not. I have a part in this for both of you." They busied themselves setting up the slide projector, sales portfolios and brochures. Magdelene prepared the refreshments.

In short order the room was ready, a projector screen at one end of the small conference table and a selection of chilled Family Roots drinks on a sideboard. Two gentlemen from the Port Authority arrived. The men, both wearing dark pants and white shirts, seemed to be fraternal twins.

"I'm Thomas, and this is Porter, the blond-haired man said, shaking Linton's hand. Porter, who had dark hair, acknowledged Linton with a nod, but did not offer his hand.

"Please have a seat," Linton said. He introduced Clarence as his nephew and Magdelene as his daughter.

While Clarence referred to her script, Magdelene sat motionless in a chair, burning with righteous indignation. Midway through the presentation, Clarence stopped to ask for a glass of water.

"Magdelene, please get refreshments for us, will you?" Linton asked.

Magdelene felt belittled and humiliated. She served samples of roots with a broken smile and returned to her seat, in the eye of an emotional hurricane.

Clarence talked for thirty minutes. The men were so impressed both with the proposal and the roots, they agreed to whole-heartedly recommend that a contract be signed.

While the men shook hands, Magdelene began to clean up. Once the Reps were safely out the door, Linton and Clarence gladhanded each other on their success.

"Come on, Magdelene," Linton said, "we did it! Now is time fe big lunch!"

"I have to go back to the hotel," she said.

"Why? I was looking forward to having lunch with the new CEO of Family Roots. I cannot tell you how proud I am!"

Magdelene stood there, her jaw slack with surprise. Clarence hugged her, but she was numb. For the first time she had what she so desperately wanted and worked to achieve, control of Family Roots.

"Why yuh so surprised? Me getting old, and is time to slow down."

"I... I..." Magdelene threw her arms around Linton.

She promised her father that she would not let him down. Since then, Magdelene's success as CEO of Family Roots earned her Linton's absolute trust. She was sure that after Linton heard of her idea to sell the formula and brand name, he would be proud. What a way to exit the business, Magdelene thought, exiting with massive profit, just as her teachers encouraged in business school. She could hardly contain herself. *Get the formula.* The drink's popularity had already led to several inquiries. Magdelene knew there was indeed interest in acquiring the formula. Family Roots stood to gain millions of dollars. It would not be difficult to make a deal. Soon they'd all be on easy street. It was fitting that a quarter century had passed since her father had introduced the drink. She thought of revealing her idea to sell the formula just before the celebration. Perfect timing, Magdelene thought. Daisy would agree to sell the formula, with Daddy getting sick. Reaching for a pair of tongs, she began to carefully pull the fried chicken out of the pot and put the pieces in a serving bowl.

As the days passed, preparations for the anniversary celebration went into high gear. The chartered yacht was docked in Oakland, the catering arranged, and Linton spent thousands on liquor for an open bar. Banners were printed. Finally it was almost time and out-of-town guests began to arrive. Daisy's sister, Iris, now a widow of many years, arrived and stayed at the McMann home. The night before the party, Daisy stood in her bedroom doorway, gazing at Linton.

She was worried about her husband. At first his forgetfulness was hardly noticeable, but with growing frequency he began to miss appointments, would not remember where he left something, and would insist a conversation had not occurred when it had. She knew something was seriously wrong when, two weeks earlier, she received a late night call from Linton, in New York. He sounded lost, confused.

But what really scared her, caused the hair on her arms to stand rigid with alarm, was that Linton asked her to remind him of the recipe. She understood all too well what that meant. Daisy told Magdelene and asked her to make a doctor's appointment for Linton for the following week. Iris, too, was alarmed when Daisy gave her the news.

"How long has this been going on?" she asked.

"A couple of months. Recently he got confused driving home. Maybe it's not serious. We'll just wait till the appointment and they will probably order some tests."

"When?"

"Day after the party."

Iris put her hand on Daisy's shoulder. "Don't worry. He's going to be all right."

Magdelene glanced at her watch, wondering where Linton and Daisy were. There was little time to waste. Everyone had to be at the Family Roots Celebration soon, and she had scheduled the meeting so that she could make her proposal on what was to be a festive evening. After what seemed like an hour, they walked in, oblivious to the time.

"You're late," Magdelene said. She had not expected Samson to be with them and was forced to contain her shock.

Everyone took a seat and Magdelene took the floor, her heart pounding.

"Why I've asked you to come here before tonight's celebration is that I want to open negotiations to sell the roots formula and the brand name, Family Roots." She paused and glanced at her father. "I've done some research and the roots formula along with the Family Roots brand is valued at seven million in cash. We could easily get the rights to eleven per cent of all future revenue from sales. The best part is that Family Roots will finally be made available beyond the New York and San Francisco metropolitan areas. We might even expand our distribution to include Kingston and London. It will generate millions in profits over the years. It will both broaden and provide longevity to the Family Roots brand, and will give us an extremely profitable exit strategy. What do you think?"

Magdelene's question was met with breathtaking silence.

She looked at Daisy's stony expression.

"Exit strategy? What type a rasclat foolishness a dis?" Linton demanded. "Who said we need any exit? Who says we need to expand? Who told you I would even think of *selling* Family Roots? It nuh fe sale! We don't work like this to hand it over to you and see you sell it off!"

"But Daddy, what we have is worth more in someone else's hands! Let's cash out!"

"Maybe you don't understand, Magdelene. I started Family Roots in 1961. But the formula from which it is made was created long before. I learned it as part of a tradition, a tradition born in Africa and brought to Jamaica where rebellious slaves struggling for their freedom passed the recipe from generation to generation. Now it is a part of me, *a part of us*. I can never sell it."

Magdelene tried to explain. "Daddy, seven million dollars is a lot of money. This is what we call an exit strategy in business school."

"What de hell dem teach yuh!" Linton roared. "After all these years, you should know that I would never sell the formula or the company."

Magdelene stamped her foot. "You just won't listen!"

Linton shook his head. "No. I am not going to listen. Look at how much money we have. How much more do we need?"

"You don't go into business to be sentimental," Magdelene said. "You do it for a profit."

"Don't you understand," Samson interjected. "It's more than a business for Dad, it's who he is."

Magdelene, fighting back tears, acknowledged her brother for the first time since he had come in the door. "You! What the hell are you doing here?"

"Magdelene," Daisy said, "Samson is going to start working here again. Dad had intended to discuss it with you today."

Magdelene picked up her purse and got her coat from the closet. She wanted to go home and be alone. Her potential triumph had turned into a debacle.

Linton got to his feet, calling to her, "Profit is not everything young lady, but family is."

Infuriated, Magdelene drove home to change for the party. She may have lost the battle, but one day the formula and the company would be her's.

The twenty-fifth anniversary of Family Roots had been a splendid evening celebrated with hundreds of guests. Linton appeared happy and Daisy was a gracious host. But the mirth of the evening evaporated once they came home. Already in bed, Daisy was dozing off when Linton sat next to her.

"I can't sleep until I say this. I––we–– have made a serious mistake. We've been blind. It became perfectly clear to me this evening, that while Samson has always been in love with roots, Magdelene is only in love with money."

"What should we do?" Daisy asked, putting her arms around him and pulling him closer.

"I don't know yet," Linton replied. "Let's sleep on it."

The next day, after nightfall had wrapped its arms around town, Samson knocked on the door of his parents' house. When no one answered, he rang the bell and heard chimes echo though the darkened hall. A few moments later Linton turned on a light and opened the door for his son. They went into the kitchen and sat down at the table. Linton poured two glasses of roots. He was nervous and found it difficult to start the conversation. Samson did not push him.

They sipped their drinks in the soft incandescent light until Linton blurted out, "If yuh won't cut yuh dreadlocks, how about yuh beard?"

Samson laughed. Would his father ever give up wishing?

"After five years you should know that I'm never cutting it…

Dad? I wanted to tell you how proud I was at the meeting yesterday. For a long time I thought all you cared about was money."

Linton snorted. "Raising you children left me worried about money every day." Unbeckoned, Linton recalled Major ordering him to work in the distillery. To his horror he realized that he had become that man, his father, whom he'd hated for all those years. Major had refused to let him into his life. Indeed, he recalled parroting Major's words to Daisy about family honor and duty. He would not make the same mistake with Samson. But was it too late?

"Samson, I want to tell you about my past. Do you drink rum?"

"I've been known to."

Linton produced a bottle of rum and two more glasses, poured, and began telling Samson about his concealed past. He told him about Major, about Pauline and Misti and Andrew, about growing up on the plantation and about Sheila. He shared with his son some memories he had never even expressed to Daisy. He told Samson about living with Timothy in Bessanworse, of his being a Rastafarian, and of his smoking ganja. As Linton confided in Samson, he experienced a joy he had not felt since he had told Andrew about being his brother.

"Why have you waited so long to tell me this, Dad?"

"I thought it was behind me. I was convinced I had escaped the past," Linton said. "When you became interested in Rasta, it all came right back. I thought being an American required of me to leave it all behind... to raise my children without mentioning my past, your heritage." He put his hand on Samson's. "I forgot that no matter what, I'm still Jamaican."

"Why are you so against me being involved in Rastafari?"

Linton sighed. "I wanted to control you. I thought I knew what was best for you. My father never let me close, but he still wanted to run my life. And I wanted to run yours. But you chose something else, just like me."

Samson's voice trembled, "You understand that I can't work for Family Roots and not continue playing music. Our band is doing well, you should come and see us."

Linton smiled. "Yes. I'd like that." For the first time in nine years Linton sat with his son, basking in a glow of mutual respect. "I've waited for *thirty* years to talk with yuh like dis," Linton said.

"What?" Samson was puzzled.

"It's been at least thirty years since we've really enjoyed each other's company."

"Dad, I'm only twenty-nine!"

"Oh, that's right!" Linton said. But Samson could not help but notice the look of discomfiture on his father's face. He picked up the rum and put it away, then went to get Daisy and they put Linton to bed.

"What's going on with him?" Samson asked Daisy.

"We have a doctor's appointment tomorrow. He's been forgetting things, and acting strangely."

"I want to go with you." Samson hugged his mother and left for home. He felt buoyant, pleased by how much his father shared with him.

They took Linton to the doctor and that evening, after making Linton dinner, Daisy joined Magdelene on the porch.

"Mom, I'm worried," the Family Roots Chief Executive Officer said.

"Your father is going to be fine." Daisy said it with enough conviction to convince herself.

"C'mon Mom. You know he's not. The doctor said he was suffering from pre-senility dementia. People don't die from dementia. But I'm not talking about that." Magdelene hesitated. "Dad's forgotten the formula hasn't he? You're the only one who knows it. You should tell me now."

"Magdelene, we were very disappointed in you trying to sell Family Roots from underneath us."

"Disappointed?! Here we are sitting on a company that can't grow because an old man refuses to share a formula that could lead to untold riches. You know as well as I that if more people knew the formula we'd have more plants, more manufacturing and more market share. But Dad's stubborn! He's sentimental! He insists on flying to New York every three months like a crazy man. Well it doesn't look like he's going to make that trip again, does it? What's Clarence supposed to do?"

"If I must go, I will," said Daisy.

Magdelene stamped her foot. "I don't understand your reluctance."

"One day you'll understand," Daisy said. "And your father and I are going to create a position for Samson."

Magdelene's face twisted in frustration and anger. "Dad won't give me a raise, but he'll hire that no-good Rasta?"

Daisy got up. "Don't talk about your brother like that. At least he's been true to himself." With that, she went into the house.

In her car, Magdelene smacked the steering wheel. Samson's joining the company wasn't good news. What if they decided to tell him the secret instead? After years of cutting roots and scrubbing kettles, he understood the roots even better than she. She had to get the formula. Goddammit!

There was still a chance.

She reached home and tried to put it all out of her mind. She made dinner for Gaylord and herself, watched T.V. and went to bed. But once there, she was unable to sleep. Her mind raced until, at 2 a.m., the phone startled her.

It was Daisy and she was frantic. Linton had been taken by ambulance to the hospital.

It was a long night for the McMann family. Linton lay in intensive care, while the doctors ran a battery of tests. He had experienced a shortness of breath and chest pains so intense it left him unable to speak. The tests revealed that Linton was suffering from angina. They prescribed some medicine and sent him home with instructions not to work for the next week.

One morning, a few days after Linton returned home, Samson looked in on his father, saw him sleeping peacefully, and went out to the garden to work on the flower beds. Daisy and Magdelene were grocery shopping. Knowing how much his mother loved roses, Samson had bought three bushes to plant.

Linton was awakened by a crushing pain in his chest. He rolled over on his side and reached for his heart medicine. But he only succeeded in knocking the bottle off the nightstand. The container fell on the floor and rolled away beyond his reach. Collapsing back onto the bed, he gasped for breath. He could hear his son, in the garden, the spade slicing the earth asunder, but his feeble cries went unheard. No one came to comfort him.

He understood he would not live to see his beloved family again. Indeed, he was forced to let go, entering into the whorl of time, lost in a maze, that moment of reflection beyond perceived life, the acquiescing to a time and place that is at once sorrowful and soothing.

Now. Forever. The press of forgotten memories: the spicy Jamaican dishes, sugarcane waving lazily in the breeze, the pungent smell of fresh rum, Sheila watching with her aching sad brown eyes, Timothy and his golden smile, Andrew, a welcoming gale of laughter, and Busby, offering a glass of spirits.

Finally, in the distance, Major in his prime, tall and strong, emerged from the house. Linton's heart leapt with joy as his father embraced him. Without saying a word they walked over to the distillery where Busby was waiting, glasses of rum in hand. The three men clinked their glasses and drank, satisfied in silence.

Wearily, Linton closed his eyes. Standing before the distillery at the crest of the hill, he felt the warm, humid breeze across his skin, melting his pains away and bringing much-needed energy. He watched the evening sky grow darker over the canefields that seemed to stretch as far as he could see.

Daisy reached out, her arm searching for the warm body that belonged next to her. But as her fingertips tentatively touched the sheets, searching for Linton, she woke up. Moments ago, in her dreams, Linton had held her hand and whispered in her ear, making her laugh. Opening her eyes and seeing the vacant bed filled her heart with sadness. Five days had passed since Linton's death.

During the day Daisy was treated like a queen bee in a busy hive. Samson and Magdelene were at her side, assisting around the house and helping with the guests who came for the funeral. Their old friends spent time with her, leaving little time to reflect. But grief waited for Daisy in her bed, between the sheets, where after a long day she would lie down and wait woefully for sleep to bring Linton back to life.

Daisy's world was turned upside down. Despite Iris's age, she flew to California immediately to be by Daisy's side. Iris was her rock, the older sister and friend she had always been able to rely on.

When she arrived, she shocked Daisy with some unexpected news.

"Callie is coming to the funeral."

Daisy couldn't believe it. They had had no communication in over twenty-two years.

"Callie?"

"She wants to be by your side, Daisy. You both have just taken this grudge too far. You're sisters for crying out loud. Callie's plane arrives this evening, a taxi will pick her up and bring her to the funeral parlor for the wake."

Later in the evening, after getting Iris situated in her room, they took a cab to Mooney's Funeral home for Linton's wake. Daisy was nervous.

"Don't worry Mom," Samson said.

"You have nothing to fret over," Iris insisted. "This is why the Lord created funerals, to keep the living coming together. This is a time for you and Callie to repair your broken relationship."

"I just don't know how to start over. I've tried." Daisy looked out the window. The taxi sped past the dreary, rain-soaked landscape.

"Just walk in there and start by saying hello," Samson replied. He squeezed Daisy's hand.

The cab jerked to a stop, bringing Daisy back to the present. Her heart was filled with dread.

Inside the mortuary, they were escorted to the chapel. It was a plain room with a skylight above the open casket. Bathed in soft bleak winter light, Linton lay in peaceful repose, his face frozen, his makeup perfect. He wore a blue and white three-piece suit, his hands clasped upon his chest, the simple gold band, a symbol of the love that bound him to Daisy for eternity, gracing his left finger.

Daisy glanced at the flamboyant, diamond-studded ring on her own hand. She shuddered. She saw Janet and Lissette seated near the front of the room. "I paid dearly for this ring," she thought. "Too high a price."

When she was finshed at the casket, Daisy approached her daughters.

Lissette hugged Daisy. "It's good to see yuh."

"Hello Daisy," Janet whispered.

Daisy hugged Janet. "I'm so glad you came," Daisy said.

Someone tapped on her shoulder.

It was Callie.

Without hesitation, the sisters embraced. Daisy caressed Callie's gray hair. "Oh God, me so happy fe see yuh," she said.

"After de service yuh mus' come wit' us fe something to eat." Callie looked at her nieces, "We all go eat together. Wouldn't dat be nice?"

When the ceremony ended they took taxis to Daisy's hotel, where Samson got them a table in the hotel restaurant and then excused himself.

After Samson left, a pall of uneasiness hung over the table. Daisy was grateful to feel the warmth of connection surging from Callie, but Janet kept her distance.

The dinner conversation was brittle, formal. Daisy inquired about Janet's life and she gave perfunctory answers, never amplifying on anything. Janet showed little curiosity about Daisy, and did not ask at all about Magdelene. During dessert, Daisy summoned her courage.

"I know I've been less than perfect," she said. "But tonight, permit me to beg your forgiveness. I let you down. I thought that I was achieving something, that money was all you needed. Callie, I want also to apologize for how I've treated you."

Callie pressed her sister's arm. "Daze, nuttin bad is between us. De past a de past. We'll talk later."

Taking Daisy's hand Lissette added. "Mom, we've had this conversation. I've come to understand you just simply tried to do your best. I forgave you long ago."

Daisy looked at Janet.

"Forgive you?" Janet asked. Her voice was calm. "Why do you need my forgiveness? Aunt Callie said it all, what's past is past. What if me say yuh forgiven? Is it a magic wand that now you can get a good night's sleep?"

"I think maybe Lissette and I will take a little walk," Callie said.

When Lissette and Callie were gone, Janet continued.

"You gave me life and that was it! Why didn't you visit? You never gave me the chance to make you my mother! I was so young I barely remembered you."

"I'm sorry Janet, God knows, I wish I'd done things different. But you must know that I love you." Daisy looked at her entreatingly. "Please forgive me."

"No one wishes you'd have done things differently more than me. When Mother's Day comes, I don't think of you, Daisy. Is Dearma me thinkin' of. She was there. I can't speak for Lissette, but what you ask is so difficult for me, not because I don't want to forgive you. I don't need to forgive you. When I arrived in the States you never meant that much to me. Sure, you were there for me financially. But that was just the point, I never cared about money, as much as I loved you. Was it worth it? Really?"

For a moment, the tinkle of silverware seemed to resound loudly.

"No," Daisy whispered, "it wasn't."

Janet took Daisy's hand. "It's not worth holding a grudge either. I came here... to start over... to support you–– *Mom.*

They embraced and Daisy felt Janet's tears on her cheek for the first time since that day in 1950 when she left Jamaica for Miami.

Dinner was over. Minutes later, Callie and Lissette rejoined them and Daisy paid the bill.

"We'll see you at the funeral tomorrow," Janet said, waving good-bye.

Callie accompanied Daisy home. Iris was already asleep. Daisy helped Callie settle in a room, and then Daisy sat in a chair and wept.

"People warned me, Callie, that I would lose everything. I wouldn't listen. I wanted to deny that whole Jamaican side of my life. People warned me."

"You were having such bad luck. You went through so much with Miles."

Miles.

Quite some time had passed since he had crossed her mind. Long ago she convinced herself that she would never have married him had it not been for that terrible morning in the cellar.

Wilbur.

She still lived in his shadow cast by that monstrous, unspeakable crime. Even now she could taste the dirt in her mouth.

"Daisy?"

The mansweat assaulting her nostrils.

"Are you all right?"

Fingernails tearing her flesh.

"Daisy?!" Callie shook Daisy's arm.

Roused from a trance, Daisy said, "Not Miles. Callie, I was raped, Wilbur... he raped me at Mummaa's house."

"I know."

Daisy looked at Callie through her tears, unsure if she heard Callie correctly.

"Yes, yuh hear me. I know him rape you…*An' me kill 'im, wit' obeah!*"

Speechless, Daisy stared at her sister.

"Yuh nuh haffi tell me," Callie continued. "What happen come to me long ago inna dream. Me try fe see if I could get yuh fe chat 'bout it, but yuh wasn't talking. But I could tell from the way yuh act an' de way him carry himself, crowing like common fowl! I hated him. I hated him being wit' Mummaa. And I hated him fe hurtin' yuh. When yuh marry Miles, I was sure."

"Why?"

"Feelings. I saw how he looked at you, like him was plotting to rape you again, and me, I promised myself that he was going to be *dead* before he could ever touch yuh again. So me go down a May Pen Cemetary––"

"Oh, God!"

"And I waited for the full moon, to collect some soil from a grave." Callie's voice was steady, her face relaxed. She showed Daisy a scar on the palm of her left hand. "I drew blood from me hand by the light of the moon and mixed the blood with the dirt." Callie paused, unsure of how to go on. "I can't tell yuh 'bout what I did next. It was an incantation that must remain secret. After I finished casting the spell, I took a little of this magic powder and sprinkled it on Wilbur's food. A month after that, he start to vomit blood, and a few month later him *blood-clat* dead. And I'll never do dat again, *ever*." Her emphasis on the last word made Daisy jump.

"I remember when yuh got the visa and left. Everyone was so mad, but I knew. I understood. How could yuh stay inna de house where yuh was raped? Only I couldn't say a ting! As long as Mummaa live, we couldn't say a bad word against Wilbur. I never unnerstan' dat."

"Me either." Crying, Daisy said, "I always told Mummaa 'bout how Wilbur look pon me over the years when I was growing up, making me feel so uncomfortable. But she just brush it aside. I tell you, though, I think she knew."

The women talked for hours, catching up, then the first signs of dawn began to lighten the sky

"All dis time I've held this grudge," Daisy said. "It all started with this." She raised her right hand. The faint scars from Callie's smashing her hand with a rock were still visible. "One grudge led to another, and another, until we forgot we're sisters."

"Finger mash no cry," Callie called out. In unison they chanted, "Remember how we a play!" They fell down laughing, lying prone on the bed and soon were asleep on the bedspread, still wearing their clothes.

"Life is an incomplete sentence," Samson said, eulogizing Linton, his father. "Pain comes to us from seeing a life incomplete, its loose ends waiting to be gathered together by the surviors. And so it falls to me to try to put a full stop on my father's life."

He paused. The closed oak casket was situated before the alter. Looking at the small group gathered in the center of the cavernous church, Samson went on, "For death, we are told, is not the end, but a new beginning. At the end of his life, Linton McMann left a living legacy. As his son, only now am I beginning to understand his aim in life. Only now am I coming to appreciate it. He wasn't perfect. But like the saying goes, If every fool wore a crown, we should all be kings.'" He looked at Daisy and Magdelene, sitting in the front pew. Their eyes met. "Our father will live on in my heart and in the hearts of all who loved him."

With his voice still echoing, Samson paused to wipe a tear. He had not used his notes, choosing instead, to speak from his heart. The audience waited for him to continue, but he could not.

"Thank you," he said and took his seat in the congregation.

At the cemetery, mourners gathered beneath the crystal blue sky to see Linton McMann lowered into his permanent resting place. Iris was the first to throw dirt upon the casket, followed by Callie, Clarence, George, Ethel, Lissette and Janet. One by one they filed past, each paying their respects. After everyone passed, Daisy, Magdelene and Samson were the last to throw handfuls of soil onto Linton's casket.

XX

OCTOBER 1986, HAYWARD, CALIFORNIA

The next day, Daisy and Callie went shopping at Macy's in San Francisco. Callie had never seen such immense and well-stocked department stores and, because of her sister's generosity, was able to buy things she could not otherwise afford. Her unbridled excitement thrilled Daisy. Their only lament was that Linton was not there with them.

That night, Daisy accompanied Callie to the airport and saw her off with a promise to visit Jamaica soon.

Slowly, over the next few days, the visitors stopped coming. Lissette and Janet left for New York, promising to visit. But Daisy's life, already strange without Linton, bewildered her. She had depended on him for a routine. His absence left Daisy sitting on her sofa, watching television listlessly.

During this time, Iris remained with her sister. She became the anchor holding Daisy fast against the currents of sorrow. One evening, after doing their laundry, the sisters sat in the bedroom, folding clothes.

"I can't thank you enough for staying with me," Daisy said.

"Daisy." Iris stopped folding. "When Tom passed away, I don't know what I would have done without you. Even after all these years I wake up wanting him, feeling him--" Iris halted, her voice choking with emotion. "I wished we lived closer to one another. I'm going to miss you."

The women embraced. The phone rang and Daisy tried to ignore it but the ring continued, insistent, until she answered.

"Mom! We have to talk."

"Magdelene, I'm doing laundry with Iris."

"This can't wait Mom. *When are you going to tell me the recipe?*"

"Now is not the time," Daisy said.

"Then when?"

"Thusday at the bottling plant."

"Promise?"

"Yes." Daisy hung up the phone.

"Have you decided what you are going to do?" Iris asked.

"Announce the heir to the secret. I told Magdelene that twice already. I don't know what is wrong with that girl."

"Really?" Iris stopped packing her clothes.

"When she said she wanted to sell Family Roots we were shocked. Linton couldn't believe it."

"Come on, Daisy. It's no mystery why Magdelene would choose money over tradition."

"What are you talking about?"

"Look at how you've lived your life, Daisy. Magdelene learned that money was the most important thing in the world from you. Long ago I warned that your pursuit of money and things was blinding you to the things that really mattered. All yuh ever stressed to Magdelene and Samson is money and education and what neighbors might think. Samson rebelled, but Magdelene's been a good student. Too good."

Daisy picked up a neatly folded blouse, shook it out, folded it again. "Magdelene became Linton's hope after Samson disappointed him. Samson's insistence on growing dreads, not going to college and living a Rasta lifestyle with all the ganja, was a huge disappointment to us."

Iris threw up her hands. "You must believe you're still in Jamaica. Only in Jamaica do parents think they *own* their pickney." Iris grasped Daisy's shoulders firmly. "Samson and Magdelene are Americans, and if you wanted to raise them like Jamaicans you should have stayed there."

Daisy glanced at her sister. "But I didn't."

"You know who you plan to share it with?"

"Sure do."

Later, in bed and unable to sleep, Daisy felt dreadful. She remembered her promise to Magdelene, indeed, remembered whispering in her ear after graduation about being the heir to the secret that was the heart of Family Roots. But the promise was made before any of them had an inkling of Magdelene's intentions; before they realized that she really had no understanding or interest in the foundation that earned the name Family Roots.

Daisy remembered Linton saying what she had refused to see, that while Samson had a true love for the history and the tradition of the roots, Magdelene's entire focus was on money. I failed, she thought. Yet again. In her mind she pictured Janet and Lissette, still teenagers. Hindsight made everything so clear.

After telling Callie of the rape, and speaking about it with Iris, Daisy realized how much Wilbur's shadow had dominated her life. Her experience in that cellar made her blind to the fact that she had lived her entire life reacting to his crime: her marriage to Miles, how she treated her daughters, her obsession with America and being American. But none of it had ever brought her the relief she finally found when she opened her mouth and spoke of it. Only then did Daisy realize how she had ignored Janet and Lissette and why.

She flashed back to the conversation with Linton when she sealed her daughter's fates. Of course they could have bought the house and sent for the girls, but how would they have afforded private school for Magdelene and Samson? But her biggest mistake, she admitted, was thinking that by sending money she was sending them her love. She equated bringing them to the United States with being enough, when it should have been just the start of repairing the past. Mummaa's fear was justified. Daisy finally felt shame.

She had put money above all else. But not this time. I'm going to make Mummaa proud, Daisy resolved, pulling the covers up over her.

Wednesday afternoon, Magdelene and her husband, Gaylord, went to the Family Roots headquarters. Magdelene busily cleared out Linton's file cabinet and chattered nonstop to Gaylord about her plans for Family Roots.

"Do you know how long I've waited to find out the secret?" Pulling old papers and folders from Linton's files, she threw them away. She threw what she deemed garbage on a pile that Gaylord stuffed into plastic trash bags. "Every time I asked Daddy he would just laugh." She paged through a notebook before tossing it aside. "That was the problem with Dad, his sentimentality. I keep thinking I'll stumble across the roots formula."

"When is Daisy going to tell you?"

"Thursday," Magdelene replied. "And Friday I'm meeting with Ike Collins, the CEO of Collins Soft Drinks. The deal is as good as sealed. We are simply going to merge our production into his facilities in Los Angeles and keep this office open as a subsidiary."

Gaylord tied up a plastic bag and carried it over to the corner, dropping it with a thud. "I don't know, Maggie. One of the last things your father said was not to do that, and I'm sure Daisy is dead set against it."

Magdelene pulled a black and gold velvet bag from the back of Linton's desk drawer. "I'm not worried about what Mom thinks. Honey, what you don't understand is, *we* have educations. We went to the best schools. We have our MBA's. Mom doesn't understand business like we do. The best part is we all win, there's plenty for everyone in the deal."

"Indeed there is," Gaylord said. "You talk to Samson about any of this?"

"Hell no!"

"Magdelene!"

"What's he going to do?" Magdelene made a face. "I don't need his dreadlocks and Rasta nonsense around me."

Magdelene opened the velvet pouch and found an old, cork-stoppered blue bottle, an antique key, and ten English shillings. She frowned and tossed them all into the trash pile.

"Worthless. Just some old coins. God! there's a ton a junk in here. My father was a pack rat."

In a scant two hours they had cleared the office of any hint of Linton

When dawn broke in Hayward, Daisy and Iris got in the car and drove to the Family Roots plant. Inside they found the usual, smooth-functioning flurry of activity. Clarence and Samson were already outfitted in white jackets, hair nets and hardhats. Tall kettles were connected to a central reservoir by steel conduits. In the corner of this cavernous room was a small, well-ventilated, windowless structure where Linton used to conduct the mix.

"Everyone," Daisy said, "I am going to announce who I am sharing the secret formula with after I get dressed to work in the mixing room." Daisy put on her protective clothing and came out of the dressing room. She glanced at Magdelene, who smiled at her. Samson looked at her gravely.

"Are we ready?" Daisy asked.

Everyone nodded.

Daisy looked at the people assembled before her. Clarence, Samson, Magdelene, Iris, and the entire staff of Family Roots. Daisy thought of Linton. He would have been proud, Daisy thought, for Family Roots will survive.

"Samson!" she called, "come on."

Samson! Magdelene threw her clipboard on the floor.

"We need to talk. *Now*," she demanded. "Let's go to the office."

Leaving the group of employees gathered around Samson, congratulating him, Magdelene led Daisy down a hall where Daisy grabbed Magdelene's arm.

"Talk to me 'ere." Daisy said, stopping.

"How could you do this to me?"

"Oh Magdelene, we were so wrong, me and your Dad. You never loved roots. We taught you to love money. *Money!* Look at what it cost me. I lost my two eldest daughters and I almost lost my soul. She looked sadly at Magdelene. "Samson is goin' learn the formula today."

"We were going to be on easy street!" Magdelene shouted.

"You still don't understand. We already are on easy street. You think you know better than everyone. Well, the formula isn't for sale."

"So what now? Is Samson going to run the company?"

"No, I'm making Clarence the new CEO. He's earned it. Samson will be President and only he will have the formula. They will work together to keep the company growing.

"You, my child, are free to pursue the career you have dreamed of, somewhere else. You'll receive a lifetime monthly payment from Family Roots and I am setting up accounts so that my other children will get monthly payments."

Frustrated, Magdelene threw up her hands. "Dad is rolling in his grave."

"Please leave, Magdelene. I'll see you later."

Daisy walked back into the room and motioned to Samson.

"You're making me the mixer?" Samson looked at his mother incredulously.

"Me can't think of anyone else who deserves to know more than you," Daisy replied.

They went into the mixing room. As she closed the door, she thought of her true love, Linton. At that exact moment she felt something stir in her heart.

The tree may have fallen, Daisy thought, *but the roots are still alive.*

THE END

GLOSSARY

a .... to or at

a fe me .... our's, my, mine

bangarang .... argument or fight

buccra .... white people

duppie .... ghost or spirit

dutty .... dirty

fe .... for

haffi .... have to

nuh .... not or no

obeah .... black magic or witchcraft

unnoo .... you all

ACKNOWLEDGEMENTS

I must thank first of all my long suffering wife, Leanne Marie Francis who supported me as I brought From Rum to Roots from an idea to a finished product over the past ten years. I'd like to also thank my mother-in-law, Patricia Henigman for her support and for always believing in this book.

I would like to thank all those who helped me. Donnell Alexander, Pamela Berkman and Amy Alexander are all mentors and writers I look up to, my developmental editor, Ricky Weisbroth who became a more of a teacher than an editor, Alan Rinzler, an editor who served as a midwife to help give birth to this book. My deep gratitude to Cary Dakin who helped guide me. I must thank Rodrick Groves, one true friend who through the years watched over 200 movies and spent hours discussing literature with me. He was another teacher. John Orr, a kindred spirit who helped me with crucial copyediting. And I will never forget Narendra Nandoe's advice before writing this book: reading is indeed more important than writing. Also a big thank you goes to Susan Ragan, I'll never use an extra adverb again… seriously.

I must thank both Aunts, Bernice, Aunt Dottie, and Aunt Resna, who along with all my elders contributed to who I am and spoke to me about my history. Lorna Chamber's and Ouida Dyer's, help proved indispensable, and a special thanks goes out to Kirk Prince who along with Donnell was present when the germ of the idea of this book was born in 2002.

I'd like to thank the people who read my manuscript, Jon Gausman, Elena Marie Bridges, Heather Crawford, Marinell James, Reginald Spence, Judi Spence Wills, Deborah Spence, Bryan Moss, Seraiah Avalon, Ruth Johnston, Cameron Galloway, Mark Romyn, Erik Grettir Jacobs, Jennifer Fountain, Joan Estrada, Brian Chambers and Arlene Chambers, and Jason Roden.

I'd also like to thank my friends in Roaring River Jamaica who extended hospitality and warmth to me while I wrote the book there: Judith Higgins, Diann Higgins, Pauline Hemmings, Rose, Martha, Ann Marie, Simone Dobson, Robbie Forester, Sherman Holmes, and Christopher. Also a special shot out to my boy, Dwight Francis. Rest in peace brother.

But most of all I must thank my parents, Lloyd Francis Sr. and Udel Francis nee Wilson. They insisted I write well.

CPSIA information can be obtained at www.ICGtesting.com
Printed in the USA
LVOW11s2233020914

402149LV00011B/153/P